I0760327

VENGEANCE *of a* MAFIA QUEEN

USA TODAY & WSJ BESTSELLING AUTHOR

SIOBHAN DAVIS

ISBN-13: 978-1-959285-22-9

Editor: Kelly Hartigan (XterraWeb)

Cover design by Shannon Passmore of Shanoff Designs

Cover imagery and interior imagery © Depositphotos

Formatted by Ciara Turley using Vellum

Falling for the enemy was never part of my plan…

Losing my innocence at thirteen, in the most brutal way, changed me. My kidnapper stole my childhood and tried to break me. The knowledge my father orchestrated the entire situation hardened my heart, and instead of grieving his death, I celebrated it.

One down. Many more to go.

My burning need for revenge has only grown over the years, keeping me focused on my goals and enabling my rise to power.

Made men are weak. A pretty face and the promise of a good time easily distracts them.

Now, I'm in charge.

Men bow before *me*.

Except for *him*—the brother of my abductor. Massimo fights me every step of the way, but I'm not about to let the explosive chemistry between us deter me from my chosen path. His family is my enemy. *He* is my enemy, even if he doesn't know it yet.

I won't stop until all those who wronged me are punished.

By the time they realize I'm coming, it will be too late.

They tried to take everything from me.

But where they failed, I will succeed.

Unless *he* becomes *my* weakness.

Note from the Author

This is a complete **stand-alone dark mafia romance** set in my *Mazzone Mafia* world. It is NOT necessary to read that series before reading this book as it's an entirely new story with a new couple not featured previously.

For readers who have read my *Mazzone Mafia* series, this book is set one year after the epilogue in *Scared to Love*. (From Chapter 1 onward.)

This is a mafia romance with dark themes and it's only recommended to readers aged eighteen and older. It may contain triggers for some readers. Check out the trigger warning page on my website at www.siobhandavis.com. Please note this trigger list contains spoilers.

Mafia Glossary

- Bratva – The Russian mafia in the US.
- Capo – Italian for captain. A member of a crime family who heads/leads a crew of soldiers.
- Consigliere – Italian for adviser/counselor. A member of a crime family who advises the boss and mediates disputes.
- Don/Boss – The male head of an Italian crime family.
- Donna/Boss – The female head of an Italian crime family.
- La famiglia/famiglia – Italian for the family/family.
- Made Man – A member of the mafia who has been officially initiated/inducted into a crime family.
- Mafioso/Mafiosi – An official member of the mafia.
- Mia amata – Italian for my beloved.
- Mia regina – Italian for my queen.
- Na Zdorovie – Russian equivalent of cheers (when toasting a drink).
- Pakhan - Boss/leader of the Russian mafia in a particular jurisdiction.
- Regina – Italian for queen.
- RICO laws – The Racketeer-Influenced and Corrupt Organizations Act, a federal statute enacted in 1970. It allows prosecutors to seek tougher penalties if they can prove someone is a member of the mafia.
- Soldati – Italian for soldiers.
- Soldier – A low-ranking member of the mafia who reports to an assigned Capo.
- The Commission – The governing/ruling body of Cosa Nostra, which sits in New York, the organized crime capital of the US.

- The Five Families – Five crime families who rule in New York, each headed by a boss.
- The Outfit – The Chicago division of Cosa Nostra.
- The Triad – Chinese Crime Syndicate.
- Underboss – The second in command within a crime family, and an initiated mafia member who works closely with, and reports directly to, the boss.
- Vor – The Bratva equivalent of a made man (singular).
- Vory – The Bratva equivalent of made men (plural).

VENGEANCE *of a* MAFIA QUEEN

FIVE NEW YORK FAMILIES

MAZZONE

Bennett Mazzone
Current don & president of The Commission

Son

Rowan Mazzone
Heir

GRECO

Gabriele Greco
Don

Brothers

Massimo Greco
Future don

DIPIETRO

Josef DiPietro
Current don

Son

Cruz DiPietro
Heir

ACCARDI

Luca Accardi
Current don

Cousins

Caleb & Joshua Accardi
Heirs

MALTESE

Roberto Maltese
Current don

Son

Fiero Maltese
Heir

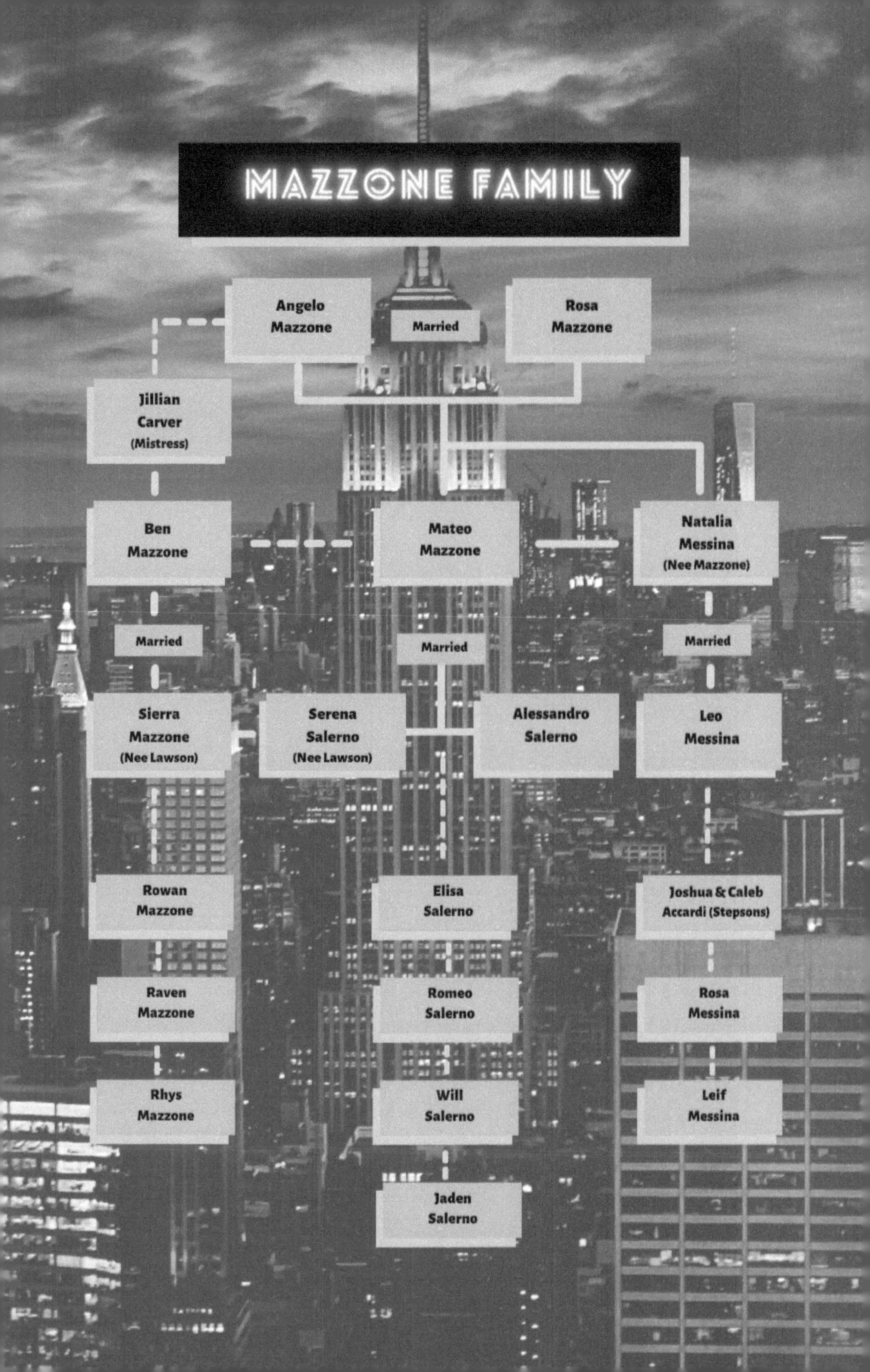

MAZZONE FAMILY

Angelo Mazzone — Married — Rosa Mazzone

Jillian Carver (Mistress)

Ben Mazzone

Mateo Mazzone

Natalia Messina (Nee Mazzone)

Married

Married

Married

Sierra Mazzone (Nee Lawson)

Serena Salerno (Nee Lawson)

Alessandro Salerno

Leo Messina

Rowan Mazzone

Elisa Salerno

Joshua & Caleb Accardi (Stepsons)

Raven Mazzone

Romeo Salerno

Rosa Messina

Rhys Mazzone

Will Salerno

Leif Messina

Jaden Salerno

GRECO FAMILY

Maximo Greco — Married — Eleanora Greco

- Carlo Greco
- Primo Greco
- Gabriele Greco
- Massimo Greco

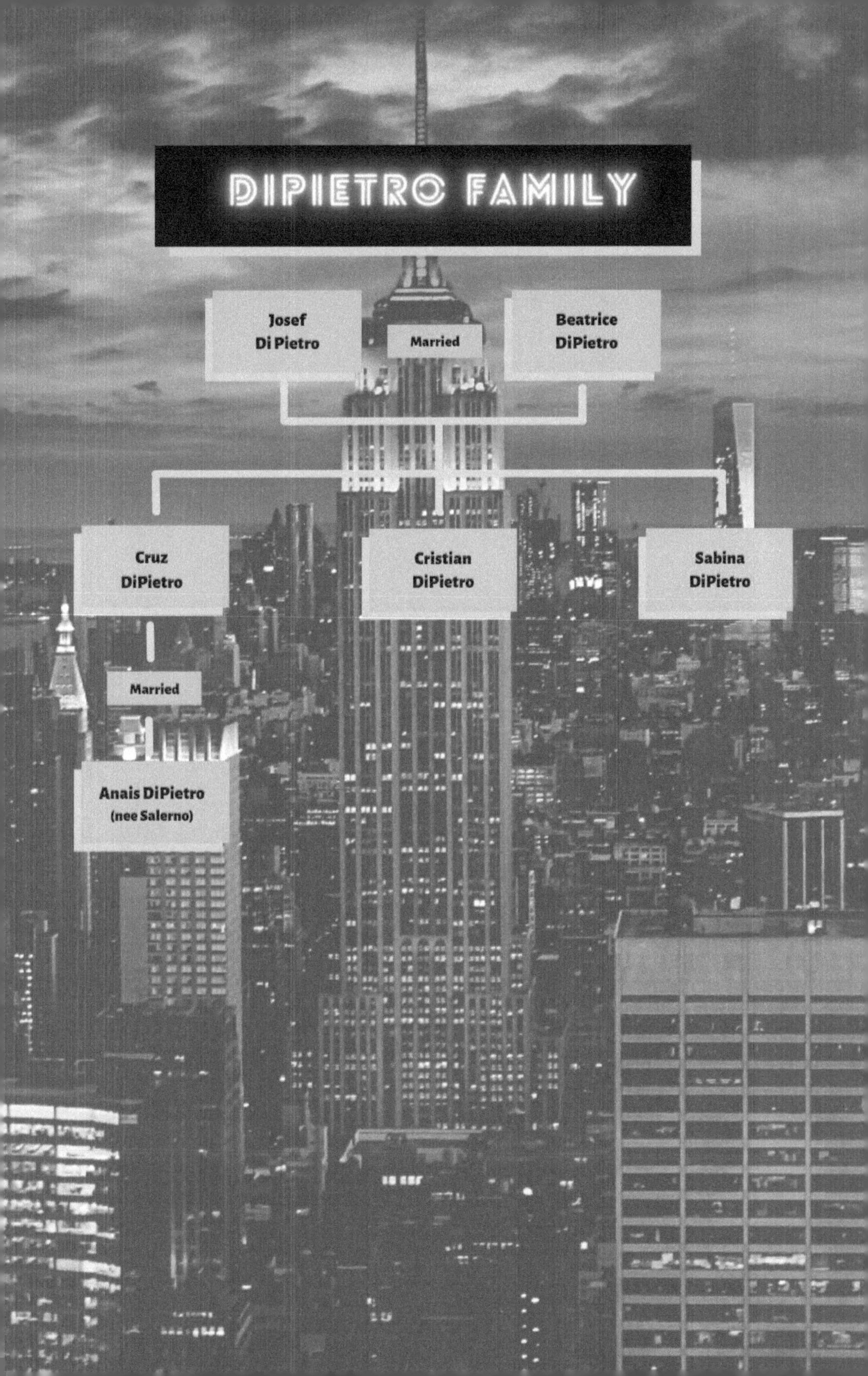

DIPIETRO FAMILY

Josef
Di Pietro

Married

Beatrice
DiPietro

Cruz
DiPietro

Cristian
DiPietro

Sabina
DiPietro

Married

Anais DiPietro
(nee Salerno)

MALTESE FAMILY

Roberto Maltese — Married — Ingrid Maltese

- Fiero Maltese
- Zumo Maltese
- Sofia Maltese
- Tullia Maltese

ACCARDI FAMILY

Natalie Mazzone

Gino Accardi

Married

Juliet Accardi

Married

Caleb Accardi

Twins

Joshua Accardi

Leo Messina

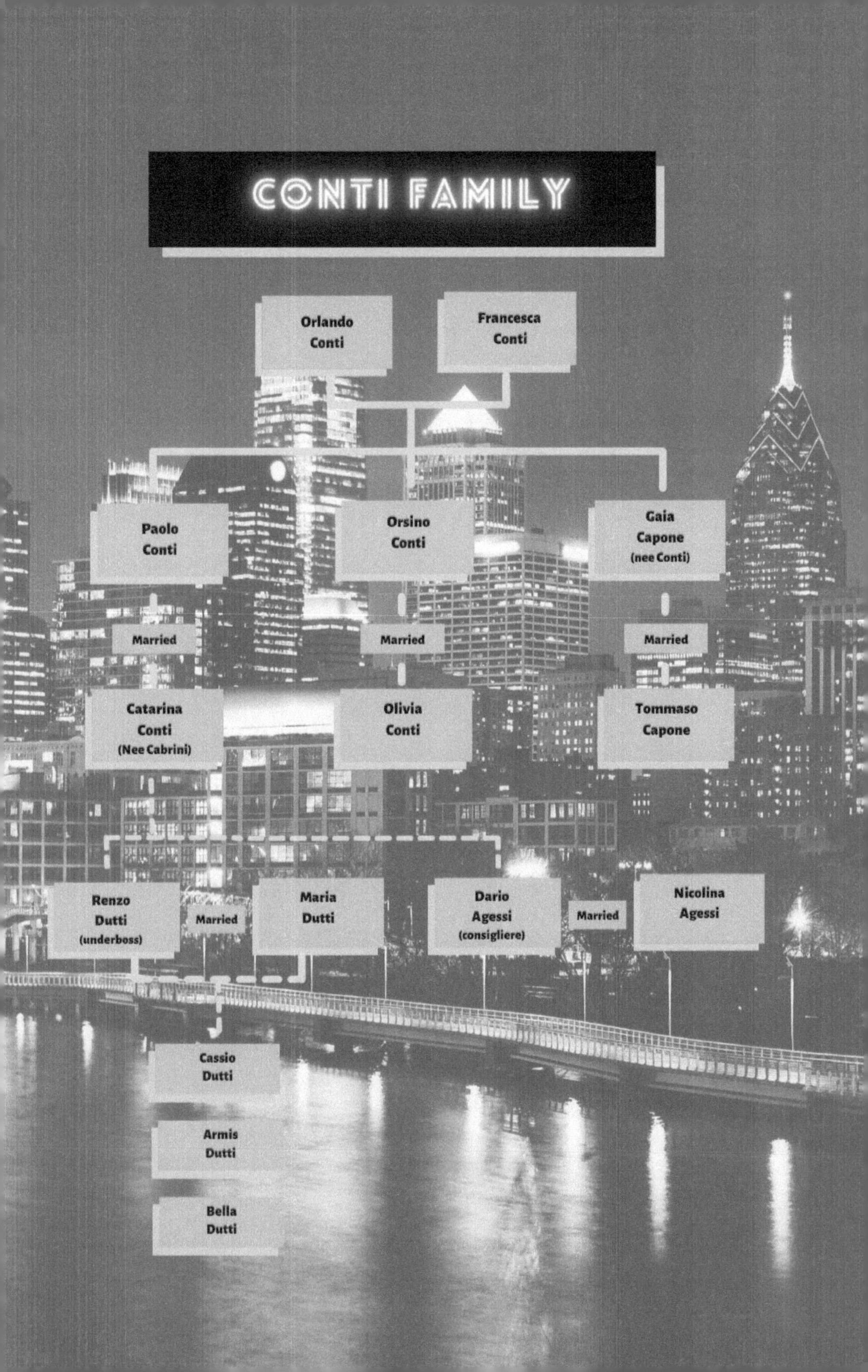

CONTI FAMILY

Orlando Conti

Francesca Conti

Paolo Conti

Orsino Conti

Gaia Capone (nee Conti)

Married

Married

Married

Catarina Conti (Nee Cabrini)

Olivia Conti

Tommaso Capone

Renzo Dutti (underboss)

Married

Maria Dutti

Dario Agessi (consigliere)

Married

Nicolina Agessi

Cassio Dutti

Armis Dutti

Bella Dutti

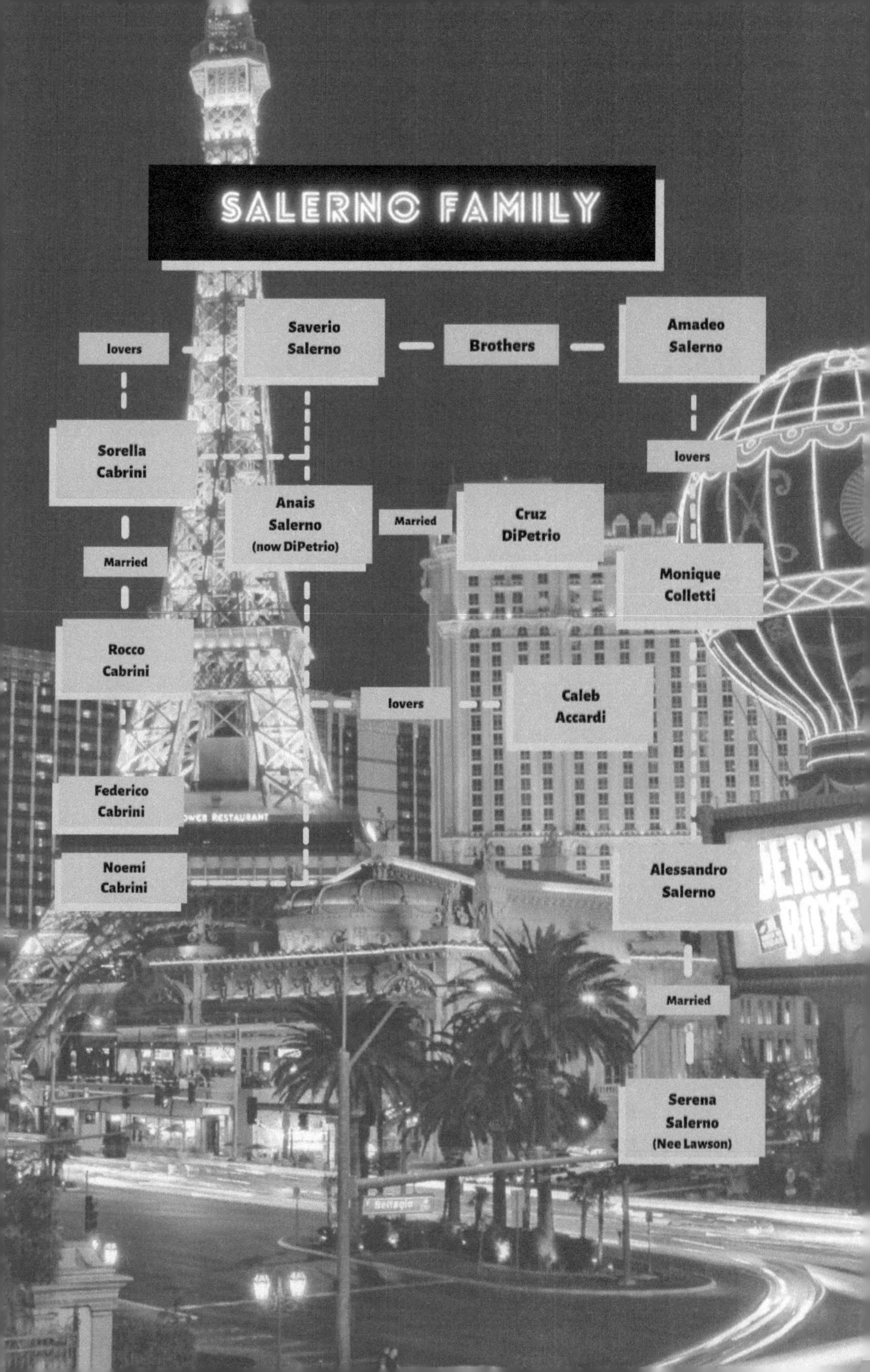

SALERNO FAMILY

Saverio Salerno — Brothers — Amadeo Salerno

lovers

Sorella Cabrini

Married

Rocco Cabrini

Federico Cabrini

Noemi Cabrini

Anais Salerno (now DiPetrio)

Married

Cruz DiPetrio

lovers

Caleb Accardi

lovers

Monique Colletti

Alessandro Salerno

Married

Serena Salerno (Nee Lawson)

Prologue One

Catarina - age 29

"Is this seat taken?" a man with a deep husky voice asks, and I don't need to look up from my drink to know who it is.

"I think you already know the answer," I respond before bringing the glass of Macallan 18 to my lips and taking a sip. I stare straight ahead, my gaze skirting around the barman pretending not to listen. I don't blame him for his nosiness. He must be pulling a double, if not a triple, shift. As the busy private airport lounge has cleared out, I have noticed him glance at his watch, with the worn brown leather strap, a total of thirty-seven times. He's clearly itching to get out of here. It is Christmas Eve after all. The platinum band encircling his ring finger suggests there's a wife waiting at home, maybe kids too.

"It's never smart to assume," the handsome stranger standing on my right says.

Setting my glass down on the polished marble counter, I swivel on the bar stool as I slowly lift my head. Inquisitive forest-green eyes latch on to my face, widening with growing interest as he drinks me in. "True." I deliberately part my lips as the tip of one finger elegantly traces the rim of my glass. His gaze rakes over my face before lowering to my body as he blatantly checks me out. "But you have been staring at me long enough to know I'm alone."

That's not technically true. Renzo accompanied me on this business trip, and he's currently watching these proceedings with hawk eyes from his position at the small table by the window.

We have worked together long enough for Renzo to understand how I like to do things. He knows boredom set in hours ago, as we wait impatiently for news of our flight to Philly. Unlike my underboss, I have zero desire to get home in time for Christmas. But Renzo knows I can't sit still for any length of time without growing agitated.

I need something to take the edge off.

And the perfect distraction has finally made his move.

I know what this stranger sees. I am aware of my allure. It has taken many years and dedicated investment to cultivate it. To hone it into a weapon I regularly use against men. Slowly tipping my head to one side, I allow a soft smile to dance over my lips as I conduct my inspection of his handsome features and hot body.

He's sexy as sin with attentive sultry green eyes and lush full lips. His chin and chiseled jawline are coated with a thick layer of dark hair, neatly trimmed and extending around his mouth, as is the fashion these days. Along with the eyebrow slash and the way the blue-black hair on his head is shorn tight at the sides and worn longer on top. High cheekbones, a strong nose, and olive skin hint at European origins.

Ink creeps out from under the cuffs of his crisp white shirt and covers his hands. More tattoos are visible on his neck, disappearing beneath his collar. The shirt is stretched snugly across his broad shoulders and bulging biceps, and the material is high quality and clearly expensive. Designer black pants hug muscular thighs, and black dress shoes complete the look. I know his suit jacket rests on the back of his stool, and he's not wearing a tie.

If I had to bet on it, I'd say he's *mafioso*. Though he's no one I know or have come across, which means he can't be anyone important. I would know because I have made it my life's mission to know every key player across the US.

His tempting lips pull up at the corners in arrogant satisfaction as he watches me take my time ogling him. This man is seriously gorgeous, and he knows it. He's even better up close. I spotted him checking me out the minute he entered the lounge an hour ago. Most other men would have approached me before now. But a man who looks like him doesn't often have to chase women—if ever.

It's obvious he was waiting for me to approach him.

I smother an internal laugh.

As if I would ever lower myself to such a travesty.

Men crawl to me when I beckon them. It's never the other way around.

"You're married," he says, finally cutting through the tension building between us. His stunning eyes drop to the constrictive gold band wrapped around my fourth finger.

I cross my feet at the ankles, ensuring his eyes are drawn to my long slim legs, showcased perfectly underneath the fitted white Chanel dress I'm wearing. It hits just below my knee when I'm standing, but seated as I am now, it rests above my knee, offering a glimpse of toned tan thighs.

He doesn't disappoint.

Men never do in this situation.

Flash them a pretty smile, a hint of smooth silky skin, and feign interest, and they fall for it every time.

Not that I'm doing much faking on this occasion. This man is sex on a stick, and lust coils low in my belly, for the first time in a very long time.

Sex is rarely for pleasure.

Most always it's business.

On the odd occasions where I indulge, purely for the release, it usually disappoints.

Something about this man tells me he won't let me down.

"So?" I shrug, maintaining eye contact as I take another sip from my drink.

His grin expands. "I guess I have my answer."

And I guess I have mine. *La famiglia* have many traditions. Not all are adhered to by everyone. But there are exceptions. Like mafia wives. There is a code which most made men abide by: You don't mess with the wives.

Either this man has no honor or no moral compass or he has no clue who I am. Most likely it's all of those. Which suits me fine. I don't need to respect him to fuck him, and I seldom like the men I let into my body.

His attention is laser focused on me as I drain my drink and stand. "A woman with discernible tastes," he says, his approving stare locked on my curves as I straighten to my full height. "Color me intrigued." With supreme confidence, he cups my face with one hand while his fingers trace a path over my hair. "What's your name?"

"Let's not waste time with such trivialities," I say as he removes the tie from my hair, freeing my long dark-brown locks from my ponytail.

"Beautiful," he murmurs, weaving his fingers through my hair as it tumbles down my back in straight sheets. "You should always wear your hair down."

"I don't take orders from men." Grabbing my purse, I subtly nod at Renzo.

His lips twitch. "Is that so?"

"Yes." I drill him with a look as I remove his hand from my face and the other one from my hair. "If you want this, it happens on my terms."

A deep chuckle rumbles from his chest, the sound doing weird twisty things to my insides. "Are you always this forthright?"

"Are you always this slow?" I trail my fingers up the hard planes of his impressive chest through his shirt.

"There is this thing called foreplay." He waggles his brows, and holy hotness, I can barely drag my eyes from his face because his features have come alive, and he truly is a sight to behold. He's like a reincarnated Adonis—a creature designed to snare women with just one look.

"There is this other thing called time." Reluctantly, I tear my gaze from his, looking over his shoulder at the digital board mounted to the wall. "They have just called boarding for my flight."

Clasping my hand, he holds it firm as he ushers me toward the exit. "I can be quick."

"Don't I fucking know it," I mumble under my breath, yanking my hand from his. Usually I'm grateful for the two-pump chumps, but I would enjoy more than a quickie with this man because I already know he won't disappoint.

For that reason alone, it's best this is over with fast.

Out of the corner of my eye, I spy Renzo approaching.

The stranger chuckles again. "Say the word and I'll skip my flight and book us a hotel room." He moves in closer, pressing his mouth to my ear. "I want to worship your body all night long and hear you screaming my name until you have lost the ability to speak."

Delicious shivers skate over my body as his warm breath tickles my flesh and the wicked intensity of his words covers me like a second skin. Liquid lust dampens my panties and I discreetly squeeze my thighs as my nipples harden, pressing against the thick material of my dress.

"Do you usually pick up strange women in airports and take them to hotels?" I inquire, handing my purse to Renzo as he reaches my side.

"Do you?" he asks, eyeing Renzo with a mix of curiosity and wariness.

"No. I never pick up strange women in airports," I deadpan, grabbing his hand and tugging him toward the door.

"Not bisexual. Got it." His gaze drifts to Renzo's hand on my lower back as we walk toward the door. "Who are you?" he asks, eyeballing my right-hand man.

I decide to have some fun with this. "He's my husband." I level a look at Renzo, warning him to play along.

The stranger's eyes pop wide. "What the fuck is this?"

"Relax," I say, pulling him out through the door, my gaze skimming the hallway in search of the nearest wheelchair-accessible bathroom. "He won't be joining us. He'll just wait for me outside."

He opens and shuts his mouth in quick succession before shrugging like it's no biggie.

Huh.

Finding a single bathroom, I stride toward it, enjoying the feel of the man's strong, warm, callused palm wrapped around mine. Every few seconds, he glances at Renzo, and I know he's trying to figure me, *us*, out.

We reach the bathroom, and I'm relieved to find it empty. Keeping the door propped open with my hip, I turn to face my underboss.

"Be quick," Renzo says. "I will call the gate, but they won't wait forever." Flying commercial sucks. Perhaps I shouldn't have given my pilot the night off, but he has a young family, and I didn't want to keep Petro from them at Christmas. Renzo slaps my phone in my hand along with a condom, piercing me with a look.

"We won't miss the flight," I promise because I know he wants to get home to his wife and kids too.

"Try anything and you're a dead man," Renzo warns the stranger. "Hurt one hair on her head, and you won't make it out of that bathroom alive." There is no disguising the intent in his tone.

"You have nothing to worry about. Your wife is safe with me," the stranger replies before I yank him into the bathroom and lock the door.

"Those are some of the weirdest words to ever come out of my mouth," he admits, looking highly amused while I tug at the belt holding his pants up.

"Shut up. We're here to fuck, not talk." Unbuttoning his pants, I let them fall to the ground as I dive my hand underneath his boxers, gripping his semi-hard length.

He hisses as I stroke him, his erection solidifying in record time at my touch. He's big, and I'm salivating at the anticipation of feeling him inside me.

He cups my breasts through my dress, kneading me hard. "I was hoping these were real."

"Like I'm hoping you know how to use the gift God gave you." I drag his boxers down his muscular thighs and toned legs. Saliva pools in my mouth at the sight of his magnificent cock. It's long, thick, and beautiful, jutting out straight from his body, primed and ready to give me pleasure. Swiping my thumb across the tip through the bead of precum lodging there, I wish I had time to suck him off.

I'm surprised at my thought, reminding myself again it's for the best I don't. These types of reactions are not usual for me, and I already know this man would be dangerous for my sanity.

"Trust me, you'll have no complaints." Circling his hand around his hard-on, he gives it a few quick pumps while watching me with hungry eyes as I shimmy my lace panties down my legs.

"Just so you know," I say, walking over to the sink. "I am armed." I flip the button on my cell phone, revealing the hidden knife inside. I hold it up, showing it to him. "I know how to use it too."

"Who are you?" he asks, walking toward me, loosely holding his boxers and pants up. Fresh curiosity is etched across his face.

"The woman you're about to fuck." Gripping his chin with my free hand, I bring his face down to mine and claim his mouth in a searing-hot kiss I feel all the way to the tips of my toes. His pants and boxers pool at our feet, and I feel the heat from his cock as it presses against my belly through my dress.

Unconcerned I am holding a knife to his stomach, he responds enthusiastically, angling our heads and devouring my lips in a punishing kiss that has my insides rejoicing and my pussy pulsing with potent need.

This man knows how to kiss a woman, and I can't remember ever being kissed so thoroughly.

"Turn around," he growls against my lips. "Keep the knife in your hand if you need it, but you aren't in danger from me. I won't hurt you." Diving to my neck, he nips at my skin. "Unless you want me to."

His words irritate me, and I move my knife up, pressing the tip against his throat. "I thought I told you to shut up. Put your cock in my cunt and fuck me or get the hell out."

Most men would run for the hills right about now, but this man once again proves he's no ordinary man. He grins, almost blinding me with a dazzling white smile. "I think I might love you," he says as I nick his skin and a fine line of blood rises to the surface.

I snort out a laugh, instinctively knowing I don't need the knife. "I think you must be as fucked up as me." I'm rarely honest with men, but it's the truth. Spinning around, I place my hands on the counter as he yanks my dress up to my waist and slaps my ass. My pussy is drenched in a way it never has been before. "That's for cutting me," he snarls, slapping my ass again. I glare at him over my shoulder as he lowers to his knees.

"FYI. I didn't ask, or want, to be slapped."

"Liar." He plunges two fingers deep inside me. "You're fucking soaked. You liked it. Probably want more."

I don't wish to explore those words or what they might mean to me. "You're all talk and no action." I bait him, biting my lip to stifle a moan of pleasure as he scissors his fingers inside me.

"Your pussy is beautiful," he says before shoving his face up against me from behind. Ripples of pleasure wash over me as he licks my slit and plunges his tongue inside me. I want him to make me come like this and then fuck me and make me come again. But there isn't time, and I can't miss this flight because that wouldn't be fair to Renzo.

Reaching around, I grab fistfuls of the hot stranger's hair, yanking hard on the thick strands until he stops what he's doing and looks up. "There isn't time. You have three minutes to fuck me or I'm leaving."

He climbs awkwardly to his feet, reaching out to hold on to the wall to steady himself, his lower legs tangled in the wrinkled pants. "If you were mine, I would never share you with another man." He snatches the condom from my fingers and rolls it over his hard shaft. "But your husband's shortcomings work to my advantage." He grabs my hips and tilts my ass up before slamming his cock inside me in one hard drive.

A scream tears from my throat. Predicting my reaction, he covers my mouth with his hand, stifling my scream of passion, before Renzo bursts in here, all guns blazing. I can only hold on for dear life as the handsome stranger fucks me into oblivion.

The sounds coming from me are wholly new, along with the sensations he coaxes from my body, as he pounds into me with savage need. Every thrust of his cock sends sparks flying over my skin, and my climax is steadily building. He commands my body like a man who knows his way around a woman's body. One hand possessively holds my hip in place while he wraps my hair around his other hand, tugging my head back as he rams into me.

I'm not even shocked I have relinquished all control to him. I'm too lost to sensation to fully recognize it or to care. My skin is flushed, and I'm hot all over, my muscles quivering and limbs turning to jelly, as he fucks me hard and raw, like he can't get enough. My walls clench around him as he buries himself deep, and I'm pushing back against his dick, in synchronization with his movements, greedy for more.

"Fucking hell," he grunts while driving deep inside me. "Your cunt is so hot, so tight, so warm. I could live in here until I die and be completely and utterly happy."

A laugh erupts from my mouth. Oh my God. Who the hell is this guy? I'm not laughing two seconds later when his fingers find their way to my clit, and he skillfully rubs me in time with the thrusts of his cock.

I shatter explosively without warning. Stars burst behind my eyelids as waves of bliss crash into me, over and over, and I'm vaguely conscious of him roaring behind me when he finds his own release.

I am momentarily stunned. Incapable of moving. Frozen in time as my body slowly comes down from a heavenly high. The pounding on the door snaps me out of it, and I push him away as he slides out of my body. I instantly miss the feel of him inside me and the warmth of his body pressed against my back, but I lock those feelings up tight and shove them aside to comprehend later.

Lowering my dress down over my hips, I fix it back into place and brush knotted strands of hair away from my face as he disposes of the condom and gets dressed. Snatching my panties from the floor, I shove them in the trash and grab my cell phone. "Thanks for the fuck." I stretch up to kiss him one last time, lingering for longer than I should.

"We should swap numbers."

I shake my head. "That wouldn't be a good idea."

I turn to leave, but he grabs me, reeling me into his arms as his lips descend. He kisses me passionately while Renzo hammers on the door.

No man has ever made love to my mouth the way this man is.

I don't know how some woman hasn't slapped a ring on him yet because he is completely addictive in a way that wouldn't be healthy for me.

We break apart at the same time, staring deep into one another's eyes, and for a teeny, tiny second, I allow myself to dream.

The dream disappears into a puff of thin air as I shuck out of his hold. "Goodbye." I hold my shoulders back and my head up as I stride toward the door, refusing to look at him again.

"What a shame you are already married," he says.

Stalling with my hand curled around the door handle, I look over my shoulder at him, arching a brow as my curiosity is piqued.

"If you were single, I would marry the fuck out of you."

Prologue Two

Catarina

"Do you want to talk about it?" Renzo asks two and a half hours later when we exit Philadelphia International Airport. I'm grateful to have left the snow back in Maine. Though I'm less sure about leaving the hot stranger behind without exchanging numbers.

Which is reckless and uncharacteristic for me.

I *have* done the right thing.

Even if it doesn't feel like it.

Turning away from the dreary view out the window of the car, I look my underboss in the eye. "Why would I want to talk about it?"

His Adam's apple bobs in his throat, and that's the only indication he is feeling something about what went down in the bathroom. "You seem melancholy."

"I'm not," I coldly reply, turning my head and staring at the back of the driver's head. Renzo is the only other man who has made me orgasm during sex, and he's the very last person I would discuss this with. "I'm just thinking of what's to come," I lie.

"Are you changing your mind?"

I narrow my eyes at him. "You know me better than that. I haven't worked my ass off to get to this moment only to chicken out at the last minute." I rest my head back against the leather headrest, briefly closing my eyes. "I have counted every second of the eleven years I have been married to that insufferable pig. I have minimal seconds left in me."

I am not worried about the two *soldati* in the car hearing this conversation—Ezio, my driver, and Ricardo, my personal bodyguard—for both men are loyal to me. Ninety percent of the Conti *famiglia* is loyal to me now. The ten percent who remain loyal to my useless disgusting husband are not long for this earth.

"You've got this." Renzo reassures me, loyalty and determination shining in his eyes.

Reaching along the back seat, I squeeze his hand. "I couldn't have done this without you."

He tilts his head to one side, squeezing my fingers in return. "It has been my greatest honor to watch you grow into the woman you are today. As it is my great honor to serve at your side."

Retracting my hand, I settle it on my lap. "You saved me from myself." I peer straight into his eyes so he can see it's no lie. I don't often indulge emotion or sentiment, but we are on the cusp of great change, and I'm feeling oddly emotional after my bathroom encounter. "I'm not sure I thanked you properly."

"I know you're grateful. You don't need to say the words, and it's never been a chore."

"Are you happy?"

"Yes," he replies with only the briefest hesitation. "You have given me a good life, my donna. I would not have been afforded the same opportunities had I stayed working for your stepfather. The gratitude works both ways."

I purse my lips as the wrought iron gates of the Conti family home open to grant us entry. My mood instantly plummets. Gravel spins at the tires as the car slowly maneuvers the long winding driveway. Tall spruce trees line the private road on both sides, looming over us like ominous sentinels.

We round the bend, and Castle Conti comes into view. A shiver tiptoes up my spine, like always.

I hate coming here.

I hate staying here even more.

But it's Christmas. It's tradition we spend Christmas Eve through New Year's Day with my in-laws. My parents are dead. My stepfather hates my guts, and my sister will be spending the holidays with her in-laws, so it's not like I can make any excuses. Besides, this will be the last Christmas I have to endure this bullshit. I can stomach one final charade.

The drab gray-brick two-story monstrosity with copious turrets and towers and creeping ivy covering a lot of the walls is like something from a horror movie. I will never forget my first impression of this place. I instantly hated my new home, and that's saying a lot because my stepfather's Vegas property is a creepy gothic mansion straight from a nightmare. Before I was forced into marrying a man old enough to be my father, I already knew I was exchanging one hellhole for another. However, being confronted with the macabre reality almost sent me spiraling into a new depression.

Instead, I set myself a challenge. To convince my husband to extract himself from his mama's apron strings and buy us our own home. It took me two years to achieve that particular goal, and I endured two years of sheer hell until it was time to move out.

The car pulls into an empty space in the garage, and Ezio cuts the engine. "Stick around." A sixth sense suggests I could need the three men.

We all climb out of the vehicle, and Renzo cocks an eyebrow as he moves to the trunk to retrieve my bags. "What's up?" he asks, handing the bags to Ricardo.

"I'm not sure," I murmur as I enter the house from the side of the garage. My instincts are razor-sharp, and I have learned never to disregard them. I walk across the kitchen into the west hallway, transecting the dark lobby and striding along the east hallway, in the direction of the family room.

Francesca Conti, my bitch of a mother-in-law, is a creature of habit. She entertains friends on Christmas Eve night, expecting her two sons, her daughter, and their families to be in attendance. I'm sure it irks her to no end I missed the festivities. The fact a ton of planes were grounded in Maine due to snowstorms will pass over her head, and she'll find some way to blame me for embarrassing the family by my absence.

I loathe the woman with the intensity of a thousand suns.

She should be on her knees worshipping at my feet for how I have transformed the fortunes of the ailing Conti family and finally put them on the map. But she would rather choke on her tongue than utter those words.

She will get her wish soon enough.

Without knocking, I open the ornate engraved mahogany double doors and force my way into the room, knowing it will rile Francesca up even more. There is little opportunity to have fun in my world, so I seize the moments wherever I can.

All conversation ceases immediately. My mother-in-law's friends are long gone, and the kids are tucked into bed, so it's just Paulo's mother, brother, sister, and his siblings' spouses in the room. My husband is missing, and I grind my teeth to the molars, guessing where he is.

Paulo's brother, Orsino, is the only one whose eyes light up at the sight of me. That's because he's a lecherous brute, just like his brother, and he covets something he can't have. I let him fuck me one time to enhance his torture. Now he knows what it's like to be inside me, he craves more. I have been knocking him back for years, watching him get more and more wound up. It thrills me to no end, knowing he can't throw me to the wolves, not without risking his own death. My husband is as stupid as he looks, but even he wouldn't let that slight go without the ultimate punishment.

I enjoyed letting that secret "slip" to Orsino's judgmental, vacuous wife. She was added to my shit list the first day I arrived in Philly from

Vegas. Like the rest of his family, she treated me like dirt underneath her shoe, looking down her nose at me, like I was unworthy.

All because of the things that were done to me as a child.

Things I didn't ask for.

Things that were out of my control.

Things that almost destroyed me.

Blood boils in my veins as I fist my hands at my side. Keeping a neutral expression on my face, I subtly wrangle my breathing under control and force those emotions aside, adopting the façade the public has come to expect of me.

Francesca's beady eyes narrow to slits as she stares at me, her gaze darkening when she spots Renzo at the rear. "You can't just barge in here without warning," she blurts.

"Why ever not? I'm family." I stride across the room to the liquor cabinet, helping myself to the whiskey. It's the cheapest Irish whiskey on the market because Francesca thinks I'm not good enough for the more expensive scotch I prefer. Never mind that the cash lining her pockets comes from my initiative and hard work, not her lazy good-for-nothing son.

She mutters under her breath as I pour two glasses. Turning around, I hand one to Renzo, purposely leaning in close to his side. Without knowing our history, everyone in the family thinks I'm fucking him. Paulo tried to have him killed one time—until I pulled him aside and showed him my little video collection. His face had drained of blood so fast it was almost comical.

It's how I have made him toe the line and let me run the show. But I have grown tired of ruling from the shadows. It's time to move my plan to the next phase, and that means Paulo and his family have got to go.

We were planning to do this on New Year's Eve.

Usher in a brand-new year with a brand-new leader and a new way of thinking.

If Paulo is where I think he is, I am all out of patience, and I suspect I will be moving those plans up to tonight.

"What was that, Francesca?" I ask, drilling her with a look that lets her know exactly what I think of her. "I couldn't quite hear it."

"You think you're so smart." Her snide tone rolls off me like water off a duck's back. "I don't know what you're holding over my Paulo, but one day, you'll get your comeuppance."

"Not unless you get yours first." I waggle my brows and grin at her. "Speaking of the degenerate, where is my husband?"

Gaia glares at me, poking her insipid husband in the ribs. "Are you going to let her talk about my brother like that? He's Don Conti! No one gets to disrespect him, especially not *his wife*." Her husband looks at her with an expression that says yes, he will totally let me talk about Paulo however I like. Tomasso might be bland, but he's not stupid. He knows I run the show. He knows most of the men are loyal to me. He's not about to cross me. It will pain me to kill him, but I can't leave him alive because he's not loyal to me, and I can't be sure he won't go to the authorities.

"Out with a decent woman, if he has any sense," Francesca hisses.

"That's a no then," Renzo deadpans, swallowing the cheap whiskey in one mouthful.

"You know where he is." I storm across the room, jabbing my finger in her face. I see where my husband got his priggish looks from. His mother is as ugly on the inside as she is on the outside. "You know what he does, and you have stood by and said nothing. Done nothing." All the blood leaches from her face. I have never been this blunt before, but the gloves are off now. D-day is approaching, and I have zero fucks to give anymore. "You should be ashamed of yourself."

Since I discovered the truth, I have been torn to shreds with the knowledge. Wanting to turn my husband in but knowing I can't. The harsh reality is most made men would not care, and a lot of the cops are on the Conti payroll. I haven't had a chance to earn their loyalty yet, and I know they would bury the evidence in return for a cash bribe. So, I can't do anything about it. Not without collapsing the empire I have painstakingly built.

I have to remember my end goal. That goal will ensure no other child suffers at the hands of the mafia. Women will no longer be treated as second-class citizens. When I am president of The Commission, I will enact real change. Not talk about it endlessly and only go halfway with measures, like the current president, Bennett Mazzone.

Until then, I do what I can for these girls and boys. I get them as far away from my husband as possible, and I keep him locked up for as long as I can without drawing suspicion.

But no more.

It ends now.

"What is she talking about?" Orsino asks as I stride from the room, my resolve set.

"I'll call in the troops," Renzo says when we are out of earshot, already reading my mind.

"I'm sorry to ruin your Christmas Eve, but this has to happen now."

"Agreed, and no apologies are necessary."

"Where were you tonight?" I ask the instant my husband steps foot in his bedroom. I kicked him out of the house he bought us the second I had ammunition to use against him. We haven't lived together for years. The pathetic prick moved back in with his mother, and he has never been to the house I purchased when we effectively separated. Flipping the lock on his bedroom door, I step out of the shadows, ready for this final confrontation.

"Get the fuck out, whore." He doesn't bother to look over his shoulder at me as he starts undressing.

I press the pre-typed text and send it to Renzo, letting him know it's time to set this in motion. We have teams all over Philly, ready to strike at Paulo's loyal supporters at the same time. No one will be expecting us to attack tonight, so I'm confident we will have the element of surprise.

"What have I told you about raping little children, Paulo?" I deliberately soften my tone as I pad quietly toward him. "What did I tell you the last time I caught you?" I have used various threats and incentives over the years to stop him from targeting young girls and boys, and I have surveillance on him. But he still has men loyal to him. Men who aid him in hurting children. I will celebrate their deaths later tonight when we have taken complete control. I won't waste a single second feeling any remorse.

Today we expunge some of the vile monsters who prey on the vulnerable.

Paulo whips around, shirt open, exposing his grotesque swollen belly and the smattering of curly gray hair on his wrinkled chest. He was forty-five when I was forced to marry him, and he's an old man now. I laugh as he points a gun at my chest. "We both know you won't pull the trigger." Doing so will sign his own death warrant and that of his family.

"The worst day of my life was the day I agreed to take you off that bastard Salerno's hands," he snarls, spit flying from his mouth. "He knew he was selling me a dud. That you couldn't give me an heir, and he didn't care."

In a lightning-fast move, I steal the gun from his hand and pistol-whip him across the face. He loses his balance, and his legs go out from under him as he crumples to the carpeted floor. I kick him between the legs before pressing my booted foot under his chin, tilting his head back, and restricting his air supply. Tears leak from his eyes as he curls his legs up, and a strangled whimper escapes his mouth.

"I can't have children because of men like you." I press down on his neck as he claws at my foot with both hands. "It's poetic justice you leave no heirs, and I really like the irony of you dying at my hands," I say, removing the pressure from his neck and stepping back. There is no fun in killing him like this. While I don't have time to linger, I intend to make this as painful as possible. I point the gun at his head. "Get up on the bed, you disgusting piece of shit." I kick at his leg when he doesn't move.

"Fuck you, whore." He swipes at me with a dagger he had tied to his leg, but he really should know better.

Darting to the side, I level a swift powerful kick to his chin, relishing the snap as his jaw dislocates. He drops the knife automatically, and I shoot him in the foot, gaining enormous satisfaction from the animalistic howls he emits as he writhes on the floor while clutching a hand to his chin. Shooting him in the other foot, I crouch over him, quickly checking for other weapons, but he's clean.

Blood oozes from his feet as I step over him, and I'm glad I changed into black pants, a matching top, and boots, because if I got blood on my new white Chanel dress or my Jimmy Choos, I most likely would've killed the bastard on the spot—and we can't be having that.

Opening the door, I find my *soldati* waiting outside as expected. "I need you." My gaze bounces between Ricardo and Ezio as I step aside to let them enter. They stride to where Paulo is whimpering on the floor, hauling his shivering hulk up onto the bed. "Tie his wrists and his ankles to the bedposts," I instruct, throwing them lengths of rope from my kill bag. This room is a throwback to the turn of the century and in dire need of modernization, but the four-poster bed comes in handy for what I have in mind.

"Keep a lookout," I command my men, after they have finished securing him to the bed. I wait until they depart the room before I get to work. I strip my husband bare, trying not to puke at the sight of his flabby flesh and limp dick.

"I'm sorry," he whines in a garbled voice, struggling to speak with his dislocated jaw. His eyes plead with me as I remove my precious serrated-edge Stryker from my bag, stroking it lovingly.

Men consistently disappoint me, but my arsenal of weapons never lets me down.

"Beg for your life, and I might reconsider," I lie, hovering over his hideous body.

He spews garbled lies from his disfigured lips as I mentally count all his crimes in my head. His begging is as pathetic as everything else he does in life, and I'm done listening to his sniveling. Striking fast, I shove the tip of my knife deep into his balls, jumping back as urine projects from his dick as he pisses himself. "Asshole," I say, taking care of the problem when I slice his cock cleanly from his body. Tears pour down his cheeks, and his face is contorted in pain.

It only spurs me on.

Jabbing my knife repeatedly into his balls, I ravage his manhood until there is nothing left but shredded skin. "That's for all the innocent children you victimized," I confirm, watching the blood seeping from his groin in twisted fascination. He attempts to scream, but the sound is trapped inside, emerging as choked, staggered breaths.

"This is for all the times you hurt me," I continue, gliding my knife across his chest in a horizontal line. "For all the times you violated me until I was strong enough to take control and outmaneuver you." I make a succession of cuts along his chest, blood cascading from the wounds as he thrashes on the bed, his survival instinct kicking in.

I slash at every inch of exposed skin, hitting my stride. "For all the people you cheated, lied to, and betrayed." Slash, cut. "All the men you had killed for no reason other than you didn't like them." Slash, slash, cut. "For all the cruel words directed at innocents and those who were vulnerable." Slash, slash, cut, cut. "For daring to exist." I step away and retrieve a pair of plastic gloves from my bag. "I wish I had time to draw this out more, because it's what you deserve, but the rest of your family is waiting for me," I say, putting the gloves on.

Anguish races across his face, and I'm a cruel bitch because it warms my heart to see it, knowing he's in pain, that he feels fear, and he can't do anything about it. Let him die knowing what it is like to suffer at the hands of another. Let him die feeling some of the pain his victims surely felt.

"At this very moment, your loyal *soldati* are suffering the same fate. I can't leave any of them alive," I lie because I won't kill innocent women and children. The cunts downstairs don't count. They are far from innocent and deserve to die, but they are the only women whose throats will be slit tonight. Everyone else being terminated is a man. They cannot live because they cannot be trusted.

Plans have been made to get their wives and children out of the country. I will ensure they are taken care of, provided they don't cross me. I expect a few token idiots will try to betray me, and we'll make an example of them. That will keep the others in line. Eventually, they will forget and move forward with their lives. In time, they may even come to thank me.

"The men who are loyal to you will be joining you in hell," I explain, trailing the tip of my knife up and down his straining arms. "They were given a choice, and they chose wrong." I level him with a cunning smile as I dig the knife into the inside of his lower arm, dragging it all the way through his skin, up to his armpit. Then I repeat the motion with the other arm, deeply satisfied with the inhuman sounds gurgling up my husband's throat as blood spills from the jagged cuts. I'm not sure what it says about me, but I am deriving enormous pleasure inflicting pain on him.

Without warning, I rip into his stomach, peeling back the flesh and yanking his entrails out. I let them hang over his body, draping them like a myriad of venomous snakes are climbing out of his insides. I feel nothing as I stab him repeatedly in the thighs, his legs, and his arms and slash across his face.

I should have put some opera on. A majestic symphony to accompany my artistic endeavors, I think as I step back and survey my masterpiece. Paulo is barely recognizable as a human, his body ripped apart with my sharp blade. I see the moment the light leaves his eyes, and a blanket of relief washes over me.

He can't hurt anyone anymore.

The world is stripped of one more evil prick.

Depositing my soiled gloves on the ground, I pick up my cell and call Renzo. "Bring them to the living room for me."

I snap a couple of pictures of the gruesome scene, planning to share this around. I want men to see this. To know what I am capable of. To understand what fate awaits them if they dare to double-cross me.

Tossing my cell on the table, I cross the bedroom and stare at my reflection in the mirror, scarcely recognizing the image peering back at me. The innocent girl with the bright, laughing eyes is long dead—

replaced by a bloodstained face that was crafted to seduce men and a body that burns with fiery intensity from the inside out.

Vengeance is a never-ending fire that refuses to extinguish.

As long as there is breath in my body, I vow to exact revenge on the men who have wronged me.

I will not be at peace until I have eradicated every single one of them from existence.

For years, I have plotted and planned with military precision. Now, the time has come to properly set things in motion. It will still take time, but I can be patient. Failure is not an option, and I won't cut corners. This will be a slow and methodical process, and by the end, I will be in control of The Commission and the entire Italian American mafia.

My spoken name will spread fear.

I will be talked about for years after I have exited this mortal realm.

No made man will dare to betray me.

All men will bow before me or die.

Chapter One

Catarina – 5 years later

"It is time to make move," Anton Smirnov says, straightening up in the high-backed leather chair behind the desk of his private home office. Unlike a lot of Russian diplomats in the US, Anton chose not to live at the Russian Diplomatic Compound in the Bronx, preferring a plush penthouse apartment on Park Avenue with stunning views over Central Park. Security is premium at this modern building, and he is guarded by a team of loyal *vory*.

"I agree. Pennsylvania, Florida, Ohio, Illinois, Washington, and Nevada are all running smoothly. It's time to shift our focus to Boston, New Jersey, and New York."

I have no doubt mention of Nevada is the reason for the tightening of his thin lips. Animosity between the Bratva and Don Salerno is as hostile as it has always been. Anton is the main *pakhan* presiding over the restructure of the Russian mafia within the US. While he was not here when things were at their bloodiest between my stepfather and the Russians over control of Las Vegas, he is well versed in the recent history and determined to exact revenge.

On that, we are in perfect alignment, but these things take time. It's a protracted game of chess, and every movement on the board requires deep analysis, strategic thinking, and copious amounts of patience.

"I will talk with Moscow and arrange meeting with Colombians to discuss expanding supply," he says in a distinctive authoritative voice, his tone still heavily accented despite his strong grasp of the English language and the voice coaching he availed of.

"It's already a foregone conclusion." I fold my hands neatly on my lap. "They have been trying to infiltrate the New York market for years. They won't turn us down, and I'm confident we can secure a good price. Part of getting Don Mazzone to agree will depend upon them undercutting the competition."

"The quality of their product trumps the Paraguayans', and they have proven their reliability," Anton supplies, rising majestically from his chair and heading to the liquor cabinet.

"That helps too, but the main obstacle I face is Don Mazzone's reluctance to get involved."

Bennett Mazzone is the head of the Mazzone *famiglia*—the most powerful of the five families who rule New York. Greco, Accardi, Maltese, and DiPietro make up the other four. All of them sit on the governing board of The Commission, led by Bennett as their president. Currently, all Italian American mafia organizations are members of The Commission, and we have enjoyed relative peace and prosperity for several years, thanks to their strong governance.

"He should want to clean up the mess," Anton replies, gesturing for me to join him at the window. "It's bad business for everyone."

"I agree, and it doesn't matter how much he has legitimized his business operations or that there are no ties to him on the streets. The FBI won't care. They are still aggressively pursuing the mafia via the RICO laws, and Don Mazzone has a big target on his back. His contacts can only do so much if they come for him. While I understand his reticence, he doesn't have much of a choice." I climb to my feet and join my ally at the window.

Anton hands me a vodka shot. "Na Zdorovie!"

I chink my glass against his. "Na Zdorovie."

We knock back our shots, standing companionably side by side as we survey the glorious view of the city and Central Park from Anton's fiftieth-floor penthouse.

To look at him, you would never suspect he is a powerful figure within the Bratva and the most powerful Russian in the US. The cut of his tall thin frame underneath the expensive suit is that of a confident man who is assured of his considerable talents and his place in the world. His dark hair is always neatly trimmed, and the streaks of gray threaded throughout give him a distinguished look that is nonthreatening. He looks nothing like the stereotypical mobster and everything like the diplomat he is. He's ex-military, and like a lot of his comrades in Russia, he has been heavily involved in the criminal world for many years, working a dual role for government and the underworld. They are not always easy to separate.

"What do the other families think?" he asks, cutting through my inner monologue. He tips his chin down to look at me.

"From the reports I have received, they are conflicted. Don Mazzone washed his hands of the street trade many years ago, focusing on supplying top-quality narcotics to VIP clients through his network of casinos and clubs and concentrating on his property development and tech businesses. The other families have always supported his decisions because they are all filthy rich, thanks to his shrewd thinking. But the current drug war on the streets is making most of the dons uneasy. Don DiPietro is already calling for action. When I sweep in, offering a solution, Bennett would be mad to turn me down."

"Your track record speaks volumes."

"*Our* track record speaks volumes."

Anton was introduced to me almost four years ago by a mutual contact. He had only recently relocated to the US through diplomatic channels. We connected instantly, recognizing a common goal and a shared philosophy for achieving it.

Through his strong leadership, the Bratva is finally achieving their potential in the US, but there is a lot more to do. What we have achieved thus far has been done on the down low, but that won't appease *Pakhan* Smirnov forever. He understands the need to do this in a structured piecemeal fashion, and he is less arrogant than most of the *vory* or made men I have encountered, but he is still a *man*.

There is only so long their ego can be contained.

"Has your brother-in-law mentioned anything about Greco marriage contract?" he asks, ushering me back to my chair, oblivious to the immediate panic that one word invokes in me.

Anton and I have a great relationship, but it's strictly professional. When outlining my reasons for wanting to form a working relationship with our enemy, I was deliberately vague about the events of my childhood, giving him only what he needed to know to be convinced of my sincerity.

He has no idea how that name instills true fear in me.

I brush a piece of lint off the leg of my white pants suit before reclaiming my seat, needing a few seconds to compose myself. Intense pressure sits on my chest, and a painful lump lodges in my throat until I focus on my breathing and get a hold of myself. The entire time I've been fighting an inner battle, my outward expression has remained composed, thanks to years of practice shielding my emotions. I clear my throat and shake my head. "Cruz hasn't said anything." I meet Anton's steely brown eyes head on. "What have you heard?"

He leans forward on the desk, clasping his hands in front of him. "It's your in." A pleased smile creeps across his mouth. "This is opening we have been waiting for."

"Are you going to tell me why you look close to puking?" Renzo asks the second we emerge from the elevator into the underground parking garage under Anton's building.

"Dario needs to hear this too," I explain, nodding at Ezio as he opens the door for me. "I'd rather not repeat myself."

The ninety-minute journey back to Philadelphia is quiet but fraught with all the things I haven't yet revealed. I need this time to come to grips with the solution in front of me. It's the obvious answer, but it will take iron-strong willpower to pull it off, and I'm not sure I have it within me to go through with it.

A layer of stress lifts from my shoulders as the car approaches the high wooden gates surrounding my two-story modern home. Nestled in a secluded area within the affluent Chestnut Hill area of Philly, it is my sanctuary, the one place where I can fully let my guard down and relax.

It's a glorious July evening, and I'm itching to pour a glass of chilled wine and sit out in my beautiful, landscaped garden, but this is the kind of conversation that must take place indoors. Even with all the security measures I have in place and the twenty-four-seven team of men stationed around the perimeter of my home, one can never be too careful. Drones are getting more sophisticated, along with surveillance equipment and other monitoring tools.

"You look pale, Donna Conti," Dario Agessi says, greeting me in the hallway of my home, when we step foot inside.

"You will understand when I tell you the latest development." I don't miss the concerned look Renzo shares with my *consigliere*, and I don't think it takes much for either man to connect the dots.

There is only one topic that has the power to rattle me, even after all these years.

Renzo, Dario, and his wife, Nicolina, know the truth about what Carlo Greco did to me when I was thirteen. Anais—my sister—was too young to understand, and I never told her when she got older.

No point in giving her nightmares too.

Her father—my stepfather—Saverio Salerno, the Las Vegas don, has been blackmailed into keeping silent, and Cruz DiPietro, my brother-in-law, is the only other person who knows, but I trust him to keep it a secret. He has his own ambitions and a vested interest in playing this game. He's pissed at the Mazzone *famiglia* for several reasons including my sister and her inability to keep her legs closed when it comes to Caleb Accardi. Caleb is Natalia Mazzone's stepson, but she is now Natalia Messina having married Leo—her brother Bennett's underboss—six or seven years ago.

It's a complicated mess that is vastly getting out of control, and I'm a complete bitch for stoking that flame to aid my agenda.

You won't hear any apologies from me.

Vengeance has no conscience, rules, or limits, and it is the greatest form of freedom. There is little I won't do to have my revenge.

"Tell us why you are so shaken," Agessi says when we are seated in my office, nursing matching glasses of scotch.

"There is good news and bad news." I pause to take a long drink of my whisky. "The good news is, we have a way to legitimately infiltrate New York." My gaze bounces between the only two men I trust in the world. I know this will not go down well with them. "The bad news is, it involves marrying into the Greco *famiglia*."

Shocked silence initially greets me. Renzo recovers his voice first. "No fucking way!" He grips the arm of his chair with tense fingers. "You are not marrying another weak pathetic piece of shit, and you are not putting yourself directly in the line of fire."

"I don't like it any more than you do, but this is too good of an opportunity to pass up. This is what we have been working toward all these years. Everything we have put into motion has led us to this point. Only a fool would turn it down."

"Everything we have been working toward is of no use without the woman who spearheaded this from the start," Agessi says, piercing me with troubled blue eyes. "The personal cost is too great. It is something we can't ask of you."

"I'm not asking." I drill both men with a sharp look. They advise and support me, but ultimately, the decision will be mine.

"Think about this logically," Renzo says, his Adam's apple jumping in his throat. "How could you ever step foot in that house again without revealing your true identity? How could you fuck that man knowing what his brother, *that fucking animal*, did to you?"

"I didn't say it would be easy, but it's mind over matter, and I have had years of practice handling the fallout from those seven months. I didn't endure the things I've endured to give up now I am getting closer and closer to my end goal." I throw back the rest of my scotch and stalk to the liquor cabinet to refill my glass.

I am careful when it comes to alcohol, always remaining in control because my enemies can strike at any time. But tonight, I need to get blistering drunk. I want to blot it all out before I am forced to confront it.

"Gabriele may be weak, but he is not unkind," Agessi supplies, already reading my determination clearly. "If the rumors I have heard recently are true, I don't think you need to worry about him sharing your bed."

I have heard those rumors too, but that is neither here nor there. "Mazzone isn't seeking a marriage contract for Gabriele Greco. He is looking for a bride for his younger brother, Massimo."

"The Ghost?" Renzo blurts, his eyes popping wide. "You're considering marrying a man no one knows any fucking thing about?" His tone rises with every word, and I can't recall the last time I saw him so agitated.

I dump more scotch in my glass and bring it to my lips. "I'm not *considering* it. I'm doing it. And there is nothing you can say or do that will stop me."

Chapter Two

Catarina

"You're drunk," Nicolina says, casting a shadow over my bikini-clad body as I lie stretched out on the sun lounger by my pool.

"And you're blocking my sun." I jerk my head at the lounger beside me. "Sit your skinny little butt down."

My only female friend lies beside me, setting an empty wineglass down on the circular glass table between us. Nic shoves the hem of her cute blue summer dress up to her thighs and closes her eyes as she tips her head back, lifting her face to the sun.

"Dario sent you to babysit me," I surmise, conscious I may be slightly inebriated. After three large whiskies, I grabbed a bottle of Sancerre from the refrigerator and came out here to relax. Not that it's working, and despite what my friend thinks, I'm not nearly drunk enough.

"He's worried about you. He told me what happened and how Renzo stormed out of here."

I heave a tired sigh. "I know Renzo's concern comes from a good place, but he's thinking with his heart, not his head."

"He's still in love with you," she says, opening her eyes and sitting up straighter.

"He was never in love with me," I scoff, pouring my bestie a large glass of crisp white wine. "He has been many things to me over the years. My trainer. A friend. My closest confidant and a trusted colleague. He's my family. He was only my lover for a short time, and he doesn't love me, at least not in the way you are implying."

"You have a warped view of love," she replies, accepting the glass I hand to her. "That's why you don't see it."

"I don't believe in love, so how can I see something I don't believe exists?"

"You don't see the love between me and Dario?" she inquires, quirking a brow. "Because that is definitely the real deal."

"I'm not getting into a philosophical debate with you about love. My acceptance that you two have a good marriage is not a declaration that I believe in love as a concept. More that I believe in you two as soul mates."

"You're splitting hairs, Rina, and we both know it."

"We're getting off topic. Not that it matters. I'm doing it, and Renzo will just have to get used to it. I'm the boss. I make the decisions. Period."

Nic swings her legs over the side of the lounger, shielding the sun again as she pins me with a knowing look. "Retract those claws, girl. This is me you're talking to. I know you've got to be scared shitless."

I sit up, mirroring her position so we are facing one another. "I am, but that has got nothing to do with this. This is a means to an end, and I have never shied away from challenges."

"I know you are strong. You are the strongest woman I know, but this is going to dredge up all those emotions you have worked so hard to bury. This will not be a cakewalk."

"You think I don't know that?" I hiss, gulping back a mouthful of wine. "I know this will be one of the hardest challenges I have faced, but what doesn't kill us makes us stronger."

"Dario says there is little known about this man. Walking into the unknown will make it harder."

"It could make it easier." I shrug, because the truth is we don't know.

"What is known of him isn't that favorable. He has shirked his responsibilities to his family, leaving his brother to run things alone when he's clearly incapable of providing the necessary leadership. While reports say Massimo is the ultimate playboy, there are literally no pictures of him anywhere. I googled him before I left the house, and all that came up is he's an enigma. He could be a worse monster than Paulo. Worse than—" She cuts herself off, cursing softly under her breath.

"You can say it. Worse than his brother though I honestly don't believe there is a man walking this earth who could ever exceed the creative depths of Carlo Greco's depravity."

"I don't want you to go into this with blinders on."

Irritation churns in my gut. "I never go into anything without being fully cognizant of all the angles. This will be no different. I will request a meeting with Don Mazzone, outline my proposition to restore peace to the streets of New York, and when he declines my help on the grounds I have no jurisdiction, I will propose myself for the marriage contract. No commitment will be made until I sign on the dotted line, and I will only do that after I have met the man and seen what I will be dealing with." I stand, snatching the almost-empty bottle of wine in my hand. "If you came over to lecture me, you know where the door is."

"Shut the fuck up and sit your cranky ass down." Nic swipes the bottle from my hand and pushes me back onto the lounger. "We care about you, and you want us to challenge your decisions. You were the one who said you didn't want to be surrounded by yes men. That means you can't get mad when we question your choices to ensure you have fully thought things through."

I exhale heavily, knowing I'm being unfair. "You're right."

"I always am." Nic bobs her head and waves of bouncy golden-blonde curls frame her gorgeous face. Occasionally, I am envious of her blonde locks, wishing I didn't have to dye my natural dark-blonde hair a deep rich brown.

"No one likes a smug asshole," I remind her, holding out my glass for a top off.

"It works for Fiero Maltese," she retorts, and I bark out a laugh.

"Fiero is the quintessential mafia playboy. I'm pretty sure Massimo Greco would fall short of the mark when compared to the Maltese heir."

"What about the bathroom hottie from Maine?" she randomly asks, pulling out her cell and swiping her fingers across the screen.

I roll my eyes. "That was five years ago, Nic. Get over it already." I'm such a freaking hypocrite, but you will have to ply me with copious whiskies and rip every nail from my fingers before I'll admit I think of the hot stranger more than is normal after all this time.

A few seconds later, she thrusts his image in my face.

"Why the hell do you still have his photo on your phone?" I ask, reluctantly taking it from her.

Fuck, he is seriously hot, and I still get shivers remembering how incredible the sex was. Which is why I deleted his pic from my phone a long time ago. Men like him are a distraction I don't need and can't afford.

"After I got Renzo to send it to me, for you, I couldn't quite make myself delete it." My underboss had snapped a pic of the man when he wasn't watching. It's standard protocol for the random men I pick up for sex. Insurance in case they try anything. No one ever has, but I can never let my guard down.

I arch a brow. "Does your husband know you drool over pics of other men?"

"Pfft." She waves her hands about. "If you think Dario doesn't check out hot chicks, you don't know him very well. We're allowed to look as long as we don't touch."

Dario and Renzo are both loyal to their wives; a rarity in the world we inhabit.

I hand the phone back to her. "I don't know why you even mentioned him. What the hell has he got to do with anything?"

"He is the only man I have ever seen you show any interest in." She stows her phone back in her purse. "I thought maybe something would happen." Her features soften as she squeezes my hand. "Don't tell me you're not lonely because I won't believe it."

I shrug, unwilling to enter into this conversation. "I'm too busy to be lonely," I lie. "I find a man to fuck when I want sex, and the rest of the time, I'm content doing my own thing. I'm not unhappy. I live my life the way I like it."

"That makes me sad for you. I want you to experience love because no one deserves it more than you do."

"I don't like you going in alone and unarmed," Renzo says, staring glumly at me as I hand him my Stryker and my gun from the back seat of my blacked-out SUV. We are parked in the secure private parking lot of the building The Commission operates out of.

"Relax. I'm meeting The Commission—not going before The Triad to explain why I blamed them for something I orchestrated." I flash him a wicked grin, grateful it didn't take long to get an audience with Don Mazzone and his esteemed colleagues.

Calling my brother-in-law helped to fast-track the meeting. Don DiPietro, Cruz's father, is close to retirement, and increasingly he is bowing to his eldest son's decision-making. I talked to Cruz, and he put a word in his father's ear. It was Don DiPietro who proposed a meeting with me to listen to my ideas for resolving the turf war that has broken out on the streets.

"You have many irons in the fire," Renzo says. "Be careful you don't get burned."

"Don't worry. I know how to handle myself," I say before exiting the car. Renzo insists on coming up in the elevator with me, and I don't object. I know he needs to do this for his sanity. To say things have been a little tense between us this past week is an understatement. Repairing our relationship is at the top of my priority list after I make my pitch and watch the dominoes fall into place.

"Shit," I mutter under my breath when we step out of the elevator onto the twentieth floor, spying Leonardo Messina striding this way.

Bennett's underboss is a smart man, and I bet he never forgets a face. I hope he doesn't remember the broken, battered, frightened girl he carried from the Greco's basement twenty-one years ago. I'm confident I look different enough not to be instantly recognizable, but there's still a smidgeon of doubt.

Thrusting my shoulders back and lifting my head, I skim a quick hand down the front of my white and gold Prada skirt suit and walk forward with a poise gleaned from years of projecting an image of power and control.

His gaze is appreciative and respectful as he watches me approach, slowing to a stop as we meet in the middle of the hallway. Leo extends his hand. "Donna Conti. It is a pleasure to finally meet you."

I am guessing Bennett must have told him about our meeting because there are no pictures of me online. I have made sure of it. Thanks to Bennett's tech companies, most of the families now have the resources to ensure there is no footprint on the internet. Guarding our identities, and our movements, is vital with the FBI breathing down our necks all the time.

I clasp his hand in a firm handshake. "Likewise, Mr. Messina. Your reputation precedes you."

"As does yours."

"I'm hoping that's a good thing." My lips lift at the corners.

"Absolutely," he replies without hesitation, his brow puckering as he glances over my shoulder at Renzo. "Have we met before?" he asks, and all the tiny hairs on the back of my exposed neck lift. I turn around and subtly glare at my underboss.

"I don't believe we have," Renzo coolly replies.

While I'm reluctant to offer his name, without knowing why Leo has made that observation, I have no choice but to introduce him now. "This is Renzo Dutti. My underboss from Philadelphia."

They shake hands, coolly assessing one another. "You won't be permitted to enter with Donna Conti," Leo confirms, casually thrusting his hands into the pockets of his pants. "All meetings are closed."

"I am aware," Renzo replies. "I will wait for her in the hallway."

Leo nods, staring vacantly at my underboss before seeming to shake himself. His brow smooths out, and I release the breath I was holding when he returns his attention to me. "It was an honor to meet you. I hope your meeting goes well."

"You too and thank you."

We part company, and Renzo walks quietly by my side until we hear the ping of the elevator doors closing. I slam to a halt, casting a glance over my shoulder to ensure the hallway is empty. Spying cameras mounted to the wall, I walk to the bathroom and enter with Renzo trailing behind me. He checks the stalls are empty before locking the door.

"What don't I know?" I ask, working hard to rein my anger in.

"I met Leonardo and Bennett one time in Vegas, but it was like eleven or twelve years ago. It was during that time when Saverio had pulled me away from you. I didn't think Leo would remember me as our contact was fleeting."

"Why is this the first I'm hearing about this?"

"Honestly, I didn't think about it until we ran into him." He runs a hand along the back of his neck. "Now that I recall the circumstances, I'm pretty sure it was the night Bennett met his wife, Sierra." He at least has the decency to look ashamed.

"You being here could have jeopardized everything." I am beyond livid.

"He didn't recognize you. That's more important."

I shove his shoulders, slamming him back into the wall. "Don't bullshit me. If he connects you to Vegas, he could connect me too."

"I'm sorry, Catarina. It was negligent of me."

I narrow my eyes at him. "You don't mess up. What's really going on?"

"I've been distracted since you dropped the bomb last week." He grabs my hands in his, holding them tight. "Don't do it. Please, I'm begging you."

I forcibly remove his hands and step back. "I am not discussing this with you again. The decision is made, and this conversation is over."

A muscle clenches in my jaw as I stalk to the sink to check my reflection in the mirror. I touch up my nude lipstick, inspecting my chignon for any stray strands. Renzo hovers behind me, the weight of unspoken words thickening the space between us.

The front of my suit jacket dips low, showcasing the upper swells of my breasts. I purposely didn't wear a camisole, aiming for sophisticated seduction. Strings of gold-colored pearls adorn my neck, matching the gold borders edging the lapels and cuffs of my jacket and the hem of my skirt. Skyscraper pale-gold stilettos elongate my smooth legs.

I know I look the part; now I just need to execute it.

I turn around, staring wordlessly at my underboss, silently questioning if he is losing his nerve. I hope not because I need him. He has always been my rock, and he's important to me.

Renzo follows me to the door, flipping the latch and unlocking the door. "I haven't forgotten what you were like when you first came to Vegas," he says in a low voice, staring at the door as he talks to me. "You may have banished it from your mind, but I will *never* forget it." He thumps his fist against his chest before turning around. Pain is etched upon his face, fear shining from his eyes. "I cannot bear the thought of seeing you like that again. If you do this and they hurt you, I will raze New York to the ground."

Chapter Three

Catarina

The door to the conference room opens, and Bennett Mazzone greets me with a warm smile. "Donna Conti, welcome."

"It's a pleasure to meet you, Don Mazzone," I say, shaking his hand.

"Likewise, and please call me Ben."

"Only if you call me Catarina," I reply with a genuine smile. I like that he doesn't stand on ceremony. It seems to affirm everything I have heard about the man. "Thank you for seeing me on such short notice."

"Please join us." He steps aside to let me enter, and I feel Renzo's burning gaze at my back.

The room is long and wide with a glossy rectangular walnut table, housing sixteen chairs, occupying prime real estate in the center. A couple of flip charts are stowed in the top corner of the room to the left of a long cabinet mounted against the wall. The scent of freshly brewed coffee lingers in the air, tickling my nostrils. An impressive coffee machine with accompanying supplies rests beside a tray holding bottles of water and pastries. Floor-to-ceiling windows offer clear views of the building across the road. No blinds cover the windows, but it doesn't surprise me. Ben owns this building, and I know the windows are constructed of special glass that looks clear from the inside and tinted from the exterior. I also have it on good authority that it's bulletproof glass—a sturdy structure that is patented by one of Don Mazzone's own companies.

"Allow me to introduce you," Ben says, closing the door and steering me toward the table where the other dons wait to meet me. He announces them one at a time, and I pass the usual pleasantries, working hard to keep my façade firmly in place as I greet Gabriele Greco. Discreetly wiping my sweaty palms down the side of my skirt, I force a fake smile as I formally meet one of the men I despise.

I saw him one time, staring at me from the doorway of the basement of his family home. I was lying on the cold, steel floor of the cage I ended up calling home for seven months, soaking in a pool of my own blood and urine. Every inch of my skin was aching and throbbing, and my scalp was stinging where Carlo had torn clumps of my hair out the night before. I couldn't move a muscle or force my vocal cords to work to plead with the man at the door for help.

By then, I knew no one was coming to my aid.

All I could do was stare at the man with the worried frown as he silently watched me. Then he turned on the leather soles of his dress shoes, and I heard the distinct clacking sound as he retreated, taking the stairs as fast as possible so he could get away from me.

I never saw him again, and it was at least two months later when Leo and Mateo rescued me.

My heart is racing, my palms are clammy, and blood is pounding in my ears as I exchange words with him. He smiles, showing no hint of recognition, which is a relief but only a minor one.

"Take a seat." Ben pulls a chair out for me, but before I can sit, Don Maltese clears his throat.

"She should be checked for weapons." His lips kick up at the corner. "I volunteer as tribute." His greedy old-man gaze roams the length of my body with zero shame as a couple of the others shuffle awkwardly in their seats. I guess the apple hasn't fallen too far from the tree with his son.

Ben levels a harsh glare at his colleague. "I will not dignify that comment with a reply, only to apologize for your ungentlemanly conduct." Ben turns to me with a sincere expression, and I can already tell his reputation hasn't been exaggerated. "Please accept my apology, Donna Conti. Roberto was way out of line."

All hint of humor fades from Don Maltese's face, and I smother a smile. "It's fine. It's not exactly original, and I have been subjected to far worse," I coolly reply, elegantly lowering myself into the chair and placing my cell on the table. At least it has diverted the surge of panicked adrenaline that was coursing through my veins being in the same room as the brother of my abductor.

"I am sorry to hear that." Ben claims a seat at the top of the table. "I genuinely hoped our organization had moved beyond the sexist archaic treatment of the past, but it's clear I have more work to do." He levels another cutting look in Maltese's direction.

I want to suggest it's a hopeless endeavor as long as men like Don Maltese sit on the governing body of The Commission. From the things I have heard about his son, I'm not sure his successor will be much of an improvement.

"My son speaks very highly of you," Don DiPietro says, clawing a meaty hand through the shock of thick silver hair on his head as he focuses the conversation.

Ben studies me for a few seconds. "How do you know Cruz?"

"We met through mutual colleagues at an event in Cincinnati a few years ago," I lie.

I purposely didn't attend Anais's wedding to Cruz DiPietro six years ago. Protecting my identity so I could execute my plan was greater than my desire to see my half-sister get married.

Anais and I communicate mainly via phone or FaceTime, and she knows to keep our relationship a secret. She, too, has her own reasons for wanting to retaliate at Ben. I only took Cruz into my confidence a couple of years ago when I knew I could manipulate him into helping my cause and could trust he would go along with it. Of course, he doesn't even know the half of it. I have fed him the right amount of information, and no more, to ensure he does my bidding.

"My understanding is you have intel about the war that has broken out over the supply chain on the streets and you have a proposal to resolve it." Ben's keen gaze traps me in place.

"I do." I maintain eye contact as I relax a little in my chair and pop the cap on a bottle of water. With slow, steady hands, I pour some water into the glass and take a sip while my gaze bounces confidently between the men. Setting my glass down, I part my lips, letting my tongue peek out to lick my bottom lip. Then I inhale deeply, the movement drawing subtle notice to my chest.

I now have the attention of all the men in the room with one exception I'm not unhappy about.

The key to projecting confidence is body language. Intelligent conversation and holding my own among a group of men would only get me so far if my body betrayed my fear. So, I have learned how to hold myself in such situations. I remain upright but relaxed as I let my gaze flicker across the five most important Italian American men in the US while they wait for me to pitch to them.

Hidden fear is hot and fiery as my eyes briefly linger on Gabriele's. He looks a lot like Carlo with the same dark hair and chocolate-brown eyes, but where Carlo had an evil cold glint in his gaze, his younger brother's eyes are a warmer brown. Still, looking at him is like staring the ghosts of my past in the face, and it has the power to unnerve me.

If I let it. Which I won't.

"You have the floor," Luca Accardi says gently nudging me with his words and a quick tilt of his head.

A screen lowers from the ceiling at the other end of the table as I tap into my phone. Ben gave me the technical specifications before the meeting so I could deliver a visual presentation. I learned from experience that made men won't accept what I say without proof, and I came prepared.

I pull up the first set of photo files, and they load quickly on the screen as all five men lean forward in their seats with undisguised interest. "The Triad has cut a deal with the Paraguayans, which sees them receiving the lion's share of the supplies coming into the city," I say, omitting the part where I orchestrated it from the shadows. "The Irish and the Mexicans have been arguing with the Paraguayans over missing shipments and delayed orders until they recently became aware of Lee Chang's betrayal. They confronted him to resolve this peaceably," I add, moving through pictures showing The Triad leader meeting his Paraguayan contact under the cover of darkness and several trucks leaving the port laden down with cocaine and marijuana.

My next picture shows Chinese warehouses piled high with a variety of narcotics and chemicals. Ben curses under his breath as I display close-ups. "They have also cut a deal to bring heroin and MDMA in through Canada. The Chinese are known for mixing drugs with chemicals to produce an inferior product that causes a higher incidence of accidental overdoses. When they were working with the Irish and the Mexicans, there was a quality control standard. Now they are doing things their way. It was this intel that ultimately started the war."

Ben and the other dons exchange looks, and I can tell this is news to them. A ripple of excitement goes through me. I love when a plan comes together. "The Irish and Mexicans remain allied, and they are determined to wipe The Triad from existence in New York and split their turf. A reliable source has confirmed The Triad is expecting a heavy shipment of arsenal next month. The bloodshed you have witnessed on the streets recently is nothing compared to the chaos that is due to be unleashed."

"How is it you are aware of this?" Don Mazzone asks. "This isn't your jurisdiction."

"We're neighbors. It's natural I would hear things. I have spent years developing a reliable network of contacts who keep me informed across the US."

"Impressive." He stares at me in quiet contemplation, his face betraying no hint of the concern he must be feeling. He's not confirming my intel is better than his either. Not that I blame him. I would keep that close to my chest too.

"Our reluctance to intervene has cost us," Don DiPietro says.

"It needs to be dealt with before this war brings heat down on all of us," Don Accardi adds.

"What is your proposal?" Don Greco asks, and I try not to hiss at him as I reply.

"It's quite simple really. Give me full control, and I will take The Triad, the Irish, and the Mexicans out and run the supply in New York on your behalf."

Rumbling laughter erupts from Don Maltese, and I really want to gut that motherfucker until his intestines are coating the floor. "Simple? Are you insane? There is nothing *simple* about eliminating the three main suppliers on the street. The blowback alone would result in a war just as bloody."

"This is not my first rodeo. How else do you think I have achieved control across several US states?"

"I can understand eliminating The Triad. Those assholes have disrupted the peace, but the Irish and the Mexicans have coexisted with us for years without any trouble," Don DiPietro says. "Turning on them without due cause is bad for business."

"My track record begs to differ."

"You can't tell me you didn't endure threats and challenges when you wiped out rivals in other states," Ben supplies, eyeing me with abject intrigue.

"Of course, I did, but the trick is to anticipate it and to act first. There are several smaller gangs operating in pockets around New York who will jump at the chance to cut out the middlemen and control the supply." A list Dario compiled uploads on the screen. "None of these local gangs are serious competition. We wipe them out at the same time we hit the others, installing our own men in each location and buying their loyalty."

"It's way too risky if it backfires." Don Maltese slants me with a superior look.

"It won't." My voice projects confidently around the room. "My strategy works. It's well tested." I haven't introduced the other element to this plan yet, needing to secure agreement first.

"None of those states are New York," Greco says.

"I am aware." I drill him with a sharp look before redirecting my attention to Ben. "My team has been working on this for months. We have surveillance intel we can share with you, as well as lists of names and addresses, distribution routes, and the locations of warehouses and safe houses. Inspect it for yourself if you need more convincing."

"I would like to study it," he concurs, and I swipe my fingers across my phone, sending him the preprepared email with all the information. His cell pings. Ben glances briefly at it, nodding once in my direction.

"The Paraguayans will never go for it," Don Maltese says, determined to get my idea rejected. "They can't supply the quantities we need for our VIP clients plus service the entire street business."

"We can't risk pissing them off and disrupting our supply," Don Accardi agrees.

"We don't need them. My supplier is willing to distribute to New York. They deliver quicker, they have the volume we need, and their product is better quality."

Ben's mouth pulls into a thin line. "You're talking about the Colombians." I haven't hidden who my supply partner is on purpose. I want them to believe the Colombians supply most of my product when the truth is it's the Russians who supply the bulk.

I nod as Don Accardi hisses under his breath. "Over my dead body will we partner with them."

That can be arranged, I think as I stare neutrally at him. "Business decisions based on emotion are unwise. I know there is bad blood between New York and the Colombians, but—"

"With good reason," Don DiPietro says, cutting across me as Don Greco shifts uneasily in his seat.

"Those bastards can't be trusted," Don Accardi adds.

"I have worked with them for four years, and I can vouch for them. They can supply us with the quantities we need, and they are reliable."

"We got out of the street trade years ago for a reason." Ben drums his fingers on the table. "We need to step in now to resolve this, but that doesn't mean we want to manage it going forward. It's a headache we don't need."

"Which is where I come in. I am skilled at managing this. You won't need to lift a finger. I will run this for you."

"What's in it for us?" Don Maltese asks.

"I have negotiated a significant discount with the Colombians, which will save you money on your existing orders and enable you to skim ten percent off the street trade for yourselves." All heads perk up, and I know I've got them. Profit always trumps objection. "You will benefit considerably just by approving me and my plan."

"If we were to agree," Don Accardi says, "and that's a big if, you would be reporting directly to us. Why would you want to do that? You're your own boss. By all accounts, you are wealthy and powerful in your own right. Why start answering to someone now?"

"I want more," I plainly state. "My hunger for success is the fuel that drives me," I lie because my sole motivation is revenge. I eyeball Ben. "I believe in the vision you and The Commission have for all Italian Americans. I believe I can add value and play a part." I lean forward, my eyes sparkling with the requisite excitement. "Imagine a US where all the drug supply is managed by The Commission. We'll be the biggest market in the world, serviced by two or three key suppliers who only sell to us. We can take advantage of the technological and financial resources at your disposal to digitize the distribution and payment in a way that keeps us off the radar and eliminates the need to wash so much cash."

"You think you can legitimize narcotics?" Disbelief threads through Ben's tone.

"Not in the way you and I have legitimized other parts of our businesses, but I believe there is a smarter way to manage this that affords us more protection." I return my attention to the other men around the table, who are still not fully sold on the idea. "This is a long-term plan. This isn't something that can be achieved overnight. We start by regaining control in New York, building a new team and new processes, and once that's nailed down, we talk about reaching out to New Jersey and Boston, Chicago, and other territories. We build a model that works and sell that until all the supply is under our control."

I pause to take another drink of water before continuing. "So, to answer your question, Don Accardi, that's why I want this."

"You have given us much to consider," Ben says, "and there is a lot worthy of merit, but we have one key concern."

"Trust," I supply.

He nods. "I know you have proven yourself. I know what is said about you amongst the families. You are hardworking, and you deliver on your promises. But you are an outsider."

"And a woman," Don Maltese adds.

I deliberately look down at my chest before lifting my chin and pinning him with a flirtatious grin. "Last time I checked."

"Women are weak," he retorts, fixing me with a smug grin. "Respected only for what's between their legs, not what's between their ears."

"A misogynist. What a surprise," I deadpan, rimming the edge of my glass with the tip of my finger.

"Your sexist, ageist remarks are becoming tiresome, Roberto. Show Donna Conti the respect she deserves," Ben says to Don Maltese, earning my admiration. There are a lot of things I admire and respect about Bennett Mazzone.

I won't enjoy killing him.

"I understand trust and loyalty are earned," I say, keeping the conversation on track. "I fully understand what I'm asking is a big risk for you to take, so I have a potential solution I think you will be happy with." I deliberately let my eyes wander to Gabriele Greco.

Ben sits up straighter, awareness ghosting over his face.

I stare directly at the president. "I believe you are looking for a bride for Massimo Greco. I will marry him and handle this situation for The Commission"—I pin my gaze on my startled enemy across the table—"as a Greco."

Chapter Four

Massimo

"No." Leaning back in my chair, I face off with my brother, daring him to keep pushing me.

"No?!" Gabriele strains forward in his seat, propping his elbows on the desk.

It's still weird to see him sitting in father's seat, at the desk that's a family heirloom, in an office that holds nothing but bad memories for me.

Steam billows from his ears, and his nostrils twitch as he glares at me. "You dare to say no to me after everything I've done for you?" he roars in a heightened tone that is most unlike him.

"I told you I will come into the business earlier than planned and work with you on a transfer of power, but that doesn't include you choosing a bride for me. If I ever marry, it will be a woman I select."

He slams his fist down on the desk, rattling the bottle of Old Rip Van Winkle perched in front of him.

"Papa was too soft on you," he says, shaking his head as he refills his glass with more bourbon. I declined because I don't plan to stick around after I check in on Mom, and unlike my weak, spoiled, unobservant brother, I don't have a personal driver.

"Do not mistake neglect for tenderness." I grip the sides of my chair, my knuckles blanching white. "Maximo Greco didn't have a single soft bone in his body. The beatings I endured in this very office are testament to that. Don't pretend like you don't remember."

Fuck, I would kill for a drink, but my desire to return to my home trumps that need.

"You are lucky he ignored you as much as he did." Gabriele stares off into space, looking lost in memories. Tense silence bleeds into the air. My brother turns his head, eyeballing me. "Neither of us is cut out for this life."

I wouldn't agree in my case, but I don't refute him because I'm not ready to reveal my truths yet. "You are lucky Don Mazzone has been in charge during your reign. He's smart, and he has achieved peace and prosperity. It could be a lot worse. If Papa or Carlo or Primo were in your shoes, they would have butted heads with Bennett a long time ago."

"They would never have accepted him as the president of The Commission in the long-term," Gabriele agrees. "Especially Papa and Primo after the brutal way the Mazzones killed Carlo."

"Let's get real, brother," I say, sitting more upright. "Carlo had that coming to him. If you ask me, they did the world a favor."

I was only fourteen when Carlo was murdered by Mateo Mazzone and Leonardo Messina, but I remember the sheer relief I felt when I heard the news.

We didn't know the identity of his killers for years, much to Papa's consternation. When he discovered the truth, he plotted with Gino Accardi to double-cross Bennett, but it ended up backfiring when they were killed, along with a ton of other dons and their heirs at the warehouse bombing in Chicago, orchestrated by members of The Outfit who were still loyal to the DeLucas. It was a total shit show, and it's how Gabriele ended up as don when he had zero desire for the job. It was always supposed to go to Carlo or Primo as the eldest sons.

"You shouldn't speak ill of our brother or the dead."

I stand, stretching my arms up over my head and rotating my right shoulder, which still aches after my last job. "I hope he's rotting in hell. It's no less than he deserves."

Gabriele sighs as he stands. "He wasn't a good man, but I still don't wish that on him."

We walk to the window, standing side by side as we watch Mama enjoy afternoon tea in the garden. She's alone, like usual, but she looks content. I still remember the shell of a woman she was when my father was alive. While it's too late for her to bloom, now he's dead, at least some semblance of life has returned to her frail form.

"She isn't happy I want to move out," he says.

"I doubt it will make much difference. It's not like you are here that often." Guilt splays across my brother's face, and I feel instant remorse. "I didn't state the obvious to make you feel bad. She will be fine. It won't be much of a change, and you deserve to live your life."

"I do." He leans into the wall, facing me on his side. "I'm not cut out for this, Massimo. I know you don't want to do it either, but you'll be better at it than me."

Gabriele is too soft for this life, which is one of the reasons I made a pact with him when Papa and Primo were killed and he was next in line to head up our family. "I told you I will honor our agreement, and I don't mind stepping up earlier, but I won't be forced into marriage with a stranger. Not by you or Bennett Mazzone."

"War is coming, brother, and it's going to get messy. This woman could be the key to restoring peace." He clamps a hand on my shoulder. "I think you will like her. She's smart, ambitious, and beautiful. She runs several territories, and she could be the perfect buffer to cover your shortcomings until you are up to speed."

I grind my teeth to the molars, trying not to let my irritation show. It's not my brother's fault he has no clue who I am. I have hidden it from everyone for a reason, but the gloves will be coming off soon.

"We know nothing about her." I intend to conduct some research and put some feelers out, but I don't expect it to turn up much.

"We are aware of that fact. It's the main reason Ben supports this plan. He was impressed with her, and if she can deliver what she promises, she will be a formidable ally. But he suspects there is more she isn't saying. Having her marry into the *famiglia* is the best way to keep her close and weed out her hidden agenda. As your wife, she'll have to bend to your decisions. You will keep her in her place."

"*You* marry her then." My lips fight a smirk.

"If she had a dick between her legs, instead of a pussy that has Don Maltese all riled up, I would totally go for it." He slaps me on the back. "We both know I couldn't satisfy a woman like that, but you can."

"So, I'm to be nothing more than a glorified gigolo?"

"Seduce her into giving up her secrets and ensure she's fully on our side. I doubt it'll be a chore." He chuckles. "If she is planning to betray us, you can kill her and marry whoever the fuck you like. I really don't see the problem."

I can't explain it without coming off like a total wimp. What man jerks off to memories of a random woman and a fleeting bathroom quickie that happened years ago? I still can't explain it to myself. "I'm not committing to anything until I have met her," I say, knowing I have to at least agree to a meeting.

Gabriele grins, like he knows something I don't. I feel a childish urge to give him a wedgie. "I'll set it up. You won't regret it."

"How are you, Mother?" I ask, bending down to kiss Mama on the cheek before I claim the seat beside her. Slouching in my chair, I lean back and tip my face up to the sun, absorbing the warmth and the Vitamin D.

"I am good, son. How was Rome?"

"Overcrowded, overpriced, and overrated."

"I doubt it's overrated." She pours two glasses of iced tea from the jug chilling in the cooler box. Our housekeeper knows how much

Mama enjoys sitting outside in the summer, and she caters to her needs with a dedication that is commendable. "Perhaps you could take me the next time you visit."

"That sounds like a plan," I lie. Mama thinks I've spent the past seventeen years traveling the world for pleasure. Occasionally, she asks if she can come with me, and I hate turning her down. But the line of work I am in means it isn't safe.

"Did your brother tell you he's moving out?" she asks as I take a long gulp of my iced tea.

I kick my booted feet up on the legs of the table. "He's forty, Mama. It's time he moved out." I know Gabriele has stayed here for her, but it's made things awkward in his personal life. Being a gay made man is not acceptable, less so if you're a don. Sneaking around is hard for my brother, especially when he can't bring his lovers home. I don't blame him for wanting a place of his own.

"I will miss him."

"He will visit regularly like I do." I make it a point to check on Mama often when I'm not overseas on business.

"My boys are good to me." She pats my cheek before sipping her drink, and I wonder if she is truly happy or if she just puts on a front for Gabriele and me.

I'm sitting at the glass table in front of the rock pool at my house a few hours later when the security system alerts me to an impending visitor. Drinking from my beer, I pull up the camera feed on my laptop, grinning as I watch Fiero drive his Ducati Panigale up my driveway. Parking alongside my Ducati ST, he removes his helmet and hangs it off the handlebars.

Running a hand through his chin-length white-blond hair, he forgoes the front door, sauntering around the side of my five-thousand-square-foot bungalow. Hidden among the forest, on four acres of land in Oyster Bay Cove, Long Island, my home is my fortress. Only a handful of friends and family has ever been here. I have high-end security systems and a team of armed men guarding my property, and a secure secluded pathway that leads to the private strip of beach I own at the rear of my land.

Snagging a cold beer from the outdoor refrigerator behind me, I pop the cap as my oldest friend rounds the corner of my property and comes into view. "Dawg, you've been holding out on me," he says as he approaches. "I hear congratulations are in order."

I roll my eyes as I hand him the beer. "Made men are worse gossips than women."

My best buddy chuckles as he sinks into the seat beside me. "Damn straight. Catarina Conti sure has my old man frothing at the mouth."

"Any woman trying to challenge norms would have your old man frothing at the mouth," I reply, pushing my laptop and my research aside for now.

"So, it's true? You're marrying her?"

I shake my head. "I told Gabe I'd meet with her, but I have promised nothing more."

"Pops said she's sexy as shit."

I bring my beer to my lips and swallow a couple mouthfuls. The cold bitter liquid glides pleasantly down my throat. "That would make it more palatable, but I'm not being forced into marriage."

"It would interfere with your contract work."

"That's coming to an end anyway."

He arches a brow. "Already? That's a little ahead of our schedule."

"Gabe wants out now. It's time to step up."

"Are you ready?"

"As ready as I ever will be."

He flashes me a grin that regularly has panties dropping all over the city. He clinks his beer against mine. "Soon it will be our time to shine. Our time to lead. That motherfucker DiPietro won't know what's hit him."

"Has your old man relented yet?" I inquire, my gaze automatically drifting to my open laptop.

"You know he's a stubborn fucker. Claims he has plenty of years left in him yet." Fiero shrugs, but his jaw pulls tight. He endured a lot of the same shit I did growing up. The difference is, he's the eldest son in his family while I was the youngest. I was never destined to rule, but it's always been his destiny. Don Maltese is a sour motherfucker who never loses an opportunity to whale on his heir. He had that in common with my father.

I can't wait to prove everyone wrong.

"If he won't back down, we might have to help him along." I stab him with a solemn look.

Fiero's Adam's apple bobs in his throat as he slowly nods. "The thought has occurred to me."

"You'd do it?"

"If that's what it comes down to? Yeah." He exhales heavily, pinning me with ice-blue eyes clear of indecision. I nod, respecting his lack of hesitation. His eyes flick over my head. "What are you up to?" he asks, dragging my laptop toward him.

"Research on Donna Conti."

"And?" He scrolls down the page.

"I can't find anything."

"That's not unusual within our organization these days. You can't find something if it isn't there even with your superior tech skills."

"I can usually find something even if it's fake and purely there to cover tracks. But there is literally no footprint online for Catarina Conti. Mazzone thinks she's hiding something, and I tend to agree."

"It only adds to the intrigue," my buddy says, closing the laptop. "If you won't marry her, maybe I will." He waggles his brows.

"You'd give up your bachelor ways to marry a stranger in an arranged contract?"

He shrugs, tipping beer into his mouth. "It's gonna happen sometime." He cocks his head to the side. "I know you're opposed to it, but marriage to someone like her would help our agenda."

"Maybe, but the lack of intel makes me uneasy. I don't like dealing in uncertainties."

He barks out a laugh. "You're such a fucking hypocrite." Rumbling laughter spills from his mouth at the dour expression on my face. "When you think about it, it's really perfect. You're a ghost. She's a ghost." His blue eyes twinkle with mirth. "You two are a match made in heaven."

Chapter Five

Catarina

"I want everyone on high alert tonight," I say as our car approaches the rendezvous point in Manhattan where we will meet Don Mazzone's men.

"They won't pull any shit at Mazzone's home," Nicolina says, snuggling into Dario's side. "His wife and kids live there."

"That's not what Catarina means, hon," Agessi replies. "We're not sure who will be there and who might recognize her or Renzo."

I thought about not taking Renzo with me tonight, but his absence would probably raise more suspicion. Still, I can't take chances. I phoned my stepfather and warned him not to take any calls from New York. We also concocted a story in case anyone should recognize my underboss and query how a former Las Vegas *soldato* is now my right-hand man. I intend to pay Saverio a visit in person to ensure he repeats the same story, should he be asked.

"Leonardo and Natalia live on the grounds of Ben and Sierra's estate," I explain. "Alessandro and Serena too." Ben goes to great extremes to keep his private residence top secret, but it is widely known all three couples live on the same sprawling estate. The exact location is a closely guarded secret, and all visitors are forced to arrive in the same manner as we will. "While we have never met Alesso and Serena, he is a Salerno. He meets Anais regularly, and he has made several trips to Vegas. My stepfather has a couple of pictures of my mother on the walls. He could spot some resemblance."

"He won't make the connection," Renzo says, staring absently out the window as the busy streets of New York flash by. "You look nothing like your mother or Anais." He turns to face me, looking handsome in his black Burberry suit and pale-gray shirt. His eyes sweep over me quickly.

I am wearing my signature white. My fitted, sleeveless, knee-length silk Givenchy dress has a scooped neckline offering a mere hint of cleavage. It dips low at the back, resting just above my ass, with three looped diamond chains holding the sides together. Silver and black stilettos and a matching purse complete my outfit. My hair is straightened and pulled back in a high ponytail. Subtle makeup complements my ruby-red lips and smoky eyes.

I know I look good. I made sure of it. A lot is hinging on tonight.

"You obviously take after your father." He reaches across the leather seat to squeeze my hand. "You look stunning, and he doesn't deserve you," he adds through gritted teeth.

"Renzo." My tone carries considerable warning. I am sick to death of arguing with him about this.

"Nothing has been agreed yet," Dario reminds him.

"He will take one look at her and offer to say his vows on the spot," Renzo retorts, withdrawing his hand from mine.

Nicolina is as subtle as a brick when arching her brows. It's her "I told you so" face.

"This will be my decision. I'm the one with the power in this situation. The Commission might be nervous because I'm an outsider, but they need me, and they know it. He will agree to it."

A muscle pops in Renzo's jaw, but he raises no further objection.

We park in the private parking garage at Ben's Caltimore Holdings building where one of his men is waiting to escort us to the chopper on the roof.

As soon as we fly out of the city, we are handed eye masks to wear. Two of Ben's men sit with us to ensure we don't peek.

Forty minutes later, we land on the grounds of the impressive Mazzone residence. We hand our weapons to one of Ben's *soldati* before we exit the helicopter. It's standard protocol apparently and a directive straight from the boss. We don't argue. This is his family home, and I would expect nothing less.

Bennett and his gorgeous wife, Sierra, are waiting for us. Sierra is the person I am most concerned about. After Renzo explained how he met her, Ben, and Leo in the basement of one of the clubs Saverio owns in Vegas, I became worried she may remember my underboss.

On the don's orders, Renzo had taken her from a table in the club and brought her to Saverio under duress. It was twelve years ago, and Renzo looks different, so she might not remember him. Back then, he was younger, leaner, and had hair. Now, he's bald and broader with a beard and massive amounts of ink he didn't have the night they met. We are hoping she doesn't recognize him, but given the circumstances, she could.

I can't execute my plan while keeping Renzo hidden. So, we might as well introduce him now, and if any of them recognize him, we'll feed them the story we have devised. We'll say Renzo only discovered his familial ties to the Contis after he was in Saverio's service, and that he came to me, looking for work when Saverio let him go, and quickly moved up the ranks. My tech guy is planting the fake seeds online in case anyone looks for verification. I am hoping it's enough to deflect them from digging deeper, especially if Saverio sings from the same hymn sheet.

Renzo keeps his hand on my lower back, his sharp eyes peeled, as we walk toward our hosts. "Welcome." Ben shakes my hand as he greets us. "We are delighted you could join us."

"Thank you for inviting us to your lovely home and for facilitating the introduction." I smile politely at Sierra. "It's a pleasure to meet you, Mrs. Mazzone."

"Please call me Sierra." She leans in, enveloping me in a warm hug. A delicate floral scent tickles my nostrils as her summery perfume wafts in the air. She is truly stunning with gorgeous golden-blonde hair tumbling in soft waves over her shoulders, expressive green eyes, and a bright smile. Her maxi dress is made of white silk with a chiffon overlay stamped with vibrant pink and purple butterflies. The thin spaghetti straps showcase her slender arms and the delicate curve of her collarbone. Looking at her flat stomach and slim hips, I can't believe she only gave birth a couple of months ago.

"I'm Catarina, and this is my *consigliere*, Dario Agessi, and his wife, Nicolina; my underboss, Renzo Dutti; and Ezio, who is one of my most loyal *soldati*." I gave Ricardo the night off to take his girlfriend out dancing. There are enough of us tonight that I can do without my regular bodyguard. Ben and Sierra shake hands with everyone, and I watch her closely as she shakes hands with Renzo. He doesn't prolong the greeting, and I don't see any trace of recognition on her face.

"The Greco party is due to arrive shortly," Ben confirms. "Why don't we enjoy a pre-dinner drink while we wait for them?"

I purposely fall into step beside Sierra while Dario moves up to talk to Ben. Nicolina, Renzo, and Ezio trail behind us. "I can't believe you only gave birth a couple of months ago or that you are a mother of three. You look amazing," I truthfully tell Ben's wife.

"You are so sweet, thank you. You look amazing too. That dress is stunning. White really suits you."

"Thank you. My wardrobe contains a lot of white. It's kind of my thing."

She cocks her head to one side, looking contemplative. "Was that a strategic choice?"

I nod.

"Ah, I love that!" Exuberance exudes from her tone. "The symbolism is powerful."

"I think so." There's a brief pregnant pause, which I quickly fill.

Earning Ben's trust will be easier if I win his wife over. "What did you name your new son?"

Her face lights up at the mention of her baby. "Rhys. His older brother is Rowan, and his sister is Raven, so I insisted we had to give him an R name too."

"How old are your eldest children?"

"Rowan is twelve, and Raven is six."

She's quite disarming. Genuine too, which is a surprise, because a lot of women resent me and are hostile. From the things Anais has said about her, I wasn't expecting her to be so welcoming. My sister painted a totally different picture, saying she is always rude and unfriendly toward her. Knowing Anais, she did something to cause Sierra to treat her that way. Like me, Anais is not the kind of woman other women want to be friends with—for some of the same reasons and for completely different reasons too.

She loops her arm through mine, as if we have been friends forever. "Do you have any children?" she asks.

I shake my head, deliberately not elaborating.

"Ben has been telling me about you," she continues. "It is hard to impress my husband, but you have impressed him. I can only imagine how difficult it must be, as a powerful woman, operating within the confines of a regime that is still so archaic. Ben has been trying to effect change, but it isn't easy."

"It's not. I share your husband's philosophy, but implementing that vision is a tall order. I have encountered a lot of prejudice. As a donna, I need to constantly prove myself, and even then, most of the men I do business with still consider themselves superior to me when I could outfight them, outmaneuver them, and outsmart them nine times out of ten."

"You must be highly intelligent with thick skin and nerves of steel to even consider going up against them. I don't envy you, but I applaud you." Her smile is genuine as she looks me in the eye. "We need more women like you in our world."

"We do," I agree, trying not to gape as we round the back of the majestic mansion, onto a large paved area in front of exquisite manicured gardens. A massive wooden canopy, decorated with rows of twinkling string lights, presides over the elegant outdoor table and chairs. Vases filled with roses and lilies line the top of the table, interspersed with a myriad of lit candles glowing behind glass covers. Soft music plays in the background as Ben pours Cristal into flutes at the outdoor bar tucked into the corner alongside an impressive kitchenette and industrial grill. "Wow, this is beautiful. You have a gorgeous home."

"Thank you." She beams at me. "Nat, Rena, and I have done a lot of work in the garden over the years, and Nat has even cultivated an orchard and vegetable patch, like she had growing up."

"You are talking about Natalia Messina, Ben's sister?" I make a show of looking around. "Is she here?"

She shakes her head, and soft waves of golden curls cascade around her shoulders. "Ben thought it would be more relaxing if we kept dinner confined to us, but they might join us for a drink after."

Goose bumps sprout on my arms at the thought, but I know I will have to meet them sometime. It is best to get it over and done with to see if there is any hint of recognition from any of them. "That sounds lovely. I look forward to meeting them."

Ben hands the ladies glasses of champagne and offers beer to the guys, and we move to the plush seated area on the left, just in front of a large outdoor pool. It is currently covered but illuminated via a border of lights embedded into the stone surrounding.

Ben takes a seat beside me with Dario on my right. Nicolina is across from us, chatting with Sierra, while Ezio and Renzo stand off to the side, both men fixing their gazes in my direction. "Your men are very loyal to you." Ben observes, flicking a loose thread off his black pants.

I turn my head so I'm facing him. He's a very good-looking man, and I can see why the ladies of New York were disappointed when he showed up one day with a wife and son in tow. "I expect and demand it. I'm sure I don't have to tell you loyalty is not always guaranteed despite the oath. I have to work harder than most dons to earn it and keep it, so I won't accept any deviation. If you swear loyalty to me, it *is* for life."

"I respect that." His blue eyes penetrate mine as if they are probe lenses, digging deep. I hold his gaze confidently, used to this kind of analysis. "I am aware of how you rose to power."

"I think most people are."

His lips twitch. "Ah, yes. The photograph."

"You saw it, and yet you never held me accountable. Why is that?"

"Conti was a sniveling idiot who held power only because of those who were loyal to his father. Like you said, we are neighbors. I knew you were steadying the ship and building it. I knew you would seize power one day. We don't tend to get involved in other families' business unless it's necessitated. The Commission was in its infancy with many other pressing problems to deal with."

"Timing was my ally."

He nods. "Yes, but we also learned your husband was a sick pedophile who preyed on innocent children. You rid the world of a monster. I lost no sleep over his death, and I'm glad you made him suffer."

Goddamn it. Why does this man make it so hard to hate him?

"Boss," a man says, materializing behind us. "The Grecoes are here."

Ben drains his beer before setting it down on the coffee table. "Stay here. I will escort our guests." He fights an obvious smile. "Take a few moments to prepare yourself."

Well, that's reassuring.

"Remember you haven't committed to anything," Dario says in a low tone, moving in a little closer. "Only the inner circle knows your true goals. You can back out without shame. No one would blame you if you can't go through with this. We will find another way."

"I'm not backing out, but I appreciate your concern. I would rather you diverted your efforts to getting Renzo on board."

"He will respect your decision," he says, looking over his shoulder. "They are here." He stands, offering me his hand. I hold on to him and pull myself to a standing position as Renzo walks toward me.

"Remember what we discussed," I warn him in a low tone. He has never made a scene before, but I have never seen him like this.

"No fucking way," he hisses, his eyes popping wide as he glances behind me.

Slowly, I turn around, and all the air punches from my lungs when I lock eyes with the man approaching alongside Ben.

My memories haven't done him justice, or perhaps he has gotten even hotter since I last saw him. Words escape me as I stare at the man who has had a starring role in my dreams for the past five years.

His startled gaze mirrors my own, and Ben's brow puckers as his gaze bounces between us. They come to a standstill at the back of the couch as I struggle to grasp the reality of the situation. If that man is Massimo—and there's a ninety-nine percent chance he is—I can't go through with this marriage. Disappointment churns with confusion and desire as we stare at one another.

I don't even notice the other men from their party coming up at the rear. I can't tear my eyes from the hot stranger.

"Okaaaay." Ben's eyes dart from the stranger to me. "I'm clearly missing something here." He turns to the man beside him. "Are introductions required, Massimo, or do you already know Donna Conti?"

The most dazzling smile stretches across his mouth. "Oh, we most certainly know one another."

His tone is suggestive in the extreme, leaving no one in any doubt of how we are acquainted. I level him with a sharp look. "It was a long time ago. I barely remember."

He chuckles, and the sound reverberates in every part of my being. "Liar." He wets his lips and moves forward, walking swiftly around the couch until he's standing right in front of me. "You are even more beautiful than I remember." Taking my hand, he raises it to his lips, planting a firm kiss to my knuckles. "Not married this time." His eyes dart over my head, and I can tell his glare is directed at Renzo. I'm vaguely conscious of Sierra whispering to Ben from behind us. Massimo keeps a firm hold of my hand as he bends down, pressing his hot mouth against my ear. "I recall the last words I said to you that day at the airport. Do you?" Mischief dances in his eyes, and I don't want to play this game.

This has thrown me for a loop, and I need to regroup.

"I said 'If you were single, I would marry the fuck out of you.'" He nips my earlobe with his teeth. "Is it irony or fate that it's now coming true?"

Chapter Six

Massimo

"Absurdity is the word you're looking for," she coolly replies, seeming to compose herself. She was definitely rattled when I first appeared, and I can relate to the sentiment. It blows my mind that *she's* Donna Conti, and it changes *everything*.

"I prefer destiny." I waggle my brows and flash her a flirty smile.

"It's more like a travesty," she retorts, yanking her hand from mine and stepping back.

"It's karma."

"It's a disaster."

"Kismet."

"Calamity," she hurls without missing a beat.

"Providence," I volley back.

"Misfortune," she hisses.

"Entertaining as this is, I feel someone needs to be the adult around here," Ben says, fighting a grin.

"What's going on, Massimo?" Gabriele asks, moving around to my side. "Is this wedding happening or not?"

"Yes," I blurt the same time she says, "No."

I slap a hand over my chest as I smirk at her. "You wound me, *mia amata*."

"Do *not* call me that. I am not your anything."

I press my lips to her ear again. "Not yet, but you will be." I straighten up and flash her a cocky look that has her rolling her eyes.

"Dinner won't be served for a while," Sierra says, injecting herself into the conversation. "Perhaps you two should go for a walk to discuss the situation in private."

Ben slides his arm around her waist, tugging her into his side as he pins proud eyes on her. I have had the pleasure of meeting the woman who tamed Don Mazzone a few times over the years, and she is as smart as she is empathetic and beautiful.

"What a superb idea." Winding my hand around Catarina's, I pull her into my side. She glares at me, attempting to remove her fingers from my grasp, but I hold on tighter, refusing to let her go. The asshole who was with her at the airport straightens up, his hand automatically moving to the empty holster at his hip. I return his glare and some.

"There are some walking trails in the forest over there." Sierra points around the far side of the house. "The paths are well lit."

"Perfect. Thank you." I look down at the woman simmering with rage at my side. "Shall we?"

"Oh, I get a choice now, do I?" Hostility bleeds into her tone.

"I will be right behind you," the dick says in a barely concealed venomous tone.

"That won't be necessary." I drill him with a challenging look. "I am pretty certain my wife-to-be has a concealed weapon somewhere on her person, and she assured me before she knows how to use it."

Ben stiffens at my words, opening his mouth to say something, but I subtly shake my head, silently conveying I've got this and he has nothing to worry about. He offers me a curt nod, clamping his lips shut.

"It's fine, Renzo," Catarina says, cautioning him to back down with a pointed look. "He won't hurt me." She looks up at me. "If he tries, he will soon learn the error of his ways."

I chuckle under my breath. She's every bit the spitfire I remember.

Something akin to excitement flows through my veins for the first time in a very long time.

"I have armed men all over my property," Ben says, looking at Renzo as he speaks, but the message is for the woman still trying to wrest her hand from my grip. "Nothing will happen. They will ensure it."

"Come have a drink," a pretty blonde with bouncy curls says, looping her arm through Renzo's. She shoots me a curious look. "Our queen knows how to handle herself."

"Let's go." Catarina leads me forward, and I raise no objection.

Gabe lifts a brow in amusement as we walk off, leaving the gathering behind.

The second we are out of sight, she digs her long nails into my palm in an unexpected move. My hold on her loosens, and she withdraws her hand. Spinning around, she shoves me with more strength than I would've believed, pushing me up against the wall at the back of Ben's house.

"I like where this is going." I waggle my brows and grin at her.

"Shut the fuck up." She prods one slim finger into my chest. "Let's get one thing straight, Massimo."

"Fuck! Say my name again." I cut across whatever she was about to say.

She blinks, caught off guard. "What?"

Tilting my hips up, I press my groin into her stomach. "You saying my name gets me so fucking hard."

Brow furrowing, she steps back, creating space between us. "You have issues."

Closing the gap between us, I reach out and cup her face. "I'm seriously attracted to you. I see no issue with that."

Swatting my hand away, she moves back a couple more steps, looking flustered for a few seconds until she refocuses. Her dark glare is meant to be menacing, no doubt, but it only adds to her appeal. "No one touches me without my permission. If you ever manhandle me like that again, I will slice your dick off and feed it to you in pieces."

"Manhandle you?" I quirk a brow. "I only took your hand and touched your cheek. Let's not exaggerate."

"You don't touch me, got it?"

"You had no issue with me touching you before. You practically strangled my cock you were so greedy for it."

Fire blazes from her eyes, and I am going to enjoy this so much.

I came out tonight determined not to agree to this marriage. Now, I want to throw her over my shoulder and frog-march her to the nearest church.

"This will never work. I won't make it to our wedding night without putting a bullet in your skull." She turns around, ready to walk off, and I dart out in front of her.

I hold my palms up. "I won't touch you, and we can discuss this like civilized adults. I apologize if I was out of line. Seeing you again has caught me off guard."

Wide expressive eyes stare intensely at me. I had thought them brown the night I met her, but they are more green than brown today, and I'm guessing she has hazel eyes.

"I wasn't joking back there. This has disaster written all over it."

I open my mouth to speak when a tall figure emerges from the shadows, and I instantly shove Catarina behind me, shielding her from the man who steps toward us. "My apologies, sir. Ma'am. I didn't mean to startle you." The *soldato* steps forward, holding out a pair of tennis shoes. "Mrs. Mazzone thought Donna Conti might like to borrow these."

Catarina sidesteps me, forcing a smile as she accepts the shoes from the man. "That is very considerate of her. Thank you."

The man walks off while she shoots daggers at my face. "I think you are incapable of obeying orders."

My brow puckers in confusion, and she rolls her eyes as she leans against the wall and slips her stilettos off her feet. My much taller frame almost dwarfs her, and I feel an uncharacteristic protective urge wash over me out of nowhere.

"You touched me literally seconds after I asked you not to," she explains, slipping her feet into the flat shoes.

"You can't expect me not to protect you. You will be my wife, and it's my duty to ensure you come to no harm."

"That is not a foregone conclusion, and I can protect myself." Her eyes narrow as she stabs me with a cold look. "Most every man who was supposed to protect me has let me down. I expect you would be no different." Hooking her stilettos around her fingers, she stalks off in the direction of the forest, leaving me to chase after her.

"What does that mean? Who has disappointed you?" I ask when I have caught up to her side. She is powering toward the woods like a woman on a mission.

"It doesn't matter." She steps onto the main path leading into the dense woodland. "I have no expectations when it comes to men, and you will be no different."

"And the hits just keep on coming," I murmur. She spears me with a sharp look as we pound the path through the forest. Sierra was right, and it's well lit, guiding our way.

"If we do this, it is purely a business arrangement."

"Naturally," I lie because I have no intention of keeping things strictly business, but I need to get her to agree to it. Then we can negotiate terms.

She slams to a halt, lifting her head to look at me. "Why do you want this? I thought you have nothing to do with the business. This will curtail your lifestyle."

"Don't believe everything you have heard."

"That's a nonanswer." She tilts her head to the side, and the moon highlights her stunning face in all its breathtaking glory. With her high cheekbones, well-proportioned nose, intriguing, expressive eyes, and a mouth that has been the epicenter of my every fantasy since I met her, she is truly exquisite.

Lightly freckled, tan, smooth skin glows in every place it's exposed, begging for my touch. Her slender body has curves in all the right places, and her beautiful dress showcases her figure to perfection. Her gorgeous rack gives way to a narrow, slim waist, shapely hips, and legs that would look perfect wrapped around my shoulders. She snaps her fingers in my face. "Stop eye fucking me. We're trying to have a serious discussion."

"I can't help it. You're fucking beautiful. It's only natural to stare."

She blinks repeatedly, looking momentarily stunned, and I wonder why. Surely it can't be my words? Men must be tripping over themselves to rain compliments on her.

"Why are you prepared to do this?" she asks after a couple of silent beats.

I give her the explanation that is for public consumption, opening myself a little in the hope she will do the same. "Neither Gabe nor I were ever supposed to be don. Circumstances forced it. We made a deal after our father and our brother Primo were killed in the warehouse explosion. Gabe would take up the mantle, and I would be free to live my life until it was time for me to take over." I shrug casually. "That time has come, and I'm getting ready to step up."

"You don't need a wife for that."

"It is frowned upon to lead without a wife and without heirs."

Calculation glints in her eyes. "Your brother has managed it."

"Barely," I truthfully reply.

"Is Don Mazzone forcing this because of your brother's sexuality?"

Her observational skills are not lacking. I would be impressed even if I wasn't concerned for my brother. That secret is a secret for a reason. Fear sluices through my veins, but I keep it hidden behind a mask of neutrality, neither confirming nor denying it.

"I know he is a forward-thinking man, but our organization is still backward-thinking when it comes to the role of women and gay men." She steps up closer, and the spicy scent of her perfume tickles my nostrils. "There is only so much Ben can do. I suspect you are being dragged into this as an unwilling party and you are agreeing to protect your brother."

There is some merit to her assessment, but it's not my main motivation. Still, it suits me to have her believe it. "What if I am?"

"I won't marry another weak man. It damages my reputation and sets me back. I think this contract has the potential to derail my hard work, and I won't put myself in that position."

"Don't bullshit a bullshitter, *sweetheart*," I say, purely to piss her off. "You need this contract as much as I do. I lend legitimacy to you in the same way you do for me. It's of mutual benefit, or it wouldn't have been suggested. By *you*, might I add." Folding my arms over my chest, I smirk at her, wondering if this supposed hesitation is all for show or if she's purposely trying to talk herself out of it. Which wouldn't make sense. She is hungry for a bite of the Big Apple, and she knows she needs me to secure the support of The Commission.

If she *is* trying to get out of it, it's because she's either running scared at the prospect of being married to *me* or she is hiding something she's fearful I might uncover.

Either way, I'm as intrigued as ever and even more determined to make her mine.

"Don't fucking insult my intelligence," she snaps, poking her finger in my arm. "You need me way more than I need you, and your petty taunts prove my point perfectly. I eat pathetic pricks like you for breakfast. I need a *king*. Not some playboy prince who has spent years fucking his way around Europe while the rest of us work for a living. It's almost an embarrassment to weak men to group you in the same category."

Irritation prickles my skin, and anger surges through my veins, quick and pointed. I step forward, clamping my arm around her back and pulling her into my body, trapping her arms at her sides so she can't retaliate. Fuck her and her "no touching" rule. Wrapping my free hand around her ponytail, I yank her head back and glare at her. "*Mia amata*. That is the last time you'll ever suggest I am weak. Don't make me demonstrate how I am the complete opposite because I don't want to hurt you. Challenge me, and you won't like it. That I guarantee."

I lower my face to hers as she wriggles against me, spewing poison from her eyes. My mouth hovers an inch from her lips, and we are pressed so tightly together I can feel the rapid beating of her heart against my chest and see the pulse throbbing at her neck. Air spills from her lips as her furious eyes pin me in place. "We both know this is happening, so quit fighting me. You can save that for our wedding night," I say, brushing my lips briefly against hers before moving my mouth to her ear. "I look forward to a proper reunion."

Chapter Seven

Catarina

"You look like you're ready to unleash holy hell on your intended," Nicolina says, working hard not to smile as she tops off my wineglass.

"He unsettles me," I honestly reply. "He has me off my game, and that's not a good thing for any of us."

"It's a momentary blip," my bestie says, slurping from her wineglass. "The bathroom hottie caught you off guard, but you'll regain the upper hand. Massimo is no match for you."

"I wouldn't be so sure. Something tells me there's a lot more to him than meets the eye," I murmur, watching the new arrivals as they stride toward where we are congregated, standing around the cozy seated area, chatting and drinking.

Dinner was delicious, but it was difficult to enjoy it with the heated stares leveled my way by my new fiancé. Unfortunately, Massimo and Gabriele were seated directly across from me. Dario engaged Gabriele in conversation while Nicolina almost single-handedly carried the conversation with Massimo while I quietly fumed.

"At least he doesn't look like you know who. That's got to help," she whispers in my ear.

"It does," I truthfully admit. Massimo takes after his mother while his other brothers favor their father. It's the only explanation as to why I didn't spot a resemblance before. His deceased brothers and Gabriele have dark-brown hair and brown eyes, and Massimo has blue-black locks and forest-green eyes. He is also taller and broader, and he seriously works out because every inch of his body is taut, toned, and ripped to perfection.

Which leads me to my other problem. How can I manipulate him when I'm so attracted to him? Usually, it's easy for me with men even if they are hot. But the intense chemistry between me and Massimo could cause me to lose focus, and I can't ever take my foot off the controls. I have a lot on my plate—so many elements I'm juggling—and I don't know if I have the capacity to handle my fiancé on top of everything. It would be a cakewalk if there was no simmering attraction and he wasn't so invested in pushing my buttons. I am quite likely to murder him the next time he goads me, and that wouldn't be smart. I need to stay my hand until all my ducks are lined up.

When I kill Massimo, Gabriele, and their mother, it will be when the time is right and I'm poised to take control of The Commission.

"Donna Conti," Leo Messina says, approaching me with a stunning brunette on his arm. "It's lovely to see you again. I wanted to introduce you to my wife, Natalia."

I already know who she is. I met her one time, but I was only ten, and it was a fleeting visit to her house with my papa, so I'm not expecting her to remember me.

My feelings when it comes to this woman are complicated. Natalia is the reason I was kidnapped, and while it wasn't her fault, and I don't even know if she knows what happened, it's hard to look at her and not feel bitter. My ordeal could have been hers if things had played out how they were supposed to. Yet I'm glad she didn't have to endure a life with that monster even if I suffered in her place. Women get a raw deal in our world, and it doesn't feel right to harbor resentment toward another innocent woman, yet sometimes I can't help how I feel.

My emotions veer back and forth like this any time I let myself think about my past.

It's a clusterfuck of confusion I don't know if I can ever unravel.

Plastering a sociable smile on my face, I dampen down all my errant emotions as I stretch out my hand. "It's a pleasure to meet you."

"Likewise." Natalia shakes my hand in a firm handshake. "I hear congratulations are in order." Her eyes twinkle with mischief as she glances in Massimo's direction. "At least he is easy on the eyes. You could do a lot worse."

"I did," I deadpan, taking a sip of my wine. As much as I want to gulp the whole drink back, I can't lose control.

"Ah, that's right. You were married to Paulo Conti." Sympathy splays across her face. "I can't begin to imagine what kind of nightmare that must have been. My father considered him for me for a brief period," she says.

"I am aware. Paulo loved to bring your name up any time I failed to please him. He never let me forget you were his first choice." It is ironic how entwined Natalia's history and my history are.

"He was an awful man. I had nightmares for weeks after he came to dinner, terrified Papa would give me to him."

"Ben would never have let that happen," Leo says, shooting me a mournful look. "How did you end up promised to him?"

"After he lost Natalia to Gino, he approached my father. He had always had an unhealthy obsession with me," I lie.

"Oh my God." Natalia lifts a hand to her face. "He didn't..."

I shake my head. "He didn't touch me as a child. I count my blessings for that."

"How is it you were given to him? Who is your father?" Massimo asks, stepping forward from behind Natalia. I had seen him approaching and wondered when he would join the conversation.

"My father is dead now, but he was one of Conti's most loyal capos." That's a blatant lie, but the evidence is there to corroborate my story should anyone go looking. I conveniently borrowed the identity of a man who passed two months after I assumed control, and I trot his name out any time I need to explain my parentless status. "He raised me alone after my mother died giving birth to me."

"Any siblings?" Massimo asks, and I shake my head.

"That must have been lonely growing up," Natalia says.

I shrug. "I didn't know any different."

"I am sorry for what you must've endured with Paulo. I feel somewhat responsible."

I can tell she is genuine. "It's not your fault. Count yourself lucky you didn't have to marry him. It wasn't a good marriage."

"I know what that's like," she replies, resting her head on Leo's shoulder. "My first marriage was horrible and lonely, but I had my sons to pull me through."

I know her backstory, thanks to Anais and Cruz. "Caleb and Joshua, right?"

"Someone has done their homework." Massimo circles his arm around my waist.

"Are you deaf or just stupid?" I snap, forcibly removing his arm from my body.

"Rebellious," he replies, replacing his arm around my waist. "And I don't like being told what to do."

"That makes two of us." I thrust his arm away.

Leo chuckles. "Do I sense trouble in paradise already?"

"Nothing has been set in stone yet," I say. "And our deal is strictly a business arrangement."

"She's delusional," Massimo says, finishing his beer and setting the empty bottle down on the table behind us. "We're madly in love, but she's afraid to admit it."

I glare at him. If this continues, he'll give me wrinkles around my eyes. "There is only one delusional person in this scenario, and it's most definitely not me." Someone raises the volume on the music, and Ben hauls Sierra out onto the large circular patio area, and they start dancing. Out of the corner of my eye, I spy Dario leading Nicolina over to join them as another couple approaches our little group.

I tense a little as Alessandro and Serena come up to us, praying he doesn't spot any connection to Anais. But he doesn't give any indication he sees a familiarity when Leo makes quick introductions and I shake his hand. We talk casually, and every muscle in my body locks up as Massimo's arm snakes around my waist again. My body fights an internal war as I battle the urge to melt against him.

This isn't me, and I'm growing increasingly alarmed the more he's around.

I dig my nails into his wrist as I remove his arm this time. Amusement dances across his face, and I'm tempted to stab him with the knife concealed in my cell phone. "You must have a death wish," I growl, shooting an apologetic look at the others.

"Let's dance," he says, ignoring my ire. Linking his hand in mine, he tugs me across the garden toward the circular, paved area.

"I am this close to stabbing you," I warn, utterly annoyed when he throws back his head and laughs.

"*Regina*, I would expect nothing less." He sweeps me into his arms when we reach the makeshift dance floor. I have no choice but to hold on to him, circling my arms around his warm neck as he sways us in tune to the music. Nicolina grins at me as we dance, and I briefly wonder whose side she is on. Renzo has a face like thunder as he watches Massimo twirl me around in his arms, but his animosity is nothing new. He has been steadfastly stubborn with regards to this marriage deal.

Heat rolls off Massimo's body in heady waves, lulling me into a bit of a daze. Instead of fighting him, I go with the flow, indulging myself for once. He is an excellent dancer, and while I can easily hold my own on the dance floor, on this occasion, he is the commander, and I am merely along for the ride. We float across the stone floor, turning and twisting and spinning, and every time he reels me back into his gorgeous body, it's hard to remain immune with the feel of him this close. He is all hard muscle, flexing hips, and intoxicating warmth. Spicy, citrusy notes of his cologne waft around me, adding to the addictive pull of this man.

He is dangerous for me, and I need to regain control. "You're making me dizzy," I rasp a few minutes later as he twirls me around before hauling me back into his arms.

"Are you always this grumpy?" he inquires, holding me close as we sway from side to side.

"Never. You bring out the worst in me."

"I don't believe that for a second. Do you want to know what I think?"

"No."

Of course, he ignores me. "I think you don't know how to enjoy yourself. I think you work too hard and you need to let loose more often. I think I will be good for you because I will force you to stop and appreciate life, to feel things you have closed yourself off to, and those thoughts scare you to death."

He is eerily close to the truth. Not that I'm admitting it. "I think you have an overinflated sense of your own importance and you know nothing about me."

"The latter might be true, because there is nothing on the internet for me to find, but I'm a good judge of character, and I know what I see when I look at you."

Yeah. I'm not touching that. "No *mafioso* worth his or her salt leaves anything to be found on the internet. You have minimal footprint too, so stop talking shit."

"Keep this up, *mia amata*. All it does is turn me on."

"Stop calling me that." I'm beginning to sound like a broken record, and maybe I need to mix it up.

"We need to discuss specifics of the contract. I can drop by your house tomorrow to talk about it," he says, dipping me down low.

I tighten my arms around his neck and cling to him as my hair trails the ground. "There is nothing to discuss. I will have my attorney send a draft agreement to your attorney tomorrow. You can raise queries on anything you don't like and suggest your own additions."

"We should hash it out between us first and then have the attorneys draw up the paperwork," he refutes, keeping a tight hold on me as he straightens us up.

"I am out of town for a couple of days, and we should start this as we mean to go on. It's a business agreement, and all negotiation should go through our legal teams."

"I want to discuss sex and children. I am not doing that through my lawyer. Let's talk about it now."

"There is nothing to discuss."

"Bullshit," he says, subtly pivoting his hips so I feel his erection pressing against me. "That is what you do to me, and I'm betting if I pushed my fingers inside you you'd be equally turned on."

"Your arrogance is outrageous and wildly short of the mark." I narrow my eyes to slits, pretending my panties aren't soaked and I can't feel his cock jerking behind his pants. "Sex is off the table and nonnegotiable until it's time to procreate. Children will have to wait until the timing is right."

"Neither of us is getting any younger, and I need heirs. I will be requesting a full medical exam and inserting a timeline into the contract for pregnancy."

The feminist in me is livid, but it's the way of our world, and causing a ruckus will only draw attention to a topic I need to keep on the down low. "Women are having babies well into their forties. There is plenty of time for us to start a family," I lie. "But if you want a timeline, I will suggest one I think you'll be happy to agree to." I can't fulfil it, nor would I want to if I could. But it doesn't matter. He'll be dead before that clause comes into play, so I can agree to it.

The no-sex clause is the bigger issue. I can't sleep with him on the regular because it's too risky. I still remember how hot we were together, and it can't happen. "The only time we will have sex is when we agree to start trying for a baby."

He maneuvers us over to the quieter side of the patio, away from the other dancing couples. "If sex is off the table, that means exclusivity is too."

"No fucking way. You will not embarrass me by fucking whores on the side."

"Plenty of made men keep whores and mistresses. It isn't that unusual." His lips kick up at the corners, and I narrow my eyes.

"I hold a position of leadership, and you won't disrespect me in front of my men. Just like no don would allow his wife to disrespect him."

"I'll be a don, and I have needs. Either you ride my cock or I'll find someone who will."

"No, you won't, and this is nonnegotiable. If I can remain celibate, so can you."

He barks out a harsh laugh. "You're such a fucking hypocrite. I can't be the only bathroom hookup you indulged in while married. You don't get to have your cake and eat it too, and I loathe double standards. Either we fuck each other or we fuck other people. It's really quite simple," he says, snapping a pic of my face.

"What the fuck?" I reach for his cell, but he has slipped it back into his pocket already.

"Spank bank material."

I am instantly enraged, and I'm tempted to slap him across the face, but I muzzle the urge because I won't lower myself. "You're disgusting. I hate you."

He slants me with a smug look I instantly want to claw off his face. "You wish you did."

I shuck out of his arms, working hard to leash my temper. No one has ever rattled me as much as this man. He follows me as I stride toward the table where my purse is. "We're leaving," I tell Renzo when I reach him. "Please inform the others." Snatching my purse up, I remove my phone and thrust it in front of my fiancé's face. "Add your number."

For once, he complies without argument. He punches in his digits and hands the phone back to me. Our fingers brush in the exchange, and I want to punt kick myself between the legs as fiery tingles rip up and down my arm from his touch. Why can't my body get the memo he's the enemy?

If I didn't think I'd go insane, I might imagine he's his despicable older brother any time he touches me. Carlo's touch always repelled me, and my skin would crawl like a thousand fire ants were marching across my flesh. That would surely cure me of this strange craving for Massimo's touch. But imagining he's Carlo would likely lead to me killing Massimo in a fit of rage or fracture my patched-up sanity and rip the cracks in my heart wide-open again. I would be of no use to anyone like that.

I send the picture of a mutilated Paulo to Massimo's phone before dropping my cell in my bag. His cell pings, and he opens my message, staring at the photo with an impressive ambivalent expression. Grabbing a fistful of Massimo's shirt, I drag him toward me. My eyes lower to his mouth for a fleeting second before lifting to his eyes. They are dark with lust, which is more than a little concerning, and I see the truth of his desire staring back at me. "I call the shots, Massimo. Never forget that." I release him, giving him a little shove, as Nicolina and Dario come up alongside us. "Stop pissing me off unless you want to suffer the same fate as my last husband."

With those parting words, I walk away to thank our hosts before getting the fuck out of here.

Chapter Eight

Catarina

"Where is he?" I demand, slanting my gaze between the two armed men guarding the double doors of my stepfather's dark, drab living room. My patience is in limited supply, and Saverio is really testing me.

"Don Salerno said to escort you here and he would join you shortly," one of the men says.

Neither man is part of the group loyal to Renzo, who provide intel in our absence, ensuring we always know what is going down in Vegas.

"He is disrespecting Donna Conti," Renzo says, his hand going to the gun at his hip. "And that won't be tolerated. He needs to remember his place." There is little love lost between Renzo and his former don because of the way Saverio has treated me in the past.

"It's been fifteen minutes, and I'm a busy woman." I stand and stalk toward the burly man with the cropped dark hair. "Tell Don Salerno if he isn't here within the next five minutes I will be sending the video to Don Mazzone." I glance at the Tag Heuer watch on my wrist. "You have four minutes and forty seconds. Go."

The man takes off, returning in the nick of time with a mutinous-looking Saverio.

"You are lucky she lets you live." Renzo levels a lethal look at his former don.

"And you are lucky I let *you* live," Salerno barks, dropping his large form into the worn leather chair.

"You look like shit," I tell him, pleased to see the steady stream of booze, narcotics, and women I ensure he is supplied with is working like a charm.

When I first moved here with my mother, after we had to flee New York, he took pride in his appearance. With the ugly slash across his face, he had his work cut out for him. But he kept himself fit and healthy even with an unhealthy drug habit. Now, he has completely let himself go. His belly bulges over the waistband of his pants, his hair is thinning, and the bad dye job does little to disguise the gray. Dry, pasty skin and bloodshot eyes attest to poor nutrition and bad sleeping habits. His lifestyle may kill him before I get the chance, which would be a shame as I have a cocktail of torture lined up for my stepfather.

"And you still look like a pain in my ass," he says, snapping his fingers in the air.

"If it wasn't for Donna Conti, your bank balance would not be as healthy and the chaos on the streets of Vegas would see you lose your territory again," Dario says, reminding him of how I have restructured his business, cleaned up his streets, and lined his pockets.

"If it wasn't for me, she wouldn't have anything." He jabs his finger in Dario's direction as one of his men brings him a glass of scotch. He doesn't offer me or my men anything, such is the disdain he holds me in.

He knows I have him by the balls, and he hates it.

"I made you," he hisses, swinging his gaze in my direction. "Anything you have now, you have because of me. You'd do well to remember that."

The last shred of patience evaporates, and I hop up and lunge at him, lifting his chin with the side of my knife. His men withdraw their weapons the same time my crew does, and they point guns at one another over our heads as both factions face off. "You sold me to that pig Conti at eighteen to get rid of me. You weren't doing me any favors. You knew what he was like, and you still gave me to him. Anything I have now is because of *me*. You'd do well to remember that."

"You think I'd any other choice?" he roars, and I press the edge of my knife into his throat, nicking his skin. "You were unpure, broken, and bitter. Damaged goods. No one else wanted you. I took you and your whore mother in when you had nowhere to go! I paid for all your cosmetic surgeries. I gave you back your looks. I let my man train you and later let you have him for your underboss. I secured a marriage contract for you when no one wanted you. The deal I made gave you a purpose and power, and you have the nerve to give me shit?"

I dig the knife in deeper as his men glance anxiously from side to side. "I should slit your throat right now, just like you slit my mother's throat when you grew tired of her."

"Yet I still kept you. You give me no credit."

"I was nothing more than a glorified babysitter. You kept me for Anais. You didn't do it for me. You would just as soon have slit my throat too, only Anais was attached to me. She loved me the same way I loved her. I raised my sister for four years when you were out murdering and fucking and double-crossing your allies as well as your enemies. Don't pretend it was anything else."

I remove the knife and straighten up before I murder the bastard ahead of his time. "Back down." I stare at Saverio's men before nodding at Dario, Renzo, Ezio, and Ricardo. All the men lower their weapons and put them away. I snatch the undrunk scotch from Saverio's hand, knocking it back in one go. Then I throw the glass at the wall, watching it shatter with aggravated satisfaction. "Understand one thing, Saverio."

His nostrils flare at the slight.

"You live because I allow it. I have a direct hotline to Don Mazzone now. If I show him that video, he will know you planned to betray him and that you haven't forgiven him for taking Alessandro from you. He won't hesitate to kill you."

"What do you want?" he spits, removing a soiled handkerchief from his pocket and dabbing at the trickle of blood leaking from his neck.

"I am here to remind you to keep quiet about Carlo Greco and to reaffirm my story if Leo, Ben, Alesso, or anyone else from New York asks about me." I tell him the story we have concocted about my background and how I came to be Paulo's wife.

"I won't say anything." He has no choice but to agree.

"I know you won't. While I don't understand it, Anais loves you. If you die, she will be devastated. Especially if it's at my hand. Remember that if you are tempted to betray me." The only thing in this world Saverio cares about—more than himself, whores, and drugs—is my half-sister. They have a fucked-up relationship I will never understand.

"All bets are off if you renege on your word," he reminds me, awkwardly climbing to his feet. "I want a seat on The Commission when you have control."

"And you shall have it," I lie. "As long as you stick to the plan."

He nods, gesturing to his man for another drink.

My men move around me as we prepare to leave. "Keep your nose clean and your head down, Saverio," I remind him, knowing he will do the exact opposite.

"I like this one," Nicolina says, fingering a wedding dress with a strapless neckline and a heavy layered skirt as I lift my head from the printed document in my hand.

"Don't you know me at all?" I already gave a list of my likes to the owner of the high-end bridal boutique, and she is currently setting up a few for me to try on in one of the dressing rooms. Nicolina made the booking, insisting on an appointment after hours so we have complete privacy. "I want something simple but elegant. Something breathtaking without looking like I have tried too hard."

"I know you like clean, sophisticated lines, but this is your wedding day." A dreamy look crosses her face. "If there is one day to throw the rule book out, it's the day you get married."

"I have been married before, and I didn't get to choose my gown. That bitch Francesca did, and she put me in this godawful high-necked heavy meringue creation that scratched my skin and almost smothered me in the heat. This time, I'm doing it my way."

"Fair enough." Her eyes skim over the rails of beautiful gowns. "Oh, look at this one. You would totally kill it in black."

My gaze drifts over the exquisite figure-hugging black lace and organza gown with feathers. "That would make a statement for sure, and I'm almost tempted, but I want to draw attention to this marriage for all the right reasons."

"Massimo is going to look so hot in a suit."

I shake my head as I scroll through the terms of the legal agreement while we wait for the bridal owner to call me in. "You have an unhealthy obsession with him. I think I need to have a word with your husband."

"Come on, girl. Admit it. He's sexy as fuck and a drastic improvement over your last husband."

"Most men would be a drastic improvement over Paulo. That's not a good comparison."

"I'm just saying it could be a lot worse."

"How exactly?" I glance over her head to ensure no one is listening. "He's the younger brother of the man who stole my innocence and tortured me in the most horrific ways. This should be straightforward. I marry him, and when the time is right, I kill him. But it's not straightforward because he's infuriating and sexy and enigmatic and I can't stop thinking about him and how fucking amazing the sex was between us." Her eyes light up, and sometimes I wonder if Nic is missing a few vital brain cells. "Trust me, this is not a good thing."

"Would it be so bad to let yourself enjoy him for whatever time you do have with him?"

"Yes, it would."

"Why?"

"Because I might start to feel something for him, and that will only make my task harder."

Her eyes pop wide. "Oh my, wow. You already feel something for him."

"Don't be ridiculous. The only thing I feel is an irritating craving to fuck his brains out. Which is why I can't agree to this absurdity." I wave the contract in my hand. "He has added a sex clause."

Her eyes widen so far I'm afraid they might pop out of her head. "Lemme see." She grabs the document out of my hand before I can stop her. "Ho-lee fucking shit." She fans herself with her hand as she reads the list of his sexual demands, including how he wants it twice daily, access to my mouth, my pussy, and my ass, and I'm to subject myself to bondage and other kinks he's in to. In an attempt at equality, he has left a space blank for me to add my own list of sexual demands. "You've got to agree to this!" she shrieks, almost bouncing in her seat. "You can't turn a man like this down!"

"I need to for my sanity, but I can't have him fucking other women while he's my husband." He's not being unreasonable stating I fuck him or let him fuck other women. I do know that, but I can't find a workable solution that will safeguard my sanity and my goals.

"He has you by the proverbial balls," she agrees, casting her eyes over the rest of the document. She taps her finger on a section farther down the page, the pregnancy and medical clause. "How are you going to manage that?"

"I'll bribe the doctor to lie on his report. Massimo is requesting I attend his own guy for a full medical, and your husband dug up some shit I will use to make the not-so-good doctor agree to my demands. Trust me, Massimo won't know I'm infertile. He'll get a glowing report confirming I'm prime breeding ground." In the interests of fairness, my husband-to-be is also undergoing a full medical, and I appreciate his attempt at equality. It is not usual for made men to offer such a thing, and it only makes me more curious about him.

"Ew. Do you have to put it like that?"

I don't explain how I must be clinical or crude when raising the topic because it has taken me years to discuss the subject at all and years to condition myself to hide the pain. One of the worst things Carlo did to me was taking away my ability to have children. If I allow myself to think about it, I get all up in my feels, and emotions are a death sentence for a woman in my position.

"Yes. I do," I say in a clipped tone as the owner walks toward us with a broad smile on her face.

"I know you do. I'm sorry." Nic pulls me into a hug before easing back to examine my face. "I hate you have to do all of this. I truly do. I hate this life for you. You deserve so much more."

Nic doesn't quite agree with my approach to vengeance. She understands why I plot and plan, but she worries about the long-term consequences and whether I will feel more at peace after it's done. She would rather I let it go and advance my career for *me* and not as a means of exacting revenge.

"I do, but we work with the cards we've been handed the best way we know how. This is how I chose to play the game, and there is nothing or no one who will steer me off course now."

Chapter Nine

Massimo

The site manager shows Fiero and me the latest progress, and I exchange a wide grin with my best friend and business partner as we walk around the large waterfront property we jointly own, growing more excited as we inch closer to completion. Everything we have been working toward since we graduated high school is coming to fruition, and soon it will be time to make our move.

"Thank you," I say, shaking the man's hand when we end up back on the lower level in the large space that will become our personal office. "Everything looks perfect. Exactly how we envisioned it."

"We appreciate you are keeping us on schedule and within budget," Fiero adds as he shakes the man's hand. "Don't forget there will be a nice fat bonus waiting for you if you finish on time and on budget."

The man nods before quietly slipping out of the room, leaving us to our own devices. I remove the hard hat on my head and place it down on the large rectangular desk in the center of the open space before walking to the floor-to-ceiling windows.

I stare at the soft ripples of the Hudson River outside, flowing into

Upper New York Bay, with a mounting sense of contentment. A large cargo ship with colorful stacked containers lies motionless at the side of the terminal a few miles to our right. Farther up, tall red cranes stretch skyward as they ferry containers from ship to land. On our left are a couple of other industrial premises. The northern tip of Staten Island buzzes with industrious energy, and I can't wait for the day we are operational and our output matches our neighbors'.

"Did you ever visualize it like this?" Fiero asks, coming up alongside me. He shoves his hands deep in his pockets. "When we were holed up in your bedroom, concocting wild plans to show our fathers we were worthy successors, did you ever dream we'd own a property like this? Have access to our own shipping port and unlimited potential for expansion and control?"

"I didn't have the imagination or the experience to conceptualize anything like this," I truthfully admit. "I knew I wanted to rule from the very top, but getting from point A to point B was less clear."

He slowly nods. "I know what you mean. It's surreal, but at the same time, we have worked our butts off for this. We deserve this." He lifts his clenched fist, and we touch knuckles. "We're doing it, man. We're really fucking doing it." His grin is so wide it threatens to split his face.

I shoot him a matching grin. "Fuck your old man for never believing in you."

"I hope your prick of a father is turning in his grave, regretting the day he called you a mistake and made you invisible."

I rub the back of my head as my gaze eats up the stunning view outside. "In a warped way, we owe this to our fathers. If they weren't so stubbornly blind and doggedly cruel, we might not be here. Their dismissal and lack of faith pushed us to achieve this."

"Nah, man. I refuse to give either of those motherfuckers any credit. This is all on us."

"Damn straight." I turn to my best friend, the guy who has been by my side practically my entire life, more my brother than any of my brothers have ever been, and I acknowledge how grateful I am to have Fiero in my life. "I couldn't have done this without you, brother."

He pulls me into a hug, slapping me on the back. "That goes both ways." He clamps his hand on my shoulder before shucking out of our embrace. "We have always done everything together. This is the first time one of us is branching out into unchartered waters completely alone. I'm not sure I like it."

"We attended different universities in different European cities, and our career paths went in different directions," I remind him.

"That was by choice, and we were still doing the same things at the same time. Still working toward the same end goal."

"Marrying Donna Conti ties into that goal. This marriage will elevate my status."

"You know I'm not talking about that!"

My lips twitch. I know exactly what he's referring to. I just love yanking his chain. "If you're feeling left out, we could always find you a bride."

"I was thinking more along the lines of sharing yours." He waggles his brows and slants me a wicked grin.

"Not a fucking chance in hell. I knew I'd end up regretting showing you Catarina's picture."

"The old man was right. She's sexy as sin, and I'd definitely be down to tap that." Leaning against a pillar, he crosses his legs at the ankles while he baits me. "It's not like we haven't tag teamed before."

"You cannot compare random women to my fiancée. I'm not sharing her with any motherfucker." I jab my finger in his face. "Including you."

"You're not in any position to make such a statement. Unless she's finally relented and is granting you access to the holy land?"

I bark out a laugh. "Oh, she'll relent all right. Even if she refuses to sign the contract with that clause included, mark my words, I will have her begging for my cock in record time."

Fire dances in his eyes. "Care to put your money where your mouth is?"

I straighten up as my lips curl at the corners. "When have you ever known me to back down from a wager?" I arch a brow. "Set your terms and prepare to lose, asshole."

"One hundred K if you bang her on your wedding night."

"Deal." I have the utmost confidence in my seduction skills, and I believe in the power of our chemistry, so I shake hands on it, assured I'll be richer, and not poorer, come my wedding night.

Fiero chuckles. "That infamous Greco arrogance is still strong, but you're going down! You haven't even gotten her signature on the dotted line!"

"Formalities, man. By this time Friday, the contract will be signed, the medicals will be done, and a date set for the wedding. You can bank on it."

His eyes pop wide. "You asked her for a medical?"

I lean my back against the window. "Of course, I did. It's standard with these things."

"Yeah, when the brides are younger and of less standing."

"The fact she's older means it's more of a necessity. I'm having a medical too. The Greco bloodline will die with me unless I produce an heir."

A deep chuckle rumbles from his chest. "I wish I could've been there to see the look on Donna Conti's face when you brought that up!"

"She was actually fine about it. My sex clause is the bigger issue." I can't contain my grin. "I added a ton of kinky shit to the contract purely to rile her up. I expect it to come back completely redlined."

He cracks up laughing, clutching his stomach. "Man, you are something else." He thumps me in the arm. "And you make it far too easy for me. I am already compiling a shopping list to spend my one-hundred-K windfall on."

We spend the afternoon at the waterfront property, sitting side by side at the only desk in the space, poring over the architect's designs for every floor in the vast fifty-thousand-square-foot, four-story building. The upper levels will accommodate our various real estate businesses and the ancillary companies we have set up to support our interests over the years, and the lower levels will house our import-export business. While the real estate and ancillary businesses are legit, and it's how we have funded this project, the import-export business was set up purely as a front to hide our drug operation.

"Allante has sent through his first surveillance report," Fiero says, lifting his head from his laptop to glance at me. Clicking out of the file I am presently working on, I open my inbox and retrieve the email from our PI.

I peruse the image files taken at the private airstrip, examining the photos of my fiancée and her team as they board a jet.

"She went to Vegas," Fiero confirms, skimming through the written report as I zoom in on a pic of Catarina talking to that asshole Renzo at the bottom of the airplane steps. She is wearing a white pants suit, and her hair is down; the wind blowing errant strands across her face. Large designer shades cover her eyes and half her face, but her lips are painted the same red she wore last night, and her makeup is flawless. She looks hot as fuck, and my cock is already straining behind my zipper. I only have to look at her and I grow hard, which could be problematic.

"You're a lucky bastard. She's stunning," Fiero adds.

"She is, and I am. Why did she go to Vegas, I wonder," I muse, tapping a finger on my chin.

"It's one of the states she supplies, so it must be business related. Pity we didn't have a man on the ground to know exactly what she was up to."

"We need to secure a contact in every state she has business in," I say, deciding on the spot to extend the surveillance. "We need eyes on her everywhere."

"I'll get Allante on it."

Allante has worked with us for years, and we have a significant investment in his PI firm. We have helped him to develop his network and quickly grow his business, funneling plenty of work his way.

Fiero fires off a quick email as I gather up my things. I told Mama I would take her out to dinner tonight, and I don't want to be late. I need to break the news to her about the wedding, and I want to do it in person because I'm not sure how she will react.

Most Italian mamas dream of marrying their sons off from the cradle. Not our mama. She is very attached to me and Gabe and solely reliant on us. After losing her husband and two eldest sons, we are all she has.

I blame my dead father for her ongoing anxious disposition because he did his best to break her. Although she is learning to live again, she is fragile and will never be whole. The internal scars she bears won't ever fully heal. Mama leans on us out of necessity and fear. She may worry a wife might divert my attention, but I want to reassure her that won't be the case. I would like it if both women in my life could get along. Truth is, I think they need one another.

"Done." Fiero leans back in his chair, watching me pack up. "I thought you were planning to shadow your fiancée yourself?"

"That is still part of the plan, but I am heading to Berlin tomorrow. I have one final job to take care of, and with the wedding and other work, I'm too busy right now. I'll let Allante continue to watch her for the time being."

I have just dropped Mama back home after dinner when I receive a call from Allante. "Massimo, I think you should see this in person."

"Send me your coordinates, and I'll be there as quick as I can."

My cell pings with the details as I park at the side of the road and retrieve my duffel bag from the trunk, pulling out the items I need. I quickly get changed into black cargo pants, a long-sleeved black top, black ball cap, and a pair of black sneakers. Then I head across the city to Manhattan, meeting up with our PI on the street across from a row of busy restaurants.

Opening the passenger door, I slide into Allante's car, removing my ballcap and running a hand through my hair as I look in the direction my PI is facing. "What's going on?" I ask over the successive clicking of his camera as he takes pics through the tinted glass.

"Take a look for yourself." Sitting back in his seat, he hands the Nikon camera over to me. Scrolling back to the start, I flick through the pictures of the two women embracing on the sidewalk before heading inside the French restaurant. "Your fiancée is with Anais DiPietro," he supplies.

"I know who she is." The wife of my enemy is my enemy too. "Send those to me and cc Fiero," I instruct, leaning across him as the door of the restaurant opens and the two women emerge behind their bodyguards. Catarina is not wearing her usual white. She's wearing a simple fitted black dress that would look plain on most women, but on her, it looks magnificent. Her hair is down again, cascading in soft waves over her shoulders, and I wonder if this is her natural look or if the straight lines she usually sports is her actual hair.

The men watch the street, their eyes skimming over Allante's car without interest, as the women exchange words. Carefully veiled annoyance is evident on my fiancée's face while blatant anger is crystal clear on Anais's face. Allante snaps more pics as I analyze their body language for signs I can decipher. Catarina holds herself with confidence while Anais crosses her arms around her chest and juts out her lower lip. It's obvious who is in control, and prickles of apprehension skate across my chilly flesh.

My phone pings, and I accept Fiero's call. "What the fuck is she doing with DiPietro's wife?"

"I don't know, but I don't like it."

"You think this is Cruz's doing? Is she working with him to undermine us? Spy on us?"

"It's something we can't rule out. We know Don Mazzone suspects

Donna Conti has an ulterior or additional agenda. She is the one who suggested herself for the marriage contract. Perhaps this is why."

"Maybe you shouldn't marry her."

"This is even more reason I should."

"How the hell do you figure that?"

"There is a lot of merit in keeping your enemies close. If Cruz has put her up to this, this could work to our advantage too. There are several ways sleeping with the enemy could work to our benefit."

Chapter Ten

Catarina

I pause *The Last Kingdom* on the TV as a knock resounds on the living room door. "Come in," I call out, unfurling my legging-clad legs from underneath me and planting my bare feet on the ground. It's late, and I'm trying to relax and forget about the marriage contract I signed earlier today.

It's done.

I'm marrying Massimo Greco in a week, and I'd be lying if I said I wasn't tied into knots and conflicted over the decision I've made. As Ricardo enters my private space, I stand, pushing my long wavy hair off my face and tugging on the hem of my off-the-shoulder sweater.

"Donna Conti. Apologies for the interruption, but we have an issue at the front gate."

I'm instantly on guard, jerking my head up as I stride toward him. "What kind of issue?"

He drags a hand through his hair. "Your fiancé is at the gate demanding to be let in."

I blink a couple of times and tug on my ears, not sure I heard that correctly. "Are you telling me Massimo Greco is at the gate?"

He nods. "Yes, ma'am."

I let loose a string of colorful expletives. "How the fuck does he know where I live?" I didn't tell him on purpose, readily agreeing to live with him at his house in Long Island after we are married. This house is my sanctuary, and I won't have any man intruding in my safe place. While I don't go to the lengths Don Mazzone does to keep his residence a secret, the location of my home is not exactly common knowledge either.

"I don't know, ma'am. What do you want me to do?"

"You might as well let him in. He's stubborn as fuck, and he won't go away easily."

He nods. "As you wish. I will escort him personally."

"Thanks, Ric." I move to follow him out of the room—to head to my bedroom to get changed and make myself more presentable—when I think better of it. Fuck him. If Massimo is rude enough to show up unannounced this late at night, he can take me the way I am.

Maybe if he sees the real me, it will defuse his attraction and he'll give up his conjugal rights.

Against my better judgment, I agreed to a modified sex clause. Three times a week instead of twice daily. Vanilla instead of his list of kinky shit. And he can have my mouth and my pussy, but no man is taking my ass ever again. I expected him to protest more, but he was annoyingly agreeable to all my changes.

I don't trust it or him.

He's a Greco, after all.

No one with that name can ever be trusted.

I suspect he thinks I'll be unable to resist him and I'll come crawling to him for sex more often.

Ha! He can think again! The devil will dance on my grave before I'll ever beg that man to fuck me. As it is, I only agreed to three times a week to get the contract signed. I have no intention of screwing him that regularly. It's not like he can do anything about it. Once we marry, it is for life. Only death can sever our ties. Something that will happen sooner than expected for my husband-to-be.

Dropping back onto the couch, I top off my wineglass and unmute the TV, working hard to dial back my aggravation because I refuse to lose my cool in this man's presence again. Massimo has an uncanny ability to rattle me in a way no one else does, and I don't like it. I need to remember who I am and what I am here to do.

A few minutes later, Ric knocks on the door again. I pause my show for a second time, pissed Massimo is interrupting my Alexander Dreymon swoonfest—fuck, that man is sex on legs, and I have a newfound appreciation for fictional Viking warriors.

Drawing deep breaths and cautioning myself to remain composed, I walk toward the door and open it slowly. The man I am betrothed to stands behind my bodyguard and looks like butter wouldn't melt in his mouth. "Thank you, Ricardo. You can remain out here." I step aside to let Massimo enter, refusing to look at the good-looking bastard as he saunters into the room like it's not rude to show up unannounced and uninvited.

I close the door behind him, watching as he drinks the room in. This is the first time I have seen him in casual clothes, and I hate to admit he looks hot, but there is zero point lying to myself.

Dark denim hugs his shapely ass and highlights his strong thighs and long legs in his designer jeans. A long-sleeved gray Henley is stretched across his large biceps and muscular back. Ink covers both sides of his neck, crawling down underneath his top, and I wonder how much of his body is tattooed.

I guess I will find out in due course.

The thought equally thrills and terrifies me.

"Nice place you've got here," he says after a thorough inspection of my tastefully decorated personal living room, slowly turning around to face me.

"Thank you. I think so." Fuck, his top is pulled so tight across his chest and abs it almost looks painted on. I can make out every dip and curve of his upper torso, and he's every bit a work of art. How the hell am I going to deny him? Especially if he goes out of his way to tease me, like I suspect he will? "How did you get my address?" I blurt, stalking toward the couch and my wineglass.

"I'm quite handy with a computer, and it actually wasn't that difficult to find."

I know he's lying because there is no trace of my address on the internet. I make a mental note to check with my IT guy to see if anyone has somehow managed to hack into any of my systems. "Next time, call me if you plan to drop by unannounced. I was busy."

"Indulging your Viking fetish, I see." He wears an infuriating smirk on his handsome face.

"Have a seat," I say in a clipped tone, struggling to remain calm in the face of his aggravating presence. I drop down on the couch. "And I don't have a Viking fetish. I have an Alexander Dreymon one."

"Pfft." He rolls his eyes as he stands before me instead of sitting like a normal human. "He's completely overrated. Unlike me." Bending down, he brings his mouth to my ear. "I totally exceed expectations, and you'll quickly come to realize my value."

"Your arrogance is astounding," I say, pressing my back into the couch. "And you're crowding my personal space. Back off."

"Apologies," he says, sounding utterly unapologetic as he straightens up. "I've had an idea I think you'll like." He waggles his brows, and I'm pretty sure I'm not going to like the next words out of his mouth.

"Debatable."

"We could role-play and spice up our sex life. I'll order a long wig and a Viking costume online. I can get one for you too. We can indulge our baser desires and fuck like wild savages." His eyes glimmer with a mix of amusement and lust, and I discreetly squeeze my thighs together, not in any way repulsed by the idea.

I clear my throat and conduct a stern inner talk with my wayward libido. "Role-playing is not part of our arrangement."

"Only because some party pooper redlined it, along with all my other fun suggestions. I might think you're a prude or frigid except any woman who fucks a complete stranger in an airport bathroom is clearly neither of those things."

The fucking nerve of this man! Who the hell is he to cast judgment on me? Irritation fires at me from all angles, and it's a challenge not to give in to it. But I won't give him the satisfaction of knowing he is getting to me.

At least his judgy comments have poured cold water all over my libido.

For that, I'm grateful.

"Did you seriously come here this close to midnight to discuss the deleted details of a contract we both already signed?" I ask, in a lethally calm voice.

"Nope, but I love winding you up. It's my new favorite pastime. Think of all the fun times ahead!"

Oh joy. I close my eyes and count to ten in my head. "What do you want, Massimo?" I ask in a resigned tone, reopening my eyes a few seconds later. "Unlike some I could mention, I worked a twelve-hour day, and I have a full schedule tomorrow."

A muscle clenches in his jaw, and it's not the first time mentioning his lack of purpose has struck a chord. I wonder why? If he was a true playboy, insults like that would roll off his back. My tech guy, Enrique, has been digging, trying to find out more about the man I'm marrying, but his search is turning up nothing more than the usual trivial gossip. I don't trust it or buy it. Massimo is hiding something, and I fully intend to find out what.

His jaw smooths out, and his features soften; that fleeting aggravation disappearing as quickly as it appeared on his face. I'm instantly on high alert, my spine turning rigid as I wait for him to state the nature of his visit. "First, I apologize for dropping by so late, but I just got off a plane from Berlin, and I'm tied up the next few days, so I figured this is the only chance I'll get to do this."

Berlin? Why was he in Berlin? I make a mental note to ask Enrique to check that out too. "Do what?" I ask.

"Second," he says, ignoring me because it seems to be programmed into him. "You look beautiful. I don't think you realize how utterly compelling you are. You are so fucking gorgeous you take my breath away." Taking my hand, he pulls me to my feet. I'm ashamed I let him, but his words and the intense way he's looking at me have magnetized me so much that I'm incapable of protesting. His fingers thread softly through my wavy hair. "Is this natural?" he asks, in a gruff voice that sends shivers cascading over my skin.

"Yes," I croak as his forest-green eyes lock on to my eyes.

He traces the pad of his thumb across my naked face. "You are flawless, and your skin is so soft." I blink as if in a daze, wondering what this man is doing to me. Leaning in, he presses a featherlight kiss to my cheek. "I know you are wary of me, but I mean every word of what I have just said."

"Thank you," I say, finally breaking through the haze. "But I'm sure you didn't visit to shower me with compliments." Before I can sit back down, he drops to one knee and removes a small black velvet box from his pocket.

"What are you doing?" I blurt even though it's obvious what he's doing.

He flicks the box open, and I'm almost dazzled by the large pear-shaped diamond sitting on a platinum band embedded with a row of smaller diamonds. "I know our arrangement is a business arrangement, but I want our marriage to succeed, and I want to set the tone from the outset. Every woman deserves to be proposed to, and I'm going to do this the right way."

"Get up," I snap, tugging on his arm, as panic replaces the blood flowing through my veins. My heart thumps against my rib cage, and pressure clamps down on my chest.

Why is he doing this?

He can't do this to me.

He's totally fucking with my head, and I won't let him.

"Not until I have proposed to my fiancée." He takes my hand, holding it firmly.

"This is ridiculous, and I'm not doing it." I wrench my hand from his hold, almost yanking my arm from its socket with the strength involved in extricating myself from his tight grip. "You seem to be laboring under a misapprehension," I say, grabbing my wineglass and moving away from him. I gulp back a mouthful to help steady my nerves. "Let me clear it up for you. This marriage is a business arrangement. It will never be anything more, and I'm not like other women. I don't need or want a proposal. I'll wear your ring because it's expected, but I will not entertain any romantic charade because you are fooling no one. Whatever you hope to achieve with this grand gesture, you can forget about it. I'm not buying the bullshit you're selling." I glare at him, relieved when I spot tension bracketing his face and stiffening his shoulders.

He climbs to his feet and stalks toward me with a thunderous expression on his face. "I have never met a more ungrateful rude bitch, and trust me, I have known a lot of women."

I level him with a cold sneer. "That's hardly news to me."

Snatching my hand, he roughly thrusts the ring on my ring finger. "You're welcome, *mia amata*," he hisses, projecting fire from his eyes. "You don't need to worry about any more romantic charades. I got the message loud and clear."

He storms out of the room, slamming the door behind him as I stare at the glistening diamond on my ring finger, wondering why this feels like I've lost something when I clearly won that round.

Chapter Eleven

Catarina

"You look beautiful. Elegant and regal, just like a queen," Dario says, attempting to reassure me with his words and his proud smile as if he can sense nerves firing at me from all directions. It's not like me to be this anxious, but Massimo Greco tends to set my nerves on edge and ignite an uneasy fire in my blood. It's disconcerting, and I'd be lying if I said I hadn't had second thoughts about marrying him this past week.

Dario pats my arm, and I focus on my breathing, using it to settle myself. We are waiting at the end of the aisle in the historic cathedral in midtown Manhattan, watching Nicolina stride elegantly up the red-carpeted floor toward the front of the church.

The place is packed with the crème de la crème of high society and powerful Italian Americans from across the US. The archbishop of New York is conducting the ceremony, and I truly feel like mafia royalty.

It is exactly two weeks since Massimo and I reconnected and one week since we signed our marriage contract. To pull together a wedding of this magnitude in such a short space of time is nothing short of miraculous. Nic handled the arrangements with The Commission's event planner, and I owe my friend and personal assistant a massive bonus for her hard work.

"Thank you," I say, running my free hand down the front of my wedding gown. I smile at my *consigliere* as he prepares to give me away.

I opted for a fairly simple fitted lace dress. The beauty is in the sharp lines that mold to my curves and the pretty handmade lace overlay. The neckline dips into a subtle V, flashing a little cleavage, but it's respectful, and the material sweeps over the curve of my hips, flowing in straight lines to my feet. Long, sheer lace sleeves cover my arms. At the back, a line of tiny pearl buttons runs from the nape of my neck to just above my ass. The train is a loose-fitting mermaid style because I didn't want to be too restricted when walking. I also needed some room to strap a thin dagger to my inner thigh. I never go anywhere without some form of concealed weapon, and even with the high-level security in place today, I refused to leave home without the means to defend myself.

I opted to wear a veil, as is tradition at Italian American weddings. It's constructed of the same delicate lace as my dress, and it falls from midway down my chignon to the ground. I chose not to wear it over my face because I don't hide from anyone, and I'm far from the blushing bride.

I made the decision to do this, and I will own it.

"You are far too good for him," Dario says, his features softening as we watch Rowan and Raven Mazzone walk up the aisle next.

It's kind of sad there are no kids in my family or Massimo's to act as our ring bearer and flower girl. Ben and Sierra didn't hesitate to offer their eldest children for the roles when they heard of our dilemma. This church is packed with armed made men, and security guards roam inside and outside perimeters, so it's completely safe to allow children to join in the celebrations. Natalia and Leo have brought their eldest child, and three of Serena and Alesso's kids are in attendance too. There are several teenagers in the congregation as well. Most of them are boys, which isn't surprising when they initiate at thirteen and are training to be fully indoctrinated in our world. But there are a few girls here too. Most likely daughters of important made men who will suffer this fate at some point in the future.

"I know." I agree as the pianist switches music, indicating it's time to get this show on the road. Holding on to Dario's arm, I grip my white-rose bouquet tightly in my other hand as we proceed to walk forward.

"If he makes any move to hurt you, you mustn't hesitate to call me or Renzo," he softly murmurs, keeping a fake smile plastered on his face as we walk toward my fiancé and his best man, Fiero Maltese. I'm surprised he didn't choose his brother Gabriele, but it's not an unwelcome substitution.

The Maltese heir is *very* easy on the eyes.

"He won't," I say with confidence born of nothing but gut instinct. "He's not like his brother."

Dario subtly flinches. "You can't say that for sure, and you can't let your guard down."

I hold my head up high and proud and nod and smile at several men as we pass by—familiar and unfamiliar faces; dons and their underbosses and *consiglieres*, and important contacts I conduct business with. "I never let my guard down. You know that. I'm merely pointing out I don't believe I have to worry about that with him."

Up ahead, Massimo angles his body, turning to look at me as I approach. Our gazes lock, and naked appreciation is evident in his intense stare. Forest-green eyes roam me from head to toe, eliciting a subtle thrill of excitement as my body approves of his single-minded attention.

Massimo is drop-dead gorgeous in a black tuxedo that is custom fit to his tall, broad, muscular form. He's had a haircut since I saw him during the week, and his beard is trimmed tight to his jawline.

If the circumstances were different, I imagine I could be smitten with such a man and thrilled to be marrying him. But that's an alternate universe where his brother didn't rape, abuse, and torment me, killing something vital deep down inside me.

"Besides," I murmur, keeping my eyes pinned on the man waiting for me, "I know how to handle myself. If he tries anything, he'll be sorry." A sudden bout of nausea crawls up my throat, and I pause for a few seconds until it passes. I draw a deep breath. "No Greco will ever put hands on me again without my permission. That is a guarantee."

We slow our approach as the top of the aisle is in sight. Out of the corner of my eye, I spot *her*—Eleanora Greco. Massimo's mother and my soon-to-be mother-in-law. Anger prickles my skin as I look at the small, petite woman standing beside Gabriele, looking timid and lost as she hangs her head, refusing eye contact with anyone. Memories ghost before my eyes, and a violent trembling threatens to take control of me.

Dario tightens his hold on me, instinctively knowing something has spooked me. "I've got you," he whispers. "We all have you, and we won't let anything happen to you today or ever." His words soothe the ragged edges of my nerves, and I draw a subtle breath, regaining my composure. "You are more than just a boss to me, Catarina." Dario tilts his head slightly so he's eyeballing me. "More than just a friend. You are family, and I protect my family with everything I am. If he harms one hair on your head, he will have me and Renzo to deal with."

As if he heard us whispering, my underboss turns to stare at me from his position in the second row. He brought his wife and two sons with him today. His daughter is only six, and they left her with her grandparents. I had thought of asking Armis to be the ring bearer, but Renzo is still vehemently opposed to this marriage, and expecting his eight-year-old son to play a formal part in the wedding is not something I could ask of him.

Neither could I ask him to give me away, but he was my first choice. I know he would have said yes, purely not to upset me, but I couldn't force that upon him either.

Renzo has been there for me since I was a scared fourteen-year-old, and I hate this marriage has driven a wedge between us. Honestly, it's ripping my insides to shreds. A big part of the second thoughts I have had this week relate to the man who has been my savior in so many ways. Renzo is dogged in his belief this is a mistake, and we have never been so divided. I am satisfied this is the right path to achieve my goals, but Massimo's ability to rattle me and Renzo's continuous disagreement have given me reason to reflect on my decision a lot.

After much consideration, I am going through with it because my gut tells me this is the right course of action. I can only hope, in time, Renzo will see I am right and agree to let it go. For now, I am glad he could put his reservations aside to be here today even if he is wearing a face like thunder. Our gazes hold for a few seconds before I drag my attention away, refocusing on my fiancé.

Massimo levels a dark look in Renzo's direction, and it's fair to say there is no love lost between both men. I doubt they will ever trust one another. "Thank you, Dario," I say as we stop in front of Massimo and Fiero.

Dario kisses my cheek. "It is a privilege and honor to escort you, Donna Conti."

"That is the last time you will refer to Catarina like that," Massimo says, accepting my hand from Dario. "In an hour, she will be Donna Greco." I could be imagining it, but his eyes briefly flare with heated possession as the words leave his mouth.

Dario narrows his eyes, not taking kindly to the obvious being stated. "We'll be watching you." He stabs him with a sharp look. "Make one false move, and you'll have me and Renzo to answer to."

"Your protection of my bride is admirable, so I'll let that go. But I think Catarina is well capable of handling herself. She doesn't need you, me, or any man to jump to her defense, and I have no intention of stepping out of line." Holding my hand tight, he pulls me in closer and peers straight into my eyes. "You have nothing to fear from me. I will treat you like a queen."

"See that you do." Dario pins him with a warning look that sends chills up and down my spine.

"Meet and greet is over, folks," Fiero says, flashing me a flirtatious smile. His wild bleach-blond locks have been tamed, artfully styled back off his face, highlighting his exquisite bone structure, big blue eyes, and wide mouth with full lips. Like my husband-to-be, he's sporting a thin beard with neatly trimmed facial hair. He's about as far removed from the stereotypical made man as you can get, and it's strangely endearing. He shares a similar playboy reputation as my fiancé.

Before the Accardi twins stole the crown, Massimo and Fiero were the poster boys for the mafia around New York for many years.

"The archbishop is about to throw a hissy fit if we don't get started." Fiero leans around Massimo, planting his lush lips against my cheek. "You look stunning, *regina*. A true beauty."

"Thank you," I supply as Massimo shoots him a dark glare. Fiero chuckles under his breath, and I ponder the dynamic of their friendship. Dario steps aside to let Nicolina approach, and I trade looks with my matron of honor as I hand her my bouquet.

"Ready?" my fiancé asks, repositioning us so we're facing forward. I nod, silently willing the butterflies in my tummy to kindly fuck the hell off. "You take my breath away," he says in a low, soft tone. "You have exceeded every dream I have had about this moment." His eyes appear sincere as he stares at me, and he's either purposely forgetting how I snubbed his proposal or he's accepted it wasn't appropriate given our arrangement. "I know you might hate me, but I don't hate you, *mia amata*. That couldn't be further from the truth. I don't want to begin our marriage with any anger or misconception between us." Lifting our conjoined hands, he brings them to his lips and plants a kiss on my knuckles, purposely ignoring the irritated sigh that heaves from the archbishop's lips.

It's rude to keep him waiting, and I shouldn't condone such disrespectful behavior, but I reluctantly admire Massimo for having the balls to say what he wants to say, irrespective of who is waiting.

"I want to get to know you, and I won't pressure you to do anything you don't want to do," he continues.

I gulp over the lump lodged in my throat as his eyes pin mine in place.

"I want our marriage to work. I promise I will make you happy if you meet me halfway." His fingers brush against my cheek. "My smart, beautiful *regina*." His voice cracks a little as his eyes flood with warmth. "Can you at least agree to that?"

I blink successively, ensnared in his hypnotic trap, unable to think straight in the moment. Absently, I nod while trying to clear the fog from my eyes and my head. "Yes," I finally manage to say.

He smiles, and his large, surprisingly callused hand wraps snugly around mine as we step closer to the altar and the waiting archbishop.

We hold hands as the archbishop commences with the ceremony, but I barely hear the words. I'm too busy trying to figure out what Massimo's game plan is. I can't believe his pretty words are the truth because it's too convenient, too smooth, too hopeful to be real.

We say our vows and exchange rings, and it's as if the outside world has ceased to exist. Internally, I'm blindsided and feeling too many things.

If Massimo's intention was to throw me off-kilter, he has achieved his goal.

That thought is enough to drag me kicking and screaming from that shadowy place in my head. All my senses return, in full clarity, as the archbishop pronounces us husband and wife, and Massimo reels me into his arms, dipping me down low as he kisses me passionately in front of an approving crowd.

So much for not doing anything I don't want to!

Chapter Twelve

Massimo

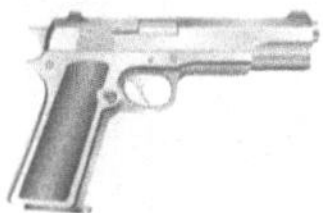

"Smile, Mrs. Greco. You don't want to wear that resting bitch face in all our wedding photos," I say, tightening my arm around her slender waist as we pose for the photographer on the steps of the cathedral. My wife digs her nails into my side as she plasters a fake smile on her face, and I chuckle.

"You will pay for that," she hisses into my ear, and all it does is spur me on. She is still fuming over the stunt I pulled at the altar, and I am floating on a cloud. Nothing gets my juices flowing like an angry Catarina, and I fully intend to cash in later.

Life is good. Life is *great*.

I am married to a smart, gorgeous, feisty, sexy woman who challenges me with every breath. I didn't realize how lacking my life was until she came back into it. She might want to slice my dick off or cut my throat, but at least it makes life interesting.

The photographer rearranges us so we are facing sideways and my wife's back is against my chest. Draping my arms around her, I lean down and whisper in her ear. "Countless women would pay to be kissed like that by me, and yet you are angry." I rub her hip through her gorgeous lace dress. "You are far too uptight, but I'll address that problem later."

"Your arrogance has blinded you to the truth, and you'll be addressing nothing later," she fumes through a forced smile.

"We'll see." I hold her tighter, reveling in the feel of her toned body pressed against mine. Blood rushes south, hardening my dick, like always in her presence, and I subtly nudge my growing erection against her.

"That's enough for now!" she calls out, wrenching out of my arms and storming down the steps. She glares at the photographer as she passes by, heading in the direction of her crew. I watch her angry stance with a full hard-on straining behind my pants, wondering if there isn't something wrong with me. Is it normal to get this turned on in the face of such blatant hostility?

"Is she still steaming over the kiss?" Fiero asks, coming up alongside me.

"She wants to rip my guts out and wrap them around my throat."

He chuckles, rubbing his hands with glee. "I am looking forward to an even healthier bank balance in the morning."

"She is holding on to her anger because it's easier than accepting the truth of our attraction." I grin at my friend. "But she won't be able to resist me for long."

"Famous last words, my friend." Fiero clamps a hand on my shoulder. "At least life won't be dull."

"That is one thing I am definitely guaranteed with my new wife."

I take a moment to appreciate my good fortune because it's not every day I get married. The church bells are chiming, the bright blue cloudless sky cushions a majestic sun, and laughter and raucous conversation surround us as our guests linger and mingle before they will head to the prestigious five-star hotel where the reception is taking place.

I was glad when Catarina readily agreed to the hotel venue because Mama is not equipped to host the event at our family home, especially on such short notice. Besides, I don't have any happy memories associated with my childhood or that house, and I would rather not start my married life with a celebration in that ghastly place.

"We should move," Gabriele says, materializing at my side. "More press is arriving, and that's never a good thing."

"Agreed. Will you escort Mama to the hotel?"

"Of course." He clears his throat and rubs the back of his neck. "I just wanted to thank you for coming through for me, for our family. It means a lot you would do this."

"It's not exactly a chore," I say, my eyes automatically wandering to where my wife is surrounded by well-wishers.

"You look good together, and I believe you are a good match." He pulls me in for a quick hug. "I hope it's a happy marriage. Maybe some grandkids are just what Mama needs to fully put the past behind her and move forward."

"That won't be happening for a while. Catarina has a lot to do in New York, and she is already busy running the rest of her operation. It will be some time before she'll be able to focus on raising a family."

Gabriele smirks. "Accidents have been known to happen."

"She has an IUD," I say because the medical confirmed it.

"Pay the doctor not to replace it the next time," he suggests, and my jaw hangs open. Gabriele is one of the most honest, noble men I know. It's one of the reasons it's been so hard for him to be a don. Being shady doesn't come naturally to him, and doing some of the things he's had to do often play on his mind.

I won't have any such qualms. I'm quite prepared to do whatever is necessary to claw my way to the very top, and I won't lose a minute of sleep over it either.

"Well, brother. I do believe you have shocked the shit out of me." I slap him on the back. "Perhaps there is hope for you after all."

"It's time for our first dance," I say, standing and extending my hand to my beautiful bride. The dinner and speeches are thankfully done, and this is the last big formality before we can let loose. God knows my wife needs it. She's as tightly wound as a ball of string, and I'd say she has lockjaw from all the forced smiling she's doing.

"Don't pull any shit," she warns, placing her dainty hand in my much bigger one. "Not unless you plan to sleep with one eye open tonight."

I chuckle as I lead her out to the dance floor, waiting excitedly for the moment she realizes I changed the playlist. I pull her into my arms when the song starts, and her head jerks up as her eyes narrow on me. "This isn't 'Livin' on a Prayer' by Bon Jovi." Her arms glide around my shoulders, and she subtly digs her nails into the base of my neck as we start to move.

"That's such an odd choice for a wedding, don't you think?" I arch a brow, stifling my laughter.

"And 'Killer Queen' isn't?"

"At least it's apt." I level her with a pointed look.

"I might just prove your point tonight, darling husband," she says, emitting a little gasp as I spin her out and reel her back in. "And this is a shit song to dance to."

"Who cares?" I twirl her around again, enamored with the growing rage glimmering in her eyes. She truly is a magnificent creature. A complete conundrum. All hellfire and prickly ice. She's a puzzle I can't wait to solve. I know I'll have fun getting there. "It's Queen. They are legends, and I think it's the perfect song choice for my bloodthirsty wife."

"I swear you want me to stab you" she says, as I dip her down low again. "Do not even think about kissing me!"

Ignoring her request, I yank her back up into my arms and slam my lips down on hers. She's seething. Her entire body is trembling with rage as I discreetly nudge her stomach with my growing erection while I angle my head and kiss the living daylights out of her. She can't do anything but go along with this.

Catarina understands the way this game is played. Everyone here may know this is an arranged marriage, but that doesn't mean they don't expect a show. Catarina is smart enough to know it's bad business not to appear happy about the deal. It's why she's kept a mask on her pretty face all day. She wants everyone to see she is pleased with the arrangement and fully cooperating even if she knows it satisfies the other made men to believe she is now beholden to a man.

They mistakenly think I can keep her in line.

I already known I can't, and truthfully, why would I want to?

Doesn't mean I can't manipulate her and blackmail her into doing certain things my way. I'm already messing with her head, and I fully intend to find out exactly what my beloved is up to.

Catarina kisses me back with brutal kisses she intends to be punishing, but I'm living for them and the feel of her sexy body underneath my hands. She sucks my lower lip into her mouth before sinking her teeth into the flesh and drawing blood. Using the opportunity, I plunder her mouth with my tongue while grabbing her ass and pressing her hot, tight body against my throbbing hard-on. I'm devouring her in plain sight, in a way that is not customary at weddings, but I couldn't give a flying fuck. She has me all worked up, and I don't back down from a challenge.

Around us, the crowd whoops and hollers as we fight one another through savage kisses and dueling tongues. Eventually, she pulls back, spitting fire from her eyes as her chest heaves and she wrangles her breathing under control.

"Keep fighting me, *mia amata*. I told you it only turns me the fuck on."

My shoulder is bumped from behind as Renzo walks around me, extending his arm toward my bride. "Dance with me, Donna Conti?"

Before she can take his hand, I grab his shirt, dragging his face up into mine as I press my gun into his stomach. "Disrespect me again, and you won't live to take another breath."

The crowd quiets around us, save for the clicking of shoes as someone approaches. "Put your gun away, Massimo," Bennett Mazzone says. "There are women and teenagers here."

"I will back down when he agrees to show me some goddamned respect at my own wedding."

"Put the gun away, Massimo," Catarina says, walking around Renzo to my side. Her eyes penetrate mine with a silent plea to trust her. I keep my gaze glued to Renzo Dutti as I shove my weapon behind my back in the waistband of my pants. She levels a look at her underboss as she circles her arm around my back. "You need to apologize to my husband."

My arm goes around her shoulder, and I tuck her in close as I wait for the asshole to eat humble pie.

A muscle clenches in his jaw as he grits out, "I apologize, Massimo. I was out of line."

"You were, and it's Mr. Greco to you."

He nods, shifting uneasily on his feet.

"My wife will be addressed as Mrs. Greco or Donna Greco. Do you understand?"

If looks could kill, I'd be ten feet under with the expression on his face.

"Ren." Catarina's cautionary tone urges him to get with the program.

"I understand, Mr. Greco." His jaw pulls taut as he glances at my wife. He wants to dance with her, but he can fuck off now and slink back into whatever slimy hole he crawled out of.

Bennett steps in to smooth things over. "If I may be permitted to dance with the bride, nothing would please me more."

I nod at Don Mazzone, appreciative of the calm resolution he brings to every situation. Filling his shoes will not be easy, but I'm determined to be an even greater president, and to push things even farther than he has.

I kiss my wife on the lips before freeing her so she can dance with the big boss man. Renzo stomps off the dance floor, not looking one bit happy. I smirk at his retreating back as I walk to the top table to ask my mother to dance.

"We need eyes on that guy," Fiero says, materializing at my side.

"Agreed. He clearly doesn't approve of this marriage, and I suspect he's in love with my wife."

"I'll message Allante, but first I've got some mischief to make." He waggles his brows before making a beeline for Nicolina Agessi. It's customary for the matron of honor and best man to dance at a wedding, so Dario cannot refuse Fiero, but he'll be wishing for blood after Fiero has charmed the proverbial panties off his wife. I have seen countless married women drop to their knees for my best friend, but I know Fiero won't take it further than flirting with the wife of any made man.

We might be rogues, but we do have some standards.

It's ironic that if I'd known Catarina was married to a don I never would have fucked her at the airport.

Fate works in mysterious ways.

I coax Mama out onto the dance floor, spinning her around the middle of the crowded space as the band we hired really gets into the swing of things. All the small kids have retired to bed, and the party is finally getting started. Mama laughs as we dance to a few songs, and I love seeing her looking happy and carefree for a change.

I had planned on introducing Catarina to Mama in the run-up to the wedding, but we were both too busy. They only had the chance to say a brief hello earlier, so I plan to take my bride home to meet my mother properly sometime this week.

"She's very beautiful," Mama says as the music slows down, and we adjust our pace. It seems I'm not the only one keeping tabs on my bride as she dances with a succession of powerful men. "But cold and closed off," she adds, somewhat apologetically.

"Why do you say that?" I gently pull her into my arms. "Catarina has been smiling and affectionate all day." Albeit forced, but I didn't think many would notice.

"It's fake. I have been watching her."

"Mama." I tilt her chin up so I'm looking into her face. "Can you really blame her? You were in an arranged marriage. Surely you were guarded at first too?"

Venom dances in her eyes. "With good reason! I was eighteen.

Completely innocent and utterly terrified. Your father did not make allowances."

A full-body shudder works its way through her, and pain splinters my heart. I am not privy to all the facts, but I know their marriage was not a happy one. I saw enough of it myself to know.

"You are not your father! You are a decent man, Massimo. You are nothing like that monster!" Tears prick her eyes as she audibly gulps. "That woman has no clue how lucky she is! A lot of made men are cruel, unfaithful bastards, but not you. You will treat her well, and she shames you acting as she does. She has no right!"

Heads turn in our direction, and I slowly maneuver us over toward the side of the dance floor. I don't know how much alcohol Mama drank today, but it's possible it was too much. She is not normally this vocal. Especially in public where the full extent of her social anxiety is usually on display. She grips my cheeks in her small, almost childlike hands. "You and Gabriele escaped the curse. You are good boys. That's why you are both still standing and the others are rotting in early graves."

"Papa did us a favor by ignoring us and focusing on Carlo and Primo instead," I quietly admit even though I did not think that at the time.

"He did, but he was stupid. You are the best of all my sons. My Gabe. I love him, but he doesn't have the heart or the stamina for this world. But you." She squeezes my cheeks. "You do. You have always been the true Greco heir. I saw it when your father was blindsided. You will be a strong, fair leader. You will not tolerate injustice or foolishness." Her eyes blaze with determination, and this is the most animated I have seen my mother in years. "Don't let love blind you, my son. If she isn't with you, she's against you. Don't let her derail your future when you have fought so hard for it."

Chapter Thirteen

Catarina

"I'm not fucking you," I say, emerging from the bedroom into the main living area of the plush honeymoon suite my husband reserved for our wedding night. It's on the top floor of the hotel with stunning views over the city and every luxury we could want.

He levels me with a smirk as he gets up and walks to the well-stocked bar. "If you say so," he says, dipping behind the counter.

"I do." Dropping down on the couch, I rub my sore ankles, grateful to be out of my killer heels and my dress. It's been a long day, and I am ready to call it a night.

"I told you I won't make you do anything you don't want to do." He strides toward me carrying a wooden box and two crystal tumblers filled with ice. "But you want to do *me*." He flashes me a smug grin, and his arrogance knows no bounds. "You just won't admit it to yourself."

My eyes pop wide in surprise when he sits down beside me and opens the box to reveal what's hidden inside. The Macallan Rare Cask is a limited special edition whisky that is expensive and hard to come by. "Where did you get this?" I ask, reverently trailing my fingers along the front of the bottle.

"Scotland," he deadpans, removing it from the box, as I roll my eyes. He sets the tumblers on the glass coffee table and proceeds to pour two generous measures. Saliva pools in my mouth as familiar aromas scent the air. "Call it a wedding gift," Massimo says, handing a glass to me. "I know you're a big fan, and I went to considerable trouble procuring this bottle."

Raising the glass to my nose, I close my eyes and inhale the intense notes of sweet raisin that give way to vanilla and dark chocolate undertones and layers of light citrus zest. "Thank you," I say as I open my eyes. "It's a thoughtful gift, and I'm impressed." I take a sip of the rich velvety scotch, savoring the smooth liquid as it coats my tongue and glides down my throat. "But you're still not getting laid."

"You know you won't be able to resist for long." Leaning his back against the arm of the couch, he swings his bare feet up right beside my thighs. "Neither will I if you insist on wearing sexy lingerie to bed," he adds, his gaze growing more heated as his gaze skims over my white silk nightie. It has a lace trim at the bust and the hem, and it hits me mid-thigh, exposing a lot of flesh. I purposely wore it to tease him because he's been riling me up all day, and it's time for some payback.

Scooting back, I mirror his position on the opposite side of the couch, bringing my legs up and letting my feet rest alongside his. "I usually sleep nude," I lie, lifting my glass to my lips. "This is a concession for you." I take another mouthful of whisky as my husband's gaze darkens further with lust.

"I don't understand why you are fighting this. It's only sex. Unless you're afraid of catching feelings?" He arches a brow as he drinks greedily from his tumbler.

"Catching a disease is more my concern."

"Ouch." He plants a hand over his chest. "You wound me." In an abrupt move, he sits up and slides down the couch until he's much closer. On instinct, I draw my knees up, and now he has a perfect view of my pristine white lace panties.

His nostrils flare, and his pupils are so dark they're almost black. "You know I'm clean, and it's been over a month since I've been with a woman." Knocking back the rest of his whisky—like the heathen he is—

he sets his empty glass down on the table and bravely places his hand on my bare leg. Heat from his palm seeps into my skin, warming me all over. "I don't know why you're resisting. I want you. You want me."

"I don't even *like* you," I coolly retort before I take another couple sips of my drink.

He trails the tip of his finger up and down my leg, eliciting a rake of fiery tingles all over my skin. "Lie to yourself all you want, but you're not fooling anyone, especially me." His palm flattens out on my leg as he starts inching it upward. Liquid lust settles in my core as he fixes me with a wicked look full of intent. His intense gaze and the feel of his strong hand moving up my leg is like being sucker-punched in the ovaries, and I'm struggling to hold on to my resolve. "That one time we shared was incredible," he adds as his hand rounds my knee and treks higher. I swallow over a sudden ball of nerves clogging my throat, hating how my chest heaves and butterflies swoop into my belly in wild anticipation. "I couldn't get you out of my head for months. I even went back to the airport in Maine to try to get a lead on you, but there was no trace."

There wouldn't be. My team is good. They know how to cover my tracks. My eyes widen, and a gasp leaves my lips as his fingers breach the hem of my nightgown and slide along the inside of my thigh. My core pulses with abject need, and my nipples harden, clearly visible against the flimsy silk.

Fire flares in his eyes as they lower to my heaving chest. "Truth be told, I have thought about you a lot since the day we met." His eyes pierce mine in place as his hand briefly stalls on my inner thigh. "No woman has ever gotten under my skin until you."

I want to believe him, but he's too smooth. His seduction tactics are slick in the extreme. He's a man. They're programmed to want sex. The large bulge in his pants is testament to that. I'm his wife, and he wants sex with me. He knows there are boundaries, but he'll do anything, say anything, to get me to give in.

Massimo already unsettles me, and I can't give him this power over me.

He needs to understand I'm in control.

"Stop," I say when his fingers brush against the front of my panties. "I don't want this," I lie because I haven't been this turned on in a long time.

True to his word, he removes his hand from under my nightgown, and begrudging admiration sweeps through me. "We need to consummate our marriage, *mia amata*," he says, reaching in to cup my cheek. "It is the way of these things."

"No one will know but us," I counter, wrapping my fingers around his wrist and pulling it away from my face. I can't have him touching me, even if it's apparently innocent, because his touch does weird things to my body and confuses my brain.

"We are stuck with one another now, Catarina. We might as well enjoy it." He inches a little closer, putting his face all up in mine. "I will make it good for you, I promise." Leaning in, he kisses the corner of my mouth.

I straighten up, fighting a losing inner battle. "I know what you are doing. These seduction tactics might work on other women, but they won't work on me."

He chuckles. "Sweetheart, I have never had to try this hard with any woman. Usually, all it takes is one look, and they're beating a path to my door."

"Ugh." I shove at his shoulders, pushing him away. "That only makes me more determined to hold out."

He exhales heavily, looking slightly defeated, but it could be tiredness forcing him to back down. It's after three a.m., and we partied hard with our guests. "Why fight me on this? We already agreed."

"We agreed to three times a week," I remind him, tucking my legs in snugly against my chest and wrapping my arm around them. "There is nothing in the contract that says we have to fuck on our wedding night."

"That was short-sighted on my part, but I don't get the big deal. What does it matter if we fuck now or two nights from now?"

Perhaps it's time I tried a different approach. Wetting my dry lips, I decide to make myself a little vulnerable in the hope he'll respond to it and back off. The truth is, he is right on a lot of scores.

I do want him.

I have agreed to sex as part of our arrangement, and sex has always been one of my go-to strategies when I need to control a man.

It would be easy to lure Massimo in and have him exactly where I want him.

But he's no ordinary man.

There is a combustible chemistry between us that can only lead to trouble.

And he's the brother of the man who destroyed my innocence and set me on this path.

Although it helps that Massimo looks nothing like Carlo, I don't know how I will react if I let him touch me more intimately. It wasn't a factor in our previous encounter because I didn't know who he was. But I know now, and I'm not sure I can handle it.

Will it conjure long-hidden memories to the surface?

Will it resurrect the nightmares of my past and reopen old wounds at a time when I need to keep my wits about me?

I am juggling far too many balls to let any man derail me like that.

Sleeping with Massimo is a risk I can't take, no matter how much my body seems to crave his touch. I will have to keep deflecting for as long as I can hold him off.

"Catarina. What is it? What troubles you?" His voice is soft, his expression concerned, as he stares at me, gently threading his fingers in mine. I zoned out, and I have no clue what emotions were playing on my face. This is further proof of how dangerous he is to me. It's too easy to forget who I am, to lower my shields, when he touches me with his magical hands. He's observant too, and I know there is much more to him than meets the eye. I can't drop my guard around him because too much is riding on it. I haven't come this far to let it all fall apart now.

"Wedding nights don't hold good memories for me," I admit before gulping back the last mouthful of my whisky.

He turns deathly still. "Do you want to talk about it?"

Reaching out, I pour two fresh whiskies, handing one to my husband before I settle back against the arm of the couch. "Are you sure you want to hear it?"

He lifts his knees, setting his glass on top of them. "I want to know everything about you, and I have a feeling it is your demons that drive your burning need for power and success."

He isn't wrong, and I hate how much of an open book I appear to be to him. But I can feed him snippets. Play on his sympathies. Let him think he is getting to know me and believe he has an understanding of who I am. Lull him into a false sense of security, and then I can strike. "I never want to be beholden to a man ever again. I never want to feel so helpless and trapped that I pray for death to take me." Shame washes over me as I think of the times in my life where I almost gave up.

"Tell me," he coaxes, leveling me with a look that suggests I can trust him. "I want to understand and ensure I never do anything that triggers or undermines you."

Chapter Fourteen

Catarina

"I was eighteen when I married Paulo. He was forty-five with a protruding beer gut, thinning hair, stained teeth, and an even uglier personality. He made it clear from the start I was only there to service him and to look pretty on his arm. I wasn't to speak for myself, think for myself, or act for myself." Pressure settles on my chest as I relive the second worst period of my life. "I fought him the night of our wedding when he tried to fuck me. I didn't want his disgusting hands or his puny cock anywhere near me."

I stare at Massimo as I speak, but I'm not really seeing him. I'm back there in that hideous room with the drab dull-green walls, dark wood paneling, and ornate four-poster bed. "I knew self-defense, and he was an unfit, overweight slob, so I successfully managed to hold him at bay." I grind my teeth to the molars as I recall the terrible events. "Until the spineless prick called out for his bodyguards, and they came to do his bidding." I take a sip of my scotch, feeling my husband's gaze on my face as he waits for me to continue. He doesn't interrupt or tell me I don't have to talk about it or mollycoddle me, and I respect that.

Drawing a long breath, I fix my eyes on Massimo's intoxicating green ones as I explain what happened. I numb my emotions, like I have trained myself to do, speaking in a cold, clinical voice. "On Paulo's orders, they ripped my wedding dress from my body and tied me naked to the four posts of the bed. They took turns raping me while he watched and jerked off. I screamed at first, only to draw attention and get help."

I learned a harsh lesson as a young teen about sick predators who get off on hurting others—they *love* it when you scream. It only gets them harder.

I force thoughts of Carlo aside, refocusing on my story. "Paulo's family were all staying in the house the night of the wedding. While they hadn't been kind to me, I still held out hope they would stop it."

Massimo tops off both our glasses, listening intently as I go on.

"Francesca Conti, Paulo's mother, barged into the room, and for a fleeting second, I thought she'd save me." I drink a healthy mouthful of my whisky, relishing the burn as it glides down my throat. I bark out a bitter laugh. "She saw what was happening. She knew I was only eighteen and I was being taken against my will, but she didn't care. She only cared I was keeping them all from their sleep. She told Paulo to shut me up before leaving. He stuffed a soiled handkerchief in my mouth, and they spent the rest of the night violating me repeatedly."

Pain tightens my chest, like it does anytime I think about the things that were done to me. "Paulo sodomized me while his men cheered and took photos." I squeeze my eyes shut as the memory of my wedding night surges to the forefront of my mind. It wasn't the first time a monster had sodomized me, and it brought horrific memories to the surface. I remembered the pain Carlo inflicted on me when he tore through my virgin ass at thirteen. That night with Paulo was like being assaulted by two different men at the same time, and it only added to my torment.

Even now, imaginary pain seizes my body, rippling through every part of me, reminding me why I never speak about these things. I don't think I will ever forget the specific details of the torture and abuse I was subjected to at the hands of men. At the hands of my first husband.

And what Paulo did to me is the lesser of the evils done to me.

Massimo plucks my hands from where they are digging into my thighs through my nightie, gently unfurling them and massaging each stiff finger. I wasn't even aware I was doing it. "He never violated me vaginally," I continue. "It was always anally. I only found out later he preferred young pussy and ass. When I think of what he did to me and I think about him doing that to young boys and girls, some as young as five, I want to dig him up and kill him all over again."

"He was a sick bastard." Massimo strokes his thumbs across the top of my hands. "I am sorry for what you endured."

I shake my mind free of the past, grateful to leave it there. The icy feeling wracking my body slowly dissipates as Massimo holds my hands, stroking my flesh and injecting warmth into my cold bones.

"It stopped when I was twenty-two and I gained the upper hand. I discovered the true extent of his sickness and gathered enough evidence to use it to blackmail him. But I knew it wasn't enough to take him down. Not with the connections the Contis had. They had local police and judges in their pockets. I worked diligently for years to gather more evidence, take over running his business, turn loyalty to me, and develop my own relationships with authority figures so I could take him down." Tears prick my eyes as I eyeball my husband. "I threatened Paulo in the hope it would slow him down, but he found ways to evade me. I knew he was still abusing children, and it killed me to let him live."

"But you had to time it correctly so he would go down and you wouldn't take the fall." Empathy and understanding splay across Massimo's face.

I nod. "It took me seven years, and every single night of those seven years I hated myself for not being able to completely stop it. I felt culpable and so powerless. I wanted to help those children, but I couldn't."

Emotion grips his face as he threads his fingers in mine. He nods slowly. "I know what it's like to be forced to stand by and witness injustice knowing you can't do anything about it. I know what that feeling of powerlessness is like."

I'm guessing he's talking about his mother. Anyone can see she's deeply traumatized. But I have zero sympathy for Eleanora Greco. I hope she dies buried under the memories of her failings and that she spends the rest of her days rotting in hell for the part she played in the horrors that took place in that house.

"The night I slaughtered Paulo and his family, I purposely had Paulo's bodyguards kept alive," I continue explaining. "My men brought them to the living room where Paulo's family awaited me. That night, I helped all the innocent women and children to escape to a new life in Italy. Every woman except Paulo's mother, sister, and sister-in-law."

Shock splays across his face, and a wry smile tugs up the corners of my mouth. "You heard the rumors."

He nods. "It was said you slaughtered everyone. Women and children too."

"I wanted everyone to believe that. I knew I would not be taken seriously as a woman or accepted as a donna if I was seen to be merciful. I needed men to fear crossing me. I needed to prove I could be as bloodthirsty as my male counterparts."

"That photo of Paulo more than proved that." Massimo's lips twitch, and amusement dances across his face.

"Aren't you even a little bit afraid that fate might lie in wait for you?"

He shakes his head and pins me with a confident look. "Paulo was a monster who preyed on innocent kids and abused his wife. I am neither of those things, and I won't hurt you, *mia amata*." He brings our conjoined hands to his lips, dusting kisses across my knuckles. "I promise. I could never treat you like that. I want to resurrect him so I can help you to kill him in even more creative ways."

"My only regret is I didn't have more time to torture him, but we needed to act fast to get the families out and gain complete control. It was a coordinated plan of attack that had to be executed with military precision."

"You're fucking amazing. You make me proud to be your husband."

His words, though sweet, unsettle me. So, I refocus on the original topic and pretend like he never said them. "It was important to me to get the families away from this lifestyle. I didn't want anyone making life difficult for them. The women would've been forced to marry other monsters, and the whole cycle would repeat itself. I wanted them to have a better life. They were all given homes and enough money to provide for them for the rest of their lives. I got them away from this life. Gave them back true freedom."

"You have only gone up in my estimation." His eyes penetrate mine. "There are so many layers to you, aren't there?"

"Not at all," I lie. "It's really quite simple. I want power and control and to pave the way for other women to ascend to positions of responsibility in our world. I'm not afraid to do the things made men do, but I will do it my way while protecting the innocent and respecting the men who work for me."

"What did you do to Paulo's mother, sister, and sister-in-law?" he asks, waggling his brows. "I'm dying to know."

A genuine smile creeps over my mouth. "I re-enacted my wedding night with the same bodyguards. I stripped the women naked and forced Paulo's men to fuck them while Paulo's brother and his sister's husband watched. Then I made Paulo's mother pleasure her son-in-law and his sister pleasure her brother before forcing the two men at gunpoint to fuck the guards and each other in rotation. I wanted all of them to know what it feels like to be violated. To have your will stripped from you. To be forced to do despicable sickening things. I positioned Paulo's mutilated body in the room as a threat of what would come if they disobeyed me. I can still hear their screams and their pleas. Oh, how they begged me."

I crank out a laugh. "Maybe I'm a sick bitch because I watched the whole thing and derived enormous satisfaction seeing them do anything in exchange for their lives. I enjoyed seeing them humiliated. I enjoyed seeing them suffer, and I enjoyed ending them."

"I think it makes you human." He chuckles. "I might be sick too, but knowing you have this dark side and that you are prepared to do whatever is necessary to get the job done gets me so freaking hard."

My eyes lower to the bulge in his pants, and I can see it's no lie.

"I respect the hell out of you, Catarina."

I shrug, shuddering as his thigh brushes against my leg, sending a flurry of delicious tremors coasting over my skin. "They were always so cruel to me, and his mother and sister knew he abused kids and did nothing to stop it. They were lucky I was short on time because I would have tied them up and had them repeatedly defiled all night long. Instead, I showed them more mercy than they ever showed me. I personally put a bullet between their skulls, and the sense of relief I felt is indescribable."

"You are unbelievably strong, and I'm in awe of you."

I arch a brow, wondering who is playing who.

"Come here." He pats his lap and opens his arms.

I shake my head. "I shared my story so it would explain my reluctance to fuck you on our wedding night. Not so you could use it to seduce me."

"I want to hold my wife and comfort her after she's relived the worst moments of her life. What is wrong with that?" He quirks a brow, reaching out for me. "Just come here."

I shake my head again. "*You* come here."

He flashes me a panty-melting grin, and liquid warmth gushes between my legs. "I'm comfortable enough in my masculinity to relinquish control if that's what you need."

I scowl as he scoots down to my side of the couch. He never acts how I expect him to act. He is unlike any man I have ever met. Before I can protest, he scoops me up, depositing me in his lap as he slides underneath me. His arms automatically band around me, and my heart thumps wildly behind my chest cavity. The spicy, citrusy scent of his cologne wafts through the air, like a hypnotic cloud, lowering my defenses and luring me into the promise of false pleasure.

He brushes hair back off my face and lightly grips my chin. Our faces are so close it would take nothing to breach the gap and kiss him.

I hate that I want to.

"I hate you went through all of that. It enrages me to know you were hurt in that way." His fingers sweep across my cheeks and warmth fills every nook and cranny in my body. "I promise you no one will ever hurt you again. I will kill any man who dares to breathe funny on you."

"Like you said earlier, I don't need any man to defend me." I am trying to ignore the feel of his erection growing under my ass and the warmth that exudes from his every pore.

"You don't, but I want to be your defender. Not just because I'm your husband. Because I want to relieve some of your burden. Hand some of the responsibility to me, *mia amata*. Let us do this together."

"You need to earn my trust before I could even consider doing that."

"Then I will earn it," he simply says, tucking my hair behind one ear.

Chapter Fifteen

Catarina

He stares deep into my eyes as tension thickens in the air. Desire coils in my belly, no matter how much I wish it didn't. It seems I can't halt my body's natural reaction to this man. "You are most beautiful to me like this." His fingers skim over my face before his eyes lower over my body. "Not hiding behind makeup or those power suits you love or the front you need to present to the world we live in." His eyes rise to meet mine. "Thank you for opening your heart and sharing some of your truths." He presses a kiss to the corner of my mouth, and I swallow a moan. "You intrigue and excite me." His lips brush against the other side of my mouth. "And I want you so very much."

I open my mouth to protest, but he silences me with his fingers. "I won't push you. I won't be like your first husband. If you don't want me to fuck you, I won't force it." Lust blazes in his eyes. "I will wait for you to come to me."

"You'll be waiting," I blurt, irritated when amusement skates across his face. I hate how he can obviously tell it's a lie. He can see I'm floundering. That his want is not one-sided.

"I have a hand, and my blue balls can be patient." A teasing smile spreads across his mouth, and I'm ensnared. Massimo is truly beautiful, and I only hope I'm strong enough to resist. I already suspect I'm not. "To a point," he whispers against my ear, sending warm shivers coursing along my flesh. I squirm on his lap, failing to ignore the hard, thick length pulsing underneath me.

Massimo groans, and his eyes darken with undeniable desire. "You were put on this earth to test me. I'm sure of it."

I can't smother my smile in time.

"One kiss," he says, his eyes dropping to my mouth as his tongue darts out and he wets his lips. "Would you deny your husband a kiss on his wedding night?"

"I have kissed you today."

He shakes his head as his fingers sweep back and forth across my mouth, making it harder and harder to resist temptation. "*I* have kissed *you*. You have gone along with it because it was expected."

He's as delusional as me if he truly believes that. I drive my hands into his hair without even thinking about it. "Will everything be a negotiation between us?"

His brows climb to his hairline and a devilish grin widens his lush mouth. "Do we know any other way to be?"

"One kiss. Just one kiss." The words feel like lies as I spout them.

"That is all I am asking." He closes his eyes, moaning softly as my fingers explore the thick strands of his black hair. "That feels so incredibly good."

I brush my mouth against his, and his eyes pop wide. His hands flatten against my back, pushing me in closer to his tempting body. Underneath my ass, his cock is hot and hard, and my panties are already wet. I can indulge in one kiss. It is my wedding night after all, and my husband is one of the sexiest men alive. It's not wrong to take this one thing for myself, right? "Just one kiss," I remind him as our breaths comingle.

"Only one."

Closing my eyes, I lower my mouth to his and descend into sheer bliss. He lets me control it, at first, and I'm surprised at the potent need driving me to take everything as I prod at the seam of his lips with my tongue. He opens instantly, letting my tongue plunge inside his mouth. I reposition myself on his lap, straddling his hips, so I can properly kiss him, and it's that moment when all bets are off.

Massimo angles his head and deepens our kiss, ravishing my mouth like he will die if he can't taste me. I grind against him as he moans into my mouth, one of his hands clasping the nape of my neck and controlling my movements. Vaguely, I'm aware of him removing his cell from his pants pocket and setting it down on the couch so it doesn't dig into me.

Arching his hips, he pushes up against me, and I whimper into his mouth, slamming my lips against his in a demanding kiss as I rock on top of him and grab fistfuls of his hair. His free hand glides down my back, landing on my ass. He kneads my cheeks, one at a time, before his hand creeps under the hem of my short nightie.

I don't stop him. I couldn't if I tried. I'm on fire. Every inch of my skin feels like it's bursting at the seams, and inside, I'm a quivering mess of hormones as my libido goes crazy. I cry out as his fingers slip under my panties to caress the bare flesh of my ass.

"Catarina," he says in a deep gruff voice, pulling his lips from mine.

I grab his face and pull his mouth back to mine. "Don't stop," I whimper in between kisses. "Don't stop, Massimo."

He growls into my mouth as his fingers start wandering, moving around to the front. I cry out again when he cups my pussy, gently gliding his finger along the trimmed hair of my mound. When he parts my folds and slides his finger up and down my slit, the most embarrassing moan escapes my mouth, but I'm too far gone to care.

"Fuck, you're so wet for me," he exclaims over my lips as he thrusts one finger inside me.

I push back on his dick as he pumps his finger in and out of me, ready to crawl out of my skin with desire.

Lowering his head, he buries it in my chest, his tongue lapping at the swell of my breasts before he sucks a nipple into his mouth through my nightgown. I throw back my head, writhing and whimpering on top of him, as he adds another digit in my cunt and alternates his mouth from one nipple to the other. He bites and tugs on the hardened peaks, and I'm seconds from begging him to fuck me when his cell pings with an incoming message, grabbing my attention. It's only on the screen for a few seconds, but it's long enough for me to read it. It's from Fiero, and it effectively douses my arousal in a bucketful of ice-cold water.

"Is it done? Bloody sheets are clearly not an option, so I want photographic proof you banged her before I wire the money."

"You fucking bastard." Tugging on Massimo's hair, I stretch his head back as I lift my hips and reach down between our bodies for his junk. I dig my nails into his dick as I grab it and twist hard. He yells out as his hands automatically fall off my body, and I hop up. Steam is practically billowing from my ears as I pace the carpet in front of the couch. "You bet your best friend you could fuck me for money?" I scream, my anger rising with each heated step I take.

Massimo rubs his dick, grimacing in pain. "It's not what you think," he pants.

"I just saw Fiero's message!" I roar, jabbing my finger in the direction of his cell. "You can't talk your way out of this!"

"Shit." He curses again as he presses a button on his phone and sees the message. He visibly cringes reading it. He climbs awkwardly to his feet, still rubbing his rapidly deflating dick. "*Mia amata*, let me explain."

"Stop calling me that!"

"I admit I made a stupid bet with Fiero, but I couldn't give two shits about it." He walks toward me, and I hold my palm up, warning him to stay back. "I told you I wouldn't force you, and I meant it. I only asked for one kiss. The rest was all you, and don't deny you wanted me because I still have the evidence of your need on my fingers." He shoots me a smug grin, and I lose it.

I pick up the nearest thing to me—a crystal glass bowl—and throw it at his head. He ducks at the last second, narrowly avoiding it. The bowl smashes against the wall, breaking into smithereens upon impact. "Jesus. Calm down."

"Don't fucking tell me to calm down!" I yell, unplugging a lamp and throwing that at him next.

Massimo jumps over the couch, and the lamp shatters on the floor. Consumed with rage, I pick other ornaments and things up and fire them at him as he pleads with me to stop, backing up toward the bedroom, trying to get out of my range. I almost throw the Macallan, coming to my senses in time to set it back down. It costs me, and I chase after Massimo's retreating form as he races into the bedroom and barricades himself in the bathroom.

"Come out here, and face me like a man!" I pound my fists on the door as an idea formulates in my mind. I stalk to the bed and open my weekend bag, rummaging inside for the small medical kit I packed.

"Stop throwing shit at me, and I will," he says through the door.

I grin as I find what I need, extracting the syringe and pushing the plunger in preparation. Padding toward the closed bathroom door, I place the syringe with the diphenhydramine liquid down on the bedside table behind me.

I have a prescription for the sleeping aid, using it at times when the nightmares keep me awake too many nights in a row to adequately function. "Explain to me how two grown men can act like immature teenagers, and perhaps I can see the funny side to it," I say in a deliberately calm voice from directly outside the door.

"It was stupid, but it's how Fiero and I roll. It really didn't mean anything, and I swear what happened with us out there was nothing to do with it."

"No, that was all *me*," I drawl, sarcasm littering my words as I work hard to muzzle my anger.

"Do you promise not to throw anything at me if I open the door?"

"I promise," I truthfully reply, retrieving the syringe and keeping it hidden behind my back.

Tentatively, he opens the door and peeks out. I narrow my eyes but hold myself still, leaning against the door frame.

"It wasn't all you. I wanted it too, but not because of some stupid bet."

I lean in closer, licking my lips and staring at his mouth. "Do you really mean that?"

"Yes." He clasps one side of my head, his gaze moving from my eyes to my lips and back again. "You felt my boner. There is no way of faking that. You only have to look at me, and I get hard. I'm hot for you, *mia amata*. Always."

I inch closer, pressing my body against his as we stand in the doorway. "Do you want to pick up where we left off?"

His eyes flare with renewed need. "Hell yeah." He doesn't even stop to question my motives. I thought he was different than other men, but perhaps he's not—he's a sucker ruled by his dick just like the rest of them.

I raise my hidden hand as I stretch up, putting my face all up in his to distract him. "Hell will freeze before I let that happen," I say, stabbing the syringe in the side of his neck and pushing the plunger all the way down.

Shock splays across his face as his hand flies to his neck, and he yanks the syringe out. It's empty, and he is too late. I grin as I watch horror race across his face. He looks from the syringe to me with mounting panic.

I want him to pay, and I should let him stew, believing I have given him a death shot, but I'm not that cruel. "Don't look so concerned. It's only a sleep shot. I gave you a double dose, so I reckon you have about ten minutes before you conk out." Grabbing his semi-hard dick, I stroke it through his pants, enjoying how fast it hardens beneath my touch. "Thank you for being a giant asshole and reminding me why I will never fuck you." I shove him down on the bed as he stares at me with a look of disbelief mixed with anger. "You can die of blue balls for all I care."

Chapter Sixteen

Massimo

"I am going to kill her. I will throttle her with my bare hands!" I yell into my cell as I pack my bag after my shower.

"You'll have to find her first." Fiero chuckles, and if he was here, I'd throttle *him*.

This is all his fault. If he hadn't sent that idiotic text, I would have fucked my wife into blissful oblivion, and she'd be none the wiser. I wouldn't have woken up in a foul mood, greeted by an empty bed and the mother of all headaches. "She won't have gone far. She knows we are meeting Don Mazzone in an hour."

"I can't believe she drugged you." He chuckles again, and I'm seriously considering bringing my M82 out of retirement and taking my buddy down. "She's my dream woman, and it's completely unfair you got to her first. If I'd known she was on the lookout for a husband, I'd have happily volunteered."

I know he is saying this on purpose to wind me up, but I'm too grouchy to put up with his crap today. "Shut the fuck up, Fiero. She's my wife, and no matter how angry I am with her, no one will talk shit about her, including you."

"Look, I'm sorry, man." Sincerity bleeds into his tone because he can tell I'm in no mood for bullshit. "It was a stupid bet, and I didn't mean for it to cause problems for you. I only sent the text because I was drunk and on a sex high."

"At least one of us got some last night," I mumble, still sulking and horny as fuck.

"She'll make it up to you when she comes around."

"I wouldn't bank on it. Catarina is a very stubborn woman and one of the most determined people I know. When she gets something in her head, I think it takes colossal effort to get her to change her mind." At least that's the sense I get from her.

"Bombard her with charm, and do the opposite of what she expects. Bamboozle her so she's powerless to resist."

"She isn't that type of woman," I say, zipping my bag closed. "She seems immune to my charms so far. With her, I'll have to dig deeper. Open up and make myself vulnerable in the hope she'll do the same."

"Be careful. You can't let her in until you know her true agenda."

"I don't need reminding," I snap, still irritated over the conversation I had with The Commission the day before our wedding. Keeping Catarina on a leash until we can trust her is the right thing to do. The smart thing to do. But I hate undermining her, and I know she's going to be so pissed when she finds out.

"You're already falling for her," he quietly says.

"I fell for her five years ago," I admit, taking one last glance around the large bedroom to ensure I haven't forgotten anything, before I head toward the door. "None of that will matter if she's got ulterior motives. It won't matter who she is to me. My feelings can't come into it. If she plans to betray us, I won't be able to stop her fate," I say, ending the call and pocketing my cell as I head out in search of my errant wife.

I have a tight rein on my anger by the time I reach the hotel lobby, using the GPS tracking app on my cell to locate Catarina through her phone number. If her tech guy was of any use, I would not be able to find her so easily. In time, if she proves trustworthy, I plan to overhaul her IT security and ensure it's up to scratch. Right now, she is somewhat exposed, and I can't figure out how or why.

Striding across the floor of the main hotel bar, I make a beeline for my wife. Currently, her head is bent, and she is deep in conversation with Nicolina Agessi while Renzo and Dario sit across from them, talking while they keep an eye on the room.

My wife's driver and bodyguard sit at a table in front of them, also keeping watch. I feel all four men's eyes drilling into my head as I approach. Renzo is wearing a predictable scowl. Dario has his usual fake smile. The other two sport bland expressions.

I don't blame them for being wary.

In fact, I would rather they were.

It shows they are not easily fooled and they have Catarina's back.

I am glad she has men she can rely on watching over her even if I loathe Renzo Dutti with the intensity of a thousand suns. I can tell the feeling is mutual.

"There you are, *mia amata,*" I say when I reach the table. Catarina's head whips up, and I lean down and kiss her quickly but firmly before she can object. "We should leave. Traffic will be murder at this time, and we can't be late." I extend my hand, and she takes it in somewhat of a daze. My eyes drift over her gorgeous body in a figure-hugging white dress with skyscraper heels. Her hair is pulled back in a tight ponytail, and her naturally wavy hair has been straightened. She is stunning, exuding bad-ass boss-bitch vibes, and I will never tire of looking at her.

"I'll come with," Renzo says, climbing out of his seat.

"That will not be necessary." I like that I have a couple of inches in height on him. I enjoy looking down at him. Sliding my arm around my wife's shoulders, I tuck her in to my side. "I will accompany my wife to the meeting, and I know how to keep her safe. Ezio and Ricardo will be with us, and my bodyguard will tail us in my car."

"I don't trust you, and if you—"

"Yes, yes. I got the memo," I say, cutting across him because I'm tired of hearing this shit. "This is the last time I will repeat myself.

Catarina is my *wife*. I have sworn before God to protect her and cherish her. I would take a bullet for her. No one will harm her, least of all me." I level a sharp look between my wife's underboss and *consigliere*. "The next time either of you question me, I will happily put a bullet in your brain."

"No one is putting a bullet in anyone," Catarina says, eyeballing Agessi and Dutti. "Massimo is right, and you will not raise this subject again. We will talk after the meeting, at my house, to begin formulizing plans for the attack. I assume The Commission will want us to take immediate action, and we must be ready."

"We will head to the house now and begin plotting a strategy," Agessi says.

"That won't be necessary. I had Catarina's things moved to my house last night. Meet us there at five."

"You what?" She narrows her eyes at me.

I smirk. "Don't act surprised. You agreed to live with me, and I wanted to have your belongings at my place so you feel at home when I take you there. You're a busy woman, and I thought it'd help to take care of that for you." It wasn't a chore. She already had her things stowed in moving boxes, so it was merely a matter of changing the date with the moving company.

Her features soften for a split second, granting me a glimpse of the woman I know is hiding behind the stern veneer she shows to the world. I'm determined to break down her walls and discover the true Catarina. "Thank you, Massimo. That was thoughtful." Her mask is back in place, so I can't tell if she really means that.

"I'm making a huge concession allowing your team access to my home," I say. "Very few people know of its existence, but it makes no sense for you to travel back and forth between New York and Philly. I have top-notch security systems and armed guards surrounding the property. You'll be safe, and I would rather all meetings took place there." I want to keep a close eye on her, but I'm telling no lie either. "You're a prominent figure in New York now, which means the target on your back just got bigger. You need to be extra vigilant, and I'd like to propose an additional bodyguard to ensure you are fully protected."

"We can talk more in the car," Catarina says, glancing at the time on her cell. She removes her purse from the table, slipping her phone inside.

Ezio and Ricardo stand beside us while I give coordinates to Agessi. My wife's driver is holding her overnight bag. "Sir, I can take that," Ezio says, reaching for my bag.

I shake my head, tightening my grip on my wife's hand. "Thank you, but I've got it." Something akin to admiration glides over his face before we make our way across the room. I'm aware we're drawing attention from some wedding guests who linger and unfamiliar men with heated stares who are blatantly ogling my woman. I level each one with a dark glare for daring to covet what's mine.

"I thought you'd be mad," she says when we step out into the lobby. I tip my head at my driver and bodyguard as they push off the wall and follow behind us to the elevator bank.

"I am mad," I truthfully reply, guiding her into the waiting elevator. Ezio and Ricardo are stopping other guests from entering. "You drugged me, and if you do it again, I'll tie you up in my basement and whip the disrespect from your body." I say it in jest, but her face pales, and she audibly gulps as the elevator descends to the parking lot.

Shit. That was a major fuckup given what she told me last night.

"*Mia amata*, I wasn't serious." Pushing her over into the corner, I cage her in with my body and lean down to whisper in her ear. "That was insensitive. Forgive me. I would never do anything like that unless you wanted it."

She tips her chin up, and a familiar fire burns in her eyes. "I will never want that."

This isn't the right time or place for this conversation, and we are getting way ahead of ourselves. "All joking aside, you drugged me, and I'm not okay with that."

"I was so angry, but it wasn't right to do what I did. I am sorry, Massimo, and I promise I won't do it again. You tried to take something from me for shits and giggles and monetary gain, and I took something from you as payback. Neither action was moral or right."

"It wasn't, and I am sorry too." I brush my fingers along her cheek because I find it hard not to be touching some part of her. "How about we wipe the slate clean?"

"I would like that," she says as the doors ping and open. My guys get out first to check the area before gesturing us outside. "I would like to start over completely," she adds, and my eyes pop wide.

"You do?"

A genuine smile crests over her mouth, blinding me with her beauty.

"Fuck, you are utterly magnetic when you smile. You should do it more often."

"There haven't been many occasions in my life where a smile has been warranted," she says, and I suspect she is telling the truth.

Placing my hand on her lower back, I check our surroundings as we stride toward her SUV. "I plan to rectify that," I promise, looking down at her.

"That would be nice."

I pause from replying until we are settled in the back seat of her SUV with the privacy screen up. "Not to look a gift horse in the mouth, but what has prompted your change of heart?" I ask as I buckle my seat belt.

She turns her head so she's looking me in the face. "I spoke with Nicolina, and she helped me to see some things more clearly. I really don't want to fight with you, Massimo. We are married, and I'd like to know what it's like to have a decent man for a husband. Someone who treats me as an equal, lets me have my say, and respects it. I have never had that with any man." She glances down at her lap for a few seconds as she stops to draw a breath. When she looks up, her face is less guarded. "I don't want to project my past experiences onto you."

Reaching out, I take her hand in mine and squeeze it gently. "I want our marriage to work. I like that you have your own opinions and you aren't afraid to voice them. I love that you are powerful and ambitious and smart. It's wonderful that you have an important job and your own goals and aims. All I'm asking is that you make time in your busy life for me. And open yourself up to the possibility of us."

"I want that too."

I wonder if she is being truthful or if this is a new strategy. Until I know for sure, I will play this game while keeping a close watch over her. "Good, because I'm dying to kiss you," I say, leaning over and pressing my lips to hers. She doesn't object, readily opening her mouth to accommodate my tongue. She matches my slow, leisurely pace as I familiarize myself with her taste and explore her mouth.

When we pull apart, her cheeks are flushed and her eyes alight, and she has never looked more enticing or more beautiful. "Have you ever been in love?" I blurt, the thought striking me out of nowhere.

"Never." Her features smooth out into an expression I'm more accustomed to. "I don't believe in love. It's an illusion worshipped by weak-minded fools with singular focus."

"Wow. That's...brutal."

She shrugs. "I have seen little which convinces me otherwise." Her all-seeing eyes penetrate mine. "Have you ever been in love?"

I slowly shake my head. "Thought I was once, but in hindsight, it was more of an infatuation. I was only a kid, and she was a gold-digging bitch."

"What happened?"

I grind my teeth to the molars, the subject still a sore point for me. "One of my so-called best friends stole her from me senior year of high school. He was fucking her behind my back for months before I found out."

She tilts her head to one side, her brow furrowing. "How the hell did that happen? I can't imagine any woman cheating on you. She must have been insane or blind or plain stupid."

I dart in and press a hard kiss to her lips. "It was a blessing in disguise. It never would've worked out, and at least I found out my friend was nothing more than a self-serving disloyal prick."

"Who was it?"

I decide to tell her part of the truth, as a test of sorts. "Cruz DiPietro."

Her eyes widen. "I expect you are aware I know him and his wife. I wondered why they declined our wedding invitation with what appeared to be a flimsy excuse. I guess now I know the reason why."

"If I'd had my way, he wouldn't have been invited at all, but he's the DiPietro heir, and there is protocol to maintain." I knew he wouldn't attend. We go out of our way to avoid one another at *mafioso* events, and I rarely attend them anyway.

"The woman you thought you were in love with can't be Cruz's wife Anais, because I know her, and she's too young to have been in high school with you."

"It's not Anais. Rita was Cruz's first fiancée. He got her killed three months before they were due to wed. I'm surprised no one has said anything to you about her. It was quite the scandal at the time. She was pregnant when she died, and her pregnancy was the only reason Cruz was given permission to marry her because she didn't have the right pedigree to wed an heir."

"I don't think Anais knows anything about her," she muses, looking deep in thought.

I spot an opportunity and jump in. "You sound close to her."

She pins me with a cool look as she stares at me. "We are close. Not as close as I am with Nicolina. I feel more protective of her than anything."

Interesting. "How is it you know Cruz and Anais?"

"I met Cruz at a *mafioso* event in Cincinnati a few years ago. Later, I discovered he was married to Anais." She eyeballs me without blinking. "You may not know this, but Renzo used to work for Saverio Salerno in Vegas. He was one of his *soldati* until he discovered his ties to the Contis and Philly. When Saverio kicked him to the curb, he came to me, and I hired him. It was Renzo who introduced me to Anais. He had been there while she was growing up, and he was fond of her. He kept in contact with her after he left Vegas."

That aligns to what I read online about her underboss, and I'm glad she is being truthful with me. I snort out a laugh. "Guess there is no accounting for taste. She's a vapid, self-obsessed, power-hungry slut who disrespects her husband by fucking around behind his back. It's ballsy but stupid. However, I like her for that fact alone. Couldn't happen to a nicer guy."

A mix of emotions briefly flits across my wife's face. "I heard those rumors," she admits. "Does everyone know?" Concern is evident on her face, and it's clear she cares for Anais, which is odd, because I can't imagine Catarina putting up with the spoiled princess's legendary attitude. She isn't one to suffer fools or a self-obsessed prima donna.

"Only those at higher levels," I confirm. "If Cruz wasn't poised to take over from his father in a couple of years, he would probably have her killed, but he can't afford to take her out right now. It would cause trouble with the Accardis and the Mazzones and be problematic for The Commission because Don Salerno would not handle it well. Everyone knows he's a reckless fool who would start a war he couldn't win purely to avenge his daughter's death."

"Whose side would you be on?" she inquires.

"Whoever is opposing Cruz," I honestly admit. "I don't care about the circumstances or the right or wrong of it. I will always stand with whoever stands against that double-crossing thieving bastard."

Chapter Seventeen

Catarina

"This is beautiful, truly beautiful, and not at all what I was expecting," I truthfully admit, staring at the stunning rock pool and magnificent outdoor space surrounding Massimo's large modern bungalow.

"I'm glad you like it. I spend a lot of time outside," he supplies, coming to stand beside me as I survey the gorgeous landscaped grounds and the forested area that rims the property on all sides.

"It feels safe here and peaceful." I wasn't relishing the idea of living in Massimo's home, but there really was no other option, short of buying a new property, and I'm too busy for that. Now, I'm glad I agreed to this. I haven't even seen inside but already this feels...right.

"There is access to my private beach through the woods," he explains. "I usually go running on the beach every morning if you'd like to join me."

"I would like that. Keeping fit is important to me." Not just for my physical health but also my mental state.

"I have a fully equipped home gym too and my property is on five acres, so there are plenty of running options if you want to mix it up."

"Sounds good." He stares at me with a soft smile that has me on edge. "What?" I narrow my eyes to slits.

"I love your fiery side, but I wasn't expecting to like this more agreeable side as much as I do."

I am biting my tongue a lot today, but Nicolina is right. Butting heads with him all the time won't get me anywhere. "I don't want to argue with you all the time. I just want an easy life."

"Amen to that." He reels me into his chest and kisses me. He's been doing that a lot today, and he's very touchy-feely. I both love it and hate it. "What's wrong?" he asks, breaking our kiss and tipping my head up so our eyes meet.

"Nothing."

He stabs me with a pointed look. "You can always be honest with me. If I'm coming on too strong, I would rather you tell me."

Fucking hell. I thought letting go of my animosity and my fear and reverting to my usual tactics would be a better strategy, but it's like he has me under a spell. I am already so out of my comfort zone with this man, and it terrifies me beyond comprehension. I decide to be honest because he seems to appreciate that. "I am not used to this. PDAs," I add when he appears confused.

"How is that possible? Have none of your boyfriends been affectionate with you?"

"I've never had a boyfriend. I have sex. Period."

He looks genuinely shocked. "That's tragic."

"Have you had girlfriends?" I ask because I know so very little about this man.

"A few. It was hard to maintain relationships after I graduated college because I moved around a lot."

"I didn't know you went to college."

"I studied computer science at Oxford."

"You lived in London?"

He nods while running his hands up and down my back. "Have you ever been?"

I shake my head.

"I love London. We should visit sometime. I can take you to all my old university hangouts."

"I haven't traveled much, and I would like that." In an alternate universe where this is all real. A pang of longing jumps up and slaps me in the face out of nowhere, only adding to my confusion.

"There you are," Nicolina says, poking her head out between sliding glass doors. "We are all in here when you're ready."

"Let's talk now," Massimo says before lowering his eyes to me. "Then I can give you the rest of the tour and make us something to eat while you are unpacking. I told the movers to put your boxes in my room, but I figured you would prefer to unpack yourself."

There he goes with the thoughtfulness again. Massimo is nothing like I expected, and it's becoming problematic. He is the complete opposite of his horrid older brother. I see no resemblance at all in either looks or personality, which should be a good thing, but it's only giving me a headache.

"How did your meeting with Don Mazzone go?" Dario asks when we are all seated between the two leather couches in Massimo's bright, modern, sparsely furnished office. His housekeeper left refreshments and snacks before she retired for the day, and I am sipping homemade lemonade that reminds me of my mama's lemonade. My mom was a lousy mother in a lot of ways, but she was a great cook, like most Italian mamas.

"It was frustrating," I admit, not holding back because Massimo already knows this. He could tell my frustration at the meeting even though I didn't outwardly show it because I can't disrespect Don Mazzone or The Commission. I must tread carefully until I have more control.

"Don't tell me they tricked you into marriage and now they are backtracking?" Renzo says, sitting up straighter. He is purposely not looking at my husband, and Massimo is blatantly ignoring him too. That is something I will have to deal with, but for now, ignorance is better than arguing or making threats.

"The Commission still wants me to take control of the street trade in their name, but they don't want to oust the Mexicans or the Irish without offering them a deal."

"What deal?" Dario asks, crossing his feet at the ankles.

"Five percent of the ten percent profits Catarina is promising will be split equally between the Irish and the Mexicans in return for them reporting to my wife," Massimo supplies.

"The other five percent will be split equally between the five families," I explain.

"They want to effect change quietly and peaceably," Dario surmises, and I nod.

"They are afraid of retaliation by the authorities even if we execute our takeover in one smooth fell swoop."

"We get a lot of heat in New York," Massimo adds. "It will be a smoother transition if we can get the Irish and the Mexicans on board."

"It's just a matter of changing suppliers, and agreeing to new routes, and locating additional storage space," I say.

"As opposed to taking out the main players and those bit players who would try to assume their turf. If we can reach an agreement, it will mean we only need to take out The Triad. It will avoid a lot of unnecessary bloodshed," Massimo says, sliding his arm around the back of the couch behind me.

"Provided our supplier is happy with that," Renzo says, and I level him with a warning look.

Conducting all our meetings here will not be viable because we can't speak openly in Massimo's home. It's why I already tasked Renzo with locating suitable premises we can use to meet on the down low.

"Why wouldn't your supplier be happy?" Massimo asks, drilling Renzo with a look.

"Because he only likes dealing with Donna Greco," he replies through gritted teeth.

"He will still be dealing with me." I step in before something is said that shouldn't be. "I will smooth things over with the Colombians." The honest truth is, I don't know how I am going to smooth this over with

Anton. The Russian *pakhan* has been blowing up my phone these past couple of days, and I need to find a window to meet with him soon.

"When are you meeting the Irish and the Mexicans?" Dario asks.

"Tomorrow afternoon," Massimo replies. "I will attend with Catarina."

Dario's brows knit together as Renzo clenches his fists.

"One of Don Mazzone's terms was that Massimo is involved with our entire plan," I explain. I share my team's frustration. This is utter bullshit, and it will make everything harder, but there was no choice but to agree.

Tense silence greets my words until Nicolina breaks it. "They don't trust you."

"They don't, but I respect that," I begrudgingly admit. "I need to earn their trust, and if this is the way it has to be done, so be it."

"So, the plan we worked out was for nothing," Renzo says, sulking like a moody teenager, and I really don't know what the hell has gotten into him lately.

"Not necessarily. If we can't get the Irish and the Mexicans to play ball, then the original plan stands, and we still need to wipe out The Triad," I say.

"Don Mazzone really doesn't want it to come to that, but if we can't secure an agreement, we have the green light. It's important we have a plan B in place so we can act ASAP if needed," Massimo says, standing. "I'd like to look at what you have been working on."

We spend the next hour going through some ideas before we call it a night. I walk my friends out to their cars while Massimo stays inside to tend to dinner.

"This stinks from the high heavens," Renzo says, his eyes scanning the outside of Massimo's home for the cameras I have no doubt are there.

"The Commission is being cautious for a reason, and we will adjust our plans accordingly."

"We'll talk tomorrow," Dario says, leaning in to kiss my cheek.

"Did everything go okay with Massimo?" Nicolina whispers into my ear.

"Your advice was good," I reply in a low tone. "He is receptive to it, but I'm still terrified. I'm so out of my comfort zone with him."

"You won't fail," my bestie says. "Keep the faith."

"He brought Anais and Cruz up, and I found out some interesting things. I'll explain when we have somewhere safe to talk."

"Does he know you know about the surveillance?"

I shake my head. "It's better he doesn't know we know. We can work around his PI, and he will be none the wiser."

I'm still annoyed his guy was able to get pictures of me with Anais. It could have been a disaster if we hadn't concocted a plan or if Massimo had called Salerno, but he didn't because he doesn't smell a rat where she is concerned. But I'm guessing he thinks there is something going down with Cruz. I'm pissed my brother-in-law didn't give me the background story when I informed him who I was marrying, and I intend to find out why.

"We should go," Dario says, jerking his head toward the house.

"Drive safe." I hug my friend and watch her climb into the car alongside her husband. Renzo hangs back, instinctively knowing I need to speak with him. "What is your deal, and don't say Massimo because I know it's more than that," I say.

"I'm worried about you." Renzo plants his hands on my shoulders. "This is veering off course, and I don't have a good feeling about it. I seriously think you need to reconsider everything."

"We can't discuss this here." I glance anxiously around. I know Massimo has men dotted around his estate, but I haven't seen a sign of anyone yet, which means they are discreet, and that's not a good thing for us.

"I found a place, and I should have the paperwork processed in a couple of days," he whispers.

"Good. The sooner, the better."

"What about that other matter?"

"Set up the meet but not the usual location. Someplace off the beaten track."

"Consider it done." He turns to walk away but stops. Undecipherable emotion flits across his face. "I don't trust him, Rina. I know you think it's jealousy, but it's not. He's hiding something."

"Aren't we all?" Made men are not exactly known for being forthright and honest in their dealings. Everyone is shady to some extent. Everyone is hiding secrets. I'm certainly guilty on both counts.

"Just be careful. I see the way you look at one another. Don't let him seduce you into a false sense of security."

"If anyone is doing the seducing, it will be me." I give him a hug because I sense he needs the reassurance. "You know this is what I'm good at."

"I have seen you in action, my donna," he says, extracting himself from our embrace. "I don't doubt your skills, but Massimo is a different beast. A formidable enemy and one you share a chemistry with. That's the difference between him and the other men who have come before. Be extra careful with him, Rina."

"I will. I promise."

As I stand, watching my friends drive off, I can't help wondering if this time I have bitten off more than I can chew.

Chapter Eighteen

Massimo

"How are the blue balls?" Fiero inquires as we wrap shit up at the waterfront property, ready to head back to the main office in Manhattan.

"Getting bluer by the day," I admit, powering off my MacBook and sealing it in my laptop bag. "I swear I'll have repetitive strain injury if I jerk off anymore."

Laughter tumbles from Fiero's chest. "I don't know how you can lie beside her sexy ass night after night and not jump her bones."

Tell me about it. It's been a week since our wedding, and I'm clinging to my sexual sanity by a thread at this point. "I promised her I wouldn't force her into anything, and she needs to make the move. Then I'll refuse her, give her a taste of her own medicine, until neither of us can stand it any longer, and finally things will happen naturally."

All this bullshit with the contract is just that. I only added that clause to wind her up and because it's expected with these arrangements. But that's not the kind of relationship I want to have with my wife. Every day, I'm growing more and more enamored with her even if she's still such an enigma and still keeping me at arm's length.

"I can come over and help to stir the pot, if you like." Fiero smirks as he climbs off the stool. "Take one for the team if needed."

That cheeky fucker is not getting near my wife. "Not a fucking chance in hell. I already told you I'm not sharing her." I have an uncharacteristic possessive streak when it comes to Catarina Greco. I don't miss the attention she garners when we're out together, and the rage I feel whenever it happens is unprecedented. I would commit murder if any man dared to touch her. Of that, I am sure.

My secondary cell pings with an incoming call as we take the elevator to the roof where the chopper is waiting for us. "Go ahead," I tell Fiero when the elevator doors open. "I need to take this."

Pressing my back to the wall beside the elevator, I watch my buddy walk across the roof toward the helicopter as I punch the answer button and accept the call. "I'm retired," I say before the other party can speak.

"We have a problem," a man with an overbearing, heavily accented voice says. I know who he is, and this is not customary.

"I don't care. I did my job as requested."

"There was an unexpected complication."

"So handle it."

A heavy sigh trickles down the line. "If this can't be resolved, you will need to come back and fix it."

"Resolve it then," I say through gritted teeth before I hang up.

"Problem?" Fiero asks when I climb into the chopper beside him.

"Maybe." I strap myself in as the pilot starts the engine. "I might need to return to Berlin at some point."

"Let me know if I can do anything to help," he says as we lift into the sky, heading for the city.

"Where did you learn to shoot?" I ask Catarina after we exit the shooting range through the side door. She's a damn fine shooter with a sharp eye, steady trigger finger, and precise aim.

"My father taught me when I was a teenager," she supplies, foisting her duffel bag over her shoulder.

Without asking, I swipe the bag from her hand, throwing it over my shoulder with my own duffel. She slams to a halt, planting her hands on her hips, and glares at me. Her snug black pants and fitted top mold to her body like a glove, highlighting every dip and curve. I've had to adjust the semi in my pants the entire hour we were training because seeing my sexy woman command a weapon like she was born to do it is a serious turn-on.

"Give that back," she demands.

"Nope." With my free hand, I grab her arm and drag her into my body, crashing my lips down on hers before she can deny me. I devour her mouth, like every time I kiss her, because I can't seem to do gentle or go slow with her. I'd blame my blue balls, but it's just her—I have an insatiable lust for Catarina that has been years in the making.

After a couple of minutes of frantic kissing, with both of us battling for ultimate control, she rips her mouth from mine and shoves my shoulders. "Ugh. Get off me." She rubs furiously at her swollen lips, like they have betrayed her. The thing is, she can protest all she likes, but she loves it as much as I do when I kiss her. I chuckle, and that only angers her more. "You can't keep kissing me to avoid an argument," she states, reaching for her bag.

I grab the strap, holding it firmly as she tugs on it, her face growing redder by the second. "Why the hell not?" Leaning down, I nip at her earlobe and swat her ass.

She yelps and moves to slap me, but I hold her wrist, using it to haul her back in close. "Stop fighting me, *mia amata*."

"Stop being so...so...chivalrous!"

I burst out laughing at the look of indignation on her face. Only Catarina would try to chastise me for being a gentleman. "Baby, there is never a dull moment with you." Dropping our bags on the ground, I band my arms around her back and kiss the hell out of her, loving how quickly she melts into my arms. I don't know why she won't just give in. We both know it's going to happen, and she wants it as much as me. Her body language gives her away every time. It's frustrating she's still resisting our chemistry despite promising to give *us* a try. To be fair, she has been polite and easy to live with, but it's not real. It goes against her true nature to be less than blunt, and I want that side of her.

I want her to stop pretending, and this is the only way I can think of to force her to drop the act.

"You drive me insane," she says when I finally stop kissing her. Her hands land on my chest, and I love the feel of her body flush against mine.

"You love it," I counter, letting my gaze roam over her enticing form. "And I love you in that outfit. Makes me want to bend you over the back seat of the car and fuck you so hard you feel me between your legs for days."

Air filters from her parted lips, and a red flush creeps up her neck as she stares at me. Electricity crackles in the air as we remain in our embrace, just peering at one another. My heart is thumping steadily against my chest wall the longer we stare at each other, and I want to scoop her up, carry her to my bed, and worship her like the queen she is all night long.

Catarina pulls back, looking away, but not before I spot the indecision and confusion in her eyes. I wait her out, instinctively knowing she needs a minute. When she lifts her chin, her mask is back in place, and she's in control. She clears her throat. "Have you heard anything from the Irish or the Mexicans?"

"I have noticed you do that a lot," I say, reaching down to grab our bags with one hand while I snag her hand with my other. "Deflect emotional stuff with talk of work."

"Just answer the question, Massimo," she says, and my dick swells painfully behind my zipper.

I will never tire of hearing her say my name. I can't wait until I have her screaming it at the top of her lungs as I destroy her cunt, over and over, while I fuck her into next week.

"Tomorrow is the deadline we gave them," she continues, oblivious to the torment I'm in. "If we're going to war, we need to know now."

"Always so eager for bloodshed," I tease as we step up to her SUV.

"It's been a while, and I'm itching to kill a few assholes." She looks up at me through hooded eyes. "Careful or I might shoot you."

I emit a low chuckle as I pop the trunk and toss our bags in. Threatening me is nothing new, and it cranks my arousal to dizzy heights like you wouldn't believe.

Ezio gets out from behind the wheel, opening the back door for his donna while I blatantly drool over my wife's shapely ass as she climbs inside. Visions of driving my cock in and out of her ass flood my mind's eye, and I'm leaking precum as I hop up beside her. Having a permanent boner around my wife is a regular occurrence and a constant reminder I need to get laid before I lose my mind.

Stretching across the leather seat, I whisper in her ear as she buckles her belt. "I know other ways you can channel that aggression." I rub the bulge in my pants, and she wets her lips as she pointedly stares at my hard dick. "While I understand you have concerns when it comes to anal sex, I promise, if you let me claim that sexy ass, I will show you just how good it can be with the right man," I purr into her ear, igniting the sexual chemistry even further. I won't be the only one suffering in sexual hell.

She bites down on her lower lip, and I groan, convinced I'm going to blow my load any second now. "Not happening, Casanova." She pierces me with a resolute look I'm determined to eradicate from her range of facial expressions. "And you haven't answered my question."

I adjust myself in my pants as the car glides forward and the privacy screen clicks into place. "You're no fun."

"We have a job to do, Massimo, and I want to do it."

"I want to do *it* too." I waggle my brows suggestively and smirk at her. The look she gives me tells me she is seriously considering shooting me.

"Tell me, and perhaps I'll take pity on you." She smiles sweetly at me. "Some time this century."

I flash her a grin, enjoying this immensely, but to continue would be immature and possibly unsafe, so I give in. I school my features into a more serious expression. "No, I haven't heard from them. You'll be the first to know when I do."

Chapter Nineteen

Massimo

I drop Catarina off at the house with the excuse I'm going to see Mama. I'm picking up reluctance from my wife whenever I suggest visiting my mother at home. I suspect it's because Catarina is already closed off to the idea of a mother-in-law thanks to her previous one. Not that I can blame her from the things she has confided in me, but I keep reassuring her my mother will be nothing like Francesca Conti. So far, she doesn't appear to be buying it, and I haven't pushed. Although I will have to soon as Mama is putting pressure on me to meet my wife.

Joining Fiero at the meet with Juan Pablo, I run over the plans for the expansion of our operation in Colombia. Our pharmaceutical plant in Cali is a front for our fledgling drug-manufacturing operation that will eventually see us become the main supplier to the *mafioso* in the US, if our time-honored plans come to fruition in the manner we hope.

Juan Pablo is paramilitary, and he has the contacts we need—within government and the military and with local gangs and farmers—to successfully run the business in absentia. The next two to three years will be critical for our long-term goals, positioning us strategically as the only men to take control of The Commission once Don Mazzone steps down when his tenure ends.

The meeting has just concluded when I receive a call from Diarmuid O'Hara, the man in charge of the Irish mafia. "We need to talk tonight," he says. "Where can we meet?"

This sounds promising. "I'll send you coordinates to a place in Queens."

"Fine. One hour."

"Will Santiago be with you?" His reply will give me a strong indication as to the reason for requesting the meeting.

"He will not," he confirms in his lyrical Irish tone.

My intel says Diarmuid lived the first thirteen years of his life in County Cork, Ireland before relocating to the US with his family when his uncle and predecessor was gunned down. Diarmuid's father ran the show for a few years before he had a massive heart attack and died unexpectedly, thrusting his eldest son into the role. He is only twenty-nine, but what he lacks in experience he makes up for with intelligence and sharp instincts. I have always liked him, and I hope he is coming to tell me he agrees to our terms and it's time to take the Mexicans down. I have little tolerance for Santiago Lopez or the way he leered over my wife at our last meeting.

We finalize arrangements, and then I call Catarina to update her while sending the location coordinates to Ezio.

I prop my butt on a stool at the bar of the sleazy Queens joint and order a beer as I wait for my wife and Diarmuid to show.

"This is a hellhole," Catarina says, arriving a few minutes later with Ricardo in tow. We fought over my desire to appoint her a second bodyguard from within my men. She was having none of it, claiming it's unnecessary. Personally, I think she doesn't want a spy in her midst, and not for the first time, I wonder what she is concealing.

"You're not wrong," I agree, snapping my fingers at the bartender. I order my wife a scotch as she slides onto the stool beside me, slowly drinking her surroundings in.

"What is this place?"

"It used to belong to the Mazzones, but my papa snapped it up cheap years ago. Back in the day, it was a sleazy sex club, but Gabriele put a stop to that when he took control. Now it's just a place for made men to hang out, drink a few beers, and shoot some pool."

The bartender places a tumbler on the counter and sets another beer for me. I slide the whisky to my wife, and she offers me a small smile, which feels like a win.

"I heard Ben cleaned shop when he came along. I can see why he'd want to offload this place," she says, swirling the amber-colored liquid in her glass.

"It's not Macallan, but it's the best scotch they have to offer," I supply as she raises the glass to her lips.

"It'll do." She sips her drink, looking relaxed despite the dingy surroundings and the skeezy eyeballs glued to her back. I spin around on my stool and level a glare at every man daring to eye fuck her until, one by one, they return to minding their own business.

Her lips kick up as she watches in amusement. "Are you always this possessive?"

"Never before you," I truthfully admit.

"I'm flattered." Her mocking tone aggravates me. Then again, most things aggravate me these days. Blame my blue balls and the gorgeous woman beside me because it's mostly her fault.

"You should be." Wrapping my hand around the nape of her neck, I pull her face toward me. My lips smash against hers with force, and I press at the seam of her mouth, demanding entry. I lick the inside of her mouth and ravish her lips as my fingers wind through her hair, removing that restrictive hair tie. "New rule," I say when I break our kiss. "You wear your hair down when it's after hours." I blatantly adjust the raging hard-on in my pants, wanting her to see it.

"Fuck off telling me what to do," she calmly retorts, removing a fresh hair tie from her purse. I watch in a kind of hypnotic daze as she wrangles her hair into a messy bun, securing it with the tie. "I have an image to maintain as well as a reputation. The way I present myself has been strategically thought out."

I don't doubt everything Catarina does is strategically motivated or carefully considered.

"Besides, it tends to get in the way. I want to be able to look a man in the eye when I shoot him between the eyeballs."

"Good to know," Diarmuid says, appearing behind us. He flashes us a wide grin. "Ma'am. It's a pleasure to meet you again." Taking my wife's hand, he brings it to his lips.

Smarmy fucker.

"I will refrain from returning the sentiment until I know what you came here to tell us," Catarina replies, sliding off her stool when Diarmuid drops her hand.

"I respect that." He turns to shake my hand.

"Let's talk downstairs." I grab my jacket and take my wife's hand before leading the way. Diarmuid and his two men follow, and Ricardo and a couple of my men trail us down the stairs and into the shabby basement office that still reeks of piss, blood, and sweat years after it's been cleaned out.

"You're either with us or against us," Catarina says, not mincing her words, the instant the door is closed behind us. "Which is it?"

Diarmuid smiles. "I like a woman who speaks her mind."

She levels him with an impatient look as she sits in the chair behind the desk. I take one of the seats in front as does Diarmuid.

"We don't have all day," my wife says, and I smother a smile.

"I need assurances." Diarmuid glances between us. "I am here at considerable risk."

"Cut the bullshit, O'Hara, and spit it out," I say.

"Lopez is planning to betray you," he admits, telling me nothing I haven't predicted. "He is going to broker a deal with The Triad and come after us."

"Let me guess," Catarina says. "He refuses to report to a woman."

"You got it in a nutshell," Diarmuid confirms, running his fingers through his reddish-brown hair.

"But it's more than that," I supply.

"It is." Diarmuid stares me directly in the eyes. "We have enjoyed being our own bosses these past ten years. Now you're asking us to report into you, and that doesn't sit well with either of us."

"We appreciate your honesty," Catarina says. "But things change, and this is the way it's going to be."

"The question is, are you with us or is this a fishing expedition?" I ask.

"That's not how I roll. I'm here because adaptability is the number-one rule in this business and only a fool would turn down such a lucrative offer."

"The five percent is yours if you guarantee us your loyalty and help to eliminate the Mexicans and the Chinese." Catarina drums her nails on the scratched surface of the worn desk.

"I need to take it back to my team, but I'm confident we can do business."

"No." Catarina leans forward. "We need an answer now. If you leave here without swearing loyalty, you are our enemy."

Pride swells inside me. I can see how she has risen to the position she now holds.

Diarmuid looks to me, pleading with his eyes. I believe he is genuine, and he just wants to show respect to his advisers by tabling it for an official vote. I suspect he deals with a lot of crap because most of the people who report to him are much older, and the fact he's a young gun probably sticks in their throat and leads them to question everything he does. That truly sucks. However, while I understand where he's coming from, there are occasions when a leader needs to lead and make decisions without a vote. I know he has the smarts to realize that.

"You heard my wife. She's the boss. What she says goes." I drill him with a look, silently imploring him to do the right thing.

He slowly nods. "Okay. Grand." He turns to face Rina as he stands. "You have a deal, my loyalty, and my word. We will help you to remove the Mexicans and The Triad, clean up any leftover mess, and implement a new structure."

She stands, extending her arm to shake his hand. "It's a pleasure doing business with you, Mr. O'Hara. I look forward to working alongside you."

"The pleasure is all mine, Donna Greco." Turning to me, he shakes my hand. "You're a lucky bastard."

"I know." I pump his hand a little harder than normal. "Try not to hate me too much."

Chapter Twenty

Massimo

The privacy screen has only just clicked into place when my wife launches herself across the back seat, catching me completely off guard. Her warm, soft, hungry lips descend on my mouth with fervor, and I'm so startled it takes me a few seconds to kiss her back.

Catarina shoves me down flat on the seat and climbs on top of me, her dress crawling up her thighs as she straddles my hips. I barely have time to draw a breath before her mouth claims mine again, and she's devouring me like I'm an all-you-can-eat buffet. Grinding on top of my erection, she clenches her toned thighs against my side as she lays siege to my mouth.

I'm not complaining, but things are escalating fast, and this isn't the way it's going to go down.

Invoking enormous amounts of self-control from some dormant place, I gently grip her upper arms and force her to move back as I sit up. She's cradled in my lap, and my spine is resting against the door, and we're both panting. My dick is rock hard behind my zipper, each throbbing ache a silent scream of frustration.

Her arms snake around my neck, and she presses her sexy body against my chest as her mouth lowers to my lips. "Woah, hold up, sweetheart," I say, placing my hands on her shoulders to hold her at bay. If she kisses me again, all bets are off, and I need to make a point. My wife turns rigid in my lap, and I brush my thumbs across the lines furrowing her brow. "Not that I didn't enjoy you attacking me like some sex-crazed femme fatale, but what's brought this on?"

Her anger flares instantly, and I band my arms around her lower back, keeping her in place as she attempts to scoot away. "Not so fast." I dart in and dust a kiss over her delectable mouth, hoping to wipe the scowl away. "I want to talk."

"Talking is *not* what I had in mind, Massimo." Her fingers toy with the hair at the nape of my neck, and it's incredibly difficult to concentrate.

"I can see that."

"I thought this is what you want? That we're finally on the same page," she purrs, batting her eyelashes, tilting her head to one side, and letting her tongue roam her lush lips in a deliberate attempt to bamboozle me.

It's almost working because I'm struggling to remember why I need to make this point.

I shake the fog from my brain and stick with the program. "I do, *mia amata*." I lift her wrist to my mouth, my lips lingering on her sensitive flesh as I peer deep into her eyes. There is no denying the lust I see there, and I'm quite partial to that flushed look on her skin, but I can't let her call all the shots.

Otherwise, I might as well hand my man card to Fiero and be done with it.

"But I'm also trying to understand you," I add. "What prompted this now?"

She rolls her eyes in consternation and mutters under her breath. I arch a brow, and she narrows her eyes to slits. "You're insufferable, you know that? By now, any other man would be writhing underneath me, and talking would be the last thing on his mind."

"I don't give a fuck what any other man would do!" Irritation prickles at my skin and I lift her off me, setting her annoying ass down beside me. I can't keep my resolve if I'm touching her. Swinging my legs around, I plant my feet on the ground and rub the back of my neck as I try to calm down. "I know what you're doing, Rina. I'm not some random schmuck you can seduce whenever you feel like it or some guileless idiot who'll lie down and let you trample all over him."

"I don't think you are either of those things, and you are completely overreacting. You're the one who said it's only sex. Are you always this dramatic?"

Her cool tone seriously pisses me off. "You seem to bring the best out in me, sweetheart." Sarcasm underscores my words as I grind my teeth to the molars.

"Fuck you, Massimo." Fire jumps in her eyes.

"I know you'd like that, but it's not happening this way." Leather squelches as I turn around and grip her chin. "This is a partnership, Catarina. I'm prepared to succumb to your will in lots of things, but the bedroom will not be one of them. I will not be emasculated by you, and I sure as fuck will not be your submissive."

"Then we'll never have sex because the bedroom is the one place I cannot and will not relinquish control." Vulnerability comingles with hurt and ire on her face before she shuts it down.

"Catarina." Releasing her chin, I sweep my fingers across her cheeks. "I understand why you feel like that, but it's the very reason why you should reconsider." I pierce her with a solemn look. "I will only ever make you feel good, and I would never hurt you. You will still steer the ship while I direct it."

"Forget it. It's never going to happen, and you have successfully ruined the mood." Wrenching away from me, she scoots over to the other side, strapping herself in and staring out the window.

After a few silent tense beats, she turns to face me with a familiar stony expression on her face. "What you did back there went a long way toward earning my trust and my respect. You are a man of your word, Massimo, and I truly appreciate that. You didn't sneak off to meet O'Hara by yourself, and you made it clear to him that I was calling the shots. That turned me on like you wouldn't believe. Me *attacking* you was completely natural and spontaneous. There was no ulterior motive, and I wasn't doing it because I wanted to be the one in control. I did it because I wanted to show you how happy you made me and I'm tired of fighting my impulses and staying away from you." She pauses to draw a breath. "Now, I wish I hadn't bothered. You don't need to worry; I won't be doing that again."

Fuck. I made a total mess of that. But I'm not sorry I broached the subject. It needs to be discussed. She can't control every aspect of our relationship and expect me to be happy with it, because I won't be. That's not who I am, and it's not the kind of marriage I want to have. "Catarina, I—"

She holds up one finger as she glares at me. "Save it. I don't want to hear it. This conversation is over."

She is unbelievably irritating at times. "Real mature," I snap, returning her glare and some. "This conversation isn't over. Not by a long shot."

Ignoring me, she resumes staring out the window, and we both quietly stew the rest of the way home.

When Ezio pulls the car up in front of my house, she thanks him before storming off inside. Ezio and Ricardo share a look and then turn narrowed eyes on me.

"Mind your own business, and get out of here," I bark. "My wife will see you tomorrow."

Without uttering a word, Ezio slaps the car keys in my hand before they walk toward their car. I lock Rina's SUV with the key fob and head toward the house.

My wife is nowhere to be seen when I enter our home. Deciding it's best to give her some space, I head to my office with a cold beer and a seething dick. I settle at my desk, quickly scanning the surveillance cameras to check the property is secure while I knock back my drink. I respond to a few work emails and tasks, and then I put some porn on and unzip my pants.

Pulling my engorged cock out, I wrap my hand around my shaft, giving it a few quick tugs. Guess I'm going solo again tonight, but it's completely my fault. If I hadn't engaged my brain back there, I'd be fucking my wife right now. Maybe I should have said nothing and enjoyed the ride, but I want to start off on the right footing. This power play between us is unequal and not sustainable, but I don't know how to talk to her without it becoming a fight.

Sighing, I lift my butt, push my boxers and pants down to my calves, and spread my thighs wider, stroking my straining dick as I attempt to focus on the screen. The busty blonde with the fake tits is on her knees, sucking the guy's cock, but she does nothing for me. Frustrated, I pump my hand harder and faster, letting my mind wander into fantasy land.

I imagine it's Catarina between my legs, visualizing her hot mouth wrapping around my shaft as she takes me deep. A groan tumbles from the back of my throat as I thrust harder in my hand to visions of my sexy wife pleasuring me with her skillful mouth. In my head, she's climbing on top of me and guiding my length into her warm inviting pussy. I stroke my dick faster, feeling a familiar tightening in my balls, when activity on one of the outside cameras captures my attention.

"What the actual fuck!?" Releasing my aching cock, I yank my boxers and pants up and scramble out of my chair. I finish fixing my clothing as I race outside, reaching my wife just as she's about to climb into the back seat of her SUV. Ezio and Ricardo are in the front, and she obviously called them to come back for her. "Where the hell do you think you're going?" I ask, grabbing her arm and pulling her back.

"Get your hands off me!" She spins around, spitting fire as my eyes rake over her body. She's poured into a tight-fitting sexy black dress that exposes far too much flesh. The neckline dips low between her breasts, down to her belly, highlighting her gorgeous rack and toned stomach. The hemline only reaches mid-thigh, and she's wearing lace-up knee-high boots that scream fuck me. Her eye makeup is heavy, and she's sporting ruby-red lips. Soft waves cascade down her back, and she has never been more fuckable.

If she thinks I'm letting her go out looking like that, she has another think coming. "No."

Lifting my chin, I reel her in to my body as I whip out my gun and point it at Ricardo when he rounds the car, preparing to intervene. I am getting sick of their disrespect toward me when I have done nothing to warrant it. "Stay the hell out of this. This is between me and my wife. And show some goddamn respect when you are at my house." He stalls his forward trajectory, looking unsure as he glances at Catarina for direction. When she fails to even acknowledge him, he falls back, his Adam's apple jumping in his throat. I repocket my gun and forget about him, staring at Rina. "What is this? Where are you going?"

"I'm getting laid. That's what's going on." In a quick maneuver I don't expect, she disarms me with a twist of her body, extracting herself from my grip. She takes a couple steps back. "You don't own me, Massimo. If you won't fuck me, I'll find someone who will." Her eyes glitter with determination.

Hell to the no. "Over my dead fucking body will any man lay a finger on you," I snarl, stepping forward and reclaiming the distance. My eyes lower to the creamy swells of her tits, and I'm painfully hard, my dick not happy to be cut off just as things were going places. "This is not the way to resolve things."

"Fuck you, Massimo. You can't have it both ways. You don't want to fuck me, yet no one else is allowed to either." She prods her finger into my chest, wearing her fury like a weapon. "I hate double standards."

"I never said I didn't want to fuck you!" I yell. "Why the hell do you think I've been walking around with the worst case of blueballitis these past few weeks? It sure as shit is not because I want to fuck my hand!" Holding her forearms, I push her back against the rear of the SUV. "Let's get one thing straight, *mia amata*. I want to fuck you. I always want that. I want to screw your tight cunt in every position known to mankind and then start all over again. I want to fuck your brains out until you don't know whether you are coming or going." My voice ramps up a few notches, along with my desire. My cock and balls feel like they're about to explode, and it's not gonna be pretty.

"I want to grind my cock into every available hole and hear you screaming my name as you come and come and come. I want you to beg and plead for more, even though you're sore, because you're fucking addicted to my dick and you can't get enough!" I am practically yelling by the end, totally losing control of my emotions.

This woman cranks my rage like no woman ever has before.

And she has the nerve to call me insufferable.

She gulps, her chest is heaving, and her bra-less nipples are trying to poke through the material of her dress. "Send your men home," I growl, moving my hands to her hips. I thrust my hard-on against her belly, and she sucks in a sharp gasp. Wanton desire splays across her face, and she can't deny this any longer either. We are both primed to explode, and it's going down now. "Unless you want them to watch me bend you over this car and fuck the living daylights out of you."

"You can leave," she says, not tearing her eyes from mine. "I'll see you in the morning."

Her men send daggers at me as they pass, and it's a cautionary warning, a reminder they are watching and reporting everything. I couldn't give two shits, and I have a childish urge to flip them off, but I restrain.

I rub up against my wife as I hear the crunching of footsteps on gravel, the opening and closing of doors, a car engine start, and then Ezio and Ricardo are leaving, and we're alone.

My lips crash down on hers, and I drop a slew of punishing kisses on her mouth as I press her spine flush to the SUV and rock my hips into her belly. Primal instincts roar to life, and an inner voice is demanding I claim her and make her mine. It's hypocritical after the stance I took earlier, but my need has pushed beyond logic at this point.

"Tell me you want this," I say as I press feather-soft kisses along her jawline before dipping down to her neck. My dick is leaking precum, and I'm dry humping her against the SUV as I struggle to restrain myself.

I need to be inside her, and I can't wait any longer, but I will never force her.

It will always be her choice.

She will forever have the power to say no, and I will respect her decision.

That's the thing about control—it doesn't always rest with the person who appears to hold it. I don't want her dictating when and where we have sex, but that doesn't mean she's relinquishing control.

I just don't know how to make her see it my way.

"Catarina," I growl, lifting my head when she doesn't verbally reply. "I need to hear the words."

"Yes," she rasps in a throaty voice grabbing handfuls of my ass. Her eyes are dark with desire as she stares straight through to my soul. "I want this. I want you. Fuck me, Massimo."

Chapter Twenty-One

Catarina

I can't find it within myself to be ashamed for how I have manipulated my husband when Massimo takes control, and we are finally getting what we both want. "Place your hands on the window and push your ass out," he commands, his voice thick with the same desire I feel flowing through my veins like a life-sustaining force. My initial instinct is to tell him to fuck off bossing me around, but I have pushed his buttons enough for one night. I can give him this. Truth is, I like this side of him. Scary as that thought is, I can't back out now. I want him too much to continue arguing.

I do as he asks, arching my back and lifting my hips and my ass. A soft breeze blows across my backside when he shoves my dress up to my waist, exposing my bare cheeks in my flimsy thong. In one masterful move, he rips my thong, and lace shreds float to the ground around our feet. An animalistic grunt escapes his lips as his hand comes down hard on my ass. My core clenches as a stinging pain races across my exposed flesh.

"That's for being a complete pain in my ass," he says before his hand comes down again. "That's for the audacity involved in leaving the house looking like this."

I yelp as he caresses my sore cheeks before landing a third slap.

"That's for daring to tempt me into fucking you when you know I'm powerless to resist."

I keep my mouth closed, trapping the natural retaliations in my throat, before I ruin this for both of us. My core aches with need, and I whimper as I hear the telltale sound of a zipper being lowered. Heat covers my back when he bends over me, blanketing me with his body. His warm breath tickles my eardrum as he moves his mouth there. "I like obedient, quiet Catarina." His teeth nip my earlobe as clothing rustles, and then I feel his skin flush against mine. A delicious shiver skates over my body at the feel of him surrounding me on all sides. "But I need to hear the words. Tell me again you are okay with this," he says, pressing his erection against my ass.

"I want this but not in my ass."

He grips my hips as he straightens up. "I know, *mia amata*," he says in a softer tone. "I want to fuck your pussy, but I'm too mad to be gentle."

"I like rough sex," I truthfully admit, and I'm glad he can't see my face to observe the embarrassment and humiliation there. Maybe I would have always liked it rough, but I'll never know if it's because of what I endured or natural proclivity.

"Tell me if you want to stop at any time, and I'll stop," he says.

A messy ball of emotion clogs my throat. Even angry with me, he is taking care to ensure this is fully consensual.

I am not worthy of him.

I can't form words, so I nod my consent, and he immediately dips two fingers inside me. My greedy cunt grips his digits tightly as he pumps in and out of me, and I moan as delicious tremors trek over my entire body. "You're fucking soaked. Your cunt is begging for my cock." The air distorts as he changes position, and I cry out when his wet tongue teases the lips of my pussy. He runs his tongue up and down my slit for a few seconds before denying it to me. "I want to devour your pussy, but you don't deserve it," he says, pulling himself upright. Holding my hips, he tilts my ass up higher. "Hold tight, *mia amata*."

His cock nudges my slick entrance, and my pussy clenches and unclenches with wanton need. "This is going to be fast, hard, and dirty."

He slams into me in one long thrust, and I scream his name, pushing back against him as he rams in and out of me. The feel of his hard, hot length pounding into me is almost enough to send me over the edge. "Jesus, fuck," he pants, gripping my hips tighter to control the angle of his thrusts. "You feel so good, sweetheart. I love the way your hot little pussy is trying to squeeze all the cum from my cock."

"Oh God," I moan as he picks up his pace, ruthlessly fucking me and slamming my pelvis into the car in a way I know will leave bruises. I don't care. All I care about is chasing the orgasm that is building and building at a steady pace. "Please," I beg.

"What do you want, *mia amata*?" He grunts, driving his cock in so deep I swear he nudges my barren womb.

"I want to come." I push back against him, gasping as stars burst behind my retinas when he ruts into me like a wild beast, digging his fingers into my hips to control the motion.

"I should deny you," he pants, running one hand up and down my spine through my dress. "I should withhold it as punishment," he adds, moving his hand to my breast and squeezing it hard, "but I promised I would always make it good for you, and I don't renege on my word. Unlike some I know." He kneads my breast a few times before his hand skims down the front of my body, and his fingers find their way to my swollen clit.

"Massimo," I scream as he rubs me in sync with the rolling of his hips and the thrusting of his cock. My climax is building higher and higher, growing more intense when he presses down on my sensitive bud, applying more pressure. A garbled sound leaves my mouth as he works my body like a finely tuned instrument, and I am putty in his hands.

"Now, *regina*," he roars, pinching my clit and flexing his hips. His balls slap against my ass when he buries himself deep, and powerful shudders rip through his strong body as he finds his release.

I scream as a crescendo of bliss crashes over me like a tsunami. Wave after wave of orgasmic ecstasy lays siege to my body, and I'm crying and whimpering as he grunts and pants while he deposits his seed inside me. I don't move as we milk every last drop of our orgasms, and I have never felt this good or more sated.

After a couple of minutes, I come down from my heavenly high, and reality rears its ugly head. Behind me, Massimo has grown still, and I feel his cock softening inside me. He doesn't move, and the only sounds are the crickets chirping in the forest and our mutual exaggerated breathing.

Slowly, he pulls out of me, cleans me up with a tissue, and lowers my dress over my ass. I straighten up and turn around, ready to eat humble pie. His gorgeous green eyes lock on my hazel ones, and time stands still as we stare at one another, the weight of what we just did and so many unspoken words lying in the space between us.

I wet my lips and go first. "For the record, I was never going to fuck anyone else."

His expression remains unchanged at my admission.

"I wasn't even going to go to a club or a bar. If you didn't take the bait, I would have had Ezio drive me around the city for a few hours."

"Is that the truth?"

"Yes. I would never disrespect you like that."

He barks out a wry laugh. "Yet you have no issue disrespecting me by manipulation."

Heat floods my cheeks as embarrassment washes over me. "It was low and completely beneath me. You have every right to be angry with me." I risk taking a step closer, and I lower my guard, letting him see my emotions. "I am truly sorry, Massimo."

"Why?" he asks, tipping his head to one side. "Why are you acting like this?"

"I don't know how to do this. I don't know how relationships work." A tight pain spreads across my chest as I make myself vulnerable to him. "All my interactions with men have been different. There are men who report to me and are loyal because they swore an oath. Then there are random men I chose to fuck, always on my terms, for one night only. With other men, usually business contacts, I used sex to manipulate them into doing my bidding. And all my early interactions were with men who forced me into sex." I move my hand between us. "I don't know how to do this, whatever *this* is."

He exhales heavily, closing the gap between us. "I'm hardly a relationship expert either. I didn't live with any of my girlfriends, and most of those relationships were brief." He threads his fingers through my hair. "What I do know is manipulation, lying, and game-playing have no place in any relationship, whether it's an agreed business arrangement or a genuine romantic connection."

"I don't know how else to be."

He wraps his arms around me, and I lean in, pressing my head to his chest. I circle my arms around his back as he holds me, closing my eyes and focusing on how good it feels to be embraced and comforted rather than the myriad of confusing emotions twisting my insides into knots.

"How about this," he says, and I tilt my head up to look at him. He cups my cheek. "We forget about the contract and any preconceived ideas we both took into this marriage, and we just go with the flow."

"Go with the flow?" A hint of amusement colors my tone as my brows climb to my hairline.

"Yes, sweetheart." He leans down, pressing a brief tender kiss to my mouth. "We just wing it."

I burst out laughing. "You make it sound so simple."

"It doesn't have to be complicated." He stares adoringly at me, and I literally melt in his arms. "We just live together and do what comes naturally. We share our lives and our bodies, our hearts, our spirits, our souls."

"That sounds complicated to me."

"Only if it's forced. We take one day at a time, and as long as we are honest with one another, we see where it takes us. How about that?"

"I like it, but you'll have to be patient with me. I'm predisposed to act a certain way, and I'm..." I stop before I blurt the true extent of my vulnerability.

But it doesn't matter.

He knows anyway.

"Scared."

I nod. "Petrified." Pulling my big-girl panties on, I admit something to him, and to me, for the first time. "I have feelings for you, Massimo. Feelings I don't know how to describe or handle. Feelings I have never had for any other man. It feels like I'm losing a part of myself, and everything I thought I knew about me is under a microscope. It makes my skin itch and my heart beat way too fast, and I'm scared of losing sight of who I am and what makes me *me*."

"I won't let you lose yourself." He is quick to reassure me. "Just stop fighting our chemistry and start working with me, not against me."

"I will try."

"We have been here before. I need you to mean it this time."

"I mean it." That is true as much as I can let it be true.

"Okay." He flashes me one of his signature panty-melting smiles, and it would work if I was wearing any.

"Okay." We grin at one another like two excitable teenagers. "What now?" I inquire, understanding this is a turning point.

A turning point to what or where I'm unsure.

His eyes instantly turn heated, and my core pulses with renewed need. "I don't know about you, but that only took the edge off for me." He grinds his hips into my stomach, and a shiver works its way through me at the feel of his hard length pulsing against me. "I have never gone bareback before, and there are no words to describe how amazing it felt to be inside you with no barrier."

I run my fingers up over his shirt-covered chest, popping a couple of buttons, revealing some of his toned, tan, inked flesh. "I'm dying to explore your body. I want to see your tattoos." My eyes penetrate his. "All of them. I want to lick each one and every inch of your skin."

Without warning, he scoops me up into his arms, carrying me

across the gravel at rapid speed toward the front door. "What are you doing?"

"Something I should've done the first day I brought you here." He stops at the door to plant a feather-soft kiss on my lips. "I'm carrying my bride over the threshold, and then we're going to christen every room in our house, if she has the stamina for it."

My heart swells to bursting point while liquid heat gushes to my core. I don't know who I'm becoming, or what I'm doing, but all I know in this moment is I want this man and everything he is offering. Nothing has ever felt more right. "Trust me, she has the stamina," I reply with confidence.

"That's my wife," he softly says, nuzzling my neck, before he hurries me inside the house to make good on his promise.

Chapter Twenty-Two

Catarina

My limbs ache deliciously as I wake the next morning, tangled in the sheets and my husband.

My husband.

For the first time, those two words don't inspire scorn or ignite rage or invoke helplessness.

My husband.

A fluttering sensation churns in my chest, and my heart swells behind my rib cage as I look over at him. An unfamiliar protective, possessive urge swirls around me as I stare at his sleeping form, and I am terrified of how quickly he is changing me and the implications of what that may mean for my plans.

I am so conflicted. Torn already at the thought of doing anything to hurt this man.

My husband.

Pain settles on my chest, pushing down on me like a ton of bricks, constricting my air supply and making breathing difficult. Before I suffer a full-blown panic attack, I consciously focus on inhaling and exhaling, drawing air deep into my lungs and feeling it fully in my core, until the slumbering anxiety has passed.

Glorious buttery sunshine filters through the gap in the curtains, casting Massimo in a glowing light. He is still fast asleep, turned toward me on his side, his arm curled around my waist and his leg thrust between mine. Propping up on one elbow, I peer at him as I recall our frenzied sex marathon last night.

We were insatiable for one another, fucking our way from the hallway to the living room, then on to the kitchen, before making our way to the bedroom, leaving a trail of clothes and bodily fluids along the way. We thoroughly indulged all our pent-up frustration, and it was the most mind-blowing experience of my life.

Sex has never been so good.

I have never come so hard and so many times, and I'm in awe of how perfectly we fit together. Not once, did I think about Carlo or my vengeance plan when we were enjoying one another.

It was all about pleasure.

Mine and his.

I'm squirming as I remember how incredible he felt moving in my pussy and my mouth, and I can still taste him on my tongue.

Intense desire twists in my belly as fresh need throbs down below. I am so screwed. I was truthful when I told him how scared I was last night. I'm even more scared now because I know I won't be able to take any of it back.

The scariest admission of all is that I don't want to.

I want this, and I refuse to consider the consequences.

I don't want anything to rain on my parade.

I have never known anything good in my life, and it doesn't feel selfish to want to keep this man.

Resting my head back on my pillow, I close my eyes as deep-centered pain flays me on the inside. What am I doing, and how the hell can it end well? I don't have the answers to my questions, and I know what I need to do. I need to talk to Nicolina, and I must clean up before the housekeeper arrives, but it's hard to tear myself from this bed.

Opening my eyes, I turn on my side. My heart beats to a different rhythm as I examine my gorgeous husband while he sleeps. Air trickles from his slightly parted lips, and his chest inflates and deflates as he breathes deeply. My eyes roam over the multitude of tattoos covering his arms, chest, and back. Tattoos I have been up close and personal with. My fingers twitch with longing, and I'm tempted to peel the covers back, kneel between my husband's thighs, and take his morning wood into my mouth.

That thought alone sets me in motion. Like a sneaky thief, I extricate myself from my husband, planting a feather-soft kiss into his hair as I slip from the bed. I pad naked to the bathroom and attend to business, grabbing a shirt of Massimo's from the hook on the back of the bathroom door. Like a bona fide creeper, I raise the shirt to my nose, inhaling deeply. The spicy, citrusy scent of his cologne wraps around me like a warm blanket, and I am seriously questioning my sanity as I slip out of the bedroom and head to the kitchen.

The housekeeper only comes in the afternoon to clean and iron, so I have plenty of time to get rid of the evidence from last night. My lips kick up in an uncharacteristic broad smile as I spy the trail of clothes dotted around the house.

After cleaning up, I decide to make my husband breakfast because I want to do something nice for him. Usually, Massimo is the one who cooks or we order takeout because he's generally home before me. I want to do this and start making amends because I have been a total bitch and he has put up with my shit without much complaint.

I have a fresh pot of coffee on, the bread I made from scratch is cooling on the counter, and I'm chopping mushrooms for our omelets when he wanders into the kitchen, yawning as he drags a hand through his messy bedhead hair.

"Something smells good," he says, smiling as he drinks in the scene.

I am momentarily stunned into silence as he walks toward me in nothing but a pair of low-slung shorts. His broad shoulders, toned chest, and ripped abs are almost too perfect. Like no man could possibly be this gorgeous. Not even the slight marks and scars on his body dim his masculine beauty.

His smile expands, and I know it pleases him that I'm blatantly ogling him without attempting to hide it. Even his arrogance is appealing although it pisses me off at times too. "I made coffee and bread," I say, explaining the aromas as I snap out of it.

Banding his arms around me from behind, he presses his body flush against mine. He pushes my hair away from my face and buries his nose in my neck, inhaling deeply. "I wasn't talking about the coffee or the bread," he murmurs, his voice heavy with lust as he rubs his erection against my butt.

"Oh," I whisper as his fingers creep under the hem of the shirt to caress the side of my bare thigh.

"I love seeing you in my shirt." He nips at my earlobe before placing a slew of drugging kisses along my neck and my exposed shoulder. I set my knife down and push the cutting board away, leaning my head back against him as his fingers roam around to my hip. "Are you too sore, *mia amata*?"

I shake my head, whimpering as his fingers part my folds, and he drives one digit inside me. "Always so wet for me," he growls as he thrusts his dick against my ass. "I love it."

"I'm making omelets," I weakly protest as he adds a second finger, slowly pumping them in and out of me.

"Breakfast can wait. I have something else I want to eat," he says, lifting me effortlessly, like I weigh nothing.

I yelp as my butt hits the cold marble of the island unit.

"Shirt off," he instructs, leveling me with fiery eyes.

I surprise myself by complying without protest. His eyes track my movements as I slowly raise his shirt up my body, pinning him with sultry eyes while I toss it aside. His eyes land briefly on the jagged, puckered skin at my hips, but like last night, he passes no comment. It's not unusual, given my position, that I carry battle scars on my skin. If anything, the lack of visible scars is probably more of a giveaway than the small few the surgeon's skill couldn't smooth away.

"Fuck." He cups his crotch, and precum stains the front of his shorts, confirming he's as aroused as me. "Lie back on your elbows," he says, and like a trained monkey, I obey. He spreads my thighs and stares at my most private parts. "Your pussy is manna from heaven." Opening my folds with his thumbs, he continues to stare at the very core of me. He leans in, and the most embarrassing moan escapes my lips when his hot tongue laves up and down my slit. "I can taste myself on you," he hums against my cunt. "I want to cover you in my cum so that's all any man ever smells on you."

My pussy visibly quivers at his dirty words. "You have issues," I rasp, thrusting my hips into his face as he shoves his tongue deep inside me, before sliding it back out.

"I am crazy possessive when it comes to you. I want to kill every man who looks in your direction."

His words light a fire inside me, and I'm practically purring with satisfaction, which is wrong on so many levels, but I can't help how I react to him. No man has ever been possessive of me in this way, and I'm shocked when tears spring to my eyes. What is Massimo doing to me?

I wrap my legs around his shoulders and watch as he eats my pussy like it's the only sustenance he needs. Even though I am a bit sore from last night, it doesn't take long for me to fall apart under his skillful tongue and magic fingers.

I have barely finished climaxing when he pushes his thick, warm cock inside me, and I whimper in contentment as he fills me up fully. I cling to his shoulders as he fucks me hard on the island unit. My legs hug his back as he pivots his hips, driving into me in long slow strokes mixed with deep fast thrusts.

Our eyes do all the speaking as we fuck, and it's wholly intimate in a way I have never experienced before. The sensations he's coaxing from my body and my heart are strange to me, both welcome and unwelcome. Sensing I need reassurance, he kisses me passionately as he fucks me, and it's not long before I'm coming again, clenching around his hard cock as he spills inside me.

After, we don't move, staying locked together as we stare at one another. I sense conflict in him. Not as acute as my turmoil, but it's there, lingering behind his adoring gaze. "Is this as confusing for you as it is for me?" I quietly ask.

He kisses me briefly before winding his hands in my hair and tipping my head back. "It is," he admits after a few beats. "I have never experienced this with any other woman." He pulls me in to his sweaty chest, holding me close. "It's strange for me too but not unpleasant." He rests his chin on my head. "I want this with you. I like this."

"Me too," I admit, and it's no lie.

Slowly, he withdraws, telling me to stay put while he pulls up his shorts and races out of the kitchen. I'm still in a bit of a daze when he returns with a warm cloth to clean me up. He helps me down off the counter and redresses me in his shirt. "If I had my way, you would only wear my clothes."

I smile at him as I roll my eyes. "I don't see how that fits with the whole 'I want to kill any man who looks at you' assertion."

"True." He walks around me toward the coffee pot. "Put me to work," he says when I resume chopping mushrooms.

I shake my head. "Nope. You will sit your delectable butt down. It's a gorgeous morning. I thought we could eat on the terrace. Why don't you take your coffee and head outside? It won't take too long to have this ready."

He pours two coffees, setting one down on the counter beside me. Then he leans in and kisses my cheek. "You are spoiling me."

"Hardly." I glance up at him, trying to tamper my giddiness. "You have been doing all the heavy lifting in this marriage. It's my turn to pull my weight." I stretch up and kiss his tempting lips. "Go relax. I'll bring breakfast out."

"Okay."

He lingers by my side, and I laugh. "What?" I inquire.

"I'm finding it strangely hard to tear myself away from you," he admits, twirling a lock of my messy hair.

Be still my heart. "You will have to tear yourself away from me at some point today. I have an important meeting, and Nic is coming over in an hour for a run on the beach."

"I have a couple of meetings myself this morning, and that suits. Considering we slept in, I won't have time to go with you today."

"I like running with you," I admit. Our early morning jogs are when we have been most at peace with one another. I think he likes that I can keep pace with him and I'm naturally quieter first thing in the morning and less likely to pick a fight.

"Perhaps we can meditate together before I leave and Nic gets here," he suggests, and my mouth hangs open in shock.

"How do you know I meditate?"

He waggles his brows and grins. "You left our bedroom door open one morning, and I caught you."

"Why didn't you say anything?"

He shrugs. "It seemed like you didn't want me to know. You have seen me meditating outside. You could have asked to join me. The fact you didn't told me you preferred to meditate alone, which is cool. I get it."

"I have never meditated with anyone else, but I could do it with you."

He looks pleased. "Where did you learn to meditate?" he asks.

"After I got free of Paulo, I started seeing a therapist to help me to deal with the trauma of the things that had been done to me. She suggested meditation and recommended a local group. I didn't like the group, but the instructor pointed me toward a few self-help aids, and I taught myself how to do it."

"Does it help?"

I vigorously bob my head as I set the mushrooms aside and begin chopping spinach and dicing the tomatoes. "Enormously. It helps to keep me grounded, and I regularly use breathing exercises to remain in control in stressful situations or when I feel a panic attack coming on."

I glance up at him. He's intensely focused on me, lapping up every word, and it's strange being the center of someone's world in a positive way. It will take some getting used to.

"How and when did you learn to meditate?"

"I spent a couple of years training with this specialist group in the mountains in Nepal. One of the first things they teach you is meditation and how to use breathing exercises to control your body and your mind."

"What kind of specialist group?" I inquire, instantly intrigued.

"I went there after graduating college to learn how to fight."

My eyes pop wide. "I have heard of those places. They train warriors and snipers."

"I wanted to learn from the best. I knew one day I would have to immerse myself in this world. I wanted to be prepared."

"I have the feeling there is a lot more to you than you show the world."

"I could say the same about you," he coolly replies.

Though there is no real heat behind his words, I detect an undercurrent of something that goes beyond mere curiosity.

Something strong enough to send chills tiptoeing up my spine.

Chapter Twenty-Three

Catarina

"This is delicious," Massimo says, moaning around a bite of omelet. "Where did you learn to cook?" he asks when he has finished chewing.

"My mother was a lousy mother, but the one good thing she did was teach me how to cook. She passed down all the traditional Italian recipes that have been in her family for generations." I point at the bread basket on the table. "That bread is an old family favorite."

He stares at me curiously for a few seconds before his features even out. "It's tasty. So, does this mean I can expect more home-cooked meals?"

"Definitely. I enjoy cooking but rarely have the time. I will make the effort to get home earlier, at least a couple of nights a week, so I can prepare dinner."

He leans in and kisses my cheek. "Thank you."

Heat crawls up my neck and stains my cheeks. "For what?"

"For trying." His fingers sweep across my cheek. "I don't think anyone would believe me if I told them the fearsome Donna Greco was blushing because I paid her a compliment."

I swat his hand away. "What happens at home stays at home, Massimo." I narrow my eyes at him.

He throws back his head and chuckles. "Don't worry, your secret is safe with me."

"I mean it." I rotate my suddenly stiff shoulders, feeling like an alien in my skin.

"*Mia amata.*" He clasps my face in his large hands. "I would never do anything to jeopardize your reputation and never divulge secrets of what we do in our private time."

"Not even to Fiero?"

"Especially not Fiero."

"I thought you two were close."

"We are. He's more my brother than my flesh and blood."

"How did you become friends?"

"As sons of dons of the New York families, we are all encouraged to form friendships and socialize together. Fiero and I were close in age, and we instantly connected from the moment we met as kids."

"That's how you were friends with Cruz," I surmise.

He nods. "The three of us were thick as thieves as young kids, but after we initiated, things changed."

"In what way?" I ask in between mouthfuls of my breakfast.

Massimo leans back in his chair, staring off into space as he sips from his mug. "Fiero and Cruz are both the heir apparent, and I was the youngest son of four. An unwanted mistake Don Greco barely tolerated." A muscle clenches in his jaw, and he looks lost in thought. "My father only had me initiated because it would've reflected badly on him if he didn't go through the motions with me."

I sit up straighter, deeply invested in this conversation. "You didn't get along with your father?" I tentatively inquire, wanting him to keep talking.

Fire blazes in his eyes. "I hated him with every fiber of my being." The venom undercutting his words and bleeding from his eyes verifies that statement. "He was a bastard, and I celebrated the night he died."

Shock splays across my face because I never even contemplated

Massimo could feel like this. From what I saw, Carlo and Primo were cut from the same cloth as their father, and Gabriele and their mother were slaves to their whims and wishes. Massimo was the unknown. Too young to be involved in what went on in the basement of their house, I always surmised.

"You think I'm disrespectful?" he asks, noting the surprise on my face.

"I'm just surprised. I didn't know you felt like that."

"I was an accident. An oops baby. The result of one of the many times that asshole forced himself on my mother." He rubs at his chest, and I don't question him because this kind of marriage is all too familiar in *mafioso* families. "He already had three sons. He didn't need an heir or want any more screaming babies. He left me to my mother to raise, keeping me separate from my brothers a lot of the time. As we got older, he focused more on Carlo and Primo. He recognized Gabriele's sensitive nature and did his best to beat it out of him." He grinds his teeth, and his jaw is locked tight.

"Is that why you are so close to your mother?" I trace my fingers along his tight jawline, softly caressing his tense features.

He nods as he works his jaw loose. "She clung to me, and as I got older, she looked to me to protect her. I tried my best to intervene, but Father would beat me to a pulp and then tie me to a chair and force me to watch as he hurt her. Often, he raped her in front of me."

I scoot my chair in closer and snuggle into his side as I thread my fingers in his. I regularly spotted bruises on Eleanora's face and arms, and I knew that monster she was married to was beating her and forcing her to do his bidding. It still doesn't excuse how she stood by and watched a young girl be victimized and violated so viciously, and I won't ever forgive her. But I had no clue Massimo was subjected to this growing up, and it only adds to my confusion.

The need to comfort him is riding me hard, and I wrap my arms around him as I tip my head up. "That sounds horrendous. I am sorry you had to go through that. What about your brothers? Didn't they try to stop it?"

"Carlo and Primo were Maximo's mini-mes. They were equally as cruel as our father, and the world is a better place without them in it." The vehemence of his tone leaves little doubt, and I am stunned again.

I don't know how to process this.

The knowledge Massimo denounced his father and brothers changes things, whether I want to admit it or not.

"They regularly beat Mom too," he continues, "though she has a selective memory when it comes to that. She doesn't like to think her eldest sons were monsters, so she chooses to forget it most of the time."

I clear my throat, unwilling to waste the opportunity. "I noticed at the wedding your mother seemed uncomfortable around people and she shuns attention."

He nods, rubbing circles on the back of my hand with his thumb as he rests his chin on my head. "She's very fragile. My father broke her spirit, and though Gabe and I have tried everything to rebuild her, her psyche is too damaged." He tilts my chin up with one finger. "I want you to meet her. Maybe having another woman to talk to will help both of you."

Over my dead body will I ever bond with that woman. I'm not a complete coldhearted bitch. I don't envy her the trauma she must have suffered in that house. But does the fact she was traumatized excuse what she did to me? Possibly to countless others? I don't think so. "No offense, Massimo. But I don't think it works like that. I have spent years in therapy working through my issues, and the memories still haunt me. They always will. Talking about them often triggers a flashback, and it's not something I like to do. The past is best left buried in the past."

Yes, I'm aware of the hypocrisy. The thing is, I feel those words deep in my soul, but I'm unable to live that truth. I'm unable to let it go. Not until those who played a part in my suffering have been dealt my special brand of justice.

"Perhaps you are right, but I still want you to meet her. You are the two most important women in my life, and I want you to get to know one another."

"I will visit her with you after we deal with the Mexicans and the Chinese."

"Thank you."

We resume eating what's left of our breakfast, and I'm deep in thought. "How did you end up so well-rounded?" I ask after a few minutes of amicable silence. Honestly, growing up in that house, it's a miracle he turned out the way he did.

"I was determined not to be like my father and older brothers even if I stupidly sought their approval as a teen. Fiero kept me grounded. We kept each other grounded. He was going through his own shit with his father."

"His father is a misogynistic prick."

"One hundred percent. He wasn't physically abusive like my father. His abuse was more of the psychological and emotional kind. Just before we graduated high school, he bypassed Fiero and officially appointed his younger brother as his heir. It's not usually the way things are done, but it's not unheard of either. It was the ultimate insult, but it bonded Fiero and me as true brothers. We relied on one another solely from that point on. We promised to always be honest and level with one another. He knows things about me no one else does."

"Like what?"

Pursing his lips, he turns in his chair to face me. "I think that's enough of the heavy for one day. We have the rest of our lives to discover everything about one another." Holding my face in both hands, he leans in and kisses me. It's a long, slow, passionate exploration of my lips and my mouth, and my heart is splintering in my chest as I'm torn between giving in to my insatiable need for him and wanting to put as much distance between us so I can stop this madness.

His cell pings, ending the moment and taking the decision out of my hands. Massimo lifts his phone, swiping his finger across the screen. "Nicolina is here. My men let her through the gate a couple of minutes ago."

A timely intervention from my bestie. "Are you finished?" I ask, standing and moving to clear the table.

Massimo spears the last piece of omelet with his fork, popping it in his mouth. I gather up the plates and cups while he chews. "Thank you for breakfast," he says, taking the bread basket and condiments. "And thanks for last night," he whispers in my ear. "It exceeded my wildest dreams and then some."

A shiver cascades down my spine. The good kind. "You're welcome."

He bends down and kisses me again as we both stand holding the remnants of breakfast in our hands.

"Ahem." A throat clearing pulls us apart. Nicolina beams at us, smiling like a proud mama, as she bounces from sneakered foot to sneakered foot. "I would ask what you two have been up to, but it seems obvious."

Massimo waggles his brows, tossing a flirtatious smile her way. "If your friend is running funny this morning, you can totally blame me."

I glare at my husband because I can't smack him with plates in my hands.

He chuckles as he sets the basket and condiments down before retrieving the items from my hands. "Go get ready for your run. I'll clear up here before I leave."

"Shoo." Nic flaps her hands in my face, moving around and grabbing the plates from the table. "I'll help your husband clean up."

Chapter Twenty-Four

Catarina

"What did you two talk about?" I ask Nic twenty minutes later as we jog at a leisurely pace alongside the shore.

"You, mostly." I implore her to continue with my eyes. She slows down to a walk. "I got the sense he was fishing for information."

My heart splutters as I stop, tucking stray strands of wispy hair back into my ponytail. It's a fabulous day, but it's always breezy by the ocean. "About what?"

"Your parents."

Something clicks into place in my brain, and all the blood leaches from my face.

"I didn't tell him anything!" Nic blurts, misreading the alarm on my face. "I stuck to the story about your mom dying during childbirth and your dad raising you alone."

"Oh. My. God." I bend over, placing my hands on my knees, hoping to offset the dizzy spell and the anxiety waiting in the wings. "Oh my fucking God."

"What is it?"

I straighten up, gulping. "I fucked up, Nic." I bark out a laugh. "I'm such an idiot!" I repeatedly slap my palms against my brow as my bestie watches with concern in her eyes. "I made him breakfast, and when he asked where I learned to cook, I told him my mother."

Her eyes pop wide. "I can't believe you slipped up. That is not like you at all."

"See!" I wave my hands around. "I knew this would happen! Getting close to him is a mistake! I'm lowering my guard without even realizing it. Fuck!" I shout as a tight pain spreads across my chest. "He's making me feel things, Nic, and this is all so fucked up."

"Sit with me," she says, lowering to the sand. I watch in a kind of numbed daze as she unties her sneakers and rolls her yoga pants up to her knees. She scoots forward on her butt, letting the gentle waves lap over her feet.

Snapping out of it, I mirror her position, removing my sneakers and placing my feet in the ocean's path, grateful I chose to wear running shorts today. "This was a major boo-boo. And I'm not just talking about my stupid Freudian slip. I mean sleeping with him. Learning more about the kind of man he is. Hearing him tell me what monsters his father and dead brothers were. Listening to him explain what they did to his mother and how they beat him when he tried to protect her. How he was invisible to his father and written off as a mistake." I pin pleading eyes on my friend. "I've let him humanize himself, and I'm so confused, Nic. What if he goes digging? What if he discovers the truth?"

"He won't find anything." She squeezes my hand in reassurance. "He can't find something that doesn't exist."

"Saverio exists."

"Then maybe it's time he didn't."

"That would mean revising the entire plan." I bury my hands into the warm sand, letting the golden strands filter through my fingers.

"I think we both already know the plan will need to be reworked," she says, turning to face me.

"Don't say it."

"You're falling for him, babe. He is falling for you too. I see it every time he looks at you, and I've got to say it. There is nothing wrong with that. Nothing at all. You deserve to have someone like him. You deserve to be happy. There is nothing wrong in veering off course if a new path presents itself."

"There is when it's all I have thought about for twenty-one years. How can I just let it go?"

"I didn't say it would be easy, but it comes down to what is more important? Living for life or living for vengeance?"

"It is not that black-and-white."

"I know, babe." She rests her head on my shoulder. "But I firmly believe you were led to Massimo for a reason. I don't think you should discount him or the feelings you have for him."

"How is this happening so fast?"

"This started five years ago. Some would argue it's been a real slow burn."

"What is he doing to me? I'm already messing up. I should stay away from him but I...I can't. Not after last night. I should stick to the plan and go through with it, but I'm not strong enough to stay away, and I...I don't want to." I thought it might be freeing admitting the truth, but it's not. It doesn't lessen the pain or the turmoil.

"You can't fight fate, babe, and he's yours. This was written in the stars. You are following the path you are meant to follow."

"How can that be? If I accept that, it means I have to let it go. You know what happened to me in that house. How can I just let that go?!"

"Carlo is dead. Maximo and Primo are dead. I know you didn't get the satisfaction of killing them. I know you feel like you haven't gotten your justice, but Massimo isn't his brother. Why should he pay for his brother's sins? Where is the justice in that? He's innocent, Rina. He's an innocent caught up in all of this like you were."

I am quiet for several minutes as I contemplate her words. "Massimo *is* innocent, and I can't kill him. Gawd, I so can't." I hang my head as I finally accept that reality. "But Gabriele isn't innocent. Neither is Eleanora. They may not have participated in my torture, but they knew I was held captive for months, and they did nothing. How can I let that go?" I look to the sky, imploring some deity to tell me what I should do. Lowering my head, I stare out at the water. "I can't forgive them. I can't let them live. But that will end my marriage and my life because Massimo will never forgive me if I kill his mother and his last remaining brother. He will kill me to avenge them, which brings us full circle—it's kill or be killed." I lift my knees and bury my head in them.

"There is another way."

I raise my head, instantly knowing what she implies. "That isn't viable."

"It is." She swivels around so she's facing me head on. "You let them live, Rina. The Mazzones too because they are innocent as well. Murder that bastard, Saverio, and take the crown you rightly deserve, but do it your way. The way you like to do everything. With minimal bloodshed and keeping the innocents protected." She levels me with a solemn look. "Do it with your husband by your side."

I am still mulling over Nicolina's advice later that night as I wait for Anton to show up at our meeting place on the fifth level of a parking lot in Queens. It's virtually empty at this time of night, and unlike a lot of modern parking lots, there are no cameras here. We are a few minutes early, so I'm sitting in the back seat of my SUV, trawling through the photos my PI sent me an hour ago.

I hired a local man to follow my husband.

He's got someone tailing me, so it's only fair.

What I am seeing on the screen is only adding to my torment.

Massimo is keeping secrets.

Big ones, I suspect.

I can't exactly throw shade at him for that, but it doesn't encourage me to change plans that have been more than twenty years in the making, no matter how conflicted I am.

I don't want to hurt my husband, but I don't see how I can backtrack from my original plan. Not without putting myself in the line of fire and not without jeopardizing everyone who works with me. I have come too far to retract now. I couldn't even if I wanted to. My actions to this point are enough to justify my death if any don were to uncover the truth.

If I don't stay the course, I risk my own life and those of my loved ones.

Those are the facts.

I was innocent when I was kidnapped, but no one cared. Not when I was taken or after I was rescued. The burning pain in my heart refuses to extinguish anytime I think of all those people who could have —should have—done better.

Who protected me when I was an innocent?

Does it make it right that I would inflict suffering on other innocents? No. But I aim to keep my casualties to a minimum. That has always been the way I have operated.

Now, Nic—and Massimo by default—has scattered my thoughts, divided my loyalties, and has me questioning everything.

"Nic says the decoy worked," Renzo says from beside me, glancing up from his cell and cutting through my depressive inner monologue. "Greco's PI is sitting outside the restaurant watching her and Dario eat dinner."

"Of course, it worked. We are the same height and similar builds. Put Nic in a white dress with a black wig and large shades, and she will pass for me, provided no one examines her face too closely."

"Dario knows to shield her face from view anytime we need to do this."

"Did the wire transfer go through on the building downtown?" I ask as I scroll through the photos of a large waterfront property on Staten Island with growing interest.

"Yes. I will collect the keys in the morning and meet Nic there with the interior designer."

"We don't need anything fancy," I say, knowing Nic will go all out with our new secret office space. "It just needs to be functional, and we need it operational ASAP. As soon as we take the Mexicans and The Triad out, we move on to the next phase."

"Have you heard from O'Hara today?"

I nod. "He called me earlier. He is playing the Mexicans and Chinese off against one another to buy us time to put our plan into motion. We should be good to go on Sunday, provided The Commission approves."

"I hate being answerable to those fuckers." Renzo peers over my shoulder with a frown. "What are they up to?" He squints as he stares at the photo of Fiero and Massimo climbing into a helicopter at the top of the modern building that is still under construction on Staten Island.

"I would like to know too." I click out of the image file, opening up the one-page summary report. "Initial research shows that the building is owned by a company called Rinascita. They are a big conglomerate with diverse interests, but their two core businesses appear to be real estate and import and export of speciality Italian foods."

"That means rebirth in Italian. You think it's theirs?"

I purse my lips as a long sleek black Mercedes pulls up alongside us. "They aren't listed as company directors or employees, but it wouldn't be that difficult to hide behind others if they wanted to keep it a secret."

Renzo shakes his head. "I can't see it myself. When would those fuckboys have had the time to build a business like that? Neither of them has the smarts," he adds, enjoying sticking the knife in. "They must be there for another reason."

I wouldn't be so sure about that.

There is a lot I don't know about my husband.

Massimo disappears every day, and he is vague about where he is going and what he's doing. When I pry, he says he's working on the handover with Gabe, but I smell a rat.

His official ceremony is set for a month from now—when he will be officially sworn in as Don Greco, head of the Greco *famiglia,* and take up his seat at The Commission.

When that happens, we will officially be the most powerful couple within the *mafioso* and a big part of me gets an enormous thrill out of that.

"We can continue this later," I say as Ezio opens my door.

"Be careful," Renzo cautions, like always.

I nod as I climb out of the car and get into the back seat beside *Pakhan* Smirnov.

"I don't like all this cloak-and-dagger stuff," he says, instantly handing me a vodka.

"Neither do I, but it's necessary. Greco has a PI tailing me. I'm using Nicolina as a decoy, but I still can't afford to take any risks. We can discuss what we need to discuss here as easily as we can at your penthouse or your office." I swallow a mouthful of the clear liquid, eyeing my business partner with a hint of concern.

Something is off.

There's a tension in the air I can't quite put my finger on. "What was so urgent we needed to meet immediately?"

"Moscow grows impatient. They need to see progress in New York."

"And they will, in due course. Everything is lined up. We will remove the Mexicans and the Chinese very soon, and an agreement has been secured with the Irish."

"That was not part of deal."

"I had to be adaptable. This plan will still see us supplying all the narcotics coming into the Big Apple. Per our arrangement, sixty percent will ship from Russia and forty percent from the Colombians."

"Yet the Italians will not know that."

"Not yet," I snap, irritated at his line of questioning. I knock back another mouthful of vodka before turning to face him. The leather squelches under my butt as I swivel around. "What is this really about? These plans were set in motion years ago. You helped to plan it. Why is it no longer good enough?"

"Like you say, we need to be adaptable." He waves his hand in the air. "There are political changes happening in Moscow. My new boss is an impatient man. He wants results now."

"You currently supply forty percent of all narcotics coming into the US."

"We want it all." He is quick to reply.

"And you will get it. In time."

"My boss needs to see more progress."

"You need to temper his expectations and stall him. We are so close to our goals, but it can't be rushed. I don't have their trust yet."

"Pfft." He swirls the clear liquid in his glass before tossing it back. "Spread your legs like you always do, and speed this up."

Indignation and anger rush to the surface, boiling my blood. "Do not cross a line you can't come back from, Anton."

"I don't see what the problem is. Fuck Mazzone. Fuck them all. Get them on our side. Do what you must to earn their trust quickly."

His insinuation that my success is solely because of my seductive ability is a big insult. As if my strategic skills, hard work, and careful planning have played no part. Has Anton always been a dick hiding behind a veil of civility and professionalism or did I just not see it? I could argue with him about the personal slight, but I know how to pick my battles. Something else is going on here, and I need to understand what it is. "Or what?" I drain my vodka and calmly set my glass down. "Is this a threat?"

He tut-tuts. "Don't be so sensitive. I am merely pointing out we need to accelerate plans. I don't call the shots, Catarina. Moscow does, and right now, they are not happy."

"You have to appease them until the timing is right. We can't show our hand too early, or it will all be for nothing."

He grips my chin between his fingers. "Is this because of your new husband? Is he in your ear?"

Why the hell would he say that? "Don't be ridiculous. He's my enemy." I forcibly remove Anton's fingers from my face, hoping the words don't ring as hollow to him. "I have Massimo exactly where I want him," I spoof. I'm in no doubt our battle of wills is still ongoing despite both of us waving a white flag of sorts.

"Prove it," he says, lowering his zipper and pulling his cock from his pants. "Suck my dick."

Rage unlike anything I have felt in a long time jumps up and bites me. "I don't know what game you're playing, but I have nothing to prove. I will not suck your dick. Put that hideous thing away." I slant a lethal glare at him, projecting controlled anger as prickles of apprehension glide up my spine.

The dynamic has altered.

I don't know why or what it means, but this changes *everything*.

I won't be manipulated.

Not by any man.

And not by the Russians.

I'm not naïve. I knew the risks when I established a working relationship with Anton, but I thought we had a mutual respect, and his way of doing things was different than his predecessors. I thought we could negotiate any future disagreements and, with the weight of the entire Italian American *mafioso* behind me, I could control the Russians and keep them where I wanted them.

I am beginning to suspect I made a grave error in judgment.

One that may cost all of us dearly.

I cannot allow his disrespect to go unchallenged. In a lightning-fast move, I slide my dagger out from where it's strapped to my thigh and point the tip at his disgusting floppy dick. "Fix yourself or I'll slice it off." The privacy screen lowers, and the two men in the front point their weapons at me. "Call your henchmen off, or you won't like what happens next," I say as he tucks his tiny cock back in his boxer briefs and zips his pants up.

He speaks in Russian, having no clue I have been learning the language these past few years.

"This is definitely not the time," I reply in Russian, enjoying the look of shock splayed across his face. It costs him, and I prod the tip of my dagger at the exact point of the jugular vein in his neck. "Make one false move against me, and you're a dead man. What I did to my ex-husband was only the tip of the iceberg when it comes to my creativity. Don't tempt me to explore it."

In Russian, he tells his men to back down. I keep my dagger pressed to his throat, but we both know I won't kill him. I can't afford to at this critical juncture, but it looks like all bets may be off for the future. "You disappoint me greatly, Anton. The man I thought I knew would never conduct himself in such a seedy, disgraceful manner. You have some nerve challenging me like this. We have a professional relationship. One I have always valued and appreciated. Now I am questioning everything you are bringing to the table."

I nick his throat on purpose, drawing a small bead of blood. "Don't make an enemy of me. It won't end well for you. That much I can promise."

His Adam's apple bobs in his throat as he pins me with dark eyes. "I don't take well to vague threats."

"Trust me, there is nothing vague about it. You are either on my side or against me. Which is it, Anton?"

He draws a breath, visibly forcing the aggression from his face. "This has gotten out of hand. I accept responsibility, and I apologize."

Slowly, I remove the dagger from his neck. "Has the agenda changed, or was this always your plan?" Has he been playing me all this time? Does he think because I'm a woman that I'm easier to betray?

"Nothing has changed on our side. Has it on yours?" he asks, extracting a handkerchief from his jacket pocket and dabbing at the little trickle of blood on his neck.

"Why would anything have changed on my side?"

His eyes bore into mine, and I hold his gaze. Is this about Massimo? It couldn't be. He doesn't know about my past with the Grecoes or my plans for them. I never confided that in him because it wasn't part of the overall scheme to take New York and control The Commission. It was his suggestion I marry Massimo, so it couldn't be anything to do with him. Could it? I tuck it away in a mental compartment to reflect on later.

"See that it doesn't," he says.

"I don't respond well to vague threats either," I say, reaching for the door handle.

He stretches across the seat, pinning me in place with his arm. "Don't be rash, Catarina. One false move could get both of us killed. We need to stick with original plan."

"I could say the same to you," I reply, prying his arm off me. "We are done here." I stab him with an icy look. "Do what you must to hold Moscow at bay. I will work to progress things as fast as I can on my end, and I'll provide a status report next week."

"See that you do," he says, sitting back in his seat as I open the door and get out. "Don't disappoint me, Catarina. You won't like what happens if you do."

Chapter Twenty-Five

Massimo

My wife is troubled. And I'd bet it's nothing to do with why we are parked in a blacked-out armored SUV outside a dingy restaurant in Chinatown. She has been on edge the past couple of days, and her crew seems tense too. I want to know what's going down, but Allante has uncovered nothing. According to his intel, my wife spends her days working from coffee shops and restaurants, usually alone although Dario Agessi sometimes accompanies her. I smell a rat and vow to go over the surveillance material myself once we put these Triad bastards down.

"O'Hara has taken Lopez down," Catarina confirms, scooting over on the seat and showing me her phone. The text is from Fiero. He was assigned to work with the Irish to ensure they played their part without deviating from the plan. The pic shows the Mexican boss lying in a pool of his own blood, a vacant stare in his lifeless eyes. "They are handling the rest of his crew now." She repockets her phone, glancing earnestly out the window. "What the fuck is taking so long?"

We sent twenty of our best men inside to handle the initial attack. "Something must have gone wrong," I say, removing my gun and unlocking the safety. "I'll take a look."

She snorts out a laugh and levels me with an icy stare. "We're doing this together." Her expression dares me to argue, but I know better.

"So, let's do this." I waggle my brows, my eyes raking appreciatively over her sexy form in her tight-fitting black top and pants. She's wearing military-style boots, and she has a myriad of weapons strapped to her body. "At the risk of incurring your wrath, should you wear a Kevlar?"

She smirks, and it turns my dick to steel. "My clothing is bulletproof."

"Where the fuck did you get your hands on that?" I know a couple of companies have prototypes, but it's not on mass market sale yet.

"It's actually a Mazzone tech prototype."

"Bennett has only given those to a select number of his *soldati* to test in the field."

Her grin expands. "I'm well connected, Massimo. There isn't much I can't get my hands on."

Grabbing her to me, I slam my lips down on hers. "Your smarts turn me the fuck on."

She cups my junk. "I can tell." She traces her tongue around my lips, and precum leaks from my cock. "Let's take these motherfuckers out and go home to celebrate."

Her flirtatious tone and suggestive look confirm her thoughts are aligned to mine. Still, I want verbal affirmation. It will make the killing all that much sweeter. "Tell me your plans involve both of us naked, sweaty, and fucking our way through the Kama Sutra."

She giggles, and I stare at her in awe. Her face is flushed and her eyes bright, and she looks happy and carefree in a way she rarely does. I clasp her face in my hands and kiss her tenderly. "I want to bottle that sound and listen to it on replay."

Predictably, she rolls her eyes. "I want to bottle the sound of Lee Chang choking on his own blood and play it to my enemies on repeat."

A massive grin stretches across my mouth. "I love how bloodthirsty you are. Never fails to get me hard either."

"Is there anything that doesn't get you hard?" she asks, and I'm opening my mouth to reply when the sound of gunfire emerges from the restaurant.

"Go, go, go," Catarina yells into her cell phone. Our additional reserves hop out of their SUVs the same time we leave ours. My wife races toward the front door with a gun in each hand, and I run after her with Ricardo hot on my heels. Ezio remains behind the wheel should we need to make a hasty getaway.

"Stay back," I roar, grabbing a handful of her shirt and yanking her out of the way. "Let our men enter first."

She digs her elbow into my gut, loosening my hold and spinning around in my arms. Cold metal thrusts under my neck as she levels me with a furious look while prodding me with the muzzle of her gun.

Around us, our *soldati* swarm the building, and more gunfire erupts as shots are traded.

"Let's get one thing straight, Massimo. You are my husband, but I don't take orders from anyone, especially not you." She lets me go, nodding at Ricardo.

He walks around us, entering the restaurant with his weapon out and his eyes peeled.

Rina's eyes soften a little as she looks up at me. "I know you only want to protect me, but I don't need it. I know how to handle myself."

I grab her arm, shoving my angry face all up in hers. "I fucking know that! But no don or donna worth their salt charges headfirst into a battle without scouting the lay of the land. You are too valuable and too smart to rush into the unknown. I'm not telling you what to do; I'm keeping you safe." She knows this, but she's distracted. It's beginning to worry me.

"Boss," one of my men says, poking his head out. "This level is clear. Chang and his senior associates are holed up in the basement. What do you want us to do?"

"Smoke them out," Catarina says, wrenching from my arms and turning around. "Then take them down as they emerge."

My *soldato* looks to me, and it enrages me.

When Gabe and I spoke to our men after I got married—about our plans for the official handover from him to me—I informed them my wife was to be addressed as Donna Greco and given the same respect as any don. Clearly, that went in one ear and out the other for some.

I won't have it.

My wife will not be disrespected within our *famiglia*.

"You heard Donna Greco! Her word is as good as mine, and if you disrespect her again, I'll put a fucking bullet in your head."

He gulps, looking suitably chastised as his gaze bounces between us. "My apologies, Donna Greco. It won't happen again."

She nods. "Apology accepted. Keep your wits about you. Go."

"Keep Chang alive," I call after him as he runs off. I open the door and enter the restaurant first, stepping aside to let Catarina enter.

It's a veritable bloodbath. Bodies litter the floor, and others are slumped over tables. Spicy aromas mix with the scent of gunpowder and blood as we pick our way across the room, heading in the direction of the stairs. "We had the element of surprise," Rina says, eyeing the remnants of lunch spilling across multiple tables. Several men are face-down in bowls of rice and noodles.

"O'Hara came through for us." I check each motherfucker as we pass. It's not unheard of for someone to play dead and wait for an opportunity to take a potshot.

"He did. I think he'll make a formidable ally."

"I agree."

"In time, we should look to expand his role," she says, shooting a guy who lifts his head from the table as we pass. The bullet lands cleanly in the center of his brow, and he slumps to the side, dead upon impact. "We should probably make that known now," she continues, like she didn't just kill a man. "It will foster loyalty and give him a goal to work toward."

"Good idea."

Panicked shouting filters up the stairs, as we make our descent, quickly followed by more gunfire. My cell pings in my pocket, and I remove it.

Catarina looks over her shoulder at me.

"It's from Don Mazzone. The police are fielding several reports from residents in the area. He says the police commissioner can't hold the cops off for long without it looking suspicious. We have ten minutes max."

"Let's end this." She walks down the steps like butter wouldn't melt in her mouth.

A pile of bodies rests at the bottom of the stairs, and the only man alive is the man we seek.

Lee Chang.

Leader of the now defunct Triad.

All across the city, men belonging to the five families, with support from our Irish allies, have taken down every man associated with the Mexicans and the Chinese. The organizations are wiped out. In time, others will try to move into the territory, but we'll be ready for them.

Lee is on his knees with his hands tied behind his back, surrounded by armed *soldati*, their weapons trained on his body should he try anything.

"Fucking Italian scum!"

He spits at my wife's feet, and I grab hold of his hair, yanking his head back at a painful angle. "Apologize to my wife, you piece of shit."

"Fuck you!" His eyes glint with malice and something else. "You're nothing but her bitch, and she's playing you!"

Catarina acts fast, removing a sharp knife and shoving it into his stomach. "Have you no honor?" she asks, circling him. "I can gut you like the traitorous pig you are or give you a quick noble death. Which is it to be?"

"I know it was you." He narrows his beady eyes at her. "You did this. You s—"

My wife rains bullets on his body, and he slouches forward, face-planting on the pile of dead bodies, blood oozing out of copious wounds. Deathly silence surrounds us as I stare at my wife.

"What?" She coolly holds my gaze. "Time is of the essence. We need to leave."

I nod, but something about this doesn't sit right with me.

Chang was about to say something important.

I feel it in my bones.

"Everyone out now," I command, bending down to retrieve the bullets from my wife's gun. We don't usually leave any bullets behind, even if we use untraceable weapons, but there isn't time to do a proper cleanup of the scene. Still, I'm making sure to remove all the bullets from my wife's gun as I don't want anything linking back to her. As for the rest, Don Mazzone has the police commissioner on speed dial, so I'm sure he'll make sure any remaining evidence never sees the light of day.

Our men troop past us as Catarina bends down, joining me in the hunt for the bullets.

"What was Chang about to say?" I ask as we work quickly together.

"I'm not a mind reader." She doesn't look up as she speaks. "But I think it was pretty obvious. He knows my coming to the city set all this in motion. He knows I was the brains behind this operation." She straightens up as I do, holding out her hand for the bullets I collected. I dump them in her palm. "Does it matter?"

I watch her deposit the bullets in a small clear Ziplock bag and tuck it in the back pocket of her pants. "No." I take her hand. "Come on, let's get out of here."

Upstairs, the room is half cleared out. Ricardo and a couple of my men are holding fort at the door while a few other *soldati* are checking the bodies to ensure they are all dead.

We are making our way across the space when Catarina pivots and sends a dagger flying across the room. It lodges in the heart of a small man wearing a white apron. His startled eyes meet mine as the gun in his hand drops to the ground, and he crumples in a heap on the floor. A high-pitched yell emerges as a taller, younger man charges from behind the man from a door that must lead to the kitchen, I'm guessing. He is also wearing a white apron and wielding a baseball bat as he rushes toward my wife.

She yells, "No!" when I lift my weapon, training it in his direction. I watch in horrified shock as she runs toward him, leaping over dead bodies strewn on the ground. She ducks down as he swings the bat, jumping up and landing a punch on his nose before he can swing it again. "I don't want to hurt you," she says, sweeping his legs out from under him. He loses his balance, slipping on blood, and takes a tumble, landing hard on his back. Rina grabs the bat in her gloved hands and shoves it under his neck as she sits on his chest. "Stop fighting if you want to live."

"Get off me, you bitch!" He spits in her face. "You killed my bà! You killed everyone. I will tell the cops! You are going down for this!"

"*Mia amata*," I say, stepping up behind her.

"I know." Her voice holds resignation as she withdraws her gun. "It didn't have to be this way," she says as the man spouts a string of words in Chinese. The shot is precise, and he dies instantly.

Sirens wail in the near distance. "We must go."

I nod at my men. "Check the kitchen. Ensure there are no more survivors."

Taking my wife's hand, I lead her out of the restaurant. "I know you wanted to save him, but we can't leave any witnesses."

"I know. I just hate killing innocents. He only worked in the kitchen. He didn't have anything to do with this."

Ezio opens the back door, and we climb into the SUV.

"You don't know that for sure. Anyone who works for criminals, no matter in what capacity, understands the risks."

"Let's go home," she says, nodding at Ezio when Ricardo is seated and we are ready to leave. The privacy screen goes up, and I relax in my seat. I move in closer, sliding my arm around her back, pleased when she rests her head on my shoulder. "I know you might not feel like celebrating, even if it was a great win, but how about a distraction?" I waggle my brows as I cup her pussy through her pants.

Some of the stress leaves her features as she peers at me with an instant lustful look. "I like how your mind works, husband." She leans up, planting a lingering passionate kiss on my lips. "Distract me, Massimo. I would like to forget."

Chapter Twenty-Six

Catarina

I'm on edge, and Massimo can tell. He is way too observant, and it concerns me. The Mexican-Chinese takedown was a massive success. The Commission is pleased and has approved me to implement the new supply chain model. It has gone a long way toward earning their trust. I should be pleased, but this unexpected Russian complication has me so worried I have been having trouble sleeping.

Twice in the past week, I've had bad nightmares, waking Massimo in the middle of the night when I come out of it, sweating, shuddering, and screaming. I twisted the truth when he asked what was causing them, saying memories of what Paulo did to me often return to torment me.

The truth is, my nightmares are rarely about my ex-husband.

Carlo Greco is the monster who haunts my dreams.

A combination of therapy, meditation, exercise, and melatonin or my prescription sleeping meds usually keeps them at bay. Times of heightened stress can dredge them to the surface, like now. It doesn't help that I'm not feeling like myself. I'm still torn over what to do about Don Mazzone and Massimo and his family.

Nicolina is right, to an extent. Massimo and Ben played no part in what happened to me.

Angelo Mazzone, Bennett's father, was the one who is worthy of my anger. He arranged the marriage contract for his daughter Natalia to wed Carlo Greco, which set the whole thing in motion. I know it was Angelo who gave the order to have me rescued, and he sent Leo and his now-deceased son Mateo to fetch me.

Angelo killed my father, denying me that vengeance. He never took Don Greco to task over my kidnapping, and he never came to check on me. I was handed back to my self-centered mother, broken and damaged beyond all recognition, and left to rot.

Angelo died before I could kill him, denying me that revenge too. Inheritances, including debts, pass to the eldest son in our world, meaning Ben assumed all of Angelo's responsibilities.

In my mind, it was clear he would have to pay for Angelo's failings.

Now, it is much less clear. Bennett is a good man, a devoted husband and father, and a wise leader, and he has been fair to me. The waters are muddled, and killing him no longer feels right. How could I deprive Sierra of her husband? Take Ben away from their children?

I can't justify it.

But how can I just let it go?

It is all I have known.

Who will I be without my vengeance?

These questions, and more, keep me up at night until I fall into a troubled sleep where I'm ripped to shreds by ghastly beasts who keep me chained in a cage. I wake screaming and gasping for air, my heart pounding so hard at having revisited the darkest time in my life.

Which is why I'm going to visit the place where it all started. Perhaps a physical reminder will help to make the path clearer because there is one thing I know with certainty—indecision leads to mistakes, and I can't afford any of those.

"What is this?" I ask, walking out of the closet I share with my husband holding the suspicious-looking plastic package in my hand.

Massimo's grin is so wide it threatens to split his face. He stalks toward me like a predator eyeing up its prey. "Were you snooping, wife?"

"They were on the floor by your suits," I truthfully explain. "Is this what I think it is?"

He reels me into his arms, still grinning. "I took them out last night and must not have put them back on the shelf correctly."

"Stop deflecting," I snap, nerves getting the best of me.

He tweaks my nose, and I glare at him. "Yes, those are your panties from the airport bathroom." He squeezes my ass through my dress. "I was surprised you would leave them behind."

"They were on the floor of a public bathroom. I was hardly going to put them back on, but yes, it was stupid of me to put them in the trash. I should have taken them with me to dispose of later. I am not usually so flippant when it comes to my DNA." It is proof Massimo distracted me from the very beginning.

"Damn. When I was searching for you, I never thought to have them tested for DNA."

The frantic pounding in my heart calms a smidgeon at his words. It was my initial thought when I found my lace panties preserved carefully in a sealed plastic bag. My DNA isn't on any official database—I have been painstaking in ensuring I never leave evidence behind—but I can't know that with one-hundred-percent certainty.

"Why did you keep them?" I cock my head to one side, inspecting my husband's face for any telltale signs of lying.

"I wanted a memento. It was the only reminder I had from that day, besides my memories." He fixes me with a wolfish grin that is downright wicked. "I used to jerk off daily with them wrapped around my cock, imagining you on your knees, gagging on my dick."

"Are you being real with me now?"

"Straight up." He rubs his erection against my belly. "See what even thinking about it does to me?" Bending down, he bites on my earlobe. "I had to stop doing it when the lace started to fray. That's when I had to jerk off with just my memories. I put them in the sealed bag to preserve them."

"Like a serial killer does with mementos of each kill," I deadpan, scrutinizing his face. "Are there more of these? From different women? Do I need to worry about finding other random panties in plastic bags lying around the place?"

His wolfish grin expands. "Careful, *mia amata*. That almost sounds like jealousy."

"You wish," I murmur as an unfamiliar emotion gives way to a fluttery sensation in my chest, and the vein in my neck pulses at a more rapid pace.

"You can relax," he says, grinding his pelvis into me. "I had no interest in preserving any woman's panties except yours."

That is oddly endearing, and my body seems to agree as I feel a layer of stress lift from my shoulders. "You're such a perv."

"Guilty as charged, and I feel no shame." Taking the package from my hand, he removes my old panties. Bringing them to his nose, he inhales deeply. "I can still smell you on them. Hmm." He makes a thrumming sound at the back of his throat as he buries his nose in the skimpy material.

You would have to torture me to ever get an admission, but the sight of him sniffing my panties is doing dangerous things to my body. Crazy, scary, arousing things. My skin is on fire. Tension twists low in my belly as my libido is cranked to the max. My nipples are standing to attention, the hardened peaks sharp enough to cut glass as I ache down below.

"Delicious," he murmurs, locking eyes with me as he takes a couple more sniffs, looking like a drug addict indulging in the ultimate high. He rubs the material all over his face before lovingly returning my panties to the sealed bag.

"You have serious issues."

He flashes me one of his disarming smiles, not in the least bit ashamed.

I like that about him. He completely owns who he is without apology. Still, he can't keep them. "The panties have got to go."

"Abso-fucking-lutely not," he protests, setting the package back on the shelf before he grabs handfuls of my ass.

I'm trying to ignore the heat flooding my panties, and he's making it hard. Pun intended. "I can't have evidence of my DNA just lying around the place."

He chuckles as he grips my chin with his long, slender fingers. "You're too cute sometimes."

"Massimo," I growl, growing irritated.

"Sweetheart." He kisses me, knowing it will soften me up, and I both hate and love how predictable I have become. He sweeps his fingers across my face as he breaks our kiss and peers deep into my eyes. "Your DNA is all over our house, and I want it all over my body right the fuck now," he adds, slipping his free hand under my dress.

"Your mother is expecting us for lunch," I remind him.

"We have time." He skims his fingers along my inner thigh.

"Fuck." I shudder, and my legs turn to Jell-O at his touch. I have never had this before, and the craving to feel his hands on me is almost becoming unbearable. At times when we are apart, it's often all I can think about. "You are such a bad influence."

"I'm a good influence, *mia amata*, and you know it." He slips his fingers underneath my panties and rubs my folds. "I turn you on as much as you turn me on," he says, driving a couple of digits inside me. I moan as he slowly pumps his fingers, melting against him, needing to feel his dick filling me up. Before I can ask, he removes his hand from under my dress and shoves one finger into my mouth. "Taste how sweet you are."

I suction my lips around his finger, sucking my essence down as I hold eye contact with him.

"Fucking hell, Rina. That's so hot." His mouth replaces his finger as he devours me before he pulls back, sucking his other finger into his mouth, groaning as he drinks my juices from his skin. "So delicious." He starts pushing my dress up. "I need more."

"Not so fast, sexy." I drop to my knees and reach for his zipper. "I thought a reenactment might be in order." I lick my lips and roll my hips as I lower his zipper and free his large cock.

"You're so perfect," he says as I wrap my lips around his straining shaft and begin sucking. Blowing him turns me on as much as it pleasures him. My panties are soaking as I work him quickly. He thrusts into my mouth, and I gag when he hits the back of my throat. "I need to come in your cunt," he says, pulling out and lifting me up.

"From behind," I say, walking to the bed and crawling up onto it on all fours. "Don't mess me up. I don't have time to get changed."

"As you wish, wifey." He slaps my ass, as he is fond of doing, and I glare at him over my shoulder.

He chuckles as he winds his fingers around his dick, guiding it to my entrance. I hold on to the headboard as he plunges into me in one hard thrust and fucks me to within an inch of my life. The headboard slams repeatedly against the wall as my husband pounds into me, and I seriously don't think I will ever get enough of this.

I never thought sex could be this good or that I could become so addicted to it.

Since we had our talk, we have been fucking like bunnies, and we are equally insatiable.

I never want this to end.

Sadness accompanies that thought before Massimo moves his fingers to my clit, and all logical thought flees my mind. My limbs quiver with the force of my impending climax, and I push back against him as he thrusts inside me, our movements in perfect sync. "Will never get enough," Massimo pants, rubbing my clit harder as he ruts into me, driving deep and nudging my cervix. "Love fucking you," he grunts as he pinches my clit.

Stars explode behind my eyes, and I scream as an intense climax thunders through me, sending ripples of pleasure cascading over every part of me. Massimo roars as his release hits, continuing to thrust until we are both done.

"Stay still," he says, withdrawing slowly and pressing a tender kiss to the back of my bare neck. His cum leaks down my thighs as the bed dips and he climbs off. He fixes his clothing before entering the bathroom, returning a minute later with a warm washcloth and a soft towel.

Tears build behind my eyes as he cleans me up with tender loving care. He is always considerate. Ensuring I come—usually several times—and he always cleans me up afterward and insists on snuggling. He makes me feel desired and cherished, and I am addicted to the feeling and to him.

I know what this means, even if I'm terrified to articulate the truth.

"Every time gets better and better," he says, enveloping me in his strong arms when I'm all fixed up and I get off the bed.

"I know," I whisper while hugging him. It doesn't feel weak clinging to him like this. If anything, in recent times, it seems like holding him gives me strength.

I'm fucked if I understand it.

"We're good together, *mia amata*." He tips my head back so we're looking at one another.

"We are."

"I don't know what's troubling you, and I know you won't tell me, but I want you to know I'm here if you need to talk. I won't judge. I couldn't ever do that with you. I just want to help. We might not have married for love or the usual reasons, but I firmly believe we are exactly where we both should be. We belong together. I feel that truth deeply in here." He places a hand over his heart, yet it feels like mine is the one being exposed.

"You can be incredibly romantic when you're not being an ass," I tease, needing to lighten the moment.

"Shush." He kisses my lips. "Don't tell anyone. I have a playboy reputation to maintain."

I playfully swat at his chest. "Your playboy days are in the past. You're mine now."

"And you are mine."

As I nod, I fully believe it. I don't know how I'm going to pull it off, but I will achieve my goals without hurting my husband. It's no longer a choice.

It's the only truth that matters.

Chapter Twenty-Seven

Catarina

My hands shake as I clutch the box on my lap with an iron grip. Bile crawls up my throat, and acid churns in my gut when Massimo's family home comes into view as he drives us up the sweeping driveway. Our bodyguards are in my SUV behind us.

"Hey." Massimo reaches across the console to squeeze my hand. "There's no need to be nervous. She's not going to bite."

Smothering my fear, I plaster a fake smile on my face as I look over at my husband. "I don't have a good track record with mothers-in-law."

His eyes drill into mine for a second. "I know and I promise this will be fine. Mama is looking forward to meeting you." He refocuses on the path ahead, slowing down as we approach the large gray two-story building.

I attempt to ignore the anxious fluttering in my chest and how my heart picks up speed when he rounds the huge stone water fountain. The vision returns unbidden.

I'm screaming as Carlo drags me down the front steps and across the gravel toward the fountain. The skin abrades on my knees, and my bare feet are torn and bleeding. I'm naked and shivering all over, my bruised and battered body aching like I've been run over by a semi.

I lost track of time ages ago. Days and nights roll into one in the dark, dank basement I now call home. I haven't seen sunlight in so long, and my body craves the Vitamin D.

My eyes lift to the dark sky, and I make a silent plea for someone to rescue me from this hell. I stopped crying out for my daddy after Carlo told me he knows where I am and hasn't come for me.

I don't understand. Daddy has always been good to me. Sneaking me candy sours behind Mom's back. Ferrying me to and from dance classes and the pool where I trained with a local team. Overruling Mom when she didn't want to let me have sleepovers with Jessa. Memories of late nights playing Xbox, indulging our shared passion for action movies, and him proudly clapping from the bleachers as I excelled at dance recitals and swim meets flood my mind, adding to my despair.

Why hasn't he done anything? Why is he letting this pervert do these horrible things to me? I thought I was Daddy's angel, but he's left me here with this monster, and every day that passes, I die a little more inside. I am no longer the same girl who was bundled into the back of a black van from the front of the shopping mall many months ago.

That girl is a stranger, and I very much doubt I will ever be the same person.

Hunger gnaws at my stomach, but I have learned how to ignore it. He keeps me malnourished on purpose so I don't have the strength to continue fighting him. But I'll never stop. There are other ways to fight back without physical strength.

I love goading him on what a pathetic sick bastard he is, and I never willingly partake in the things he does to me. I scratch and bite and hurl obscenities at him until he ties me up and gags me. Then I glower at him, my eyes promising retribution. Sometimes the complete opposite works. Staying mute and motionless. Looking like the empty shell I feel. Letting him do despicable things to me and acting like it has no impact on me.

I like to mix it up to annoy him, even knowing he will beat me until I'm bloody. Most days, the pain is the only reminder I am human.

"Quit screaming, bitch!" Carlo snarls, digging his nails into my arm as he pulls me closer. "It's the middle of the night, and no one is here. No one is coming to help you."

"One day, someone will come," I say, glaring at him as he forces me to my knees at the fountain. Yanking my arms back, he ties them behind me. "One day, I will have a knife in my hand, and I will pay you back for every cut, every bruise, every hurt."

He barks out a cruel laugh. "No one is coming for you. No one cares." Grabbing my knotty hair, he wraps it around his fist and tugs my head back at a painful angle. "You're my toy. Mine to do with as I please." Reaching down, he grabs my nipple, twisting it hard. My breasts have grown during my time here, much to his delight. I don't know how they're so big when he only feeds me one meal a day. Pain radiates across my chest, but I stifle my cries, unwilling to give him the satisfaction. "You're a stupid bitch who never learns. Lucky for you I like teaching lessons."

He shoves my face into the icy water, and I try not to panic, knowing from experience it gets me nowhere. Water fills my orifices, and my cheeks feel like they might burst from holding my breath. Thanks to swim lessons, I can hold my breath longer than the average person, but there are limits, and I have reached mine now. Despite my resolve, I thrash about as panic rushes in, and I'm struggling to breathe.

Carlo presses my face down farther in the water, only hauling me up when it feels like I'm drawing my last breath. He's laughing as he pulls my head up and I'm gasping, sucking in greedy lungsful of air. "You will submit to me, Noemi Cabrini. You will obey my every command like a trained little pussy. The only other option is death, and it won't be a pleasant one."

Right now, death would be welcome because I just want this torture to end.

. . .

"*Mia amata.* Sweetheart, you're scaring me." Massimo is rubbing my arms as I come to, horrified to discover I'm shaking all over and close to giving the game away.

"Sorry," I croak, clearing my throat as I force my body to stop trembling. I prayed I was strong enough to do this, but now I'm not so sure. I should have taken the Valium Nicolina gave me, but I wanted to be in full control of my faculties.

"What is it? You looked like you'd seen a ghost, and you completely zoned out." Concern is splayed across his face, and I don't know what emotions he witnessed on my face when I was out of it, but it's enough to coax me to get a grip. I know he'll need an explanation, and it needs to be a good one.

While I can't give him the full truth, I can give him most of it.

"It's the fountain," I say, turning to look at it. "It is similar to the one at the Conti house. When I didn't behave, Paulo would drag me out to it, in the dead of night, when no one was close enough to hear my screams, and dunk my head in the icy water over and over until my throat was raw, my lungs were burning, and all the fight had left my body."

"Fuck." Setting the cake box on the back seat, he hauls me over into his lap and wraps his arms around me. "He was a cruel prick, and he's lucky he's dead because I want to burn the bastard alive."

"I wanted to go to the Olympics," I admit. "I loved swimming, and I was good, but he took that from me too. Now, I can't even take a bath let alone get in a pool. Every time I do, it feels like I'm drowning." I bury my head in his shoulder as he presses kisses into my hair.

"He took so much from you, but you survived, and you're so strong. As much as he took, he enabled you to take something too."

I wonder what he would think knowing it was his family who did this to me. If he finds out, what will it do to him?

"We can go home," he offers after another few minutes when my trembling still hasn't subsided. "I'll tell Mama you have a bug."

As much as I'm tempted, I'm here now. I need to get this over and done with. Maybe, in a weird way, this might help. I lift my head. "I don't want to go home. Just give me another few minutes to compose myself."

Emotion glitters in his eyes as he gently holds my chin. "Are you sure, *mia amata*?"

"I'm sure."

He places a feather-soft kiss to my lips that is infinitely tender. "You are so strong and brave." Lifting my arm, he brings my wrist to his mouth. "I am not worthy of you." His lips brush against the sensitive flesh at my wrist, eliciting a whole new rake of tremors. This time, they are the good kind.

"You're worthy," I tell him, meaning it. I hold on to him as I focus on my breathing, inhaling and exhaling as I cajole my body into relaxing.

When I feel composed, I ease out of his arms and back into my seat. I grab the cake box and eyeball my husband. "I'm okay now."

"Stay there," he says with his hand on the door handle. "Let me come get you."

I use the extra few seconds to give myself a silent pep talk, reminding myself I can't fall apart and clue them in to my identity. I am a little concerned Eleanora might remember me if she sees me back in their surroundings. However, I think it's a long shot. It was clear by her demeanor back then that she was heavily traumatized and using drugs and booze to cope. Most days when she came down to deliver my one daily meal, she seemed out of it.

Massimo opens my door and reaches for me, lifting me down by my hips. He closes the door and kisses me, circling his arm around my shoulders and holding me tight. Warmth creeps into my chilled bones, and I lean against him as we walk past the hideous fountain. "I always hated that monstrosity," he says, noting where my gaze has strayed. "I'll get it taken away."

"You don't have to do that."

He stops walking, turning me in his arms. He tilts my chin up. "It's nothing, and you're everything. You're my wife, and I don't want you having flashbacks every time we visit my mother. She won't care."

Tears well in my eyes. Massimo is extremely good with small meaningful gestures and so thoughtful. Is he right? Is Nic? Has fate pushed us together because he is what I need to truly leave my past behind? How ironic is that? "Thank you." I stretch up to kiss him. "You're pretty good at this husband stuff."

"I have the most amazing, most gorgeous wife. She makes it easy to be a good husband to her."

I laugh. "We both know that is far from the truth, but I'll take it."

I clutch Massimo's hand in my free hand and hold the cake box in the other as we follow the surly butler through the house toward the rear of the property.

It's not how I remember it. It's been completely redecorated. The dull wallpaper and dark wood paneling have been replaced as has the old carpet with the crown pattern. In its place are light-colored walls and varnished hardwood floors, and all the doors have been sanded and stained a brighter color. The ornate chandeliers overhead are the same, as is the sweeping double staircase we passed a couple of minutes ago. It too has been sanded a lighter color, and the creepy old family paintings have been replaced with modern artwork.

The butler leads us outside to a vast stone patio situated in front of a large pool. Beyond the pool lies an exquisite rose garden I'm sure wasn't there before. To the right of it is a greenhouse and what appears to be a vegetable garden. On the left is the orchard I remember.

Carlo used to let me loose out here sometimes, when his family wasn't around, purely to taunt me. He would give me ten minutes to escape, before he'd hunt me down. It was cruel because there was no way I was ever getting off these vast grounds, but every time he started the game, I played it. Pushing my weak limbs as fast as they would go as I raced through the orchard toward the driveway and the illusive promise of freedom.

Massimo squeezes my hand as we walk toward his mother, and I snap out of my head. It's a beautiful day. The sun is beating down upon us, casting shimmery rays over the crystal clear water of the pool. Floral scents waft through the air mixing with fragrant pungent fruity smells. The aroma of freshly baked bread has my mouth watering and my tummy rumbling. I couldn't stomach any food before we left, but now I need sustenance to give me the strength to survive this ordeal.

Massimo's mother stands as we approach, smiling nervously as she clutches a napkin in her hands. The circular table is shaded from the hot August sun by a wide umbrella. It's set for lunch, and a bottle of champagne is chilling in an ice bucket at the side. Massimo lets go of me to hug his mother, kissing both her cheeks. "You look good, Mama. Well rested."

She smiles softly, her gaze adoring as she stares up at her son. She looks so petite, fragile, and thin against her strong, sturdy son. Massimo reaches for my hand, tugging me back into his side. "Catarina baked you an apple cake," he says, encouraging me with his eyes.

I force a fake smile on my face as I pass the box to a woman who had the power to save me yet did nothing. "I hope you like it. It was my father's favorite." That's no lie. Natalia Mazzone used to bake it for him. He liked it so much he asked her for the recipe to give to my mother. Their marriage was already on shaky ground by then, and my mother was not predisposed to do anything nice for her husband. So, I was the one who baked him the cake. Every Saturday for months before I was kidnapped.

She pries the lid off and inhales the cake. "It smells delicious. Thank you." Her voice is soft and timid like her smile.

"You're welcome."

Lifting her head, she inspects my face with an intensity that scares me a little. I hold my ground, keeping a smile plastered on my face. "It looks like marriage is agreeing with you," she finally says, after a few beats of tense silence.

"It is," I truthfully reply, glancing up at Massimo. "Your son is definitely growing on me."

Chapter Twenty-Eight

Catarina

"Is Gabe joining us?" Massimo asks as he pulls out a chair for me to sit.

His mother shakes her head. "He is furniture shopping for his new home." A veil of sadness washes over her features.

"Massimo explained that Gabe is moving out. I'm sure you will miss him," I say as a young woman dressed in a white uniform pours three glasses of champagne.

"I will," she quietly replies, looking to Massimo as the woman hands her a flute. Massimo subtly nods, and I wonder what that is about.

"It must get lonely in this big house all by yourself," I add, wanting to draw this woman into conversation. I want to get a read on her. I smile at the young woman as she hands me a flute, mouthing "thank you." I hate being waited on by servants, but it's something I've had to get used to. All the important *mafioso* families have a host of staff to attend to their every whim.

"It does but it's not like I have a choice. This is my sons' ancestral home. It's been in the Greco family for generations."

Massimo frowns, setting his flute down. "You don't have to live here, Mama. We can find you a smaller place if you like."

"What would you do with the house?" She leans back as another woman sets a plate down in front of her.

Massimo shrugs, nodding as the woman sets a plate of chicken salad in front of him. "We can burn it, for all I care."

"Massimo!" She gasps. "You don't mean that!"

"I haven't given it much consideration, but let's get real, Ma. This house holds no happy memories for you, me, or Gabe. Why should we hold on to it?"

The two women retreat inside after ensuring we have everything we need.

"It's the done thing," she quietly replies, looking down at her lap.

"We could tear it down and rebuild a new house. One to your specifications. That way you don't have to lose access to your gardens." My husband turns to me as I cut up pieces of my chargrilled chicken. "Mama is an avid gardener." He sweeps his hand in the direction of the gardens behind the pool. "Practically everything you see there was planted by her."

"It's very impressive," I admit.

"Thank you." She peeks at me from behind thin lashes. "It was my one indulgence after my husband died."

I don't miss how Massimo's jaw tenses at the mention of his father. "Maximo wouldn't let Mama tend to the gardens when he was alive," he explains, angrily cutting up his chicken. "He said it was beneath her to do work the help was paid to do."

"Massimo, you shouldn't say such things about your papa."

"Why not?" Massimo levels a stern look in his mother's direction. "It's the truth."

"It's family business, and you should not speak of these things in front of others."

Massimo's fork clangs to the table. "Catarina is my *wife*, Mother. She's *family*. I won't hide the truth from her. I may have to keep up a front in public, but in private, I will speak however I please about that asshole sperm donor."

This moment cements it.

There is no way I am harming a hair on my husband's head.

Which means I have to find a way to make peace with the fact I can't harm Gabriele or his mother either.

She visibly flinches, seeming to cower into herself. "I don't like to talk about it," she whispers, and her hands shake around her knife and fork. "Please, Massimo."

His anger evaporates as quickly as it came on. "I'm not here to upset you, Mama, but don't ask me to hide things from my wife."

"I don't see what good could come of talking about the past," she quietly says, putting her silverware down and clutching her flute in trembling hands. "Let's just have a nice lunch and talk about other things." She drains her champagne in one go, instantly reaching for the bottle to refill her glass.

Massimo's Adam's apple bobs in his throat, and his fingers grip his silverware tight. I slide my hand under the table and squeeze his thigh. Lowering one hand, he threads his fingers in mine and holds me tight.

"You too seem closer than at the wedding," she says, and I detect a hint of jealousy and some other emotion behind her words.

"We worked things out," Massimo says, never taking his eyes from mine.

I kiss his cheek before withdrawing my hand and returning to my lunch. I eyeball his mother, pinning her with a pleasant smile as I say, "You were in an arranged marriage too. I'm sure you understand it's challenging at the start."

"My marriage was nothing like yours," she hisses with a fire that has been lacking in her dialogue to date.

"Mother." Massimo's tone is firm. "Catarina was only making an observation."

She gulps back more champagne, seeming to have abandoned her food. Judging how her clothes hang off her skeletal frame, I'm guessing she's more accustomed to liquid lunches. "I apologize, Catarina," she says, looking dutifully sorry. "I was married to Maximo at eighteen. He was considerably older than me, and he wasn't kind."

"I'm sorry." I find I genuinely am. I could tell by their behavior that was the case, but I wasn't sure if it had always been like that. She spent a lifetime married to that prick. I endured his perversions for a short period of time, and they still haunt me. It goes some way toward explaining her actions, but is it enough to excuse it?

"My first marriage was like that," I explain, "and it wasn't a pleasant experience. I would not wish that on any other woman, but unfortunately it is all too common in our world. One of the reasons I wanted to become a donna was so I can help to change some of the archaic rules. Women should be free to marry who they want."

"Yet you married for business not love." She arches a brow as she drains her second glass of champagne. Massimo and I have only taken a few sips of our first glass. "That's hardly a ringing endorsement for change."

Massimo opens his mouth to speak, but I silence him with a pointed stare. I don't need him to defend me, and I don't want him to have to take sides.

"I can't effect change unless I'm in a position to do it, and it was still my choice to marry your son. No one forced me into it. Our marriage was strategic, for both of us, but we genuinely like one another, and we are committed to making it work."

"I wasn't forced into it either, Mama." Massimo slides his arm around the back of my chair. "Gabe asked me to do it, and I said no—until I met Catarina. This isn't common knowledge, but we met before, and there was an immediate chemistry. I married her willingly, and I'm happy to call her my wife." He leans in and kisses me, and I have never felt more cherished or more supported than I do in this moment.

"Well, that's great," she says, sounding like it's anything but. "I'm pleased for you." She offers us a tight smile before reaching for the champagne bottle again.

"Mama, don't you think that's enough?" Massimo levels her with a look. "You should eat. The salad is good."

She immediately puts the bottle down and picks up her silverware. I eat my salad as an uncomfortable silence settles around us. After a few minutes, she excuses herself to go to the bathroom.

Massimo sighs when she is out of earshot, rubbing a hand across the back of his neck.

"Are you okay?" I ask, rubbing his thigh.

"I worry about her," he supplies, finishing his champagne and reaching for the bottle of sparkling water. "I can only imagine what you must think of her," he adds, looking into my eyes. "Don't judge her too harshly. She has had a hard life. My father never loved her. She was a breeding machine, and the rest of the time, he abused her. He fed her a diet of alcohol and pills to keep her firmly under his control. After Maximo died, Gabe and I got her into rehab. She doesn't take prescription meds anymore, but the drinking is still a bit of a problem."

"Why don't you ban all alcohol from the house and forbid the staff from buying any?"

"We tried that, but she is sneaky, and she always finds a way." He chews slowly on the last piece of chicken. "Gabe and I do a lot for her, but at the end of the day, she's a grown woman. She is fragile, and she relies on us a lot, but we can't tell her what to do. We won't control her like that. We encourage her with her garden, and she likes sewing tapestries."

I noticed a few framed on the walls and wondered if it was her work.

"We try to encourage her to make good choices when it comes to booze, but she is lonely and lost since papa died. He ruled over every aspect of her life. Telling her what to wear, what to eat, who to socialize with. He had her so terrorized she barely spoke whenever he was around or whenever we left the house. She has improved since his death, but she will never fully recover. The damage is too deep-seated."

As a woman who has suffered severe trauma, I feel her pain, but I still can't find it in my heart to forgive her.

Eleanora returns, and the young women appear to cut the cake and pour coffee. "This is delicious, Catarina." She fixes me with her first genuine smile of the day. "I wish I could bake, but I'm terrible in the kitchen."

"Really?" I'm surprised. "Massimo is such a good cook. I thought for sure he must have learned his kitchen skills from you."

"Our housekeeper taught him. Where she failed with me, she succeeded with my youngest son." Blatant adoration coasts over her face, and it's clear she loves her son deeply.

That may be her only saving grace.

"I lived abroad from the time I graduated high school," Massimo adds in between devouring my cake. "I had to learn to fend for myself. Getting takeout all the time wasn't an option. I like to stay fit and healthy, and that meant cooking my own meals."

I still don't know what he was doing abroad. He has explained he attended Oxford for four years and then he spent two years with mercenaries, but what was he doing the other ten years? I know he has traveled a lot, and the gossips would have you believe he was off philandering, but I'm not buying it. Not since I got to know the man. He likes to keep busy, and he's smart. Too fucking smart to waste ten years absently traveling the globe in the pursuit of pleasure.

No, my husband was abroad for a reason, and I intend to find out what.

Excusing myself to go to the bathroom, I leave Massimo with his mother and head indoors. As soon as I'm inside the house, I slip off my high heels and pad quietly in the direction of the dungeon. I know the entrance is just under the staircase on the left.

Perhaps it's reckless to want to revisit my torture chamber, but I need to see it.

I'm struggling to hold on to the person I have become.

My identity has changed many times in my thirty-four-years on this planet. I left Noemi Cabrini behind the day I was rescued from this house. My stepfather wanted me to remain incognito, so he didn't protest when I insisted on being called Catarina after I moved to Vegas. It is my middle name and it was my paternal grandmother's first name.

I became Catarina Conti when I married Paulo, and now, I'm Catarina Greco.

It all started here, and now it feels like everything has come full circle.

Maybe seeing my prison will help me to reconcile the woman I am today and the woman I am becoming. Initially, I thought coming here would strengthen my resolve in terms of my goals, but my growing feelings for Massimo have already confirmed that aspect of my plans. I haven't confided in anyone yet, but I'm resolute when it comes to my husband.

I can't hurt him. I won't.

More than that, I need him. He empowers me in a lot of ways, and my gut is telling me he's on my side. I don't know if he still will be when he discovers the truth.

And he will.

Because I can't remain married to him and keep all the secrets I'm keeping.

Massimo deserves the truth.

I reach the door under the stairs and draw in a sharp breath. A tight pain spreads across my chest as nausea swims up my throat and knots twist in my stomach. My hand curls around the door handle as memories surge to the forefront of my mind. Invisible pain has a vise-grip around my heart, squeezing and squeezing until it feels like the organ no longer exists.

"You don't have to do this," an imaginary voice whispers in my ear.

"I do," I silently reply. I need to remind myself of how far I have come. I need physical evidence proving how strong I am and that I will stay the course, even if some of my plans are changing.

Without stopping to think about it anymore, I twist the handle, relieved to find the door unlocked. Opening it, I step inside and descend the stairs with my heart thumping loudly behind my rib cage.

My legs feel like Jell-O as I grip the new wrought iron handrail, putting one wobbly leg in front of another as I move closer and closer to my own personal hell. My breath oozes out in panicked spurts the lower I go, and all the blood in my veins has been replaced with ice. When my bare feet hit the bottom, a deluge of memories swarms my mind, and I squeeze my eyes shut to ward them off. I can't let them overtake me. I won't make it out of here unscathed if I do.

The purpose of today is not to drown under the dearth of memories. I want this to serve as a reminder of what I can achieve when I put my mind to it.

I flick the switch, plunging the room into bright light, and gasp at the scene before me.

Gone are the rough stone walls, bare asphalt ingrained with the stains of human misery, and the heavy cage I used to call home. I look up and there are no hooks and chains dangling from the ceiling. The old steel table and matching shelving unit that housed a myriad of different torture tools and devices is long gone.

The space has been completely transformed. Bright spotlights are dotted all over the ceiling, showcasing the gorgeous indoor garden. Water trickles down a feature in the center of the room, cascading in soft streams like an indoor waterfall. At the base is a small pool of stones. The feature transects the room. On both sides are a multitude of wooden flower beds, brimming with colorful plants. A seating area is tucked into the side with a large comfy couch adorned with an abundance of cushions. Two ornate tables with cast iron legs and marble-tiled tops reside at either end.

One wall has been replaced with floor-to-ceiling windows, letting light in from outside. The sloped side of the garden gives rise to a pretty garden full of colorful shrubs with a gazebo in the middle. It's not visible from the pool area, confirming Eleanora's green thumb extends all over the grounds.

The basement is completely transformed, and it's hard to connect my memories of this hellhole with the way it looks now. Tears stream down my face as I stand mute, drinking it all in as a host of conflicting emotions lay siege to me. The tinkling sounds of water merge with my soft sobs as I expunge some of those emotions. My vision is blurry, the image altering, flashing back to how it used to look and how it looks now.

It's like looking into a crystal ball and seeing flashes of my past while catching my reflection in the glass.

Right now, I'm both of those people. The broken little girl whose dreams were shattered the day a monster stole her from the light. And the woman who clawed her way back from the brink of death, clinging to her anger and her pain, vowing to exact justice from all those who wronged her.

I wonder what that image will look like weeks, months, and years from now. How will my past and present shape my future? I have many challenges ahead and few answers. It feels like everything I thought I knew was wrong, and I'm struggling to adapt my plans in a way that will still give me my vengeance.

The only thing I know for sure is I am a survivor.

I survived this place.

I survived the monsters who ruled over it and me.

And I will continue surviving.

No matter what obstacle blocks my path, I will overcome it.

Because the only constant that matters is survival.

Chapter Twenty-Nine

Catarina

"It's like my past has been erased," I pant, thrusting my arm out and punching the bag with lethal force. "How fucking dare that woman take it from me!" I swing another punch as Renzo holds the bag steady. "She can't overlay hell by turning it into a place of beauty. One part of me understands why she would do it, but it's not that simple. You can't just forget what happened in that dungeon, and I'm not naïve to believe I was the only young girl that monster caged down there."

I throw more jabs at the bag before wiping the sweat glistening on my brow. "It's all a fucking lie," I seethe, bouncing on my feet as I alternate punches from my left to right fist. "That bitch can't erase the role she played by covering it up with pretty flowers."

"Are you even sure it was Eleanora that did it?" he asks, calling time as he steps out from behind the bag, offering me a bottle of water.

I dab at my sweat-slickened face and neck with my towel before uncapping the water and taking a healthy glug. "It could have been any of them, or perhaps it was a team effort," I admit. It's been over seven years since Maximo and Primo were killed in the warehouse bombing in Chicago. I assume the garden was only erected after their deaths when Gabriele and Massimo were both old enough to have been involved.

"I think this reeks of something your husband and his brother would do to help their precious mama come to terms with the role she played. Covering over the dungeon means it no longer serves as a reminder of what she failed to do. What they all failed to do," he hisses, an ugly sneer forming on his face. "Let's face it. Carlo may have died while you were held a prisoner, but Maximo and Primo were monsters too. I bet they continued his work. They all know what went on down there. They are all equally guilty whether by action or inaction."

I lean over the bar of the treadmill and hang my head. I'm grateful the owner opened the boxing gym early so I could train with Renzo alone. I don't need an audience to witness me unraveling.

Since I visited with Massimo's mother, I have been in turmoil, my emotions veering all over the place. I expected, *hoped*, to find some kind of closure by revisiting the dungeon, and it's been denied to me.

Anger is my overriding emotion these past few days.

Anger at having something else taken from me.

But I can't deny there is relief too.

Mostly I'm confused and scared.

I'm floundering, clinging to the woman I used to be and unsure of the woman I'm becoming.

It's a strange place to be—this in-between space where I'm caught between the broken girl of my past, the vengeful woman of my present, and the unknown entity of my future.

What I do know is I'm tired. Tired of hurting. Tired of everything being a battle. Tired of always shouldering the responsibility.

Massimo has given me a glimpse into a life where it isn't all pain and fighting and struggling.

Where I'm not alone.

And I like it.

I like that vision of the future.

The dream of a life where I could be happy and not have to carry all the burden.

But is it enough to forgo all I have planned? Can I ever truly let it go? Can I really trust him?

"You are getting too close to him. He is changing you," Renzo says as if he can read my mind.

If anyone could, I suppose it would be him.

He is the one person who knows me the most, but he can't begin to understand the complexities of my heart when I can't fathom them myself.

I have never let myself truly feel before. Not since I was a kid. I purposely shut off my emotions so I didn't continue to feel the pain.

Now it feels like I'm drowning under a deluge of feelings I am ill-equipped to handle.

"He is," I truthfully admit, knocking back more water.

"You need to take them out now before you get more involved. We can stage it like an accident."

Pain rattles my chest and stabs me through the heart, like a hundred tiny daggers embedding deep. "No." I vigorously shake my head. "No one touches Massimo or his family."

Renzo's eyes widen. "Fucking hell, Ree-ree. Please don't tell me you're in love with him?"

"You haven't called me that in years," I softly say, the nickname recalling many fond memories.

Disappointment flickers over his hardened features. "Don't deflect, my donna. You are letting him get to you. Don't forget he's the enemy, and he's playing you as much as you are playing him. Whatever you think you're feeling for him, and vice versa, it isn't true."

"Don't try to tell me how I'm feeling, Ren!" I snap because he is way out of line.

"This is not like you!" He grips my shoulders. "He's distracting you with sex and sweet words."

I shove him away, instantly enraged. "You don't know shit about what we share."

"I know sex has always been difficult for you because of what his fucking family did to you!" His voice elevates a few notches, and I'm this close to knocking him flat on his ass.

"What you and I shared is in the past, and I've come a long way since then."

He scrubs a hand over his prickly jawline, sighing deeply. "I know you have. I've been the one watching as you fuck your way through important made men."

I punch him in the face, and he lets me. "Fuck you. How dare you cast judgment on me. How dare you use your intimate knowledge of me to make bullshit statements."

He wipes at the blood trickling from his nose before holding up a palm. "I apologize. That was way out of line, and I shouldn't have gone there. Please forgive me." He looks sincere, but I don't know what's going on with him anymore.

"What is this really about, Ren? I know there's something you're not telling me."

"I'm worried about you." He steps close, peering deep into my eyes. "Everything has the potential to turn to shit, and when you should be holding steadfast, you are backtracking."

"It is smart to hold back for now. We don't know what the Russians are planning. Anton is avoiding my calls, and I know something is afoot. We need to focus on doubling and tripling our security, and I want to fire our IT guy and recruit somebody new. He's exposed us recently, and that's not good enough."

"I'll get on it."

"Dario is handling it. I want you to work with him on reassigning some of our men. Add extra protection on all of us, and put extra bodies on the street. Tell them to keep their ears to the ground for intel. We can't afford for the Russians to attack when we are still settling things on the streets. I'll talk with O'Hara."

"I'm on it." Placing his hand on my lower back, he steers us toward the changing area.

"No one is to hurt Massimo or his family," I warn, drilling him with a sharp look. "That's an order, Renzo."

A muscle ticks in his jaw. "You're the boss," he says through gritted teeth, adding, "I hope you know what you're doing."

That makes two of us.

"I think you should come completely clean," Nic says an hour later as we chat over breakfast in a quirky retro diner a few blocks from Central Park.

"Absolutely not." Dario dabs the corners of his mouth with a napkin as he pushes his empty plate away. "It is far too risky. I know you want to trust him, and I honestly don't think he's a bad guy. It's blatantly obvious from the way he looks at you that his feelings are genuine."

"But?" I say, knowing there is one.

"There is much we don't know about him."

"I agree, which is why I'm personally following him to Berlin."

Massimo mentioned last night he has to leave tomorrow to conduct some business in Berlin. He said he would be away two to three days max. He was deliberately vague when I pushed for more details, and I know whatever secret he is hiding is tangled up with this.

If I'm going to confess everything to him—and that's where my head and my heart are leading me—I need to know what he's hiding.

"Renzo is going to go crazy when he discovers you left without telling him or taking him with you," Dario supplies, holding up his mug for a refill when the waitress reappears at our table.

"I don't trust him not to kill my husband," I admit, voicing my fears out loud.

"He won't go against your orders," Dario attempts to reassure me.

"I hope not because I really don't want to have to kill the man who has been by my side for more than twenty years."

"I think he's having marital problems," Nic supplies.

I cock my head to the side as I stir my coffee. "Why would you say that?"

Nic and Dario exchange a look and one of their silent communications.

"Tell me," I say before taking a sip of my coffee.

"You know he's trying to get Maria to relocate to the city, but she's digging her heels in. She seems hellbent on staying in Philly."

"I can't say I blame her. The kids are settled in school, and her friends and family are there." Renzo met Maria a few months after he permanently relocated to Philly from Vegas. He knocked her up fast, and they had a quickie wedding a few months before their eldest son was born. She is Philly born and raised, and I think Renzo has zero chance of getting her to move.

"I suspect there is more to it," Nic says, pursing her lips. "I have no proof," she adds without me having to ask the question. "Just call it a sixth sense."

"You think that's what's distracting him?"

Dario shrugs. "Possibly. Renzo has been very quiet with me lately. I think it's probably a combination of him worrying about you and stressing over this situation with his wife and family."

"All the more reason for him to stay here while I travel to Berlin."

"When are you leaving?" Nic asks.

"I have the jet lined up for eight a.m."

"I'll have my decoy hat ready and waiting," she says over a grin.

"Thank you. I know it's a pain in the ass, but hopefully we won't have to do this for much longer."

Massimo

"Are you sure it's not a trap?" Fiero asks as I watch him pack a bag from the doorway of his bedroom.

"I have done my research, and it seems legit, but it could be."

"It's odd timing. You've never had to do anything like this with any other job. Assholes attempt to hit our factory and you get recalled to complete one final job. It makes me nervous. I don't like it."

"Neither do I, but Jacobi says this guy won't fucking quit until he finds out who killed his brother. We don't need any loose ends right now. I'll take care of him while you meet with Juan Pablo in Cali, and we'll reconvene in a few days."

He zips up his bag and slings it over his shoulder. "Stay safe, brother."

"You too." We slap each other on the back before going our separate ways.

I text Jacobi as I exit the rooftop building in Mitte, striding briskly along busy Berlin streets, keen to escape the area before the cops show up. I punch out a message confirming the mission is complete and the target is down. Smashing my burner cell under my boot, I toss the fragmented parts in the nearest trash can and make my way toward the closest U-Bahn station.

I get off the subway twenty minutes later in Friedrichshain, heading on foot the rest of the way to my apartment in Kreuzberg. Nightfall is descending, and the streets are less crowded here. Most Berliners are inside the eclectic mix of hippy bars and chic restaurants or spending their Thursday night at home with family or friends.

I have apartments stashed all over Europe, but my Berlin place is my favorite. Kreuzberg is just outside the main tourist center, and it has an authentic vibe I love. It's local and central without the transparent commercialism of the more popular areas of the city.

I'm surveying my surroundings as I round the block toward my apartment and contemplating ordering takeout when a person with a familiar voice shouts a warning at me. "Get down, Massimo!"

Despite my utter confusion, I don't hesitate to heed my wife's words, dropping to the ground as a succession of shots whizz over my head. I'm like a sitting duck out in the open, but I'm fucked if I'm going to lie on the ground while some dickhead takes potshots at me.

Whipping my Glock from my waistband, I spring to my feet as more shots dart by, embedding in the wall behind me. Pain flares across my upper left arm as Catarina yells more commands for me to stay down. I fire blindly across the road in the direction of the gunfire, which appears to be coming from behind a large white van parked illegally at the curb.

My wife comes into view as she surges forward, running up the sidewalk, followed by Ezio and Ricardo and two other guys I don't know. The traffic lights change, and a stream of traffic flows down the road, slightly blocking my view. A short, stumpy guy I recognize takes off running as my wife gives chase. Frustrated I have no clear view to take him down, I run along my side of the street, ignoring the blood pouring down my arm and the horrified looks of the young couple I race past as I hurry to keep pace with my wife.

Chapter Thirty

Massimo

The traffic clears, and I run across the road as I watch Catarina throw herself at Ivanov from behind, tackling him to the ground. I reach the curb in time to see her plunge a syringe into his neck, and his limbs turn instantly floppy.

"What the hell?" I ask, my eyes seeking hers as she checks the sniper's pulse before turning to her men, blatantly ignoring me. "Carry him to Massimo's apartment. Do it fast and discreetly," she adds, quickly scanning the street as she straightens up. It's empty except for that couple I passed who are staring at us with ill-concealed shock. "Handle that," she tells Ezio. "Make sure they understand how dangerous it would be for them to breathe a word about what happened here."

"Catarina," I snap through gritted teeth. "What the fuck is going on?"

"You got shot," she says, still avoiding answering the goddamn question. Concern splays across her face as she tugs my shirt from my pants, cuts a strip from the end of it with a knife, and ties it firmly around my injury. "Let's get you cleaned up, find out what this idiot knows, and then get the hell out of Dodge."

Sounds like a smart plan. "You can't deflect forever," I say, giving up for now. We need to get off the streets ASAP. I can question her when we're safe.

She grabs my good arm, checking left and right before guiding me across the road. "There will be time for questions and answers later. Right now, we need to deal with this situation." She leads the way to my apartment building, stepping aside to allow me to input the code. It hasn't escaped my notice she knows where I live.

The door automatically glides open, and she nods for Ricardo to enter first, quickly followed by the two goons carrying a comatose Ivanov Rankov. There is no lobby or receptionist in this building—one of the reasons I purchased an apartment here. However, there *is* a camera—another reason I bought in this building. I will need to take care of that, along with the street cameras outside.

The men scout the area while I stare at my wife. She looks hot, dressed all in black, and I know it's her signature battle look while white is the armor she wears to the boardroom, so to speak. "You were following me," I surmise as she threads her fingers through mine and steers me into my own damn building.

"Yes. I knew you were hiding something." A beatific smile graces her delectable mouth. "I had no idea it was this. You have truly taken me by surprise and it's not often people do that. I have so many questions."

Her eyes gleam with excitement, and it does something funny to my insides to not only have her readily accept this part of my life but to get a kick out of it too. "As do I."

She nods, squeezing my hand. "We will have time to share our truths later."

The elevator pings as it arrives, and we pile inside first with the men following. The instant the doors close, I smash my lips against my wife's, kissing her hard. "Thank you," I say, reluctantly tearing myself away. "You saved my life."

"I did, didn't I?" Her expression is a strange mix of confused, relieved, and happy.

"If you hadn't followed me, I would be dead."

"How can you say that so calmly?"

"In my line of work, you accept it as a hazard of the job."

"How long have you been a contract killer?" she asks, and I sense every set of ears listening to our conversation.

"I told you I trained with some mercenaries for two years after I graduated Oxford. When I left Nepal, I did a couple of years with the US Army. Spent time honing my skills in Afghanistan and Iraq and creating a stellar reputation I used when I left to establish myself as a sniper for hire. I recently retired on my eight-year-anniversary to focus on my family duties."

"Yet you came back here to do a job," she says as the doors open and the men check the hallway leading to my apartment.

It's clear, and we walk behind them as we talk. "I had no choice. I was told the brother of the man who was my last hit was coming for me. I did my research, and it seemed legit, but I knew there was a chance it was a trap."

"They lured you back to Berlin to take you out," she correctly surmises as I unlock the door to my apartment. "Why?"

"That's the million-dollar question." I open the door, letting the men do a sweep of the apartment before allowing my wife to step foot inside.

They take Ivanov to the living room while Catarina trails me to the bathroom. I remove the medical repair kit from the wall-mounted cabinet, gritting my teeth as pain shoots up and down my arm. Blood drips between my fingers onto the cool white tile.

"Sit," she commands, taking the kit from my hand and gently pushing me down on the closed toilet seat. Using her knife, she cuts my shirt away, leaving me bare-chested. "I wondered how a playboy adventurer got so many scars on his body," she says, dabbing rubbing alcohol against a cotton pad. "Guess I have that answer now."

"Another hazard of the job." I hiss as she cleans the wound. "This isn't the first time someone has tried to take me out. The Ghost is legendary, and there are always assholes trying to steal my crown." I grind my teeth and dig my nails into my thigh as she carefully prods around my wound.

"I heard you were called The Ghost in our circles because you were always missing from the action, and it's widely known you rarely attended *mafioso* events. I had also heard of the contract killer, The Ghost, but never in a million years would I have thought you were one and the same." She peers into my wound, frowning as she says, "It's fucking genius. Hiding in plain sight."

I flash her a grin as pride swarms my chest. "I always got a big kick out of that. No one would've suspected it was me, and I have kept my identity a closely guarded secret. I am known within sniper circles, but there is a code of honor among us. We never divulge real names to outsiders."

"It's not just a flesh wound," she says, telling me something I already know. "I can see the bullet."

"You'll have to pull it out." I extract the tweezers and hand them to her. "If that won't work, use your fingers."

"It will hurt like hell."

"I know." I pull out the miniature whiskey bottle and down the entire thing. "Do it. I don't have time to go to my doctor, and I can't risk showing up at a hospital."

She gives me no warning before digging her fingers into my wound and rummaging around. I bite down so hard on my lip I draw blood. "Fuck," I hiss through clenched teeth as I dig my nails harder into my thigh.

She doesn't talk, solely focused on her work. "Got it," she says a couple of minutes later as more blood streams from my arm.

"Thank fuck," I say as she tosses the shell into the sink. She hands me a second mini bottle, but I shake my head. "I'll take some pain meds. I need to keep my wits about me to interrogate that prick, cover our tracks, and get us out of here."

"I have a plane ready and waiting, and I can organize transport to the private airfield as soon as we're ready to leave."

"Good." I nod. "Tell your pilot to log a route to London."

"Why London?" She uses a wet cloth to wipe all the blood from my arm.

"The guy who set this up is there on business right now. I need to pay Jacobi a little visit."

"He'll know you're coming as soon as he discovers the dickhead in the living room failed."

"Which is why I'm sending a crew to detain him for me." I look at the wound. "Can you clean that again so I can stitch it?" She cleans it thoroughly and holds my skin together as I stitch it up.

"You've done that before," she says when I'm finished.

"Countless times. One of the skills I picked up in the army." I stand, kicking the remnants of my shirt aside as I pull her into me and kiss her. "I should be mad at you for spying on me and following me when it was obvious it was dangerous, but I can't find it in me to hold on to my anger."

"I'm glad I was here, and that I chose not to trail you on the metro. To drive straight to your apartment. If I hadn't, I might not have realized what was happening in time to stop it." A shudder works its way through her. "You nearly died, Massimo." Her warm hand lands on my chest. "It scared me."

"I'm alive." I kiss her. "You're alive." I kiss her again. "And I'm going to ensure that's the way it stays."

"*We* are," she corrects me, and I smile.

It's the first time she has said we are a team and fully meant it.

This is a turning point.

The moment where we lower all defenses and properly open up.

I need to deal with the vermin first and then have a real heart-to-heart with my wife.

"Yes, *we* are," I say. Vulnerability splays across her face, but it's laced with the kind of happiness I rarely see on her face. "That makes you happy."

"It does," she quietly admits, resting her head on my shoulder.

I wrap my good arm around her and rest my chin on her head.

"Don't ever do that again, Massimo. I couldn't bear it if anything happened to you."

"Ditto, *mia amata*, and from now on it's us against the world."

"Yes." She lifts her chin up. "I like that."

"No more secrets," I warn.

She gulps nervously, but her face is earnest and her eyes resolute when she looks at me. "No more secrets."

"Talk, asshole," Catarina says a half hour later when Ivanov has woken from whatever substance she injected in him. His arms and legs are tied to a chair in the middle of my living room. Our men guard the windows and the front door, checking for any sign of people coming for us.

"Who is this bitch?" Ivanov snarls, glaring at me.

I punch him in the face. "Disrespect my wife again, and I'll drag this out forever."

"Your *wife*?" He spews the word like it's poison. "Now that makes a lot of sense."

I press my knife to his neck. "Start talking. Who put the hit out on me?"

Ivanov is not the sharpest shooter or the most brilliant strategist—as evidenced by his piss-poor execution of this job—but he's not dumb enough to attempt to come after me himself. None of my ex-colleagues would. I imagine there were celebratory parties when I announced my retirement. Which is why it makes no sense that anyone would come after me. Unless someone is afraid I might divulge important information.

"I don't know. Jacobi contacted me with the job. He said the client wanted to remain anonymous, but they requested me personally." He gloats, like the stupid prick he is. Ivanov isn't the most sought-after killer, so that can only mean it's personal. I have my suspicions, but I'd rather not voice them until I've confronted Jacobi.

"If I find out you're lying, I will gut every member of your family."

Ivanov comes from a large family, and I have the intel to get close to them if I need to. I have background information on every client, every colleague, and competitor and their families and friends. I have personally created each dossier with some support from Allante and Fiero. If there is one thing the *mafioso* world has taught me, it's that you always need insurance.

I show him the pictures on my phone, and his face pales. "I will ask you one more time. Who set me up?"

"I swear I don't know. I swear it was Jacobi who hired me. He's the one with the answers." His Adam's apple bobs in his throat. "I should have said no. My bad, but I swear if you let me go I'll never cross paths with you again."

"You have no honor, Ivanov." I trail my knife lower on his body. "It's no wonder the Bratva expelled you." I push the knife in slowly, driving it deeper and deeper into his heart as his eyeballs bulge, sweat beads on his brow, and he spews obscenities at me in his native Russian. When the light dies in his eyes, I extract my knife, wiping it on the front of his shirt.

"What now?" Catarina asks.

"I'll call a cleanup crew, hack into the necessary security systems to wipe all the cameras of evidence, line my London guys up to haul Jacobi in, and then we'll get the fuck out of here."

Chapter Thirty-One

Catarina

"Enough! I've had enough!" Jacobi croaks, pleading with Massimo from behind bloodshot swollen eyes. Massimo's UK contacts had the traitor good and trussed up when we arrived at the derelict warehouse fifteen miles outside London city center a short while ago. Massimo has been working him over for the past twenty minutes, knowing he would break eventually. "I'll tell you what you want to know, but I need protection. For me and my family." Jacobi's English is good though his accent is distinctly German.

"You're not in any position to make demands." Massimo punches him in the stomach before stepping back to survey his handiwork.

Jacobi is a mess.

His face is all beat up. Blood oozes from his nose, trickling down over his chin onto his bare chest. His body is hunched forward in the chair, as much as is possible with the bindings around his wrists and legs. Bruising litters his chest and stomach, and it's clear my husband has broken at least a couple of his ribs. Thin lacerations cover his skin from the flesh wounds Massimo inflicted with my knife.

I would have gladly volunteered to torture the man who helped to set up the hit on my husband—especially with Massimo injured—but I know this is something he needs to do himself.

"Then kill me," Jacobi pants, spitting blood onto the floor. "Kill me, and you'll have no one to inform you if they try to take out another hit." His breath filters out in exaggerated breaths, and I can tell it's a struggle for him to speak. "Let me live, and I'll tell you who did this. I'll be your eyes and ears on the ground. I'll let you know if they come for you again. In return, you provide protection for me and my family. Those are my terms."

Massimo looks up at me, and I nod. It seems, on this occasion, it's in our interests to keep this asshole alive. Massimo yanks Jacobi's head back painfully, staring deep into his eyes. "If you double-cross me, I will kill everyone you love, and I won't make it slow." Removing his cell from his pocket, Massimo opens a photo file, flipping through shots of what I presume are Jacobi's family and friends.

Jacobi's fear is palpable. "I'm on your side. I swear," he blurts. "If we have a deal, I'm your man."

"I'll sweeten the deal," Massimo says, releasing Jacobi from his grip. "If anyone comes offering a hit on me, my wife, Fiero Maltese, my family, or anyone connected with me or my loved ones, you come straight to me. I'll pay you double for the intel to take the challenger out."

It's a smart call because men like this communicate in cold hard cash.

"I agree," Jacobi says, nodding in obvious relief.

Massimo stands in front of the prisoner, exuding lethal power from every pore. "Tell me what I need to know."

"It was the Russians," Jacobi says without any further hesitation. All the blood drains from my face at the revelation. "The order came via a contact in Moscow, but the initial kill order came from New York."

Anton did this to send me a warning.

I will rip him to shreds for it.

"This is my fault," I admit in a low voice, eyeballing my husband. I won't shy away from the truth. Not when my mistakes are threatening his life.

Massimo frowns as he turns away from Jacobi to face me. "Why would you say that?"

I press my lips to his ear. "I've been partners with the Bratva for the past four years. Anton Smirnov is my contact point in the US. I lied when I said the Colombians were my main supplier."

Shock comingles with concern on his handsome face. "Jesus, Rina. Don't say the Russians are?"

I speak in hushed tones so only Massimo and Jacobi can hear me. "They are, but things have changed in the past few weeks. Their motives are no longer clear to me, and my own plans have altered. They tried to pressure me. I pushed back, and this is obviously a warning."

"I wouldn't be so sure." Massimo scrubs a hand over his jaw, looking deep in thought. After a few silent beats, he turns to Jacobi again. "I need to take *Pakhan* Smirnov out. I can't do it and risk eyeballs on me. It can't lead back to the Italian *mafioso*. It would bring too much heat. Can you ask The Terminator to do it? Five mil for a clean job."

"No." I step forward, placing my hand on Massimo's lower back. "That could still lead back to you. I have a better idea. Smirnov is the Russian ambassador to New York. Any hint of scandal would ruin his political career and force Moscow to bring him back in disgrace. I have intel we can use."

Massimo's eyes light up in acknowledgment. "Insurance."

I nod. "Insurance."

"Fuck, this is why we make such a great team." His lips collide with mine in a searing-hot kiss I feel all the way to my toes. It's far too brief for my liking, but there's always later.

"I'll get it set up," I continue. "He'll be recalled, and Moscow can do the dirty work for us." There is no way they'll let him live, but I can't find it in me to care.

He tried to have my husband killed to send me a message.

Fuck him.

He deserves everything coming his way.

"They will replace him," Massimo supplies.

"I know, but at least it removes the immediate threat, and it gives us time to regroup and prepare." It leaves me with an even greater problem, but I'll find a solution. I always do.

Massimo calls one of his men in from outside where they were keeping a lookout. "Untie him," he instructs, pointing at Jacobi. "Help him get cleaned up, and then take him to one of the safe houses."

"I'll need to return home tomorrow to avoid suspicion," Jacobi says, flexing his wrists as the bindings fall to the floor.

"I'll arrange it along with protection in Berlin."

Jacobi stands on wobbly legs, clutching the arm of the chair to steady himself. "I won't renege on our deal. I know how to pick the winning side, and I know I'm looking at it." His gaze dances between Massimo and me.

I truly hope he's right.

I am listening to the cryptic one-sided phone conversation Massimo is having with Fiero with interest as we travel in a blacked-out Land Rover from the warehouse to Massimo's home in Belgravia, an affluent part of London where lots of wealthy professionals and celebrities live.

"Okay. We'll see you in the morning," he says before ending the call.

"Fiero is coming here?"

Massimo nods before taking my hand and pulling me in closer to his side. "There is more you don't know." He brushes a few stray strands of hair off my face as we drive past busy London streets. It's early evening and still bright out.

"Tell me."

He tilts my chin up with one finger. "Did you mean what you said about no more secrets and us being a true team?"

I don't hesitate to reply. "I meant every word."

"Then we can stop with the surveillance bullshit," he says. I arch a brow, and he chuckles. "Sweetheart, Nicolina is parading all over New

York in a black wig and a white suit while we're across the other side of the ocean. If I didn't already know you were using her as a decoy, this little trip would've let the cat out of the bag."

"You left me no choice after you sicced your PI on me." I drag my fingers through the thick growth on his chin and cheeks. "How about you call your hound off, and I'll tell Nic to ditch the wig?"

"Deal." He kisses the corner of my mouth as I lower my hands to my lap. "You need to get rid of your IT guy. He's not working for you."

"I already had Dario fire him."

"Good. I will set up your IT systems so they're impenetrable."

"You will?"

He flashes me that cocky grin I used to hate but now secretly love. "I have an honors degree in computer science from Oxford, and I upgrade my skills on a continual basis. There isn't much I can't do with technology."

"Okay. I will instruct Dario to work with you on the handover. I suspect my guy was bought by Anton, but it would be nice to verify that. He's not the only enemy I've picked up over the years, so I could be wrong." My gut tells me I'm not, but I would like to be sure.

"I'll get to the root of it."

"Thank you."

"Look at us," he says, grinning wildly. "Working together so amicably. We're not just compatible in the bedroom."

I roll my eyes though I don't disagree. "If you're so fucking sure of yourself, perhaps you'll have a solution to my supply-chain issue because I won't be receiving any more shipments from the Russians. Perhaps O'Hara can entice the Paraguayans to come back," I muse, tapping a finger against my lips. "They were pissed at being cut out."

Massimo shakes his head as a wolfish grin slips over his gorgeous mouth.

"I fail to see what's so amusing. If The Commission finds out I was working with the Russians, they will kill me before Anton gets a chance."

The humor instantly glides off his handsome features. "No one is killing you, and The Commission will never find out you were working with the Bratva. They can't know you had an arrangement with their archenemy." He slides his uninjured arm around my shoulders and kisses the top of my head in a super sweet gesture that brings tears to my eyes. "Who else knows about the Russians?"

"Not many. I knew to keep this contained. My inner circle and a few of my trusted men are in the know. The crew who handles the shipping and distribution all believe the supply comes from Colombia."

"What about DiPietro?" he asks through clenched teeth.

I shake my head. "Cruz doesn't know." My stepfather hates the Bratva, and there is a lot of bad blood between the Russians and Vegas. I couldn't risk telling Anais or Cruz for fear one of them would let that intel slip to Saverio or that Cruz might let it slip to his father who sits on The Commission.

Relief floods his features. "Good. I don't trust that motherfucker."

There is much bad blood between my husband and my brother-in-law too. I don't relish revealing that news. Massimo will not be pleased to discover he's connected to his rival via marriage now. "I don't know how to resolve this issue." I rub a hand along the back of my neck, unknotting the kinks I find there. "My Colombian contact doesn't have the resources to supply the quantities I need. I can locate other suppliers, but it'll take time. I don't see how I can secure a new partner on short notice before supplies dwindle, drawing the attention of Don Mazzone and the others. They still don't fully trust me, and this won't go down well when they find out."

"I have the perfect solution." Massimo peers into my eyes, drilling down deep, though I'm unsure what he is looking for.

I hold his stare, shielding nothing in my gaze, and I'm curious to hear what he has to suggest.

His chest heaves and his features soften as he says, "Fiero and I have a production plant in Colombia and a shipping hub on Staten Island. Our long-term aim is to become the main supplier to all Italian American families, ending reliance on outsiders for this part of the business."

My mouth hangs open as I stare at him in shock. "What?" I splutter, sure I must have misheard him.

Pride gleams in his eyes. "Our fathers didn't believe in us, but we always believed in ourselves. We planned all this as naïve seventeen-year-olds from my bedroom, and everything we have done from the time we left the US has been working toward this goal."

"Jesus, Massimo. That's incredible. I had no idea. Even Rinascita doesn't lead back to you. Dario went digging after we discovered the waterfront property, and he couldn't find any direct links to you or Maltese, but I'm guessing you own both?" He nods, and I'm so impressed. "However you set it up, you are well hidden."

"It was the only way to do this. Fiero studied business. I studied IT. Both of us trained with the mercenaries. We wanted to ensure we had all the skills necessary to pull this off."

"What's the end goal?"

"To be the most powerful dons in the whole of the US. To control The Commission after Bennett steps down. To truly bring our organization into the twenty-first century. To modernize it and make it a formidable force."

"Ben has done a lot, but it's not enough."

"It's not, but he has paved the way for us." A muscle ticks in his jaw. "My father may be dead, but I like to think he will see what I've become. I like to think of him burning in the flames of hell regretting the day he turned his back on me. Fiero's father is refusing to agree to a timeline for when he will succeed him as heir. When we reveal everything, he'll have no choice but to concede. I can't wait for Fiero to stick it to his asshole old man."

"Please make sure I'm there to witness it."

"Of course, *mia amata*. You won't be excluded from anything." He cocks his head to one side. "I suspect Fiero and I aren't alone in our goals. Am I right?" His fingers sweep across my cheeks.

"I want to be the first female president of The Commission," I truthfully reply because there is no holding back now.

"We can rule together. We will be the most powerful couple in the entire US."

Adrenaline courses through my veins as butterflies swoop into my belly in nervous anticipation, but I'm excited too. I can alter my plans and still come out on top.

If you'd asked me a few months ago if I would ever give up my plans or share my crown, I would have shot you for daring to ask. Now, I can't think of anything I would like more than reigning with Massimo at my side. But we are a long way from achieving that goal, and there is much depending on it. "Only if we can cover my tracks and rewrite history."

"We will make this work to our advantage." He lifts my fingers to his lips. He dots kisses across the back of my hand. "In a way, the Russians have done us a favor. If this hadn't happened, our goals wouldn't have aligned. It feels like this is meant to be."

"Are you always this philosophical?"

"I like to call it romantic." He nuzzles his face in my neck, and my body instantly comes alive.

"I like it whatever label is applied," I admit, reluctantly forcing his head up. "But there is more you don't know, Massimo." Smothering my fear, I stare him straight in the face, hoping he will still feel the same way about me after I fess up. "I need to tell you everything."

Chapter Thirty-Two

Catarina

Nerves fire at me from all directions, and I gulp over the painful lump in my throat as I summon the courage I require to tell him the truth.

"You're shaking," he says in a gentle tone, immediately pulling me into his chest and wrapping his arms around me.

"I'm scared," I whisper.

"Don't be."

Lifting my head, I swim in his gorgeous forest-green eyes. "I'm scared you won't want anything to do with me when you know it all."

"*Mia amata.*" He plants a feather-soft kiss on my lips. "I know you have lied to me about who you are. Like I know you didn't partner with the Russians for no reason. I know you came to New York with powerful ambitions. I have already accepted these things. The details won't change how I feel about you."

"They might." I bite on the inside of my mouth, more terrified than I've been in a long time. The thought of losing Massimo cuts me up inside.

"Some might say it's crazy because we haven't known one another long enough, but I know you're a good person. Whatever is driving this justifies your actions. I won't judge you for that."

"It involves—"

"Not now," he says, placing his fingers to my lips and cutting me off mid-sentence. "We have had enough of the heavy for one day. I want to take you out tonight. To show you some of London. When we get home, you can tell me everything."

I wonder if he has any inkling of what I'm about to say, if he's just picking up on my scattered emotions, or if he truly doesn't want to deal with it right now. Either way, I'm relieved. It's cowardly of me to admit it and to accept his pronouncement, but I'm not going to argue. I am going to enjoy tonight with my husband and pretend like I don't have a care in the world. Like Russians aren't gunning for our heads. Like The Commission won't do the same if they find out what I've done. Like Renzo won't be disgusted with me when he finds out I have no intention of killing Massimo or his family or Don Mazzone. "Okay."

He kisses me tenderly, at odds with how he normally kisses me. "I would like to know one thing now."

Butterflies pound in my chest as I wait for him to continue.

"What was Lee Chang going to say before you killed him?"

"I suspect he figured out that I set him up. I staged everything between him and the Paraguayans so I had an in to approach The Commission. They needed to need me. I created an opportunity when one didn't naturally present itself."

He surprises me by chuckling. "You are even more devious than I suspected."

"You have no idea the lengths I have gone to, to further my aims. There isn't much I wouldn't do or haven't done."

"I like that you go after what you want and you don't let anything stop you. Fiero and me have the same bullish approach to life. I will never criticize you for that." He winds his fingers through my hair as the car pulls up in front of large black gates. "Besides, The Triad didn't have to take the bait. If they'd been honorable, they wouldn't have stabbed us in the back. What happened to them isn't on you, *mia amata*. It's totally on them."

I'm not sure I agree, even if there is some merit to his assessment.

I rest my head on his chest as Massimo's driver talks to the security guard at the gate, handing him some papers. Ricardo is in the passenger seat, but Ezio and the rest of my men are staying at a hotel tonight. My husband assured me his London townhouse is highly secure; it's on the only private road in Belgravia and behind high gates with restricted access unless you are an owner or a registered guest. His home has the best security money can buy and comes with the added benefit of a panic room.

I trust I am safe here.

I trust Massimo to ensure my protection for the duration of our visit.

I just...trust him, period.

"This is magnificent," I say, pivoting my head to look up at the ornate high ceilings with patterned coving in the elegant hall, after he has given me a whistlestop tour of his gorgeous home. It's set over three floors, and it has every luxury known to mankind. "Though my favorite is the rooftop terrace." It's a vast space with a dining area, enclosed garden, and a comfortable seating area with a TV. "Or maybe it's the marble bathrooms."

Contentment clings to him like a shroud as he reaches for me. Even injured, he can't seem to stop touching me. Nor I him. I rest my palms on his chest, smiling up at him, like I don't have a shit ton of problems waiting in the wings.

"This is one of my favorite homes. I love my Berlin apartment too, and my villa on the Amalfi Coast is another favorite. I can't wait until I get to show them all to you."

"I haven't traveled much outside the US," I admit. "I never had time for vacations, and most all of my business is conducted in the States."

"That is something I will enjoy rectifying. We can be busy and still make time for vacations." He rubs his nose against mine. "In fact, I think that should be a rule."

"Donna Greco. Mr. Greco." Ricardo slips into the hallway from the living room. "Apologies for interrupting, but I wanted to let you know the restaurant called to confirm your booking for eight thirty."

"Perfect, thanks," Massimo says. "And, Ric? Please call me by my first name. Mr. Greco makes me sound like an old fart."

Ricardo's lips twitch as I giggle. "As you wish, Massimo." He nods respectfully at both of us before retreating to the living room and giving us our privacy.

I sense a thawing between Ricardo and Ezio and my husband, and I'm glad to see it. Dario and Nic have warmed to him too. Renzo will be a problem, but he's the least of my worries right now.

"Only two weeks until you will be Don Greco," I remind him. "Are you looking forward to it?"

"I am." He tweaks my nose. "Everything is coming full circle, and I'm excited for the next phase of my life." He clasps my face in his hands. "Having you by my side is the cherry on top. I didn't see you coming until you snuck up on me five years ago and wormed your way into my heart." His eyes glisten with sincerity, and with every word out of his mouth, I fall deeper and deeper. "Now I can hardly imagine what my life was like before you."

"I know what you mean." I rest my hand on his palm on my face.

He pecks my lips before releasing my face and grabbing my ass, pulling me in closer. "I have big plans for you tonight, Mrs. Greco." I yelp as he squeezes my butt hard. "I had some things delivered for you from Harvey Nichols earlier. They're in the closet in our room. I need to make a couple of phone calls before I get changed." He kisses me again, like he just can't help himself, and I melt against him like it's my singular mission in life. "Get ready, and I'll join you shortly. I thought we could have cocktails on the terrace before we leave for the restaurant."

"Sounds like a plan." Wrapping my arms carefully around him, I hug him close. "Thank you for always being so thoughtful." Honestly, he's incredible. We were fleeing Berlin with minimal time to spare, and he still somehow found an opening to organize dinner and an outfit for me. "I still don't feel worthy of you."

"No woman has ever been more worthy. Trust me."

I run my fingers through the scruff on his face, smiling and feeling giddy, like a teenager in the first flush of love. "Do you need more pain meds?" I ask, as I extract myself from his arms and notice him wincing a little.

He shakes his head. "I'm fine. The pain is manageable, but I'll take some with me if that makes you happier."

"It does. I don't like the thought of you in pain."

"I have a strong pain threshold."

"As do I." Unspoken words hover in the space between us, but I won't let them ruin tonight. "I'm going to get ready." I stretch up on tiptoes and kiss him before dragging myself away to the master suite.

"You look ravishing in gold." Massimo tells me when I step out of the bathroom an hour later wearing the stunning designer dress he bought me. It clings to my curves in all the right places, and it's the perfect length, billowing softly around my ankles. "Like a true queen," he adds, handing me a box.

"You are spoiling me too much." I gasp as I remove the gorgeous diamond pendant necklace and lift my hair for him to put it on.

"There is no such thing, and get used to it, Mrs. Greco, because I haven't even begun."

"You look rather dashing," I say in a mock upper-crust English accent, letting my hands roam over his hard body encased in a sharply cut black suit. His shirt is black, and his tie is the same gold as my dress. "I'd do you," I add, making a slow perusal over the length of him.

"You'll definitely be doing me later," he purrs, biting my earlobe as he kneads my ass through my dress. "I'm already so fucking hard just looking at you in that dress." Taking my hand, he places it on his crotch. "Feel what you do to me?"

"I'm drenched," I say, rubbing my fingers up and down his shaft through his dress pants. "My pussy is swollen with need for your cock." He curses under his breath, and I inwardly high-five myself as I step back. "But it will only heighten the anticipation." I offer him my hand. "I believe my husband promised to show me London. I'm ready for him to make good on that promise."

"I will never go back on my word." He laces his fingers in mine. "And *that's* a promise."

I have the most wonderful date with my husband, and he stays true to his word—wining and dining me at a Michelin-starred restaurant before taking me on an open-top bus to see the main sights under cover of darkness. Massimo bought out the entire tour bus so we are alone, and he arranged for champagne to be served while we drive around London. The bus stops at The London Eye, and we have a capsule to ourselves as we enjoy a thirty-minute ride over the River Thames, showcasing London from a different perspective. I'm overcome with emotion, and I readily drop to my knees to show Massimo my appreciation. It doesn't hurt that he quickly returns the favor.

By the time we return to his house, I'm high on champagne and unending love for my husband. It encourages me to be brave. *He* encourages me to be brave. With Massimo, I feel like I can overcome any obstacle. "Take a bath with me?" I ask as we climb the spiral staircase toward the master bedroom.

His eyes drill into mine, instantly seeing all he needs to see. "I would love nothing more."

In the bathroom, he unzips me, and I help him out of his suit in silence as we strip naked while the water fills the giant tub. It's built into the alcove under the window, offering a gorgeous view outside. Massimo lights a row of candles on the window ledge and dims the overhead lights while I pour some scented oils into the tub. I'm on edge as I stare at the softly dappled water, fighting bad memories while clinging to my strength. Carefully, Massimo comes up behind me, cradling me in his arms with my back pressed to his chest. "We don't have to do this now. You have nothing to prove to me, *mia amata*."

"I do to myself." I angle my head back so I can look into his eyes. "I want to leave the past in the past, Massimo. I want to move forward with my life instead of always looking back. This is the start."

"I'll be with you every step of the way."

His words bring tears to my eyes, and I'm beginning to believe fate has indeed led me to him.

Chapter Thirty-Three

Catarina

"Are you okay?" Massimo asks from his position behind me in the tub.

"Yes," I truthfully reply, leaning back against him, careful not to touch his injured arm. "This is nice." I had a moment of profound horror getting into the tub, but the safety of my husband's arms around me helped to overcome the terror. Now, the water laps gently over my skin in rolling motions, and warmth sinks bone-deep. Jasmine and lavender tickle my nostrils, and the flickering candles cast romantic shadows on the walls.

"It is." Brushing my hair aside, he presses a lingering kiss to my neck. "I have never taken a bath with anyone before."

"Neither have I."

"I like claiming your firsts."

"I like claiming yours." I can almost taste his smile.

"I want to wash you," he says, but I shake my head, straightening up and turning around so I'm straddling his hips. "It's my turn to take care of you." I reach for the washcloth and dip it into the water to wet it.

"I had ulterior motives." He flashes me a wicked grin, and my pussy clenches with need.

"Who says I don't?" I bat my eyelashes in a deliberate manner, and he laughs.

"You are truly magnificent," I say, pouring bodywash onto the cloth and soaping it up. "Keeping my hands off you is becoming problematic." I rub the cloth around his neck and drag it down over his chest, washing him in slow circular motions.

"I fail to see the problem." He grabs my hips, tracing circles on my puckered skin. "When you tell me, will you explain how you got these scars?"

"Yes, but not now." I run the cloth lower, silently fist pumping the air when his abs tighten and roll at my touch and his erection solidifies under my ass. Rolling my hips, I gently grind on top of him, moaning as his hands glide up my body and his fingers flick at my nipples.

"Obviously not now." He grins as he kneads my breasts, his caress softer than usual.

"I want to fuck you," I say when my hand reaches his dick. Circling my fingers around his shaft, I stroke him the way he likes it.

"Ride me, *regina*. Take your cock and impale yourself on it."

"Holy fuck." I'm liquid lust as I abandon the cloth to the water and position myself over his straining cock. "Your dirty talk is such a turn-on."

"I know, sweetheart." Folding his hand around the back of my neck, he brings my face to his and kisses me passionately as I slowly slide down his length. We moan as I situate myself fully before sitting back to appreciate the moment. Massimo looks down to where we are joined, and his eyes are so dark with desire they're almost pitch-black. "I know what you need, *mia amata*, more than you realize it yourself."

Now I can appreciate the truth in his words.

"Tonight, we are going to go slow, but gradually you are going to relinquish control to me, and you're going to love it."

I am learning, when it comes to this man, there isn't much I can deny him, irrespective of my fears. "What if I don't want to go slow tonight?" I challenge him as I lift up and slam back down on his dick.

"Tough shit, babe." He slaps my ass, and my pussy quivers. "I need to make love to you tonight. I want to worship every inch of your skin all night long." He thrusts his hips upward, rotating his pelvis in a slow circular motion that has me seeing stars. "I want you to feel like a queen because you're *my* queen. You rule every part of me, and I willingly hand it over." His eyes bore into mine as we rock against one another, our hips pivoting in sync, in a deliciously languid fashion. But it's the raw emotion in his eyes that undoes me. The naked look of love in his gaze is unmistakable, and my heart beats in unison with his as the sentiment sends me over the edge, skyrocketing into a blissful orgasm that seems to last forever.

It's the first of many that night as my husband again makes good on his word. After the bath, we dry one another, and he carries me to bed where he makes love to me over and over until we both fall into an exhausted heap.

I wake before him the next morning, enveloped in his arms and a deep sense of contentment I have never felt before. Rays of golden sunshine filter into the room through the cracks in the blinds, and it mirrors my mood. Even the thought of our impending conversation can't put a dent in it.

I leave my husband sleeping, grab his shirt off the floor, and pad downstairs to make him breakfast. I love cooking for him, and he's always vocal in his appreciation.

My exploration in the refrigerator and pantry doesn't yield much of a bounty. I wish there were supplies to make fresh bread because Massimo loves it, but I can't find any flour. Massimo clearly had someone drop off groceries, but the pickings are slim. I settle on eggs and bacon I'll serve with the English crumpets I find in the bread box.

I am squeezing fresh oranges into a glass jug when the sound of approaching footsteps has me reaching for the knife at my thigh. I curse under my breath when I realize I came downstairs bare. Fiero enters the kitchen the same second I remember we are safe here and no one can get past the security at the gate or the front door.

"Will that stretch to three?" he asks, jerking his head at the skillet where the bacon is frying.

"I can make it work." I haven't had many opportunities to talk with Massimo's best friend, and I want to get to know him. "Was Massimo expecting you this early?"

He nods. "Where is he?" He scrubs a hand over his prickly jawline. "Please tell me you haven't killed him and stashed his body in the garden." A grin spreads over his mouth as he takes in the knotty bird's nest on my head and my state of semi-dress. "I would really hate to have to kill you."

I pick up the knife I used to cut the oranges. "I'm pretty skilled when it comes to gutting men who piss me off." I wave the knife at his face. "And I'm not much of a morning person, so I'd be very careful what you say to me next."

He chuckles, dropping a duffel bag on the ground before heading toward the refrigerator. "I saw what you did to your first husband. I'd say your knife skills are top notch."

"Massimo is sleeping," I finally admit as I watch Fiero open the fridge door, remove a carton of milk, and chug it back. "We have glasses."

"I'm thirsty," he says after knocking back half the carton. He smirks, wearing a milk mustache like he's five.

"And clearly not house trained," I deadpan, setting the jug of juice aside.

He wipes his hand across his mouth. "I'm a messy bastard," he admits, hopping up onto a stool as I retrieve more bacon and eggs from the fridge. "Ask Massimo. We tried living together a few times and almost came to blows on a daily basis."

"Massimo is a neat freak."

"He is. How's that working out for you?" Fiero claws a hand through his blond hair while fighting a yawn.

"I'm a neat freak too, so it's working out pretty well."

"Good." The humor fades from his face. "I'm actually glad we got this chance to talk alone."

I place a few more slices of bacon in the skillet and lower the heat. Turning around, I level him with a serious look. "Ask what you need to ask." I grip the counter behind me as I eyeball Massimo's best friend, holding my head up high.

"I need to know if you're playing him. If it's all fake. He has real feelings for you, and if you hurt him, I will hunt you down and make you pay."

Massimo is lucky to have Fiero in his corner, and I respect the hell out of him for challenging me like this. "I am not playing him, and I have genuine feelings for him too." He narrows his eyes on me, and I feel naked under his intrusive stare. "I had an agenda from the start, but that has changed. Massimo is changing me, and I want to change."

"Does he know this?"

"He knows some of it, and I'll be filling him in on the rest when we get back to New York."

He continues drilling me with that piercing stare of his, and I'm itching to move, to remove myself from the glare of his inspection, but I have never shied away from a challenge, and I won't start now. Keeping my cool, I stare back at him, reminding myself he is loyal to Massimo and doing this because he cares. "I see so much pain in your eyes," he says in a softer tone a few minutes later, finally releasing me from his intense inspection. "Guilt, shame, and fear too," he adds, like he somehow has a hotline to my innermost thoughts.

It freaks me out more than a little.

"Takes one to know one," I fire back.

"Yes, it does." He props his elbows on the marble counter of the island unit and heaves out a tired sigh. "I have battled those emotions my entire life."

"Massimo confided a little about your fathers growing up, and I have met yours. He's a complete pig."

"I'm not sure the word exists to adequately describe Roberto Maltese." He cocks his head to the side. "What was your father like?"

Pain stabs me in the chest, like every time I remember my daddy. "He was my everything until he failed to protect me and died before I could pay him back for abandoning me."

Compassion splays across his face, and I'm guessing he believes I'm talking about Paulo Conti. "It seems the three of us have that in common," he says after a few silent beats.

I nod as I turn around and flip the slow-cooking bacon over.

"Did he tell you about my brother?"

I glance over my shoulder. "How your father appointed him as his heir apparent in your stead?"

His jaw tenses. "I was rebellious growing up, but that didn't mean I was unambitious or disinterested in the future mapped out for me. I wanted to enjoy myself before responsibility meant I couldn't. My father never took the time to understand me. He didn't even discuss it with me before he announced Zumo was his desired heir. My brother was the dutiful son to my rebel heart. He was so fucking smart and so good." He wets his lips as a pained expression crosses his face. "He died in the warehouse bombing." His eyes lift to mine. "Rightfully, that should have been me. Every day I carry the guilt of his death with me."

I turn around to face him. "Why? You didn't make the decision to instate Zumo as heir, and the bombing wasn't your fault. If anyone should feel guilt, it's your father. And the blame for what happened in that warehouse squarely lies with Stefano DeLuca and those who helped him that day."

"Massimo has told me the same. Countless times. It doesn't make the guilt or the shame go away. If I'd been less rebellious, my father wouldn't have removed me as heir and Zumo would still be alive."

"You can't know that for sure. Blaming yourself for events out of your control is futile, but I understand it more than most." I chew on the corner of my lip. "I carry a lot of baggage with me too." He nods in shared understanding. Angling my head to one side, I examine him more closely. Fiero is vastly different from the image that has been portrayed of him, same as Massimo. I think I'm beginning to figure him out. "You hide your pain behind humor and your playboy reputation," I surmise, seeing this complicated man in a new light.

"And you hide yours behind false smiles and power suits."

"But the rage constantly burns. The pain is always simmering beneath the surface."

"Yes. It never goes away," he agrees.

"Well, this is depressing as fuck," Massimo says, sauntering into the kitchen in a pair of low-hanging sweats, his statement confirming he heard at least the tail end of our conversation. He slaps Fiero on the back before pulling him into a hug.

I refocus on breakfast, cracking eggs into a bowl and whisking them with a fork. Heat crawls up my back as my husband comes up behind me, his big hands landing on my hips. "Good morning, *mia amata.*" His fingers creep up along the outer edge of my thigh, and I slap them away.

"Massimo." I warn him with my tone and my eyes. He chuckles, rocking his morning wood against my ass through the shirt of his I'm wearing.

"Jesus. You two are insatiable." Fiero smirks as I level him with a smug grin over my shoulder. Someone sounds envious, and it's nice to be on the other side of that emotion.

"My wife is sexy as hell, and I can't keep my hands off her," Massimo admits, twirling me around in his arms. "Not my problem you're a jealous fuck."

"I never thought I'd see the day, but I'm happy for you, man." His eyes drift to mine. "I'm happy for both of you. You're good together."

I think I've had my fill of emotional mushy stuff. "Go talk to your friend." I shove Massimo in Fiero's direction. "Let me make breakfast before it's burnt to a crisp."

Chapter Thirty-Four

Catarina

"When did you set up Rinascita?" I ask when we are in the air, heading back to the US in my private plane.

"When we were in college," Fiero replies, sipping a glass of bourbon from the seat across from us. Massimo explained he told Fiero everything while I was getting dressed and packed, so he knows I have been taken into their confidence. I expected it might cause some issues between the friends, but it didn't. Fiero trusts Massimo's judgment—and now me, by default.

"Fiero studied business but majored in financial investment. We invested most of our money while we were in college, and by the time we graduated, we had tripled our investment. We used some of the money to set up a real estate and property development business, under the Rinasciata brand, while we continued investing in the stock market. We bought and sold properties and sites all over Europe, and a few in the US, but we wanted to build our business quickly while remaining under the radar."

I guess that explains all the traveling they were doing, along with Massimo's contract-killing work.

"Over the years, our earnings soared from both endeavors which gave us the funding to move to the next phase of our plan," Massimo explains.

"We kept reinvesting and we bought up more real estate businesses, some tech and comms companies too," Fiero adds.

"And we established an import-export business, which is the legal front for the drugs operation, which is where the bulk of our income will come in the future."

"Is that why you built the waterfront property?"

They nod.

"We are moving all our operations there," Fiero confirms. "It will look completely legit while we smuggle drugs in under the nose of the authorities."

It's absolutely genius, and I am in awe of them. "I have got to hand it to you. That's some feat. There's no way The Commission can ignore what you bring to the table. I'm incredibly impressed."

"Think of what we can do when we combine our smarts and our talents. We will literally be unstoppable." Massimo presses a quick kiss to my lips.

"Provided we can maintain a hold of the compound in Cali," Fiero says.

"What does that mean?" I inquire, threading my fingers in Massimo's when he places his hand on my thigh.

"Someone attempted to attack the plant," Massimo explains. "Fiero went to check everything is okay."

"They didn't get far. We paid a small fortune to hire the best security on the ground in Cali, and ten percent of the profits go to Juan Pablo, our local manager, on top of the lucrative salary we pay him." Fiero stretches out his legs, crossing his feet at the ankles.

"Along with the house and car we purchased for him and the college trust funds we set up for his three kids." Massimo drains his whisky.

"He's too entrenched to betray you. That's good."

"Hopefully," Massimo says. "We would like to visit more regularly, to keep a closer eye on things, but we are stretched thin as it is."

I know how hard he works. "I can help. My operations run smoothly, and while it'll take some time to settle things in New York, especially with this Russian complication, after that, I will have some free time. I can visit the compound for you or handle some things here if you prefer."

"We need to sit down and work out what you could take over," Fiero says.

"We'll have roles for Dario and Nicolina too, if they want to take on additional responsibility. We should formally amalgamate our teams and our interests," Massimo says.

"That makes sense," Fiero agrees.

"What about Renzo?" I ask because we can't ignore the elephant in the room.

"I'm sorry, *mia amata*, but I don't trust the man. I want him nowhere near our operation, and I don't want you telling him anything we have discussed."

I swivel in my seat, the soft leather squelching under my ass. "He's my underboss, Massimo. I can't just cut him out."

Tension bleeds into the air.

"I know we need to talk when we get home, but tell me what it is about this guy that has you so loyal to him? Because all I see is a guy who fights you every step of the way."

I heave out a sigh as all the muscles in my back lock up. "It's not usually like that. It's complicated right now for reasons I don't fully understand yet."

"Which is why he can't be taken into our confidence." Fiero drills me with a sharp look. "We didn't bust our asses for years to have some dick ruin everything."

"Don't be so dramatic. Renzo won't ruin anything because he won't know anything. I give you my word." I hate lying to him, but I won't jeopardize what Fiero and Massimo have built, or what we're planning to build together. Not when Renzo is such a wildcard. When things settle with him, I will smooth things over so everyone gets along.

I have to hold on to that hope because I don't want to be backed into a corner and forced to make a choice.

A muscle clenches in my husband's jaw as he presses the button for the flight attendant. "You said you have never been in love, but I know there was something between you and him."

"I'll just take a nap." Fiero stands, clearly excusing himself to give us privacy. He leaves as the flight attendant approaches, and Massimo requests more drinks and food.

"It was brief and temporary," I say, not wanting to elaborate because then we'll end up having the conversation we need to have on this plane, and it's too suffocating to discuss it here.

"He loves you," Massimo says, accepting a fresh glass of whisky from the attendant. I drain my current drink, handing the empty glass to the woman as she places a new one on the table in front of me.

"Thank you." I wait for the attendant to leave before replying to my husband. "I don't think he loves me in that way. Maybe he did one time, but not anymore. He's devoted to his wife and his kids, and if what Nic says is true, he's going through some marital difficulties."

"If I had to guess, I'd say it's because his wife knows he still has feelings for you."

Irritation rattles my skull. "Don't make assumptions, Massimo. You know what's said about them."

"Help me to understand it then."

I palm his cheek. "My history with Renzo doesn't change who you are to me. You know that, right?"

He rubs my thigh. "I'm secure in our relationship, *mia amata*. I know what you mean to me and what I mean to you. I don't think you're in love with him. I'm just trying to understand where the loyalty is coming from."

"It's tied into what I have to tell you. Renzo has been in my life for a long time. He was there for me at a time when no one else was. I was broken. A shell of a person, and he was the only one in my life who cared enough to help me to heal. Renzo is the one who taught me how to fight and how to defend myself. He encouraged and supported me.

He drove me to my therapy sessions and fought battles for me when my mother was negligent, and my stepfather was demanding. He knew to keep his distance when I couldn't bear anyone to touch me and how to comfort me when I woke up screaming from nightmares induced by the horrors I had lived through."

I pause to draw a breath as a tight pain stretches across my chest. "Remembering who he is to me is bringing it all back, and it hurts. I was so damaged, Massimo. In so much pain and he helped to coax me back to life. I owe him so much. He helped me to find purpose, and yes, we were lovers for a time, but that was his way of helping me too." Shudders rack my body, and I'm chilled to the bone. "Sex was difficult for me back then. Intimacy is still hard for me." My voice chokes, and my chest feels like it might implode with the burst of emotion swelling inside me.

"It's okay." Massimo bundles me into his arms. "I didn't intend to upset you."

"I know that." My words are muffled against his chest.

The attendant leaves plates of food on the table and discreetly retreats. "The man you see now is not the man he has been to me. For so long, he was the only man I could trust completely. Things are changing between us. The trust is more brittle. I hate it. I hate I must keep things from him, but you're my husband. You're my priority." I set my hands on his chest as I peer into his eyes. "I am placing all my trust in you, like you have done with me, but please don't force me to choose between you and him. I will get to the bottom of what's going on and we'll find a way to make this right, because the thought of losing either of you from my life rips me apart inside, Massimo."

"You don't need to make any decisions now. If Renzo is truly on your side, and his actions are protective, I will take no issue with that." He dots kisses into my hair. "I just want to ensure you're safe. You're not the only one scared to lose in this marriage."

"I'm not going anywhere." I press a kiss to the underside of his jaw before lifting my head to look deep into his stunning eyes. "I'm committing to you, Massimo, in every conceivable way."

Emotion shines from his eyes as he clasps my face in his palms. "As I am." He claims my lips in a tender kiss. Pressing his brow against mine, he looks me straight in the eyes when he says, "I love you."

"I love you too." It's the most natural thing in the world to return those words.

We hold one another without speaking, and I wish I could wrap us up in a bubble and ignore the outside world. As I cling to my husband, I pray like I haven't prayed in years. Begging whoever is listening to make him understand. To not take him from me.

Chapter Thirty-Five

Catarina

"Shit." I press the call button on my phone, knowing it's futile because we're still in the air and I have no signal. Nothing happens, and I toss my cell back in my bag, agitated and concerned.

"What's wrong?" Massimo asks, leaning over my shoulder as we emerge from the bedroom. After Fiero took a nap, we commandeered the bedroom, making love before sleeping for a couple hours. Now we are making our descent into New York, and reality is calling.

"I have some missed calls from Renzo and Dario seconds before we took off. They didn't leave messages, so I don't know what it's about."

"We'll be landing soon." He steers me toward our seats. "It'll have to wait until then."

Renzo is waiting for us when we emerge from the jet twenty minutes later. His lips are pulled in a tight line, and his eyes are hard as he watches Massimo and me walk toward him holding hands. Fiero trails behind us, keeping a sharp eye on our surroundings.

"We have a situation," Renzo says in place of a normal greeting when we reach him. "I need to talk to you in private."

"Whatever you have to say can be said in front of my husband." I will be spilling the beans on everything when we get back to our house, and I'm done concealing things from Massimo. Cutting him and Fiero out now would be a piss-poor way of repaying their faith in me. They have put a lot on the line to confide their secrets. I owe them the same in return.

Renzo's eyes probe mine and his brow puckers. "This doesn't concern either of them." His jaw tightens while he blatantly ignores looking at Massimo or Fiero, and I'm officially done with his disrespect.

Whipping my knife out, I dart forward and press it under his chin. "Don't test me, Renzo. I'm the boss. When I give you an order, you comply."

"You don't want them hearing this." His eyes silently plead, and my resolve wavers. It's so hard to stay angry with Renzo when I look in his eyes and see the comfort and security I craved as a shattered teen.

But we are not those people anymore, and the power shifted between us a long time ago.

"They know about the Russians, and they will know everything else very soon," I say, withdrawing the knife and stepping back to create some space between us.

"No, Ree-ree. No!" He grips my arms. "You cannot trust him. He's a fucking Greco, for God's sake!"

"What the hell does that mean?" Massimo steps up behind me, placing a hand on my lower back, letting me know he's here for me.

"I will explain later," I say, angling my head to look up at him. Massimo nods, immediately trusting me, and my heart swells behind my rib cage. Tipping my chin down, I level my underboss with a warning look. "Tell me now, Renzo. Disobey me again and it'll be the last thing you do."

"You're making a mistake. You're—"

"You heard Donna Greco," Massimo says in a lethal tone, cutting Renzo off mid-sentence. "Explain what is so urgent, or I'll gladly punish you for disrespecting my wife and your boss."

Renzo clenches his fists and grinds his teeth before slowly exhaling. I see the fight go when it inevitably leaves his face. "The Russians have attacked Vegas. It's a mass slaughter, but Saverio got out, and he's gunning for you. The Russians purposely let it slip that you are working with the Bratva, and he's out for blood. He's blaming you for losing his territory again, and my intel says he's already on his way here."

"Of course, he is." I bark out a bitter laugh. "I may have played a part, but he's far from blameless. That lazy good-for-nothing bastard sat on his fat ass for years while I lined his pockets, took care of his daughter, and kept his streets orderly. How dare he come for me." Anger blazes from my eyes as I straighten up and pull out my cell. "Anton has officially declared war and shown his hand now."

"He wants you dead," Renzo says, articulating what we all now know.

"He wants both of us dead," Massimo adds. Shock renders on Renzo's face for a split second before it's gone.

"This ends tonight." I level Renzo with a pointed look. "I have waited long enough to have my revenge. Call Dario and tell him to send out the alert to all our men. We move on Saverio Salerno tonight."

Renzo casts a wary look behind me. "Are you sure you want to do this now?"

"Yes." I trail the tip of my knife over my fingers, already itching to spill Saverio's blood.

"What about Anais?" he asks.

"Anais will never know it was me. We can pin it on the Russians. Give The Commission another reason to hate them. Get our men ready, and meet me at Massimo's house in an hour so we can put an attack plan in place."

"*Our* house," Massimo corrects, stepping around me to eyeball Renzo. "Do we know which plane he's on?"

Renzo tosses him a curt nod before refocusing on me. "I have the intel we need to map out a strategy. He took to the air an hour ago, so we have four hours max to formulate a plan and execute it before he lands in the city."

"Bring everything with you to Long Island," I say, reaching back to take Massimo's hand. "Go now," I urge Renzo. "And keep me updated if necessary."

"I'm on it, my donna." He walks in the direction of his car while Ezio pulls my SUV out from the private parking garage.

Fiero and Massimo climb in the back with me. I wait until the privacy screen is up to speak, knowing they have plenty of questions after the conversation outside. "Saverio Salerno is my stepfather, and Anais DiPietro is my half-sister," I announce before they can ask me what's going on.

Shock splays across their faces as they stare at me. "I know she looks nothing like me. She takes after our mother while I take after my father." Except for my natural dark-blonde hair, which is the only hint of my mother in my looks.

I clear my throat and settle back in my seat as the car glides forward. Massimo folds his hand around mine, and I appreciate the support. "She was young when I moved to Vegas with my mother." I stare briefly out the window as we drive away from the private airstrip. "I spent the first fourteen years of my life in New York," I admit, watching their facial expressions become somewhat wary. "My father was killed by Angelo Mazzone, my brother had died shortly before that, and my mother had nothing binding her to the city, so we left. I didn't know I had a sister. Anais was the result of a fling my mother had with Saverio. Apparently, she met him on a girls' trip to Vegas. She didn't come home for over a year. I was too young to fully understand. My father told me my aunt was ill and my mother was taking care of her."

I hold Massimo's hand tight. "I don't know if he knew where she was, but I'm guessing he knew something. After she returned home, things were not good between them. My mom told me later that she got pregnant on purpose because she was already unhappy with her life."

"She thought Salerno was her golden ticket," Fiero surmises, and I nod.

"Except he has no regard for women," Massimo supplies. "His reputation is notorious in our circles. He fucks women like it's his God-given right. His birthright."

"He's a disgusting pig."

Massimo stiffens alongside me. "Did he ever—"

"No." I cut him off with a shudder. "He never touched me. He took Mom and me in, but it was under sufferance. Mom threatened to fight him for custody of Anais, and he was too frightened to turn her away, even if she wouldn't have had a legal leg to stand on by then. He adored his little *principessa* too much to risk losing her."

"More than her mother if Anais ended up living with Saverio," Fiero says, leaning forward on his elbows with an intrigued look on his face.

I bob my head. "It killed my mother to know he wanted the baby and not her, but he paid her handsomely for signing her rights away. He was not pleased when she reappeared on his doorstep a few years later with a damaged moody teenager in tow." I glance anxiously at Massimo. He knows now I was damaged before I met Paulo, and I wonder if he will connect the dots before I tell him.

"Yet he let you stay until you turned eighteen," Massimo says, gentling his tone and squeezing my hand. "Even after he murdered your mother." I see he is connecting the dots to this part of the puzzle. It is widely known within the *mafioso* that Salerno murdered Anais's mother when she was a young child.

"Only because Anais was very attached to me. She loved me like a mother because I was the one taking care of her. My mom was too busy trying to get knocked up by Saverio again and attempting to convince him to marry her to have any time for either of her daughters."

"No wonder you are close," Massimo murmurs, rubbing circles on the back of my hand with his thumb.

"I wish we were, but the truth is, we aren't all that close anymore. It's not for lack of trying on my part," I say. "We were super close for those first four years until Saverio separated us. Being taken away from her was heartbreaking for both of us. By then, Saverio was jealous of our bond, and he hated me because I argued with him about everything. His solution was to marry me off to that pig Paulo, and he wouldn't let me visit with Anais. Not until the balance of power shifted and he needed me, but by then, Anais was a spoiled little bitch who purposely chose to forget everything I had taught her." Pressure sits on my chest, like it does every time I think of how that bastard twisted and manipulated my sister, turning her into someone I barely recognized.

"From what I know, she is nothing like you," Fiero says.

"Anais is the product of her upbringing. Her mother abandoned her, and then I did. It wasn't by choice, but she was only nine when I left Vegas for Philly, and I don't know what lies Saverio filled her head with. Her father worshipped her and gave her everything her heart desired, except a normal upbringing and the kind of fatherly love a man like Salerno is incapable of offering. What Anais has become is not her fault."

Massimo shakes his head. "I don't buy that for a second. You have endured things she didn't, and you are strong, courageous, noble, and hardworking." He brushes his lips against mine. "Lots of people have shitty childhoods, and it doesn't define who they are as adults."

"True. But the choices we make as adults *do* define us." I wonder how noble Massimo will think I am when he finds out I originally came here to kill him and his family and Don Mazzone. Shame washes over me, and I have never wished for a do-over so bad.

"The three of us are perfect examples," Fiero supplies.

"I don't disagree, but it's not all her fault. She truly had no one growing up. There was no one to show her a different way. I have tried but..." I pause to compose myself because thinking about my sister growing up in that House of Horrors all alone always makes me feel ill. "The truth is, Anais stopped listening to me the day her father forced me from her life. She tolerates me at best now."

"But you haven't given up on her. You still try." Massimo looks at me with admiration and understanding.

"She's my sister. My only surviving flesh and blood. I will never turn my back on her."

"She could do it to you if she discovers you killed her father." Fiero says what we're all thinking.

"That is a risk I must take. Saverio may have put a roof over my head, and he didn't abuse me, but he wasn't kind. He kept me hidden at the house. I wasn't allowed to go out for fear someone would see me and recognize me."

Their brows pucker in confusion, but I can't narrate that part of the tale yet. I know my emotions will be all over the place when I explain about Carlo, and I can't afford to fall apart now. We need a plan of attack so we take Saverio out before he makes a move on me first. "Renzo was my lifeline back then. I don't know if I would've had the strength to find this path without him."

"You would have." Massimo is quick to assert his belief. "There's a fire inside you, *mia amata*. He may have helped to nurture the flames, but it's always been burning inside you. You and you alone have kept it alive. Don't sell your—"

His words die as a loud blast erupts from behind us, and our car skids along the highway.

Massimo shoves me to the ground and covers me with his body as Fiero lowers the privacy screen and removes a gun from his back pocket.

"What the fuck is going on?" Massimo yells as I try to push him off me. We're in an armored vehicle, and while the bodywork and glass won't withstand repeated gunfire, there is no need to turn all Rambo and act like I'm some helpless woman who doesn't know her way around a gun.

"Jesus fucking Christ!" Fiero's eyes widen as he stares out the back window. "They're using bazookas."

Massimo lets loose a string of expletives as he climbs off me, offering me his hand. Our eyes lock in shared acknowledgment. "We need to get the fuck off this highway, or we're minced meat," I say, echoing what we all know.

Chapter Thirty-Six

Massimo

"Head for the next exit," I instruct Ezio as he zigzags across the road, weaving in and out of traffic, attempting to lose the black SUV chasing us. My SUV, along with my men inside, is toast, the car overturned and burning behind us in the distance. Rage consumes me as I watch the assholes leaning out of the car windows behind us, aiming fire at our vehicle.

"Let's give these motherfuckers a taste of their own medicine," Catarina says, flipping up the back seat to reveal an arsenal of weaponry.

Fiero whistles under his breath. "That's some collection you've got there. I'm guessing you know how to use them?"

"Don't ask stupid questions." Catarina quickly hands rifles to me and Fiero as a barrage of gunfire hits the back of the car, sending bullets ricocheting in all directions. Alongside us, other cars slam on the brakes while some spin out of control crashing into others.

"It won't be long before the cops show up," I warn as she punches a button on the roof of the ceiling and a pane of glass lowers.

"Put the pedal to the metal, Ezio," she shouts. "The Russians won't give a shit about innocent casualties, but I do. We need to get off this highway."

"What makes you so sure it's the Russians and not Saverio?" Fiero asks, readying his rifle.

"You heard Renzo. Salerno is in the air. This is Anton's doing. He's trying to take us out before we go to The Commission and bring the full weight of the *mafioso* down on top of them."

Fiero trades a look with me, and I know what he's thinking. I don't care what Renzo did in the past—though I am grateful he cared for her when no one else did—it means jack shit to who he is now. We've had a guy following him, and he's definitely up to something shady. I need proof before I present it to my wife because I know she won't believe it unless I have something concrete to show her.

Neither of us challenges her because this isn't the time. Escaping these assholes with our lives is the only goal right now.

Rina pushes the seat back down and kneels on it, positioning her rifle in one of the three holes in the glass that has secured into place. It's like an inner back window, fully sealed on all sides. "This is armored glass," Catarina explains, punching a second button on the ceiling. "It won't withstand a bazooka, but if we can keep them at bay until we get off the highway, we can pull over and retrieve the rocket launcher I have in a secret panel under the car." She glances at me as I climb onto the seat beside her. "You can have at them then, my love."

Dark intent shimmers in her eyes, and I fucking love this woman so much.

Instinctively, I know what she has to tell me about her childhood is going to destroy me, but I already know it won't change how I feel about her. Unless someone was to physically rip my heart from my chest, it will continue to beat for her. Nothing she says can change it, no matter how her truths might hurt both of us, and I sense they will.

Fiero and I get into position, placing our rifles in the holes as the back window lowers. The SUV chasing us comes into range, and we engage our weapons, in perfect sync, firing shots over the cars between us and them, aiming for the Russians' vehicle. Gunfire is exchanged back and forth, the shots bouncing off both armored cars.

"Fuck." Fiero curses under his breath as a guy with a bazooka propped on his shoulder leans out of the window.

"Get us off this fucking highway now!" I roar at Ezio, and the car swings a violent left, narrowly avoiding hitting a car on the inside lane. Up ahead, a semi-truck explodes the instant the projectile meant for us hits it, raining canned goods and debris on the road. It's chaos in front of and behind us as cars pile up, and screaming people leave their vehicles running back down the highway in sheer terror.

Don Mazzone will freak the fuck out when the news breaks and he discovers we are at the center of it. Though he can't get too mad because he was involved in his fair share of public shootouts when he first took the helm. He has worked hard to keep bloodshed off the streets of New York since, so this won't be appreciated. It's not something I need to worry about now though. I force the thought from my mind and concentrate on the here and now.

Ezio heads up the exit ramp at speed, and the carnage on the highway has bought us a little time as the Russians are stuck behind a line of stationary cars. It won't take them long to plow their way through, but we have a few minutes to prepare.

Ezio exits the highway onto a long wide road, speeding toward the next town. We keep our rifles trained behind us and our eyes peeled as Rina instructs Ezio to pull into the shoulder up ahead.

When the car stops, we climb out of the back seat as Ricardo climbs out of the front. "Watch from the rear," she says, eyeballing Ricardo and Fiero. "Ezio can watch from the front in case any other surprises come our way." Rina lowers to the ground on her knees before twisting around and sliding underneath the car. I quickly follow, and together we remove the rocket launcher from its case and slide back out.

I'm setting the weapon up, positioning it in the direction of where the Bratva will come from, while Rina talks to Dario and Renzo on FaceTime, filling them in on what's happened. Fiero and Ricardo watch from outside the SUV, at the rear, while Ezio surveys the road ahead from behind the wheel.

"Run!" Fiero yells just as I'm getting into position.

Looking through the scope, I spot the projectile coming our way and curse loudly. "Get away from the car!" I hop up with the launcher on my shoulder, my sore arm protesting the weight. Grabbing my wife's hand, I force her to run with me. Fiero and Ricardo race down the road, pumping their legs as fast as they can go.

Rina struggles, attempting to wrench her hand from mine. The weapon is heavy on my shoulder, but there is no way I'm dropping it or letting go of my wife. "Ezio!" she screams, casting a glance over her shoulder. "We have to go back for him! Please, Massimo." Pain underscores her words, and I get it. He was inside the car and may not get out in time. But there is nothing we can do about it. Not without risking death.

I don't get a chance to reply to my wife before the explosion hits, destroying our SUV and rocking the road, sending us all tumbling to the ground. I roll over onto my back, ignoring the pain tearing across my injured arm as I position the rocket launcher on my chest and tuck my wife into my side. I protect her as best I can as fragments from our SUV fall around us.

Behind us, our car is an inferno, temporarily trapping the Russians behind a wall of heat.

There is no time to waste.

I check my wife, but she's not seriously hurt. She speaks, but I can't hear the words. The sentiment blazing from her eyes is clear though, and I spring into action. My ears are ringing, and my arm throbs as I climb to my feet on unsteady limbs. Holding the rocket launcher out in front of me, I line it up so it's perfectly positioned to take those Bratva bastards out the second the flames clear, giving me a clear view of them.

It happens a couple of minutes later, and my arm is steady, my resolve undeniable, as I take my shot, and it hits the target. The Russian SUV erupts in another fireball that rocks the New York skyline, lighting it up in hues of orange and red as darkness slowly creeps in.

I set the rocket launcher down and walk toward my wife when a car screeches behind us. Whipping out my Glock, I shove Catarina away as I spin around, ready for whomever has come for us now. But it's Renzo who pops his head out of the black van, yelling something we can't hear. Fiero grabs Ricardo, and they run toward us with blackened faces and torn clothing. Snatching my wife's hand, I steer her toward the van while sending a silent question to Fiero from over my shoulder. He shakes his head, and a pained sigh escapes me.

Rina glances back with tears in her eyes, and I know Ezio's loss will haunt her for years to come. Losing loved ones in such circumstances always does.

We scramble into the car, and it careens up the road at high speed as the sound of sirens echoes in the background.

It takes some time for the ringing in our ears to fade enough that we can speak. Until then, we communicate via text. My wife doesn't want to meet at our house now. She's afraid of drawing the enemy to our home. I don't disagree, so I send everyone coordinates to a warehouse by the docks that has been in my family for years. We can reconvene there and make plans.

Fiero and I summon our men, and I send a message to Don Mazzone with a brief explanation, promising to call him when I can hear properly to update him more fully. Rina taps away on her phone, sending instructions to her team, and within the hour, we are at the warehouse and making plans.

My head is pounding, and I'm grateful when Rina's doc shows up, handing me some pain meds. He attends to our injuries and gives us a quick inspection. We all have cuts and grazes, slight pain in our ears, and matching headaches, but it's nothing serious. He advises us to come in next week to have our ears checked for any permanent damage. Once the good doc is gone, we get down to business.

"I suggest we split into three groups," Rina says, instantly taking the lead. Fiero and I are happy to let her do it because she needs this. "We don't know if Anton will send more men after us or if he'll go for Saverio himself the instant he lands." Using the coordinates Renzo has provided, I am tracking Salerno's plane as it heads for New York. He's about an hour and forty-five minutes out now. "The only person killing that bastard is me." She slams her fist down on the table.

"Dario." She jerks her head at her *consigliere* as he enters the warehouse with a ton of her capos. "I need you to push the button on the file on Anton. We need him out of the US ASAP."

"Consider it done," he says, punching digits on his cell and stepping back to make a call.

"My men will wait at the private airfield for Salerno and attempt to capture him there," she says.

"He'll be expecting an ambush," Fiero supplies.

"Most likely, but he's reckless when he's angry, and that's when he makes mistakes. We try to take him there, but we also station a group of the Greco *soldati* on the road outside the airfield, so if he makes it that far, we ambush him there." She eyeballs my best buddy. "Fiero, your men will guard us here. If Salerno makes it past the first two groups, we will leak our whereabouts to him and take them out when he arrives."

"Divide and conquer," I say, considering all the angles in my head. "It will work. We have the local knowledge and the numbers. I doubt he'll make it past your men at the airfield."

Chapter Thirty-Seven

Massimo

My words are prophetic, and it's pathetic how easy Salerno is captured at the airport when he lands.

"ETA in five minutes," Rina says, putting her cell down. She's been pacing the floor of the warehouse like a caged animal for the past two and a half hours, angry and on edge, while I have done my best to pacify Don Mazzone and The Commission.

We have to attend a meeting with them tomorrow to explain the shit show that went down. Thanks to Bennett's police commissioner buddy, news of our involvement has been kept out of the media reports. I told Don Mazzone it was the Russians spearheaded by the Russian ambassador to New York who attacked us and we have intel which confirms they have been planning to move into our territory for some time. The Russians seizing Vegas and attacking my wife adds authenticity to my words, and Bennett swallowed it fully. It makes sense they would try to take out the woman in charge of the drug-supply chain on the streets for the *mafioso*, in the hope they could step in and backfill the gap her presence would leave.

Nicolina hands my wife a bottle of water, fixing an errant strand of hair that has slipped out of her ponytail. Rina's best friend showed up an hour ago—much to her husband's disgust and clear fury—with clothes for all of us and supplies to freshen up. My wife's torn, stained white dress has been replaced with her usual black battle attire. Her makeup is intact, and her hair neatly pulled back. The usual myriad of weapons is strapped to her body, and she has set the stage in preparation for her showdown with her stepfather.

I'm still reeling over that revelation and the realization I'm now linked by marriage to that fucker DiPietro.

"Are you sure you want to do this?" I ask when she steps up to my side, discreetly threading her fingers in mine. I love how she naturally comes to me for support without even thinking about it. "I can take care of him, and you can avoid the blowback from Anais if she ever finds out," I offer.

"I know you know what my answer will be." She looks up at me with fierce determination etched upon her beautiful face.

"I had to try."

"I appreciate you did."

We share a silent communication, speaking with our eyes instead of our words. She tells me she needs to do this. I tell her I know and I am here to support her in whatever way I can.

"He's here," Renzo hollers from his lookout spot in the rafters. We have men all over the grounds, the warehouse, and the dock so there are no unpleasant surprises.

"It's time." I can almost see the stress leaving my wife's body as she utters those words. With a soft smile, she leaves my side, walking to the area in the middle of the room that has been set up for Saverio. A large plastic sheet covers the stained asphalt, and a hard wooden chair with slats awaits his reckless ass.

The warehouse doors open, and Catarina's men escort a hooded Saverio into the space. Six of them surround him, shoving and pushing him forward. His hands are cuffed behind his back as he stumbles into the warehouse. He attempts to shout, but his words are muffled behind whatever they have stuffed in his mouth. Venom burns brightly in my wife's eyes as she watches her men thrust Salerno into the chair and cuff his wrists and ankles to it.

Catarina whips the black covering off his head, and the Vegas don squints as his eyes adjust to the dim lighting. I haven't seen him in years, and he has really let himself go. His beer gut protrudes noticeably over the waistband of his pants. Fleshy arms and meaty legs attest to an unhealthy diet and steady intake of beer. His puffy face makes the scar running along one side seem less noticeable. The poor dye job can't conceal his thin graying hair, leathery pockmarked skin, and yellowed teeth.

He looks old. Worn out. Strung out. Way past his prime.

It's no wonder he has been begging Alessandro to take the helm in Vegas. Even if my wife wasn't planning to snuff out his life today, it's clear Saverio Salerno's days as a don are truly numbered.

Hard bloodshot eyes narrow on my wife as his vision focuses. "You set the Russians on me, you little bitch! You let them take my territory and steal your sister's inheritance! This is what you were planning all along!" he accuses.

I hold up a hand before Catarina speaks. "Everyone out except the inner circle," I holler. We don't need witnesses to exactly what is said or what goes down today. Our men are loyal, but everyone can be bought. The Commission would expect Catarina to hand Salerno over to them to deal with. Killing a don is not a simple matter in our world. Having justification is not always reason enough to warrant any other don or donna taking matters into their own hands. Which is why we need to stage this as the handiwork of the Bratva. The fewer who know exactly how this goes down, the better.

Rina says something to Nicolina before calling Ricardo over. Nicolina raises zero protest, allowing Ric to escort her from the premises. We wait as the *soldati* and capos in the room filter outside to patrol the grounds.

Rina stuffs the gag back in Saverio's mouth when he starts shouting shit, only removing it when the warehouse is empty of everyone except for us and Rina's inner circle. I don't like that Renzo is here, but we can't kick him out without igniting his rage. He's a pressure cooker ready to explode, and I won't force him into making an unwise move. Until we know exactly what the guy is up to, keeping him close is the smartest play.

"You can't kill me." Saverio puffs out his chest. "The Commission will have your head for it, and Anais will never forgive you."

He's such a moron. It's kill or be killed, and he overestimates his perceived value. His coming for Catarina left my wife with no choice. Salerno knows this. He also knows he would be severely outnumbered coming here. Maybe he thought he'd be handed over to The Commission and his past with Don Mazzone would buy him his life. Or maybe he wants to die. Looking at his tired, useless, old body, it's not that hard to believe.

"No one will know it was me." She walks around him, her gaze raking over him with evident disgust. "The blame will land squarely on the Russians' door."

"You always were an ungrateful cunt. After everything I did for you!"

Rina punches him in the face, and his head snaps back at an awkward angle. "You did shit for me, and you know it. You used me as a nanny for Anais until jealousy meant you gave me away. You served me up to that pig Conti knowing what he would do to me." She punches him in the gut this time, leveling a succession of precise blows to his solar plexus and his ribs.

Saverio pins her with an ugly grin as air oozes from his mouth and he struggles to breathe. "Does your new husband know who you are?" A malevolent glint appears in his eyes as he stares at me. "Does he know you—"

Catarina shoves the gag back in his mouth, silencing him. She turns around and walks over to me. "I need to be the one to tell you. He will only twist the truth and try to cause trouble between us." Her eyes are shielding nothing from me, and I know she's sincere.

"It's okay." I kiss her quick. "I trust you. I only want to hear it from your mouth."

Relieved, she squeezes my arm before returning to her stepfather. "I wish I had more time to torture you, but you're insignificant," she says, cutting the shirt off his bulging belly with her knife. Buttons pop all over the ground, and the plastic squelches as she walks around him, making quick successive shallow lacerations across his body. "You mean nothing to me, and the only person who will miss you is Anais, but I plan to rectify that. She needs to know everything, and I will tell her. In time, she'll hate you too. She will join me in dancing on your grave and celebrating your death."

My wife is delusional if she truly believes that will come to pass. I don't need to know Anais well to know she will never be swayed. I can't fault Rina her loyalty to her sister even if Anais in no way deserves it. I worry about the fallout, but that's a worry to set aside for another day. There are more pressing demands, like making sure the Russians go down for this and The Commission buys it without any suspicion. Nothing can come back on Rina. I will ensure it—even if I have to sacrifice my integrity or my life to make it happen.

No one dares to speak as we let her expunge these particular demons. Every expression contains relief as she cuts away at him while tears leak from his eyes and muffled shouts resound behind the gag. He pisses himself through his pants, and Fiero and I share a look. It's a pitiful way for a don to bow out of this life, but Saverio's poor choices have led to this moment, and he is entirely to blame.

Rina cuts away his urine-soaked pants, leaving him completely exposed. His withered dick flops between fleshy thighs, and he's a hideous sight. Trapped anguish struggles to find an outlet when Rina slides her knife into his ass through the slats of the chair, fucking him with the sharp blade. "This isn't even close to the pain I felt when Paulo and his men repeatedly violated me." Blood pools on the plastic sheet behind him, and more spills from his front when Rina carves a deep hole in his stomach.

"Wow, she's not holding back," Fiero murmurs under his breath as Rina twists the knife in deep, rotating it around his stomach, tearing his flesh to shreds. "She is level-headed and focused under pressure. How she dealt with things when we were ambushed seriously impressed me. She is one hell of a woman."

"My wife is a queen. The one true mafia queen. And she's *mine.*" I drill him with a deadly look, warning him to keep his thoughts strictly limited to professional respect.

He smirks, leaning in to whisper in my ear. "I'm still down for sharing."

"In your fucking dreams, asshole." I shove him away as he chuckles and refocus on the scene in front of us.

Catarina's hand is steady as she stabs Saverio in the thighs, purposely avoiding the arteries. "My mother was a selfish bitch, but she was still my mother," she says, withdrawing the knife only to shove it back in again. Blood oozes from several places, and he won't have much longer left to live. "This is for killing her when she dared to criticize you for moving your whores into her home." She goes to town on him then, stabbing him all over until the light dies in his eyes and his head lolls forward.

"You have done enough, my donna." Renzo squeezes her shoulder, and I instantly want to rip his arm from his body so he can't touch her ever again. "Let me handle the rest."

I storm across the space. "Get your hand off my wife," I snarl as I approach.

Renzo withdraws his hand and glowers at me.

"Touch her again, and you're dead."

Rina snaps out of wherever she went to in her head and rolls her eyes. "Calm down, tiger. He didn't mean anything by it." She leans into my side, and I automatically wrap my arms around her. "I want to go home. We have a lot to talk about." Her voice is devoid of emotion, and I suspect this took a lot more out of her than she expected.

"Fiero." I call my buddy over. "Help Renzo dispose of the body and organize the cleanup."

"You got it."

"That won't be necessary," Renzo says, looking severely irritated.

"Trust me, it's necessary." I slant him a look that lets him know exactly how little I trust him.

"Get him cremated, and send the ashes to Anais," Rina says. "She needs closure, and she'll want to organize a funeral."

I don't think it's necessarily smart, but I keep that opinion to myself because I know there's no point arguing.

Ignoring Renzo, I look to my best friend—the only man I trust completely with my life. "Plant evidence that clearly implicates the Russians. I want this to lead to Anton Smirnov. A high-profile murder, bloody shootout, and the intel Catarina has compiled will be enough to have him evicted from the US in disgrace." The Commission has contacts within the upper echelons of government. As long as we convince them this is all the work of the Bratva, they will ensure Anton is kicked back to Moscow with his tail between his legs.

"I'll make it happen." Fiero leans in and kisses my wife on the cheek. "Go home, *regina*. Your work here is done."

"I poured you a glass of wine," I say an hour later when Catarina emerges in the living room, dressed in leggings and an off-the-shoulder top. Her damp hair is piled in a messy bun on top of her head, and her face is pale, but it's not from the lack of makeup.

My wife is sad and terrified.

That much is blatantly obvious.

Her call to Ezio's wife took even more out of her, and I know whatever else she has to tell me is bad.

"Come here." I put my wineglass down and open my arms. She hesitates for a few seconds, biting down on her lower lip before she trots over to me and crawls into my lap. I bundle her up, holding her tight as I rub a soothing hand up and down her back. She buries her head in my chest, clutching my T-shirt and inhaling the fresh scent of my body wash still clinging to my skin from my shower. I tip her chin up so her eyes are on mine. "His death is not your fault. Every made man knows the risks when they swear an oath."

"I'm responsible for every man and woman who works for me, Massimo. His death, like countless before him, *is* my fault. It doesn't matter that I always ensure their families are well taken care of. The guilt is something I will carry with me for the rest of my life along with the loss." She looks unbearably sad as she peers into my eyes. "Ezio was a good man. A loyal soldier and someone I considered a friend. I will feel his loss deeply." She slides a hand over her chest, rubbing at whatever pain she's feeling.

"Your compassion is what sets you apart from your male counterparts." I press my lips to her brow. "The way you care about those who work for you and the interest you take in their families is what has sealed their loyalty to you. Ezio died with honor, protecting his queen. He died knowing you would take care of his wife and kids. I doubt he had any regrets."

"It's all such bullshit," she whispers, fisting her hand tighter in my shirt. "And I'm tired of it, Massimo." She looks so vulnerable as she straightens up, and I know I'm seeing that part of herself she keeps hidden from most others. "It's so exhausting, and it's time for things to change."

"Whatever you have to tell me will not change the way I feel about you." I kiss her softly. "I love you, and I'm going nowhere."

"You say that now, but you don't know how you're going to feel after I tell you this. You might hate me for real, Massimo, and that..." She chokes on a sob, and tears pool in her eyes. "That would kill me. I love you. I don't want to lose you."

"We'll work through this together. I promise you I'm going nowhere. No matter what you tell me, I am not leaving you."

She inhales and exhales deeply, and I watch as she wrangles her emotions until she's more in control. I protest loudly when she slides off my lap, sitting beside me. "I can't tell you this all snuggled up against you." She reaches for her wineglass and knocks back a hefty amount.

Tension bleeds into the air, and I just want her to tell me.

I know this is the final test.

The last hurdle we must pass before we can focus on building a real life together.

I want that so badly, which is why I know nothing she can say will alter my resolve.

"I need you to know that my feelings and my plans have completely changed since I put all of this in motion." There's a desperate pleading look on her face as she stares at me.

I nod, encouraging her to continue with my eyes.

"I don't think I would ever have gone through with it," she adds. "I have been too obsessed with my past. Consumed with pain and so much anger it blinded me to logic and reason. Vengeance is all I have thought about for years. I thought it was all I needed. That once I had my revenge everything would be okay, and I could start living my life." An errant tear leaks from her eye, and my heart aches for her.

I have never seen her cry.

Not even a single tear.

And it guts me.

I brush it away with my fingers while I take her hand in mine. "It's rarely so simple."

"I know that now. Nic has been saying it to me for a while, but I couldn't see her point of view. Not until I met you and I realized how deep my feelings extended. You have helped to open my eyes to the truth, Massimo. Exacting revenge would not have made me any happier. It might have given me closure, but I think I would have been left feeling directionless and lonely because this is all I have known. You have shown me there is a better way and a better life waiting for me, and I want it. I want it badly enough to have let go of the rest of my plans."

More tears shine in her eyes. "I love you, and I hope you can find it in your heart to forgive me and to let it go, but if you can't, I will respect that decision too."

"I already forgive you." The words rip from my mouth without hesitation, birthed straight from my soul.

She wipes her tears away, and familiar steely determination replaces the mournful expression on her face.

There's my queen.

The owner of my heart.

The face of my future.

The only woman I will ever love.

"Tell me, *mia amata*. Unburden yourself."

"My revenge plan had several components. Killing Paulo and Saverio was only a part of it. They weren't the only ones who hurt me. They were barely even monsters compared with the real villain of the piece."

My heart thumps painfully against my chest, and all the hairs lift on the back of my neck as things start clicking into place.

She wets her lips and squeezes my hand. "There is no easy way to say this, my love, so I'm just going to blurt it out. It will be a shock, but I beg you to hear me out."

I can only nod as ominous dread washes over me, almost knocking all the air from my lungs.

Please, God, no.

Don't let her say what I think she might be about to say. Pain lashes me from all sides and it takes every ounce of willpower to mask my emotions and keep a neutral expression on my face.

"When I was thirteen, I was kidnapped by your brother Carlo. He held me prisoner in the basement of your house for seven months before I was rescued."

Horror engulfs me as the realization of who she is slaps me in the face. "It was you! You were the girl in the cage!" I blurt as a tight pain spreads across my chest making breathing difficult.

Matching horror creeps over her face as she stares at me. "You knew?" she chokes out.

"I saw you one time. I'd been told to stay away from the basement, and it was always kept locked. Only father, Carlo, and Primo had a key. One day, I discovered it was unlocked, and I snuck downstairs." Blood rushes to my head and thrums in my ears as the vision resurfaces in my mind. I squeeze my eyes shut for a moment as pain rips through my insides, tightening and restricting until it feels like I can't breathe.

When I open them, tears glisten in my eyes. "You were in a cage. You were naked and bleeding." My voice cracks, and I'm barely holding it together. I cannot believe that girl was my wife. Nothing could have prepared me for this. "I crouched down in front of you. I asked you what your name was. You—"

"I said Noemi Cabrini," she whispers as tears trek down her face. "I thought I dreamed that. I thought I dreamed *you*. Carlo would drug me when I screamed too much. He liked when I fought him, but if I made too much noise, it would draw attention to my presence in the house. I started purposely fighting and screaming so he would drug me." She stares off into space as she speaks. I rub circles on the back of her hand with my thumb, but I really want to haul her into my arms and hold her forever.

She turns her head, and the dead look in her eyes scares me. "It was better to be numb when he hurt me. He liked to make me bleed." I am aware of the sickening things my eldest brother did to girls because rumors were rife about his depraved sexual kinks and his penchant for hurting women. She gulps, and I brace myself. "I was so out of it that day I thought I imagined the boy with the big green eyes, but I didn't."

"You didn't. It was me."

The blank look in her eyes fades as if a switch has just been flipped, replaced with potent rage. "You knew I was there, and you did nothing!" Yanking her hand back, she jumps up, towering over me, exuding anger from every pore. "You are just like your mother and Gabriele!" She begins pacing, and I'm afraid to make a move or say a word for fear of what she might do. "They knew I was down there too, and they did nothing!" she screams, picking up the wineglass and throwing it at the wall. It shatters upon impact, raining glass on the hardwood floor. "I thought you were different! But you're a monster too!" She reaches for something and rushes me. Before I can stop her, she raises her hand to my head, and a sharp pain rattles my skull before darkness swoops in and claims me.

Chapter Thirty-Eight

Massimo

"He's awake," Renzo says as I come to, strapped to a chair in the middle of my living room. I wonder when that fuck-face arrived and whether Rina called him or he just showed up at an opportune time. Pain stabs me in the brow, and my eyes feel heavy as I force them to remain open. My wife paces the floor, knotting and unknotting her hands, looking panicked and on edge.

"*Mia amata*," I croak, willing her to look at me. "Let me explain."

Renzo barks out a harsh laugh as he yanks my head back. "Too fucking late, asshole."

He lifts his clenched fist, but Rina darts forward and grabs his hand. "No. You're not to hurt him."

He narrows his eyes on her. "What the fuck, Ree-ree?"

Have I mentioned I hate he has a pet name for my wife? I am so fucking sick of him interfering in my marriage. If I get out of this alive, I am taking care of this asshole once and for all.

"Untie me." Ignoring Renzo, I concentrate solely on my wife. I hate that he's here, and I fear what bullshit he has been feeding her while I was out of it. Catarina is shattered emotionally by my revelation and not thinking clearly, which means she's vulnerable to this prick, and that doesn't bode well for me.

"Why, Massimo?" She paces frantically. "Why did you do nothing? Do you have any idea of the things your brother did to me while you slept soundly in your bed?"

All the color drains from my face at her words.

She's shaking all over, and a growl escapes my lips when Renzo circles his arms around her. She pushes him away, not looking at him, as she stares at me with the most tortured expression on her face.

Before I can explain, she launches into her story. "I was an innocent thirteen-year-old shopping for a party dress the day he kidnapped me. I wasn't paying attention because I was daydreaming about the boy who was having the party that night. Lionel was my first crush, and I was so sure he was going to kiss me at the party. My head was in the clouds leaving the mall, and I never saw Carlo coming. Next thing I knew, I was in the back of a van with three strange men, and they were binding my hands and my ankles with rope."

She sinks to the floor, sitting cross-legged in front of me. A glazed look coats her eyes as she wanders into the past. Her lower lip wobbles as she speaks. "I hadn't even been kissed at that point. Daddy had kept me sheltered, and I was completely innocent. It didn't take Carlo long to divest me of that innocence. He stripped me naked in the van in front of his men." Silent tears streak down her face. "He made fun of my trainer bra and my small breasts. He put his fingers inside me"—a shudder wracks her body as she stares into space—"and told his men to feel how tight his *little virgin* was."

She squeezes her eyes closed as pain sits heavily on my chest. "He carried me naked into your house through a back door. Your mother passed us in the hallway. She stopped for a second, and I screamed at her for help before Carlo wrapped his hand around my throat and squeezed so hard I couldn't breathe."

Her chest shakes as tears continue to stream down her face. It is torture listening to this, but I owe her my silence while she gets it all out. "She watched as he opened the door to the basement and took me down. Carlo tossed me into a cage and locked the door. It was freezing, and I was so scared I peed myself. He laughed at me before turning off all the lights and leaving me down there."

Wracking shudders rip through her body, but she holds up a hand to keep Renzo at bay when he moves toward her.

"You don't have to relive this, Ree-ree." He crouches down in front of her. "You don't owe him anything. Just kill him and be done with it."

"No!" She drills him with a sharp look. "No."

He expels a frustrated sigh, stomping over to the window and looking out into the garden and pool area.

I don't tell her to stop or say anything. I know she needs to do this, and even though it's killing me inside, I won't take that from her. She needs to get this off her chest. Maybe then she will be ready to hear my explanation, and we can try to figure out how the hell we move forward from this.

"I cried all night for my daddy," she whispers, resuming the story. "It was so cold, and Carlo left me sitting in my own piss all night. I was hungry and cold and scared. The house is so old. Pipes rattled, and the wind whistled through the vents making a creepy noise. Scuttering sounds had me screaming in terror. By the time he showed up the next morning, I was so hoarse I could barely speak."

A stabbing pain pierces my heart, and I wish I could dig my brother up and murder him repeatedly for what he did to my wife.

"He took my virginity the next morning," she says in a voice devoid of emotion. "I asked for breakfast, and he fed me his cock. He violated my mouth, my pussy, my ass. It went on for hours, and it hurt so fucking much. I called for my daddy, and he slapped me every time I said his name, taunting me that my father was the one who handed me to him on a platter as a trade until it was time to take Natalia for a test drive."

"Jesus, Rina. I'm so sorry. He was an animal. A savage, cruel bastard. If he wasn't already dead, I would kill him for what he did to you." Tears pool in my eyes, and agony twists my stomach in knots. I have never felt so helpless. I struggle against my binds, needing to go to her even knowing the last person she would want to touch her as she relives these horrors is me.

She has a faraway look in her eyes as she continues. "He called me disgusting. He had a choice vocabulary of creative insults for me. It wasn't enough to debase my body; he had to destroy my self-respect too. He would wash me in a cold bath before fucking me unless I was coated in dried blood. He loved fucking me when I was all cut up and bloody."

"Enough!" Renzo shouts, grabbing fistfuls of his hair. "I can't hear this again!"

What a fucking dick to try to make this about him.

"You know where the door is," she says in a cold tone without looking at him. "Either leave or keep your mouth shut."

Resting his head against the wall, he closes his eyes and breathes deeply, making no move to leave. Guess it was hoping for too much that he would just fuck off and leave us to deal with this alone.

Rina wraps her arms around herself as her entire body trembles. "He took videos and pictures of me to share with his men. On occasion, he let them fuck me as a reward for something they did. He regularly punched me and kicked me when I displeased him," she continues. "He almost choked me to death so many times. He used knives and other tools on me. By the time I was rescued, there was barely an inch of my skin without some mark on it."

I grip the armrests, swallowing painfully over the lump in my throat as tears fall down my cheeks. "The scars on your hips," I rasp.

She nods. "He did that. Hooked me using chains on the ceiling by my hips. Left me dangling there for hours."

Pain, unlike anything I have ever felt before, batters me from all angles, and I want to rage at a world that lets this happen. How could anyone do that to a little girl? I always knew my brother was a monster, but this...this...it's unimaginable. I attempt to control my tears as I don't want to make this about me, but it's hard to remain unmoved listening to this.

"The cosmetic surgery Saverio made me have removed most of the damage to my body, but some scars were too difficult to erase." She levels me with a dead look that pierces my skin and penetrates my heart. "I was mostly Carlo's toy, but Primo and your father abused me too."

Fresh horror crests over me in powerful waves. Nausea travels up my throat, and I think I might puke. So many emotions are running riot inside me.

My family hurt her, over and over, and I didn't know.

I didn't know the woman I love, the queen I lie beside every night, had suffered so terribly at the hands of my own flesh and blood.

I am ashamed to be a Greco.

"I am so sorry. I hated them already, but now there are no words to describe how I feel about them. I—"

"Save your sympathy," Renzo hisses, storming across the room and glaring at me from above. "This all happened while you were upstairs. Those sick pricks had her for seven months, abusing her nonstop, while you went about your life, ignoring the injustice taking place in the basement. She was thirteen! A sweet innocent teen, and your brother made her life a living hell!"

"I didn't know, Rina," I plead, ignoring the asshole and staring at my wife, beseeching her to look at me. "I was fourteen, and they kept me away from everything. I was labeled a mommy's boy. Written off as a mistake. Purposely ignored. You know this! I told you. That day I stumbled across you was the first I knew of your existence, and it haunted me."

I flashback to the past. Pain crashes through my chest as acid crawls up my throat. "I fought with my father and Carlo that day, but they were men, and I was still a boy. I was no match for their dual strength. They beat me so bad they broke my arm and cracked three ribs, and I had a head injury that left me unconscious for days. When I eventually woke up with a concussion, I didn't remember at first. Then it came back to me. You were all I thought about from the minute I woke each day, and you haunted me in my dreams. I was confined to bed for weeks, locked in my room. I cried nonstop and begged my mother to help you. She told me she tried to get a message to the Mazzones when Carlo first brought you to the house, but she was betrayed by someone she thought she could trust, and my father put her in the hospital. He threatened my life and hers. Said he would kill us both if she tried to intervene again. That is when he started heavily drugging her."

I pause to draw a breath, peering deep into my wife's eyes, hoping she knows the truth when she hears it. "She wasn't conscious much after that, and I knew she was too scared to try again, so I begged Gabe to do something. He got a message to your dad, telling him where you were being held."

"What?" she blurts. Shock splays across her face, quickly followed by confusion. "Why would that have helped? My father already knew where I was. He willingly gave me to Carlo to avoid Natalia suffering the same fate. I thought he loved me, but he loved his job and Natalia more. His commitment to the Mazzones came before me." Pain underscores her words and ripples across her face.

Fucking hell. All this time, she has believed the lie Carlo fed her. I can't begin to imagine how that must have made her feel. She needs to understand who her father was.

I strain against the ropes tying me to the chair, leaning my body toward my wife, needing to be closer to her. "No, sweetheart. That's not how it went down. Gabe overheard Carlo bragging to someone on the phone. Your father was not complicit in your kidnapping. Carlo took you to force Rocco into betraying the Mazzones. He was using you to make him spy on them for him. He didn't hesitate to do it, Rina. Rocco did whatever Carlo asked because your father was desperate to get you back."

She steeples her fingers against her chin, looking completely shell-shocked.

"Carlo was making his own power play in the background, and he needed intel. Later, he attempted to kidnap Natalia and your father, Rocco, helped. He was going to sacrifice her to save you." I let the truth of that sink in for a few seconds before continuing. "From what I've heard, Carlo had been terrorizing her in the run-up to their arranged marriage and he grew impatient. He didn't want to wait for his wedding night." A sour taste floods my mouth as I recall things I have been told and discovered over the years.

"I don't understand," she chokes out, looking lost, like her entire belief system has just come crashing down, and perhaps it has. "If Daddy knew where I was being held, why didn't he come for me?"

I cast a glance at Renzo, and I see the truth in his eyes. He shielded her from this reveal. I don't want to hurt her any more than she's been hurt, but all these fucking secrets have got to end. "He *was* coming for you, *mia amata.* He got word back to Gabe, and we were going to help by setting up a decoy to lure Carlo, Primo, and Papa away from the house while they could rescue you."

"Something went wrong," she whispers, staring at me with fresh tears clinging to her lashes.

Slowly, I nod. "I don't know why he didn't tell the Mazzones. Angelo would have intervened and helped, but Rocco chose to do it on the down low. Your brother was gathering a few friends to help, and someone sold him out to Carlo." I deliberately gentle my tone. "Carlo killed Fernando as a warning to your father. To force him to toe the line or risk losing his other child."

"No, Massimo!" A horrified sob bleeds into the air. "No! Fernando was killed in the line of duty. That's what Mama told me when I came home to discover my father and my brother had both been killed."

"That wasn't true. Carlo did it. I would never lie to you about that."

She looks up at Renzo, and sorrow trickles into the air. "He is telling the truth about this. I found out years after the fact and chose not to tell you. I didn't see how it would help. You were already in so much pain but coming through it. I feared it would set back your recovery."

She gulps, slowly nodding. "I understand, but you still should've told me."

"I'm sorry," he softly says. His feelings for her are crystal clear in this moment. He loves her, and I believe he would do just about anything for her.

I still hate the motherfucker and don't trust him an inch.

"Did your father know you and Gabe were involved?" Emotion pours from her eyes as she sits up on her knees and begins untying the rope around my ankles.

I breathe a sigh of relief. "Yeah, he knew we helped to set it up. After he punished us, he sent Gabe and me to live with our uncle in Italy so we couldn't try anything else. The farm was in a real remote part of the Italian countryside, and we were completely cut off with no phones and no way of communicating with anyone. When we were brought home a few months later, you were gone, Carlo was dead, and we were warned never to speak of it unless we wanted to die."

"Shit!" Renzo's expletive interrupts our conversation as we both whip our heads in his direction. "Donna, you are needed urgently at the front gate," he says, reading a message on his cell.

"For what?" Rina asks, stalling with her fingers at my ankles.

"Some Bratva asshole has shown up asking for you. He says he has intel you need to hear. He refuses to speak to anyone but you, and he'll leave if you aren't there in five minutes." He repockets his cell. "You go. Take Ricardo with you. I'll free Massimo."

Rina climbs to her feet, pushing her face all up in his. "Do not harm one hair on my husband's head. Untie him and then wait for me in the office. That is an order."

"Of course." He flashes her an insincere smile as he moves to my right ankle and begins unraveling the rope.

Catarina glances at me briefly before stepping out of the room.

The door has only just closed when Renzo removes a knife from his back pocket and grins at me like the sly fucker he is.

Chapter Thirty-Nine

Catarina

I can't leave like this. Not without apologizing to Massimo. I am ashamed of how I treated him, especially now I know the full story. Turning around, I reenter the room, reacting immediately when I see what's going down. My hand finds my dagger in a split second, and I hurl it across the room as Renzo raises his knife to my husband's neck. My dagger hits the target, embedding in Renzo's hand, and he instantly drops his knife, falling back as he howls in pain.

"What the fuck are you doing?" I yell, racing across the room and throwing myself in front of Massimo. Bending down, I pick up Renzo's discarded knife, waving it in front of me.

"He needs to die!" Renzo barks, yanking my dagger from his hand with a yelp of pain. "He is manipulating you, and you can't see it, or are you truly telling me you buy that load of crap he just fed you?"

I quickly tap out a message on my phone as I text for help.

"I'm not the one who is lying and manipulating," Massimo calmly says from behind me. I step slightly to the side, still holding the knife and prepared to drive it into Renzo's heart should he make one more move toward my husband.

"You know me." Renzo pleads with his eyes, switching the dagger around and offering the handle end to me. I take the dagger from him and hold on to his knife. "You have known me a long time, Ree-ree. Everything I do is for you. You are not thinking clearly right now."

I watch him carefully as I unknot the rope binding Massimo's right wrist to the chair. "I know my own mind, Ren. I also know you just disobeyed a direct order, and it's not the first time." I free Massimo's wrist and straighten up, leaving him to untie his other wrist and remaining ankle. I stay close to my husband's side, on guard, ready to act should Renzo try anything else.

"I'm doing it in your best interests. You'll thank me later."

"I love my husband," I say as the door opens and Ricardo enters the room with two of Massimo's men. "I love him, and I'm planning a future with him. The past is dead and buried now, and that's where it needs to stay." I jerk my head at Ricardo. "Cuff Renzo and remove his gun and any other weapons."

Ricardo looks blindsided, but he doesn't hesitate to follow orders. Renzo doesn't protest as Ricardo cuffs his hands behind his back and frisks him, confiscating the two guns he finds. Renzo stares at me, looking like he's carrying the weight of the world on his shoulders.

"What now, boss?" Ric asks. "What do you want us to do with him?"

"Take him to one of the safe houses. I want him guarded twenty-four-seven. All men report to you. He is not to be allowed to leave until I say."

"Ree-ree, please."

"Stop with the name!" I shout, losing control of my emotions. "That's a clear case of manipulation! You cannot fall back on what we used to mean to one another to talk your way out of this, Ren. You just tried to murder my husband. That is the ultimate betrayal."

"You can't see what is right in front of your face! Please, my donna, cut him loose before he takes you down with him. Nothing good can come from associating with a Greco! Remember who you are! Remember the things that matter."

He is beginning to sound like a crazy person, and I am done entertaining his bullshit. Nic and Massimo were right. He hasn't been able to let go of me, and it's obviously killing him seeing me happy and in love with a man who isn't him. Attempting to remove the competition is futile when I don't share his feelings, but I'm not so sure Renzo is thinking rationally anymore. I school my features into a neutral line and stab him with a cold look. "I will ensure Maria and the kids are looked after. I'll tell them you needed to go overseas on a business trip."

"They are on vacation in Mexico," he replies, looking and sounding defeated. I'm surprised to hear this news because he never mentioned anything to me. It only serves to remind me how far we have drifted apart. "Please don't say anything. It will only worry them unnecessarily."

I give him a terse nod before turning my head to my bodyguard. "Take him away."

"As you wish, Donna Greco."

Massimo stands, placing his hand on my hip as we watch Ricardo and my husband's men steer Renzo outside. Renzo glances over his shoulder from the doorway, slanting me with pleading eyes. "I am only trying to protect you. That is all I have ever done."

Ricardo drags him out into the hallway and closes the door, leaving us alone.

Massimo drops his head onto my shoulder, and I lean back against him for a moment before shucking out of his hold. I turn around so I'm facing him. "I'm so sorry, Massimo." I pick up his wrist, gently rubbing my thumb across the indents left on his skin from the ropes. "I didn't even give you a chance to explain." My fingers reach up, tentatively touching the bruise on his temple from where I knocked him out with the butt of a gun.

"It's okay." He circles his hand around my wrist.

I shake my head. "No, it's not. It's very far from okay. I just saw red. Old familiar emotions rushed to the surface, and I couldn't see anything, think anything, beyond my rage. I forgot everything we mean to one another in that moment, and I hurt you." Tears well in my eyes, and it feels like my tear ducts are broken. I have cried more today than I have cried in the past ten years. "I'm so sorry."

"It *is* okay." He draws me into his body, forcing my head to his chest. "I know you acted on instinct. Not gonna lie and say I'm happy you did it, but I understand."

"I'm not worthy of you."

"Stop that." He rests his chin on my head as he runs his hand up and down my back. "I'm the one who isn't worthy of you." Gently, he tilts my chin up with one finger. "How can you bear to let me touch you after what that monster did?" This time, tears swim in *his* eyes. "How can you even look at me knowing the same blood runs through my veins?" he adds in a whisper.

"Oh, Massimo." I cup his handsome face, letting tears roam freely down my face. "You are not your brother. When I look at you, all I see is the face of the man I love. A man who loves me unconditionally even when I have done him wrong." Even though I'm exhausted, I need to get the rest out. Might as well expunge the remaining sordid secrets. "I came to New York with plans to kill you and your family and Don Mazzone too."

"That doesn't shock me." He brushes hair out of my face, looking at me with infinite tenderness I don't understand.

"It should, and you should hate me." I attempt to wrench out of his grip, but he won't let me go.

"I could never hate you, not even if you told me your plans haven't changed, but I know they have. You would have killed Renzo right now to protect me."

"That doesn't exonerate me!" I snap. "I'm not a good person, Massimo. All these years, I have been proud of the fact I do my best to protect innocents, but it's the biggest lie I have told myself. You. Are. Innocent. So is Ben. Yet I was going to make you both pay for the sins of your families."

"All of us are tainted in blood. We all share in the sins of our families because that is the nature of our world. I would be surprised if you hadn't been planning this."

"Oh my God." Angry tears leak out of my eyes. "You need to hate me!" I cry because he's being too understanding. "I could live a thousand years and never be worthy of you, Massimo. You are too good for me. I'm a monster," I sob, burying my face in his neck, hating how badly I need his comfort when I don't deserve it. "I'm a monster just like your brother. I could say he did it to me, but I'm an adult. I'm responsible for my own decisions. I could have chosen a different path, but I didn't."

Pain obliterates me on the inside, and everything I have been keeping hidden erupts in one violent blast. I fall apart in his arms. This man I love. A man I was going to end, and it would have been for nothing.

He did try to help me.

Eleanora and Gabe too. They aren't entirely innocent, but they were victims too.

"I got my brother killed," I cry.

"No, sweetheart. That was not on you."

"And Daddy," I sob, crying harder, releasing some of my trapped grief. "I spent years hating him. Believing he abandoned me, readily handed me over to the wolves, but he didn't."

"Your father loved you. He betrayed his employer to try to save your life. The only people to blame are Carlo, Primo and my father. They are responsible for everything, and they are all burning in the fiery pits of hell. Of that, I'm sure."

Massimo picks me up, cradling me to his chest as he carries me to the couch. He holds me close, whispering comforting words and running his hands up and down my back and over my arms as I self-destruct.

I don't know how long I cry, but it's long enough to have soaked his shirt and made my eyes sting and my throat dry.

"I love you," he says when my sobbing has stopped.

"I love you," I croak, easing back so I can see his face. My fingers tenderly touch the bruise at his brow, and I really need to take care of that. "I haven't done a good enough job of showing you, but I will if it's not too late."

"*Mia amata. Mia regina.*" He caresses my cheek. "I told you there was nothing you could say that would make me change my mind, and that is the truth. I am going nowhere."

"So not worthy," I whisper.

"Catarina." The seriousness in his tone has me paying immediate attention. "I am so sorry for the horrors you endured at the hands of my family. I feel sick at what was done to you. I wish we had done more. I wish we could have freed you."

"I know now you tried. That helps, Massimo."

"I wasn't lying when I said you haunted my dreams. You have, Rina. For years, I wondered what happened to you. I tried looking, but the trail was cold."

"Saverio was always afraid someone would find out who I was. Your father was on the board of The Commission and one of the most powerful dons in the country. Salerno didn't want him to know he had taken me in. He said he was searching for me."

"He would have killed you if he found you." Massimo's jaw tightens. "I suspect that's why your mother fled New York. Angelo Mazzone's protection could only extend so far. Maximo would have come for you when the coast was clear."

"It seems there is much I didn't know about my parents. In his own way, Saverio saved my life. Before he tossed it away when he traded me to the Contis. It is all so fucked up." Tiredness washes over me, but there is a sense of relief sinking into my bones. It feels good to get everything out on the table. There is just one more thing left to say, but this will be one of the hardest things to admit.

"It is. We live in a fucked-up world." He kisses me softly, staring at me with so much love I can scarcely believe it.

I was terrified to tell him the truth, but once again, Massimo has proven what a good, compassionate, decent man he is.

"You are amazing, *mia amata*. You don't even realize it. I always knew you were strong, but your strength is beyond anything I can comprehend. To survive that. To do what you have done. To ascend to the position you now hold. It's remarkable. It is I who is not worthy."

"I don't feel very strong now," I truthfully admit, resting my head on his shoulder as I prepare to break his heart.

"Today has been exhausting, and I think it's time to call it a day."

I lift my head and pierce him with a sober look. "I have one final truth to tell you. Then you know it all."

He clasps my face in his hands. "What is it?"

Tears flood my eyes, and I definitely think I have broken something inside me. It's like I can't stop crying now. He mops up my tears and patiently waits for me to compose myself.

I suck in a brave breath and release the last truth. "The injuries I sustained as a teen mean I can't have children. I blackmailed the doctor into falsifying the pre-wedding medical report. I am so sorry, but I can't give you any heirs, Massimo."

Chapter Forty

Massimo

Shock crashes into me, quickly replaced with anger and deep-seated pain. "He took that from you too?" It takes colossal willpower to remain calm when I feel like smashing every fucking thing in this room. I can't get angry at her for tricking me with the medical report, not when my brother is the reason she had to lie.

My God, Catarina has had to endure so much.

That she is still standing is nothing short of miraculous. This woman has iron strength, and I will never stop being in awe of her.

I am enraged that Carlo robbed her of the opportunity to become a mother. I have never hated any person as much as I hate my dead brother. I wish I had a time machine so I could go back and beat that sick fuck to death myself. "That fucking bastard. That sick twisted evil prick." I grind my teeth to the molars, smothering the need to roar and shout from the pit of my lungs.

Tears stream down her cheeks and drip down over her chin. I have never seen my love look so devastated and so defeated. "He took everything from me. He left me a shell of a person. Barren. Emotionless. Incapable of feeling anything but pain and rage."

It's no wonder she's been hellbent on revenge. Carlo did his best to completely destroy her, but he didn't succeed. I feather kisses all over her face as I hold her close. "He didn't take everything, *mia amata*. He tried, but he failed because your indomitable will to survive prevailed."

She looks at me through tear-stained eyes. "I won't contest it if you want a divorce."

"I don't want a divorce. I only want you."

Shock registers on her face for a few seconds. "You can't mean that. What about children? You need an heir to carry the family name."

Perhaps it is time to let the Greco name die. It is not exactly a name to be proud of.

"There are other ways to have kids. We can try IVF and a surrogate, or we can adopt." I shrug because in the scheme of things it's not that big of a deal. Yes, I would love to be a father but not at the expense of losing my wife. "You are my everything, Catarina. Nothing else matters but you. If we can't have children, I will be fine as long as I have you."

She starts crying again, and I bundle her against me, hugging her tight, wishing I had a magic wand so I could erase all her pain and make everything right.

I carry my wife to our bedroom, and we shower together, washing away the awful events of today. After we are dry and dressed for bed, she insists on tending to my injuries. With infinite care, she rubs antiseptic ointment over the stitched wound on my arm and massages arnica cream into the raised bruise on my temple.

We snuggle close in bed, and I cradle her in my arms, watching as she falls asleep, grateful it is fast. It's unsurprising. We are physically and emotionally drained after a stressful few days. I watch her as my eyelids grow heavy, silently vowing to do everything in my power to comfort her in the challenging days ahead.

I wake the following morning before Catarina, as the first rays of daylight filter through my window. I message Fiero to meet me here while I hug my sleeping wife, inhaling the fruity scent from her hair and savoring the touch of her skin against mine. Thankfully, she slept soundly without interruption. My eyes drink her in as she sleeps.

Thick lashes brush the tops of her high cheekbones, and air seeps from her slightly parted full lips. Our crisp white bed sheet is tucked under her arms, dipping softly at the front, and her chest lifts and falls as she breathes, highlighting the swells of her magnificent tits. Smooth olive skin is soft to my touch as I risk sweeping my fingers along the elegant column of her neck. She stirs a little, and I stall my movements, not selfish enough to rouse her from much-needed sleep.

Reluctantly, I climb out of bed, careful not to wake her. Although there are many loose ends to tie up before our meeting with The Commission today, I can handle it while she sleeps. She needs the rest.

Fiero and I jog companionably side by side along the shoreline, and I push myself to my limits, needing an outlet to expel the angry energy still coursing through my veins. He doesn't speak until we are back at the house, panting and coated in sweat from our vigorous run.

I shove my wet top and sweaty socks into the basket in the laundry room, before padding to the kitchen in bare feet and my training shorts. I walk to the refrigerator to get two bottles of water, when my buddy opens the conversation.

"Spit it out," he says, removing his training top and using it to wipe the sweat from his brow.

I throw a bottle at my buddy while I knock back half of mine before I lean against the counter and contemplate how to start.

Fiero frowns, assessing the torment on my face. "It's bad."

I nod.

Recognition dawns in his blue eyes. "She told you the rest of her truths."

I gulp over the messy ball of emotion clogging my throat as I bob my head again. "It's worse than bad," I admit, rubbing my sweat-slickened chest as a tight pain unfurls across it. I stare at my buddy as I recant Catarina's story, watching his face pale and his features turn green.

"Fucking hell." Fiero claws his hands through his messy blond hair. "Never in a million years did I think you were going to say that."

Folding my arms across my chest, I struggle to breathe over the tsunami of emotions flooding my body. "How are we expected to navigate this?" I almost choke over the words. "I don't know how she can bear to be with me, but I'm grateful she is able to overlook the blood flowing through my veins."

"You're not your brother. She knows that, and she loves you."

"It's killing me, man." Tears prick my eyes. "The thought of what he did to her—in our house—when I had no clue for months." Everything I've been holding inside detonates, and I break down crying in a way I never have before.

Fiero is there, hugging me and offering silent comfort. "It's not your fault. You aren't responsible for the things Carlo, Primo, and your father did to her."

"I feel responsible. She's my wife, and my family hurt her. They stole her ability to be a mother too."

Sympathy splays across his face as he clamps a hand on my shoulder. "I'm so sorry, Massimo. Tell me what I can do to help, and I'll do it."

"We need to ensure the evidence is watertight so when we point the fingers at the Bratva there is zero doubt."

"It's already taken care of." He releases me, leaning his elbows on the counter and staring at me. "Are you going to tell her about the other issue?"

I had been planning to tell Rina because we agreed no more secrets, but it will only add to her troubles. The situation is handled, and she doesn't need to know. I must be able to make some decisions as her husband to protect her without disclosing it. I shake my head. "I can't tell her that now. She is already dealing with too much, and it's handled. I wired the money before you arrived."

"The sooner we get that Russian scum out of the US, the better."

"Fuck," I exclaim as something occurs to me. "No wonder Rina was so hesitant to visit my mother and a bit distant after we did. It must have killed her being back in that house, and I had no clue." Briefly, I bury my head in my hands as another thought occurs to me. "I'm tearing that house down, starting with that fucking fountain." I remember what she said about water, and I now know she wasn't talking about Paulo Conti.

"Don't make any rash decisions while you're emotional," Catarina says, walking into the kitchen. She's dressed in a white power suit and heels, and her hair hangs in straight sheets down her back. Her donna face is intact, and she looks in control while I'm a floundering mess. I'm determined to be strong for her because she's never had anyone to lean on, and I want it to be me from now on.

I walk toward her, wishing I could pull her into my arms, but I stink to the high heavens, and sweat clings to my body like a second skin. "Are you okay?"

"No, but I will be."

I love her honesty, and it confirms she meant everything she said. Not that I doubted her. "Always so fucking strong." I take her hand and bring it to my lips. "I love you."

Her features soften, and the look of love in her eyes is unmistakable. "I love you too, but you don't need to tear down your house for me."

"I hate that place, and I will never ask you to step foot in it again. It holds no good memories for any of us. I'm going to talk to Gabe and my mother. I don't think they'll protest."

"I don't want to cause issues with your family any more than I will when they discover the truth."

I cling to her hand. "We will get through this one day at a time." I wet my lips before I make my next suggestion. "I thought you might like to change our name. I know it must hurt to have his last name. We can take your father's name or choose one of our own."

"You would do that for me?"

"*Mia amata*, I would do anything for you."

Her eyes glaze over as her smile develops. "I'm so not worthy of him," she says, glancing over my shoulder at Fiero.

"I have never met two people more worthy of one another," he loyally replies. Taking a step closer, he stands beside me. Catarina's eyes drift over his naked chest for a split second. Of course, the fucker notices and smirks. I dig him in the ribs.

"Get over yourself, Maltese. I'm a red-blooded woman, and you're standing in my kitchen half naked. Of course, I'm going to look."

I arch a brow, not entirely sure if the emotion I'm feeling is jealousy or pride.

Catarina rolls her eyes. "Don't lose your arrogance now, Massimo. You know you're hot as fuck and the only man I desire."

"She picks me," I tease, fixing a smug grin on my face as I turn to look at Fiero.

"I see it's back to acting like five-year-olds again." She rolls her eyes when I turn my head around to her. "Maybe it's a good thing we can joke, but we have stuff to clear up before we leave." She palms my cheek, staring adoringly at me. "I love how readily you are willing to sacrifice for me, but we're not changing our name."

"We're not?"

She shakes our head. "That would be akin to letting them win. You can't sit on the board of The Commission, let alone ascend Ben as the president, if you aren't a Greco."

"I'll give it up," I reply without hesitation. "I told you you're the only important thing in my life, and I meant it."

Fiero manages to stifle his gasp of surprise before Rina notices.

"Fuck, I love you," she says before pressing a passionate kiss to my lips.

I want to reel her in to my body, but she's dressed and ready for our meeting, and I won't sully her.

"I don't know what I did to deserve you. You're amazing, Massimo, but no. You will not give up your dreams for me."

"You need time to think about it."

"I absolutely don't. I took *your* name, Massimo. *Yours*, not his. Besides, I like to think of them rolling in their graves knowing I carry their name, I married you, and I have more power than they did."

"It's the ultimate fuck you," Fiero agrees, grinning.

"I like to think so."

His expression turns tender. "I know you don't want any more of the heavy, but I need to say this. I'm so sorry for the things you went through. It sickens me. You have always been an impressive woman, but I'm only fully appreciating how impressive now I know the full story."

"You don't hate me for what I planned to do?"

"I admire you for having the courage and the bravery to follow through. You put most dons to shame. I hope you know that."

"Thank you, Fiero. That means a lot to me."

"We've got your back." He slaps his arm around my shoulders. "Massimo may not have mentioned this, but we come as a package deal." He flashes her a grin laden with intent, and I glare at him. Predictably, he chuckles. "I'm only teasing," he tells her. "Kind of."

I punch him in the stomach, only half joking. "Stop hitting on my woman."

He sobers up. "All joking aside, we have both got your back. No one is hurting you on our watch. You got me?"

She audibly gulps, smiling as she nods. "Thank you. It will take some getting used to, but I look forward to sharing the burden."

He saunters toward her, pressing a kiss to her cheek. "I'm willing to share in more ways than one." He waggles his brows before shooting me a wicked grin.

I throw one of my sweaty sneakers at his retreating back as he leaves.

"I can only imagine how the women flocked to your sides when you were younger. You two are quite the team." Catarina steps around me, striding toward the coffee pot.

"You really don't want to know," I murmur, heading to the fridge to retrieve supplies for breakfast. "Are you sure you're okay? I can attend the meeting alone. Make up a plausible excuse for you?"

"I need to work." She takes the eggs and bacon from my hands. "I can't think about all the other stuff until this danger has passed."

"I understand."

"How are you feeling about everything today?" she asks, cracking a few eggs into a bowl.

"Emotional," I truthfully reply, and she nods. "I'm glad there are no more secrets though."

"Me too." She whisks the eggs with a fork. "I thought I knew all there was to know about the past, but it's clear I don't."

"It's a shame you can't talk to Leo or Natalia." I prop one hip against the counter, watching as she adds seasoning to the egg mix. "I bet they would have more insights."

"I thought of that too, but I can't divulge my identity to the Mazzones."

"Agreed. It would be too easy for them to connect the dots. To figure out what your real agenda was." I run my fingers over her long dark hair. "They can't ever find out."

She places bacon on the skillet. "No, they can't."

"What are you going to do about Renzo?"

Pain darts across her face at the mention of his name. "I don't know. His action can't go unpunished."

I press a kiss to her brow. "We don't have to decide his fate now. I'm going to grab a quick shower before breakfast. For now, try to put it out of your mind. We'll go over our story for The Commission in the car. Let's just get through this first hurdle, and then we can discuss how to handle your underboss."

Chapter Forty-One

Catarina

Everyone piles out of the crematorium, and I'm grateful the charade is over. I'm also grateful Don Mazzone and The Commission accepted our explanation, and they believe the Bratva is responsible for everything. Ben is working closely with his contacts on an extradition order for Anton Smirnov, and he has provided additional security at the funeral today to ensure the Russians get nowhere near me or Massimo.

I stand outside the entrance with Massimo and Fiero at my side, surrounded by armed *soldati* as I watch Anais thank the guests for coming at the top of the steps. Cruz stands alongside her, supporting his wife. I didn't miss the venomous looks he leveled at Massimo and Fiero during the ceremony, and I plan to find some time to talk to him today. He is one of the loose ends I need to tie up.

I tried talking to Anais earlier in the week when I visited their house—after the ashes were left anonymously at her door—but it was impossible. She's devastated at the loss of her father and not handling it well.

"We should head to the house," Massimo says, placing his arm on my lower back. "I don't like being out in the open for too long." He's been uber protective these past few days, and I only love him more for it.

It's a relief to have no more secrets between us. I thought telling him the truth would drive us apart when the reality is it has drawn us closer. "I love you." I make a point of telling him every day because I feel so incredibly lucky to have Massimo in my life. I never want him to forget what he means to me.

"I love you too."

"Let me talk to Anais before we go. I just want to ensure she's okay."

Massimo doesn't protest, leading me toward the entrance as Anais and Cruz descend the steps. Cruz whispers something in Anais's ear before walking off as we make our approach. He tosses a snide look at us, making his feelings crystal clear.

"Hey." I walk to my sister and pull her into a hug. "Are you holding up okay?" Massimo hangs back a few steps to give us privacy.

"What do you think!?" She sniffles, extracting herself from my embrace. "My father was just brutally murdered and hand-delivered to my door in a bag of ashes like some...some commoner!" Tears stream down her face. "Of course, I'm not okay!"

Massimo passes me a tissue, and I hand it to her.

She dabs at her tears. "I don't expect you to understand," she says over a sob. "You hated him."

"He hated me too," I gently remind her. "And that's got nothing to do with my concern for you. I am sorry you're hurting." It is the most I can offer her. Guilt pricks at my skin seeing her so upset and knowing I am the cause of it.

"How could someone do this to him? He was one of the most powerful dons in the US, and he didn't deserve to die in such a ghastly manner."

She is as delusional as she is dramatic. Very few dons had much time for Saverio Salerno. He wasn't well respected or liked. And she actually has no clue how he died. No one does. It's all supposition. She's not wrong though. He did die without honor, but it was no less than he deserved. "The Russians don't share our code of honor," I say.

Her eyes blaze with potent anger. "Those fucking bastards are going to pay for this."

"They are being dealt with," Massimo says, stepping up closer. He places his hand on my back as he looks my sister directly in the face. "We haven't been formally introduced. I'm Massimo. I am sorry we are meeting under these circumstances."

"I know who you are." Her assessing gaze roams appreciatively over him from head to toe.

"Quit that shit." I narrow my eyes at her while keeping my voice low. "Massimo is my husband, and if I catch you eye fucking him or flirting with him, I will knock you flat on your ass. I don't care if you're my sister. You will not disrespect me or my husband. While we're on the subject, you need to stop disrespecting your husband before he puts a bullet in your skull."

"All that power has gone to your head," she snidely replies. "You think you're so important that everyone is out to take what you have. News flash, sis." She leans in, an ugly sneer contorting her pretty face. "No one cares. Butt out of my life. You have no say in what I do or *who* I do." She waggles her brows at Massimo and licks her lips.

His mouth curls into a snarl as disgust washes over his features. "News flash, honey. Insult my wife again, and *I'll* put a bullet in your skull. The rumors don't often get it right, but in your case, they hit the nail on the head. You should be grateful your sister gives you any of her precious time. If you were my sibling, I wouldn't waste my fucking breath."

"Are you going to stand there and let him speak to me like that?" she screeches, eyeballing me.

A few heads turn in our direction, and that's our cue to depart. "You threw the first shot, Anais. Don't dish it unless you can handle the blowback."

"Cruz!" she calls out, and it's definitely time to go. "Goddamn it." She stomps her foot. "Where the fuck is he when I need him."

"I don't want to argue with you today. I know you're upset, so I'll let it go. Maybe we can talk later at the house."

"Whatever." She waves her hand in a dismissive fashion, and I feel Massimo tense at my side. Anais pulls out a compact, grimacing as she stares at her face in the mirror. "Gawd, my makeup is ruined." Flipping it closed, she slips it back in her purse and rushes past me. "I need to freshen up." She casts a glance over her shoulder. "I'd say it was nice meeting you, but that would be a lie."

"Touché, sweetheart." Massimo doesn't miss a beat, and Anais stalks off in the direction of the bathroom. "She's awful," my husband says, not mincing his words as he steers us toward the parking lot. "I see none of you in her, and I honestly don't know how you tolerate her."

"You know why I do."

He pierces me with his stunning green eyes. "I know the why of it. I just don't know the how. She's a spoiled little bitch who never grew up."

I expel a sigh. "She's hard work, I know, but I won't give up on her. I can't."

He slams to a halt, reeling me into his arms. "You have a good heart, Rina."

"I'm not so sure you'd say that if you saw all the blackened parts."

"I know goodness when I see it." He nuzzles his nose against mine.

"I love you," I say because it's the totality of what's in my heart right now.

"That will never get old." Massimo tucks me in tighter to his side. "And I love you too, *mia amata*. So fucking much." His lips collide with mine in a hard kiss that reeks of sultry promise. "Later, sexy," he purrs in my ear, and I shiver all over.

Taking my hand, he ushers me toward our SUV. Fiero is waiting alongside it, talking in hushed tones with one of Massimo's men. I swear those two are always plotting and planning and working themselves to the bone.

Ricardo opens the back door, and Massimo playfully swats my ass as I climb inside.

We arrive at the DiPietro family home, where the repast is being held, thirty minutes later. Although I have heard Cruz's family can't abide my sister, they offered up their home because the Salerno gothic mansion is presently in the hands of the Bratva, something The Commission is planning to rectify soon.

Bennett and Sierra, Natalia and Leo, and Serena and Alessandro are exiting their cars at the same time as us, so we walk with them toward the DiPietro mansion. We are only two days into September, and the weather is still warm, so they have set up a marquee at the side of the house.

"You are friends with Anais and Cruz, right?" Natalia Messina says, stepping up beside me as Massimo falls into conversation with Ben and Leo.

"Yes." I smile as Sierra slides up on my other side.

"She seems devastated," Nat adds as a man in a black and white uniform points us around the corner toward the marquee.

"She is distraught," I truthfully admit.

"I remember they were close," Sierra says. She glances quickly around. "I know you shouldn't speak ill of the dead, but I for one am glad that perv is dead. He trapped me one time at a club in Vegas, and he would have forced himself on me if Ben hadn't been there to stop it. He had little regard for human life, trafficking young, kidnapped girls and using them for his own depraved pleasure." A look of disgust materializes on her pretty face. "He tried to force Alesso to move to Vegas after he discovered he was his nephew, and he's spent the past two years pressuring him into taking over as don."

"I doubt many here will miss him," I admit. "And I applaud you for speaking the truth. I hate the bullshit at funerals. How assholes are made out to be veritable saints just because they died. Let's call a spade a spade. He was a horrible man, and he deserved to die without honor."

Natalia grins. "I knew I liked you for a reason."

I return her grin with ease. "I worked with him for years. He was a pig. It sickened me that I couldn't do much about the sex trafficking. I tipped off the authorities a few times when I could get away with it, and he lost some shipments thanks to me. But it was never enough. I am glad it will end now." I glance over my shoulder, noticing Serena and Alesso deep in conversation as they walk hand in hand. "How is Alessandro taking the news, and do you think he'll move to Vegas once it's reclaimed?"

"He's pissed at how his uncle died without honor, but he's not overly upset," Sierra says. "They weren't close."

"He is more concerned about Anais," Natalia adds. "She's...volatile at the best of times, and this has the potential to send her over the edge."

Sierra snorts. "That's more polite bullshit. Anais is a freaking nightmare, and she's going to milk this drama for as long as she can get away with it."

"Sierra!" Nat motions in my direction. "Catarina is friends with Anais."

Sierra lifts her chin and eyeballs me. "From what I've seen, you appreciate directness. I won't pretend to understand how you two are friends when you appear to have nothing in common, but I don't judge you for it. However, I won't lie and tell you I like her when I don't. She has always been cruel to me without justification. She flirted outrageously with Ben for years and manipulated things to try to cause trouble in our relationship. I know she was close to her father, and she's genuinely upset, but she's still putting on a show. She can't help it. She craves attention as badly as I crave dick."

I almost choke on my tongue as we walk along the little stone path transecting the grass, nearing the marquee.

"You used to be such a sweet innocent thing. Look how my brother has corrupted you," Nat says, failing to hide her grin.

Sierra shrugs casually, but there's a wicked glint in her eye. "Ben can corrupt me anytime, though it's more he has helped to coax my true persona to the surface." As if he has supersonic hearing, Bennett turns around and pins his wife with a devilish look that promises lots of fun times.

Sierra giggles as Nat loops her arm through mine. "Those two are always so hot for one another." She smiles fondly at her sister-in-law. "I love how happy you have made my brother. It's all I ever wanted for him."

"He makes me so happy too," she says, positively glowing.

Massimo, Fiero, Ben, and Leo walk into the marquee ahead of us, but my husband slows down. Stopping, he looks over his shoulder at me. I walk toward him. Immediately, he pulls me into his arms and kisses me. When we break apart, his eyes probe mine silently asking if I'm okay.

I press my mouth to his ear. "I'm fine. Go talk business." For once, I'm happy to stay with the wives, gossiping and enjoying the food and drink our hosts have laid out. Massimo can talk the talk with the assholes in suits and update me later.

"We're not the only happy wives, Nat," Sierra says, grabbing my hand and pulling me over to an empty table on our right. "Spill, girlfriend. How is married life?"

I claim a seat to Sierra's right, and Nat sits down beside me. "We want all the salacious details," Nat says. "I bet it's explosive between you. No one missed those sparks that first night at dinner."

"And that wedding kiss?" Sierra fans her face. "Ho-lee fucking hotness. I totally creamed my panties! I was so turned on I dragged Ben into the bathroom when we arrived at the hotel and fucked his brains out."

We all burst out laughing, and I feel eyeballs on the back of my head. Looking over my shoulder, I see my husband smiling in my direction. He likes this for me. And I do too. It's impossible not to like these women, and I need more friends.

"You two are hilarious," I say, wiping the tears from my eyes when I've stopped laughing. "We probably shouldn't be having so much fun at a funeral," I add, sensing some disapproving looks.

"Fuck them." Nat turns and glares at the couple at the next table. "At least we're keeping it real unlike the rest of these fake-holes."

"Oh my God." I crack up laughing again.

"Quit stalling, girlfriend. How are things going with you and Massimo?" Sierra asks, a more serious expression appearing on her face.

"Things are good actually." I can't stop the smile that appears, nor do I want to. "I entered into it determined to keep things professional, but it was impossible when I was already half in love with him."

"Aww." Sierra props her elbows on the table and rests her face in her hands. "I just love hearing that."

"He's sexy as fuck," Nat says. "If he was mine, I'd be climbing him like a tree twenty-four-seven."

I toss my head back and laugh again. "If we weren't so busy, that would totally be happening, trust me." I nudge her in the side. "You are one to talk. Leo is the full package too."

She looks over at her husband with an instant dreamy expression. "He so is. I have loved him for most of my life. I never take him for granted because I spent years longing for him and wishing he was mine. Most days, I pinch myself that this is my life." The brightest smile stretches across her mouth. "When you have spent years living a nightmare, you learn to cherish every moment of the dream."

"I couldn't agree more."

"I love love," Sierra croons, staring at Ben with starry eyes. "It's the most amazing feeling in the world, and we are lucky bitches."

"They are lucky too," Nat reminds her.

"I never thought I would have this," I admit. "Even with all this shit with the Russians, I still wake up with a smile on my face, and it's everything to do with the man waking up alongside me."

"Oh, God. I'm going to cry." Sierra wells up as her sister Serena approaches.

"What did I miss?" Serena asks, claiming the seat beside her sister as Sierra begins to fill her in.

Chapter Forty-Two

Catarina

"Where do you think you're slinking off to?" Massimo asks an hour later as I slip out of the marquee.

I circle my arm around his waist and tip my head up for a kiss. He indulges me with a slow sensual kiss, and I grab a hold of his shirt, pulling him closer and deepening it. When we finally surface for air, we are both grinning at one another like lovesick fools. "You are so beautiful and all mine," he says, playfully swatting my ass.

"Forever," I promise, tugging him with me as I start to walk. "To answer your question, I am going to the bathroom, and then I need a private word with Cruz. I saw him heading inside a few minutes ago."

"You're not confronting him without me."

I slam to a halt. "Massimo, you will only antagonize him. I need to ensure he understands things have changed and warn him to keep quiet."

"I don't trust that fucker. This is nonnegotiable. I'm coming."

I surprise myself by agreeing. My husband is as stubborn as me, and there's little point arguing. "Okay."

We head into the house, and I go to the bathroom. After I've attended to business, we search the house for my brother-in-law, finding him alone in the large library. Cruz is seated on a studded green leather couch to the left of an open fireplace, nursing a glass of whisky in one hand. His lips pull into a grimace, and his eyes narrow when he spots Massimo at my side.

Cruz lifts a second glass of whisky from the end table, offering it to me. "I wasn't expecting the lackey when I poured this for you."

I accept it, leveling him with a cold look as I sit down on the matching couch to the right of the fireplace. "Play nice, Cruz. Massimo is my husband and my partner in business as well as life. He is no one's lackey."

Massimo smirks as he walks to the liquor cabinet, helping himself to the Macallan.

A muscle pops in Cruz's jaw. "You don't need a mouthpiece, Catarina, and what we have to discuss is sensitive."

"Massimo knows everything," I say as my husband sits beside me, pressing his thigh to mine and sliding his arm around the back of the couch behind me.

"Whatever needs to be said can be said to both of us," Massimo coolly replies, eyeballing his former friend with a laser-sharp look. I discreetly sniff my drink before swallowing a mouthful.

"So, it's true then." Cruz swirls the amber-colored liquid in his glass. "You have fallen for his lazy ass and cheesy charm. I must admit I'm disappointed, Catarina. I thought you had discernible taste, but I was obviously mistaken."

"Enough." I lean forward, warning him with my eyes. "These juvenile taunts are beneath you, Cruz. And you aren't the only person disappointed. How is it you failed to mention your past with Massimo to me? And how is it my sister knows nothing about your first fiancée?"

"Our past is irrelevant, just like Rita. Why would I mention some stupid whore to my wife?"

Massimo tenses beside me but only for a second.

Cruz goes in for the kill, fixing Massimo with a condescending grin. "I never had any interest in the slut except to prove I could take anything from you. I bet you still harbor notions of being president of

The Commission. I know that's why you married Rina. You think she'll give you the credibility you're lacking, but even my genius sister-in-law can't work miracles. I will enjoy taking that from you too."

"Your arrogance was always your undoing, Cruz," Massimo says, running the tip of his finger around the rim of his glass. "It's strange you wouldn't mention Rita to Anais. From what I've heard, she's a bigger whore than the first woman who stupidly wanted to be your wife. How *is* Caleb Accardi these days?"

I hop up as Cruz lunges for Massimo, stepping in between them as my husband climbs to his feet. I stretch my arms out, keeping them at bay. "Stop this!" I glare at both of them. "It's pointless and not what we need to discuss." I am going to rip Massimo a new one when we get home.

"We have nothing to discuss," Cruz hisses, straining against my hand. "If you have sided with him, you are now my enemy."

"Don't be ridiculous, Cruz. We're family."

"Maybe not for much longer," he cryptically replies, sending an icy shiver tiptoeing down my spine.

"What the fuck does that mean?" I snap, lowering my arms while cautioning them both with my eyes to stop being idiots.

"It means I am done letting your slut of a sister play me for a fool."

I prod my finger in his chest. "Touch Anais and you'll sign your own death warrant."

"Is that a threat, Donna Greco?"

"It's whatever it needs to be to ensure you don't harm my sister."

"She's my wife. I get to decide what to do with her, and no made man would blame me if I hacked her pretty tits off and made her choke on them."

Unfortunately, he's right. She disrespects an heir by cheating on him with another made man.

"Make one move on Anais, and I'll personally hand-deliver my dossier to The Commission. I know all about your shady deals, Cruz. I know you have been skimming money off the top behind The Commission's back. That stops now, by the way."

Color drains from his face, but he recovers fast. "You won't turn me in because I know too much about your agenda."

"That agenda is no longer valid, and your threat is an empty one." That's not entirely true. Cruz can cause trouble for me unless I can control him. So far, this meeting does not bode well.

"You think Don Mazzone will care about that when he learns the sole reason you came to New York was to eliminate him and wipe the Grecoes from the face of the earth? The latter part I'm still fully on board with, by the way, should you wake the fuck up and come to your senses!" He yells the last part, and I can't stop Massimo in time.

He pushes me aside and throws himself at Cruz, landing a solid punch to his face.

I send an SOS text to Fiero, knowing he's out in the hallway with Ricardo because I messaged him from the bathroom, suspecting I would need backup.

Cruz and Massimo are trading punches when my reinforcements arrive a couple of minutes later. I didn't even attempt to pull them apart because they won't listen to reason.

Fiero and Ric hold them back as I drain my whisky and slam the glass down on the table. "You are immature idiots." I glower at them. "Keep your mouth shut, Cruz. We have a mutual vested interest in keeping our secrets hidden. Neither of us gains if either of us talks."

"I won't breathe a word of it, provided you keep that dossier to yourself."

"Agreed." I rub the back of my neck as I stare at my brother-in-law. "Divorce Anais if you want to get rid of her. The shame will be punishment enough. Do not kill her, or all bets are off." I need to have another word in my sister's ear. She must end this madness with the Accardi heir pronto.

"Like I said, what I do with my wife is my business."

I push my face all up in his. "And like *I* said, touch her and I'll come for you. I will hang you out to dry. I will ruin your reputation before I gut you like a squealing pig and take photographic evidence to share with the world. Don't fucking push me, Cruz."

"Get out of my house, slut," he sneers, spitting at my feet. "You are dead to me now."

Behind me, Fiero is struggling to contain a furious Massimo as he thrashes about cursing and threatening Cruz.

I stand in front of my brother-in-law and plant my hands on my hips. "To think I used to respect you." I rake my gaze over him in a derogatory fashion. "You're nothing, Cruz. A boy pretending to be a man. It's no wonder your father is hesitating lately in announcing a date for his retirement. He knows you're not up to the job. Cristian now." I tap a finger on my chin. "Your little brother could buy and sell you, and you know it. I bet your father does too."

His nostrils flare, and I think he would swing for me if Ricardo wasn't restraining him.

"It seems to me you've got more pressing problems at home. I would watch my back if I was you." Leaving him with those parting words, I grab my wayward husband's hand, linking our fingers, as I hold my head up high, and we get the fuck out of Dodge.

Chapter Forty-Three

Catarina

I wake up blushing, palming my hot cheeks and wondering what the hell that dream was all about. I'm blaming Fiero. His suggestive remarks and half-naked status the other morning have obviously played into my subliminal mind. At least it's a welcome distraction from the painful thoughts that often plague me these nights.

My father, my brother, and Renzo feature heavily in my conscious and subconscious thoughts as I work through my emotions. Pressing business matters keep me occupied during the day, and Massimo keeps me busy all night, fucking me for hours, until I fall asleep from exhaustion. It doesn't always keep the nightmares away, but it helps.

"Morning, sweetheart." Massimo turns on his side, pressing his erection into my hip as he grabs my waist and pulls me to him. "Hmm. You're blushing." He sweeps his fingers across my cheeks as he inspects my face. "What's going on?"

"Nothing." There's no way I can tell him I just had the most erotic dream of my life featuring him, me, and his best friend in a hot threesome that has stirred my libido even in sleep.

I have never considered Fiero in that way, nor would I. I'm one-thousand-percent content with my husband, and our sex life is epic.

However, the dream has me all hot and bothered, and I need Massimo now.

Sitting up, I slowly remove my silk nightdress, flinging it over the side of the bed as I straddle my husband.

"Now, you're talking." Massimo grins, gripping my hips and helping me to get into position. He watches as I lift my body and slowly lower myself down over his hard length. Both of us moan when I'm fully situated on his cock. "Today was already shaping up to be a good day; now it just got a whole lot better," he says.

As I begin moving on top of him, he pierces me with a stunning smile that obliterates all lingering thoughts of that scandalous dream from my mind.

I stand to one side as Don Mazzone concludes the ceremony, officially confirming Massimo as Don Greco. The room breaks out into wild applause as Massimo shakes Ben's hand, wearing a satisfied smile. I stride across the stage in the conference room of the building The Commission owns, heading toward my husband with pride swelling my chest. Massimo hauls me into his arms, dips me down low, and kisses me deeply. There is definitely a bit of a showman in my husband. Catcalls ring out around the room, and I'm grinning when we break apart.

"I'd like a word with both of you before the celebrations start," Ben says. "Follow me."

Our hands move as one, and our fingers thread together as we walk behind the president out into the hallway.

"We'll talk in my office," Ben says when we are in the elevator and it's shooting toward the top level.

"Should we be worried?" Massimo's tone is cool, and his expression is unruffled, but I can tell he's on high alert, like we have been since everything went down with Vegas and the Russians. We aren't fully out of the woods yet.

"Not at all," Ben replies in an equally relaxed manner. "I have a few updates." He glances at our conjoined hands. When he lifts his gaze, his face is set in a genuine smile. "I'm really glad everything worked out with the marriage. I had a feeling it might." He emits a low chuckle. "My wife was convinced you two would fall in love. I should have known not to doubt her."

"Sierra is a very smart woman, and I enjoy her company a lot," I truthfully admit.

The elevator comes to a standstill, and the doors ping and slide open.

"She likes you too." Ben gestures at us to exit first. "We would love it if you could join our three families for dinner this Sunday."

Warmth blooms in my chest. I look up at Massimo, and he smiles, letting me know it's my call. "We would like that very much. Thank you for the invitation."

"It's our pleasure." Ben opens the door to his office, guiding us inside. "I would like to get to know you better, Massimo. Something tells me I could be looking at my future successor."

Bennett's instincts are super sharp. Without knowing anything, he can tell there is a lot more to Massimo than meets the eye.

"I won't lie," Massimo says, holding out a chair for me. "I want the presidency."

Ben grins over his shoulder as he pours drinks. Bourbon for him and Massimo and whisky for me. Massimo sits beside me in front of the desk, immediately reclaiming my hand.

I think hand-holding is so underrated.

I get a distinct thrill every time my husband links his fingers in mine.

The feel of his strong warm palm nestling against mine always calms me, and I feel invincible walking side by side with a man who is my equal in every way.

Ben distributes the drinks before settling in his seat behind the desk. Behind him, the city pulsates with energy through the window as another eventful day draws to a close. "I doubt you'll have much competition. Maltese is a stubborn bastard who won't relinquish his seat till his deathbed."

He won't have a choice. When we play our cards, Fiero will force that misogynistic prick to retire, and he won't be able to say no.

"Luca Accardi has just agreed to remain on the board for another four years, but he will definitely be stepping down then."

Surprise registers on Massimo's face. "I thought the twins were due to replace him at the end of this year?"

"There is a clause in the contract Gino Accardi constructed that allows Luca to defer their appointment until they are twenty-five if he deems they aren't ready. I don't mind admitting I approached Luca and asked him to stay on. Caleb and Joshua are not ready. They need more time."

"I bet that went down well." Massimo's lips twitch.

"Like a lead balloon," Ben deadpans, bringing his glass to his lips. He takes a slow sip while we drink our own drinks. "Twenty-one is far too young to be given all that responsibility. I'm looking out for my nephews as much as I'm safeguarding the Accardi business. Of course, neither of them sees it like that. I'm persona non grata right now. If you see them snubbing me and Leo on Sunday, you'll know why."

"They will thank you some day," I suggest. "When they are older and wiser and realize you did it for the right reasons."

"They are too busy partying to stay mad at you and Leo for long," Massimo adds.

"We'll see." Ben levels me with a solemn look. "I thought you'd like to know Anton Smirnov was put on a plane back to Moscow this morning along with a group of twenty we identified who were in collusion with him."

"That is great news. Thank you for letting me know."

"I would keep your security tight for another few months to ensure the coast is clear," Ben supplies. "But I believe the threat to both your lives has passed."

I wouldn't be too sure about that, and he's not the only threat.

Somehow, Renzo escaped from the safe house last night. He killed four of my men, and this morning, I gathered everyone and formally announced that Renzo Dutti is a traitor and no longer my underboss. Massimo and I are accelerating our plans to link our organizations together. We are agreed that Dario will remain as *consigliere,* but we need to appoint a new underboss and decide on the structure between both sets of capos.

Ben's gaze dances between us, pulling me out of my head and back into the moment. "The Commission would like to formally thank both of you for the work you have done in smoothly transitioning the transfer on the streets. We know it came at significant risk."

It's hard to maintain eye contact when he believes the Bratva came after us because we run the street trade and they are desperate for an in, but we must. I hate lying by default to Bennett and his family. It feels wrong because they have all been so welcoming and it seems like he might want to take Massimo under his wing. However, we can't admit the truth without risking everything.

"What about Vegas?" Massimo asks. "When are we attacking, and who is going to run it?"

"That is the other thing I wanted to talk to you about. We will need some Greco *soldati.* We want this to be a true Italian American operation, involving all five families of The Commission and *soldati* from neighboring states. It's important we strike hard and fast and show them the true might of our organization. That is why we plan to attack this weekend. You are both invited to a meeting tomorrow where Leo will outline the strategy."

"We'll be there," I confirm.

"Whatever you need from us, you have it," Massimo adds.

Ben nods and smiles. "The Bratva may have wised up on several levels, but they will soon learn that retaking Vegas was a dumb move."

We raise our glasses to that.

"As for the leadership in that region, it has been decided that Cruz DiPietro will become Vegas don. I need Alesso here, and he wasn't keen on uprooting his family. At least, not at this time."

My brows climb to my hairline in surprise. Not that it wasn't a potential option, but after what Cruz said at the funeral, I doubted this would happen.

"That surprises you," Ben says, looking at both of us.

"Cruz hasn't hidden his ambitions," Massimo says. "He wants the presidency too."

"I am well aware." Ben takes another mouthful of his expensive bourbon. "He would not be my choice, but his father pressed for Vegas because he believes it will give Cruz an opportunity to show what he's capable of." He clears his throat. "I also have personal reasons for wanting both of them out of New York."

I am guessing he wants Anais away from Caleb, and it's evident Sierra doesn't like or trust my sister. I honestly cannot say I blame her. Anais spotted me at the table with them at the funeral, and she's refusing to speak to me now. That could in part be because Cruz has said something to her. I don't know because she won't answer my calls. I am concerned for my sister and worried about what Cruz might do to her when she's out of sight. "I assume Cruz's appointment is reliant on Anais remaining his wife."

"You are correct, and that point has been made to him." Ben sits up straighter. "Do not worry about Anais. Alesso will be visiting regularly and remaining in constant contact with her."

A layer of stress lifts from my shoulders. I know Alessandro will not let anything happen to his cousin. Cruz knows it too. For now, this maneuvering secures Anais's safety. Perhaps in the long run, this will be a good thing for everyone. Removing Cruz from New York will smooth the way for Massimo to put his succession plans into place, and it will help to avoid confrontation.

I am guessing Cruz has his own plans, but we will anticipate them and react accordingly.

Yes, this is a good thing.

"Does that mean DiPietro will not retire now, or is he appointing Cristian to replace him in New York?" I inquire.

"I am unsure," Ben says. "But I will be strongly advising against appointing Cristian at this juncture for the same reasons I didn't want the twins taking control now."

"It seems like there are interesting times ahead." Massimo drains the last of his bourbon.

"Indeed."

Reading between the lines, it seems like Massimo is the only horse to back in the race, and Ben taking us into his confidence like this is the first strategic move on the board. It will align perfectly to our goals when we are ready to reveal Rinascita and who our main supplier actually is. For now, everything is running smoothly. But we want things fully settled and to have at least six months behind us before we approach The Commission with the truth.

Ben finishes his drink and stands. "I will let you get to your celebrations. I have a few calls to make, but I'll meet you downstairs in the ballroom in due course." He turns his head to me, wearing a smile. "Please remind that wife of mine it's her turn to get up with Rhys tonight and she should go easy on the bubbly." He grins. "It will probably go in one ear and out the other. Sierra knows I'll do the night feed, and I don't begrudge her a few drinks, but she always drinks too much and then whines about never drinking again the next day while nursing a baby and having a hangover."

Massimo chuckles as his arm automatically winds around my waist, and he instinctively pulls me in close. "Sounds like fun times."

"Just wait until it's your turn." His grin expands.

Knots twist in my gut, and I have to force the smile to stay on my face.

"We'll let you get to it," Massimo says, turning me around as he rides to the rescue. "See you downstairs, and thanks for the heads-up on everything. We appreciate it greatly."

Chapter Forty-Four

Catarina

As soon as the door is closed behind us, Massimo walks me down the hallway, pressing me up against the last door at the end. "Don't cry, sweetheart. Please. Your tears kill me."

I didn't even realize I was crying until he swipes at the dampness gathering on my cheeks. "I haven't given any thought to babies in years," I truthfully admit, placing my hands on his hips as he cages me in with his arms. "I was so angry when I first found out. It was during those difficult first few years. But I learned to accept it. I didn't see marriage and a family in my future then anyway."

"And now?" He sweeps his thumbs under my damp eyes.

"Now I want it all with you," I blurt.

"Then you shall have it." I peer deep into his eyes when he tilts my chin up. "Do you trust me?"

"Completely." There is zero hesitation in replying.

"Then trust I will make it happen."

His words fill me with warmth and light and hope, and he truly has a talent for soothing my damaged soul. "Okay," I say as a loud groan filters underneath the door alongside us.

It's followed by an ear-piercing scream and "Caleb!" shouted in a voice that's all too familiar.

I don't hesitate to open the door and barge my way inside. Caleb Accardi has my sister bent over a desk with her dress shoved up to her hips and her bare ass on display as he fucks her roughly from behind.

"Fuck off," Caleb barks, briefly turning his head in our direction as I stalk across the room, followed by Massimo.

This guy is un-fucking-believable. He has no respect for the rules, and if he keeps this up, he'll be lucky to see twenty-one.

"What the hell do you think you're doing?" I shout at Anais when I reach her. Her body jostles across the desk as Caleb continues fucking her, grunting and groaning as he thrusts his big dick into her pussy.

"What the fuck does it look like?" Caleb retorts. He turns to Massimo. "Dude, seriously. Get your wife out of here. It's none of her business."

"Get lost, Cat," Anais pants in between moans.

"You are going to get yourself killed," I say, ignoring their protests.

"You can't fuck a made man's wife. Especially not someone who will shortly be a don." Massimo attempts to reason with Caleb. "It's suicide."

It's hard to reason with either of them when they're still screwing in front of us.

"Old man, stay out of shit that doesn't involve you. You don't know what you're talking about."

I fight a smile at his "old man" comment and the dark expression that greets Caleb when he says those words to my husband.

"Jesus Christ."

We all turn to look at the newcomer. Caleb curses under his breath as Leo storms into the room like an angry thunderstorm.

"Hold on, slut." Caleb digs his fingers into Anais's hips as he picks up his pace, rutting into her like a madman. "This will be fast thanks to these interfering pricks."

This seriously has to be seen to be believed. He's a disrespectful punk with a serious death wish. I'll admit he's hot as fuck if you're into dirty-blonds with an obvious chip on their shoulder. How can Anais let him treat her like this? It's obvious Caleb is only using her for sex and to push Cruz's buttons while delivering a strong f-you to the established rules. Briefly, I wonder if Cruz did something that caused Caleb to target his wife or if it was my sister who hit on him first.

"I'll handle this," Leo says when he reaches us.

We nod and move to leave when he pulls us aside. "I'd really appreciate your discretion."

"We won't breathe a word of it to anyone," I tell him.

A tired sigh escapes him. "Thanks. I owe you."

Massimo slides his arm around my shoulders as we walk across the room and out into the hallway. My husband pulls the door shut to the sounds of Caleb spilling his wicked seed inside my equally wicked sister.

"Well, that was an eventful day and night," Massimo says three hours later when we are en route home in our car. Ricardo sits up front beside the driver, and we have a security detail of ten men escorting us home in two cars—one in the front and one behind. It seems excessive to me, but if my husband needs to do this for his sanity, I will not complain.

"When are our days ever not eventful?" I kick off my heels and pull my feet up onto the back seat, snuggling deeper into his side.

He presses soft kisses into my hair as I lean against him and siphon some of his warmth. "I'm so proud of you," I say, looking up into his gorgeous forest-green eyes. "Your speech was so eloquent, and it's obvious the men already respect you more than they did your brother."

"Leaking the truth of my contract killing past was a genius idea, *mia amata*. You are not just a pretty face." He rubs his nose against mine.

"Watch it, mister, or you'll be sucking your own cock when we get home."

"Wouldn't that be a skill." He chuckles, tweaking my nose.

I move to punch him in the junk, but he grabs my hand. "Don't damage the goods, sweetheart. It's counterproductive when we both know you're fucking soaked and dying for a spin on my dick."

"True." I give up the fight. "No point in being stupid about it." I press a lingering kiss to the underside of his jaw, nuzzling my nose in his short beard.

"It was a brilliant move, and I'm grateful to have such an intelligent wife." He loops his fingers in my hair. He loves playing with it when it's down. "My contract-killer rep has gone a long way toward garnering respect, but I will only truly have their loyalty when I earn it. When I prove I deserve it."

"It won't take long for them to see who you truly are."

"Or for them to appreciate what they have in both of us." He raises my knuckles to his lips and kisses my skin. "The sky is the limit, *mia regina*."

"The world is our oyster."

"The possibilities are endless." His lips kick up at the corner.

"There are no limitations." I stifle a giggle.

"We are smarter than cheesy clichés." Massimo gathers me in his arms as we drive through the gates of our home.

"In our defense, it's late and we're tired. We can't always be brilliant linguists."

"Who says we can't?" He kneads my breast through my dress. "We can do anything we set our minds to."

"Never let the fear of striking out keep you from playing the game."

He grins. "Good one, sweetheart, but I've got one better." He clears his throat. "Don't be afraid to give up the good for the great."

"Pfft." I wave my hands in the air in a dismissive fashion. "The most difficult thing is the decision to act; the rest is merely tenacity."

"Amelia Earhart. So, we're upping the game. I like it." His brow puckers as he searches his brain for a comeback, and I snort out a laugh at the serious look on his face. His eyes light up and his brow flattens as he puffs out his chest. "I've got the winner."

"If you say so." I'm fighting to trap my laughter.

Pinning me with a look of superiority, he says, "Throw off the bowlines, sail away from the safe harbor, catch the trade winds in your sails. Explore. Dream. Discover."

"Ah, Mark Twain for the win." I giggle, conceding defeat as I am unable to play anymore because I'm laughing too much.

I'm still laughing when Massimo lifts me outside.

But I'm not laughing when ear-shattering sirens ring out and flashing red lights surround us as Massimo's high-tech security system blares out warnings. "Fuck!" Massimo curses, reopening the back door and attempting to shove me instead. "Get in the fucking car, Rina, until I find out what's going on."

"No way," I snap back, grabbing my heels and slipping them on my feet. I remove my gun and my dagger from where they are strapped to my body. "We do this together."

"You're so stubborn." He snags my wrist and pulls me behind the car as men tumble out of the security cars and surround us. We stride toward the house as Massimo calls someone on his phone.

Before we can get safely inside, a slew of bullets flies at us from the side garden, and everyone drops to the ground.

"Ree-ree," a man with a familiar voice hollers, and I squeeze my eyes shut, pretending like I didn't hear it.

If Renzo is really here, his fate is no longer in my hands.

"Get the fuck away from me," Renzo roars.

I climb to my feet and run toward the sound of his voice because I can't see him yet.

"Rina!" Massimo shouts, racing after me. He grabs my elbow and pulls me back as Renzo continues to scream my name in between muffled shouts. "Are you fucking insane?" my husband shouts. "You can't go out there! He's unhinged and as liable to kill you by mistake as to kill me by desire."

"Tell them not to kill him, Massimo." I send him a challenging look. "Do it now. I need to speak to him."

"No, sweetheart. You really don't. Let it go. Let him go. You knew it would come to this." His face falls and I see it.

"You know something, and you haven't told me."

"It only fell into place today. I was planning on telling you tomorrow."

I jerk out of his arm and take a step back. "We said no more secrets, Massimo." Ingrained mistrust surges to the surface as I take another step back. "I want to speak to Renzo now. Give the order, Massimo."

He hesitates, and anxious butterflies swoop into my chest.

"If you truly have nothing to hide, you'll bring him to me."

"I don't have anything to hide, Rina. I'm trying to protect you."

"I don't need your fucking protection!" I scream. "When I want it, I'll ask for it. Until then, you treat me like an equal, or I walk away. I mean it, Massimo."

"Okay, okay. Relax. I'll give the order." He speaks into his cell and repeats the order through a walkie-talkie handed to him by one of his men.

Tension leaks into the space between us as we stare at one another. "I'm not your enemy, *mia amata*. I'm your husband, and I love you. You have to let me protect you and trust I'll tell you when the time is right. This past week has been a shit show. I know you're strong. So fucking strong. But you haven't dealt with any of your emotions yet, and I didn't want to add this to it."

"So, what? You were going to kill him and tell me after the fact?"

"Yes." He doesn't flinch or attempt to deny it, reminding me of who my husband is.

It's a struggle to hold myself together as Renzo appears in my line of sight. He's dressed head to toe in black, and it's hard to make out his features. But the string of colorful expletives littering the air as Massimo's men escort him across the lawn is undeniably Renzo.

"You don't have to do this," Massimo says, moving in closer when he sees how I'm trembling. "You don't always have to be strong. Lean on me. Please."

I stare up at him with tears shining in my eyes. "You know this has to be me. This is not something I can delegate."

"This will hurt, *mia amata*. Please, I'm begging you. Let me handle it."

I shake my head. "I don't shirk my responsibilities, Massimo, and I need to understand why."

Resignation crests over his face as he nods. "As you wish, *mia regina*." He steps up behind me, placing his hand on my quivering lower back. Warmth seeps from his hand to my skin, minimizing the tremors. "I am here for you. Whatever you need, just ask."

I blink successively as Renzo comes closer, sure my eyes must be deceiving me. "Is that...a wetsuit?" Disbelief threads through my tone.

"It fucking is. The crazy bastard swam up to my beach."

It shows how desperate he is. Renzo knows he wouldn't get near the house from the road, but he also knows Massimo has men stationed along his property and a security system with trip wires and cameras all over the grounds.

He knew he'd be caught, but he still came, which can only mean one thing: he needs to tell me something or he wants to confess and die at my hands.

"Get your fucking hands off me," Renzo snarls, fighting the men holding him, but it's pointless. He's outnumbered. There are armed men surrounding us on both sides. If he makes one false move, they'll riddle him with bullets.

"Has he been checked for weapons?" Massimo asks when they come closer.

"He is clean. He had a Glock on him, but we have it in our possession," a short stocky guy says, gripping Renzo's arm tight as he shoves him forward.

"Ree-ree, get away from him," Renzo yells, jabbing his finger in Massimo's direction. "He's going to kill you! It's all been a trap. Please."

Prickles of apprehension climb up my spine as I instinctively move away from Massimo. I stare at my husband. "What's he talking about?"

"The Russians put out a hit on you, Ree-ree, and he took the contract. He accepted payment to kill you!" Renzo shouts, his tone borderline hysterical, his eyes manic and darting wildly about. "Run now! Get away from him before he ends you!"

Chapter Forty-Five

Massimo

Rina's shoulders collapse, and she takes a step forward, leaning into me. Thank fuck for that. For a second, I thought she might believe the misguided crazy man in the wetsuit on my lawn. I hate Renzo Dutti with the intensity of a thousand suns, but looking at him now, it's hard not to feel a smidgeon of sympathy.

He's a broken man. His attempts to manipulate the situation to protect the woman he loves has failed spectacularly. If I was in his shoes, I'd be desperate and reckless too. He's screaming at Rina to get away from me, and I can practically feel her heart breaking. I wrap my arm around her. "What can I do for you?"

She looks up at me with tears in her eyes. "Just hold me?"

"Always."

She reaches up, dragging her fingers through the trimmed hair on the side of my face. "Jacobi came through."

I nod. "He did. I was going to tell you, but this all happened when that shit went down with the Russians, and you were under enough stress. I know you have pushed everything aside to get through this past week, but you're human, sweetheart. There is only so much one person can handle. I just wanted to shield you for a while. I would have told you when things calmed down."

"I know that." Turning around, she hugs me, clinging to me tightly. "Give me some of your strength, Massimo," she whispers in my ear as she holds on to me. "I know you have some to spare."

"I will be your strength." I kiss her, conscious of the madman screaming and shouting in the background. The longer this goes on, the more it'll hurt my wife. "Ask him, sweetheart. Ask him to tell you what he's done."

If he won't tell her, I'll shoot him myself and fill her in afterward. I wish our surveillance had discovered the truth sooner, and we might have been able to avoid some of the recent events.

Catarina turns around in my arms, and I hold her against my body, offering her the silent support she asked for.

"What have you done, Renzo?"

He continues to shout warnings, and I'm not even sure he heard her. Rina walks toward him, and my instinct is to pull her back, but he's not a threat to her. Not in a physical sense, anyway, so I let her go, remaining close in case I need to intervene.

"Renzo, you need to take a breath and start at the beginning," she says in a soft voice, the kind you would use with a child or someone mentally impaired, which her underboss appears to be at this time. "Massimo isn't going to kill me. He bought the contract so no one else would come after me."

"He's lying!" Renzo's eyes are dark as night as he glares at me.

"No, he isn't. I was with him when he made the deal with the man who organizes the contract killings. He isn't going to kill me, Ren. He loves me as much as I love him."

Renzo slumps against my men, but they keep him propped up. "I came to warn you, but it was for nothing. He has brainwashed you." He turns pleading eyes on her. "The girl I knew, the woman I fell in love with, is gone. You have changed. He has changed you."

"Yes, I have changed. I'm not the same person I was. I couldn't be. Not after everything I have discovered about the past and myself. I wish you could see my life is changing for the better. I wish you would have come and talked to me about whatever went down. All of this could've been avoided."

"I don't see how," he says in a dejected voice. All of the fight has left him, and sympathy rears its head again. "I tried to protect you. You and Maria. But I failed."

"What has Maria got to do with this?" Rina asks.

"Everything," Renzo replies. He pulls himself upright and looks a little bit more lucid as he starts explaining. "I found out a couple of months ago that Maria was cheating on me. It's not the first time. A year ago, I told her I was leaving and taking the kids with me, and she promised she would stop and recommit to me." He shakes his head. "I should never have believed her. She ruined everything."

"What did she do?" Rina asks.

"She started up with a Russian guy, a mobster. Anton placed him in her path. He had her spying on me. She was passing him intel."

"Anton was always planning to betray me," Rina says, and I know she's beating herself up for not seeing it. For trusting him when he didn't deserve it.

"Yes, but it's more complicated than that." He looks over her head at me. "He discovered Fiero and Massimo had a drug operation in Cali and they were eating up his territory in Europe. He suspected they had big plans for the US. He wanted you to marry him so you could get access to both of them."

"He was going to ask me to kill them," Rina says, quickly slotting the pieces into the puzzle.

He nods. "He intended to ask you to spy on them for him first. He wanted to ambush their facility and take control of it."

"It was the Russians who attacked our plant," I say, something else we only recently confirmed.

"I followed Maria one night," Renzo says, continuing the story. He seems determined to confess everything before he meets his maker. "I knew she was cheating again, and I wanted evidence to take with me to court. When I saw the guy, he had the Bratva marking on him, and I went ballistic. I waited up for her when she got home, and I made her tell me everything. She confessed she had been giving the douche intel on you and our plans."

"Why didn't you come to me?" Rina asks.

"I knew you would kill her. She was the mother of my children, and I did love her at one time. She hated you," he blurts, unburdening himself fully. "She knew I loved you, and she hated both of us. I didn't want her to die at your hands, and I thought, at first, I could use the situation to our advantage."

We could have if he had come to us and we ensured it was executed correctly.

"I told her I wouldn't hand her over to you if she fed specific intel to Anton."

"You gave him false intel," Rina surmises.

Renzo nods. "And I tried my best to get you not to marry Massimo. Your initial plan was to kill him, but I knew you could never do it if you reconnected with him. I remember how you were in the hours after you left him at the airport that first time. I saw the look on your face. I knew Massimo was special. I knew there was a strong chance you would fall for him and not be able to kill him, and I was right."

"What did Maria do?" Rina asks, knowing his wife was not in any way trustworthy.

"She double-crossed me. She gave them the fake info, and they acted on some of it to throw me off the scent. The rest of the time she was still spying on me. She overheard me talking to Dario, and she told them you were in love with Massimo and wouldn't kill him. That's when Anton decided to take matters into his own hands."

"Jesus, Renzo." Rina sighs and leans back against me. I band my arms around her body and hold her close.

"He held Maria hostage. He told me she would die unless I helped him to reclaim Vegas, so I did. But I tipped Saverio off so he could get out. I told him you sold him out so he would come here and you could have your revenge."

"Did you leak our location? Did you set the Russians after us on the highway?" she asks.

He vehemently shakes his head. "I didn't, but he clearly had people following me. I looked out for tails, and I didn't see any, but they must have been there." Rina must have a doubtful expression on her face because he says, "I swear, Ree-ree. I would never give you up to them. I love you. I was trying to protect you and keep the mother of my children alive."

"Where are your kids, Renzo?" my wife asks.

"They are safe. They are in Mexico on vacation with their grandparents. I have a full security detail protecting them."

"I have all the details," I say into my wife's ear because I know she will want to ensure they are looked after.

"Anton sent you to kill Massimo and me when the highway attempt failed," Rina says.

"He sent me to kill Massimo. He said if I delivered his head, he would free Maria." He chokes over a sob. "He's a lying son of a bitch. She was already dead. He killed her the day he took her."

Tension radiates from my wife in spades, and I run my hand up and down her arm in what I hope is a soothing gesture.

"He'd told me if I didn't deliver Massimo he would kill my wife and kill you next. When I didn't show up at the meet, he dumped Maria's body in our backyard and took out a hit on you. You had me locked in the safe house, and I was fucking terrified. I didn't know what had happened—just that Anton would be making a move."

"You fucking idiot!" Rina yells. "That was the time to come clean, Ren!"

"I know." His tone is meek. "It was just another mistake after a slew of them. Another bad judgment call in a long line of them."

"You killed four of my men, Renzo, and you went behind my back, conspiring with the Russians. You tried to murder Massimo. You should have just come to me at the start. If you'd told me everything, we wouldn't be here."

"You think I don't know that?" Tears glisten in his eyes, highlighted under the moon and the strength of my outdoor lighting. "You think I want to make my kids orphans?"

"You know I don't have a choice," Rina says. Her body trembles against me, and I have to try again.

"I can do this. You shouldn't be the one to do it, *mia amata*," I whisper in her ear.

"It's got to be me." Her voice is devoid of emotion as she steps out of the protective embrace of my arms.

"I know, my donna."

Catarina nods at my men, and they push Renzo to his knees. "I love you," he says, looking up at her. "I always have, and I always will. It has been an honor to watch you grow into the woman you are today. You wouldn't be that woman if you didn't do what needs to be done. I forgive you."

Rina takes a few seconds to speak, and I can tell she's struggling to hold on to her composure. But I don't intervene. She doesn't want that. She needs to handle this herself, and I will be there to help her pick up the pieces. "As I forgive you," she says. She kneels in front of him. "I love you too, Renzo. Not in the same way, but there is love in my heart for you. I will never forget what you did for me. I will never forget how you cared for me and helped me to heal." Her voice cracks, and she pauses for a few seconds. "I want to hate you for putting me in this position, but I can't hate you. You did it because you were trying to protect me."

"Don't hate yourself either," he tells her, and I respect him for not protesting the inevitable. "Can you make sure my children are okay? Their grandparents will take them in. I altered my will to leave everything to them in a trust until my kids turn eighteen."

"You have my word your children will be looked after. I will check in on them myself regularly. I will ensure they want for nothing."

"Thank you." He leans in and kisses her briefly.

I want to hate him for it, but he's too tragic a character to hate him any longer. He is the creator of his own demise—he and his wife, and it's their kids who will pay the price.

A serene sort of peace sweeps over his face. "I am ready." He clasps his hands in front of him and bows his head.

I offer my hand, and Catarina holds on to it as she rises to her feet.

She pricks his thumb with her knife before placing her hand on his downturned head. "He entered alive and leaves dead. May God have mercy on your burned soul." Removing her hand from his head, she steps back, lifting her gun.

Around us, every man has gone completely silent and motionless, watching this play out.

"Rest in peace, Ren," she whispers before pulling the trigger.

The shot is clean; straight through his skull, and he falls forward, dropping dead at her feet. The gun slides out from her hand, falling to the ground, as she turns around and walks for the front door, somehow holding herself together on the outside while I know she is self-destructing inside.

Chapter Forty-Six

Massimo

"Hey. How is she?" Nicolina asks the second she steps foot in the kitchen. I load the plate of eggs and bacon onto the tray beside the toast, orange juice, and coffee before turning to my wife's best friend.

"The same. I'm really starting to worry now. It's been four days, and she won't come out of the bedroom. I have to force her to shower and eat, and she's barely talking. She still hasn't cried." I scrub a hand along the thick growth on my chin. "I don't know what else to do to help her." I have never felt so helpless.

"I will try to entice her to take a walk or a run on the beach," she says.

"You can try again, for sure, but let me take her breakfast first." Grabbing the tray, I walk out of the kitchen and along the hallway to our bedroom.

Rina is lying on her side on the bed, staring forlornly into space, when I enter. Pain spears through my chest at the sight of her. I hate seeing her look so lost, so vulnerable, so tormented.

"Nic is here to see you," I say, rounding the bed and setting the tray down on the bedside table. Sighing, she peers up at me with the saddest eyes I've ever seen. I brush hair off her face and tuck it behind her ears. "I have breakfast."

"I'm not hungry."

"Like I've said, you need to eat, sweetheart." I kiss her softly. "You're scaring the shit out of me, *mia amata*. I hate seeing you like this."

"I don't know how to deal with it," she meekly says, pulling herself upright in the bed. "I can't reconcile what he did. What I had to do. I don't know how to feel or which emotion is the most prevalent. I'm mad. Hurt. Sad. Guilty. And I feel so betrayed."

Tears fill her eyes as she stares at me, and I hate to call it progress, because I hate seeing her upset, but it is. This is the most she has said to me in recent days, and it's the first time she has spoken about Renzo. It appears some emotion is filtering through, and that's a good thing. She needs to let it all out before she can begin to grieve and heal. She has been dealt several blows this past week, and it's a lot to take in.

"I just can't make sense of it. I keep going round and round in my head. How could this have happened? How could he do this instead of coming to me? Is it my fault because there was tension between us?" She shakes her head and rubs her eyes.

"He made his own choices, Rina. He chose to handle it alone instead of talking to you. This isn't your fault. Renzo didn't blame you. He knew and accepted what you had to do. He told you he forgave you, so you need to forgive yourself, sweetheart. You know he wouldn't want to see you like this."

She shrugs, clamping her lips shut, and I sense our conversation is over for now. I scoop up a forkful of eggs, and she opens her mouth, letting me feed her, like every other time. When she's done, she drinks some juice and reaches for the mug of coffee. "Would you like me to send Nic in? She thought you might like to go for a walk on the beach."

Rina clasps the mug in both hands, setting the base down on top of her raised knees. Tilting her head to the side, she stares at me. "Actually, could we get out of here today?"

Apart from doing some work from home, I have made no other

plans because I want to be here to support my wife. Whatever she wants or needs from me, she's got it. "For sure." I press a lingering kiss to her brow. "Do you have anywhere particular in mind?"

She shakes her head. "I just want to get away from the house."

I wish Renzo's death hadn't occurred here. Now, I fear every time we step outside she'll be reminded of what went down. Clearing my throat, I articulate the idea that's been mulling around in my head. "I thought we could buy a tree and plant it out front as a kind of memorial. If you like."

Tears well in her eyes again. "I think I'd like that."

"Okay." Clasping her face in my hands, I dot kisses all over her cheeks, her brow, and her lips. "I know the perfect place, and on the way back, we can stop at the garden center and select a tree."

"Thank you." Putting her mug down, she circles her arms around me and holds me close. "Thank you for taking care of me these past few days. I promise I'll do better. I just needed a few days."

"You're not a burden, Rina. You're my wife." I lift her onto my lap and band my arms around her. "It's okay to be sad or angry or frustrated or however else you feel."

"I don't do this. This isn't me," she says, nuzzling my neck. "I don't fall apart. I pick myself up and keep going. Why can't I now?"

"You've been dealt a lot of heavy blows, and I think you were already letting down your guard, allowing yourself to feel things you normally block. This is an extension of that." I wind my fingers through her hair. "You need to feel, Rina. You need to vent your emotions before you can begin to process them and move forward. And it's perfectly fine to do that. You loved Renzo. You loved your father and your brother. You need to mourn them in order to truly put the past to rest."

"When did you get so wise?" she asks, clinging tightly to me.

"I came out of the womb this way," I quip, silently fist pumping the air when her lips kick up slightly at the corners.

"Lucky for me," she whispers, hugging me tighter. I just hold her, burying my nose in her hair and praying we might have turned a corner. My wife is the strongest woman I have ever known, and she will bounce back from this. I'm sure of it.

I leave Nicolina with Catarina while I clean up the kitchen and check I have enough gas in my bike, and then I take a long hot shower.

The door slides open behind me, and I turn around as my wife steps under the water, tilting her face up under the showerhead. Coming up behind her, I carefully place my hands on her hips as I rest my chin on her rapidly dampening hair. "Is this okay?"

She tilts her head back so she's looking at me. "More than okay."

"Can I wash you?" I ask, reaching for the washcloth and her watermelon-scented shower gel.

She nods, and I soap up the cloth before gently dragging it across her neck, down along her collarbone, over her heavy breasts, and onto her toned stomach, desperately trying to ignore my aching cock.

I turn her around and wash her back, trailing the cloth over her shapely ass and the backs of her legs. Kneeling in front of her, I rub the cloth over her feet, along her calves, and up to her thighs before sweeping it across her pussy.

She sucks in a gasp and clutches my hair. "Please," she whimpers.

I look up at her from between her legs. "What do you need, *mia amata*?"

"You. I need you inside me."

I will never deny her. Leaning in, I swipe my tongue along her slit before pressing a finger inside her. She's already slick and ready for me, but I spend a couple of minutes feasting on her before I stand. Pressing her against the tile wall, I push her legs apart before urging her to wrap them around my waist. She obliges without question, resting her hands on my shoulders as I hold her up and line my dick up at her entrance.

Our eyes remain connected as I slowly inch inside her, leaking precum when her tight walls clench my shaft as I sink all the way in. "I love you," I say before claiming her lips in a sensual kiss. I move slowly because I don't have it in me to fuck her hard. I need to be gentle with her. To ensure she feels my love.

"Love you back," she pants over a moan as I thrust deep and slowly pull out. Her arms snake around my neck as her legs tighten at my waist. I hold her up, pressed against the wall as I make love to her while devouring her lips and pouring everything I feel for her into every thrust and every kiss.

Her breaths ooze out in sharper bursts, her walls clench me firmly, and she rocks her hips up, demanding more as she nears her climax. Picking up my pace, I thrust into her harder while rubbing her clit, reaching my own release seconds after she reaches hers.

Reluctantly, I pull out, setting her feet on the ground. She rests her head on my chest and bands her arms around me, and we stand under the water without talking, just embracing, until our skin wrinkles and the water cools. I quickly wash and condition her hair before switching the shower off and bundling her up in a big fluffy towel.

"I thought we could take a trip on my bike," I say as we dry off. "I haven't had time to take you out on it yet."

"I'd like that."

We dress in jeans, T-shirts, sweaters, and boots and head out to the garage, where my Ducati awaits us.

"I have always wanted to ride on a motorcycle." She trails her fingers along the slick bodywork. She offers me a shy smile as I fit the helmet over her head, tucking her ponytail in. "I'm glad you're claiming this first."

"You're going to love it." I predict. "It's such a rush."

I get on and she climbs up behind me, pressing close to my back as her arms tighten around me.

We take off slowly, navigating my twisty driveway and out through the gates. I take the back roads to the park, picking up speed the farther we travel. It's a stunning September day, bright and clear with enough sunshine to warm our bones without making visibility difficult.

We reach the national park thirty minutes later, and I park my bike beside a Jeep, the only other vehicle in the lot. Color is already returning to Catarina's cheeks when I remove the helmet and take her hand. "Well, how was your first experience?"

"Thrilling." She grips my hand tight and smiles. Until she remembers her pain and the smile fades.

"Don't do that. Don't remind yourself to be sad. Life is for living. It's meant to be enjoyed. It's okay to smile."

She wraps herself around me again, and I dot kisses into her hair. She eases out of my embrace a couple minutes later, still looking sad, but I spy a glint of determination on her face too.

After I stow the helmets, I retrieve my backpack and sling it on my back. We set off on the main trail, hiking along the elevated boardwalk. The park appears sunken as it's built under the dunes, but it's not. It's part of the appeal. "I like walking out here. The trails are well defined, and I love the smell of pine and the salty breeze of the ocean tickling my skin."

"It's peaceful," she supplies, admiring the view of the ocean through the trees as we walk through the forest. We stop after a mile at a bench facing the Atlantic Ocean, and I hand her a bottle of water.

"My brother had a motorcycle," she says in between sipping her drink. "He was seven years older than me and even more protective than my dad. Fernando said he'd take me out on it when I was eighteen, but obviously that never happened." Her chest heaves as she stares straight ahead while speaking.

I thread my fingers through hers on the bench.

"Renzo had one too when we lived in Vegas, but Saverio wouldn't let me leave the house unless it was absolutely necessary, and Renzo wouldn't entertain the idea anyway." A choked sob rips from her lips. "He couldn't bear the thought I might get injured. He wouldn't take that risk with me, he said, because I'd suffered enough physical pain."

I scoot in close and circle my arms around her. She's trembling, and I wish I could absorb her pain and remove her suffering. "It's okay to mourn his loss, Rina. Just because it ended horribly doesn't negate everything that came before. It's okay to remember the good times."

She sniffles and nods before continuing. "Ren would drive me to the cosmetic surgeon's office and carry me to the car after procedures. He used to buy my clothes, my tampons, and toiletries, and he was the one who got me on the pill. He helped me with my homework, taught me how to fight and shoot and how to throw a knife." Tears stream down her face. "He held me so many nights when I woke up screaming in a cold sweat, believing I was back in that dungeon. He even helped me to explore intimacy when I turned eighteen and I was ready to confront those demons."

Her chest rattles with heaving sobs as she leans her head on my shoulder. "He was so gentle with me, showing me a different side to sex."

Personally, I feel he crossed a line when things got sexual. It's predatory in a way she wouldn't have realized and still doesn't. He was her protector. A father figure of sorts, and it seems wrong to me. But it's in the past, and there's no point saying anything. It would only upset her more. I smooth a hand up and down her back as she cries, glad she's finally letting it out.

"Ren fought Saverio constantly when he wouldn't let him move with me to Philly. As soon as I had leverage and I came for him, he didn't hesitate to turn his back on the only family he'd known. He left everything behind for me."

"He loved you."

She nods. "I loved him too." She squeezes her eyes shut before lifting her face to mine. "How did it come to this? It wasn't supposed to go down in this way. Maybe if I hadn't been so focused on revenge—"

"Listen to me, Rina. This is not your fault. He made his own choices, as did Maria. Renzo decided not to come to you. In doing that, he set his own path."

"It's all so fucked up!" she yells, shaking and trembling in my arms. "All of it! I knew something was wrong, but I believed it was jealousy over you and marital problems. I should have paid more attention. If I had, perhaps I could've forced him to confide in me before he got too deep. I wasn't a very good friend to him these past few months. I didn't see what was in front of my nose."

"You had your own stuff going on. You were juggling lots of balls. Please don't beat yourself up over it."

She rubs furiously at her eyes as tears continue to fall. "I lost everyone who mattered to me all because Angelo Mazzone negotiated a marriage contract for Natalia." Anguished howls pepper the air as she falls apart. "I should have let it go. If I hadn't been so bitter and determined to make my enemies pay, none of this would've happened."

I want to say we wouldn't be here now, but she needs to purge this shit, no matter how wrong she is.

"I fucked up, and now he's dead. He's dead, and I'm the one who killed him." She sobs into my chest as I hold her, feeling utterly helpless. "How do I tell his kids? How do I face them after what I did?"

"What happened was solely their parents' fault, sweetheart, and this is one occasion where we need to learn the lessons from the past." I brush her tears away as more tumble. "The best way you can honor Renzo is to shield those kids from the ugly truth. Keep their memories intact. We tell them their parents died in a car accident. I can set the stage so that is the only truth should they go looking in the future. Let what Maria and Renzo did die with them. Let their kids remember them with pride."

"Yes." She sniffles as she nods her head. "That is exactly what we should do." She sniffles again. "My papa died without honor because he was protecting me and I spent years hating him, Massimo. I thought horrible things about him, and I was so wrong."

"You know the truth now, my love. You know he loved you so much he made the ultimate sacrifice for you. Your brother too."

Clutching my sweater, she holds on to me for dear life. "So much needless death." She wipes her nose with the back of her sleeve, staring up at me with red-rimmed eyes. "It puts so many things into perspective. All these things I've been fighting for. Revenge. Power. Success. They mean nothing. I lost sight of what was most important. The only thing worth fighting for is—love."

Chapter Forty-Seven

Catarina

A few weeks pass, and soon we are into October. Things are getting easier. Work is helping, but the grief waylays me at the most unexpected moments, sending me spiraling again. Massimo is a living saint, putting up with my mood swings and caring for me with infinite tenderness. My husband is my rock. Every day, I offer up thanks for having him in my life.

I returned to therapy, attending weekly sessions, and that's helping too. Massimo and I have a new morning workout routine. We jog along the beach or the grounds surrounding the house and then take a dip in the pool. Being in the water no longer terrifies me. It's soothing, and it feels like I'm regaining a little part of the girl I used to be.

Double dates with Nic and Dario remind me life is for living, and like my husband said, it's okay to smile and find enjoyment. It doesn't mean I have forgotten all those I have lost.

We planted a tree in the garden to remember Renzo. Sometimes, I sit out there and talk to him. It helps even if Massimo's men who guard the grounds probably think I'm crazy.

Things are working out smoothly with O'Hara, and we're establishing a strong working relationship. The streets have settled. Our supplies are delivered on time, and we have seamlessly replaced the Russians with shipments from Rinascita.

Massimo and I amalgamated our teams. Although it's still early days and there is a little disgruntlement among some of our *soldati*, we are confident things will be okay.

Massimo and Fiero are in the process of relocating all their business operations to the waterfront property on Staten Island, and Nic and I are helping get the office ready for the employees who will be transitioning there next week. I am ready for a new challenge and looking forward to working with Massimo and Fiero in their business.

Vegas was successfully reclaimed with no bloodshed. The deportation of Anton and other high-ranking Russians caused a significant political storm. By the time Cruz and Alessandro led a team to retake the Salerno territory, the Bratva had scattered. Those who were left made a quick exit with minimal fuss. They aren't a risk for now. They have suffered a devastating blow, and while they will recover, it won't be for a while.

Anais and Cruz are now living there fulltime. My sister is refusing to take my calls, and it's clear she has taken her husband's side. I'm disappointed, but I've had too much going on to do anything about it. I'll let things settle down and fly out to see her then.

I have a heavy workload, but I'm prioritizing my health and making time to look after myself more. Massimo is crazy busy with the relocation, so I ensure I'm home every evening to cook dinner. I'm enjoying losing myself in the kitchen. Cooking some of Mom's old Italian recipes takes me back, and I find I'm remembering family dinners with our parents and Fernando with fondness instead of bitterness.

I am happier than I have been in years.

My cell vibrates as I chop garlic in the kitchen, and I put my knife down to answer Massimo's call.

"*Mia regina*," he says in that deep sultry voice I love, sending shivers cascading all over my body.

"Are you on your way home yet?" I ask, putting him on speaker while I resume chopping vegetables for the primavera.

"I'm going to be late. Something just cropped up, and we need to swing by our lawyer's offices."

"No problem. I hadn't started cooking yet. Text me when you're leaving, and I'll put our dinner on then."

"Have I told you how much I love you today?"

I grin at the phone like a bona fide nutjob. "You know you tell me every morning before we part ways."

Muffled conversation happens in the background. "Fiero says I'm pussy-whipped and we're turning into one of those cheesy lovey-dovey couples."

A giggle bursts from my mouth. "I think we're guilty as charged."

"I don't give a shit," my husband says as more conversation happens around him.

"Me either. You're busy. Go, my love. I'll see you later."

I finish prepping the dinner and cover everything with Saran Wrap before I place it in the refrigerator. Then I pour myself a nice big glass of chilled Sancerre. I'm making my way to the bedroom to change out of my suit when one of the guards manning the gate calls me.

"Sorry to interrupt, Donna Greco, but we have Leonardo Messina at the front gate asking to be let in."

I frown, wondering why he would be showing up here unannounced. "It's okay to let him through," I say, making an abrupt turn and heading toward the front door.

I'm standing outside, sipping from my wineglass when he pulls up in a Lincoln Navigator with tinted windows.

Leo emerges from the back seat, walking toward me with a solemn expression on his face.

All the tiny hairs on the back of my neck lift as apprehension creeps over me. I push off the wall and straighten up. "What's the matter?" I ask when he reaches me.

He wets his lips and clears his throat. "I need you to come with me, Donna Greco."

We have enjoyed several nights with the Mazzones in the past few months, and I talk weekly with Nat, Sierra, and Serena. None of Leo's usual warmth is reflected in his gaze, and he's addressing me formally, which means this is official business. "Why? What is this about?"

"The Commission needs to speak with you urgently."

Ignoring the rampaging butterflies running amok in my chest, I plant my poker face on and level him with a direct stare. "About what?"

He shifts uncomfortably on his feet. "I'm not at liberty to say."

"This is highly irregular."

"So is the situation."

We stare at one another as an ominous sense of dread tiptoes up my spine.

"Very well," I concede. "Let me grab my purse." Leo trails me into the house, remaining quiet as I set my wineglass down in the kitchen and grab my cell and my purse.

We step outside where two Commission *soldati* are now waiting. The vein in my neck throbs as blood rushes to my head.

This is bad. Real bad. I just feel it in my bones.

"I'll need to take that," Leo says, swiping my cell from my hand as I'm midway through texting Massimo. He pockets my phone and urges me forward, steering me toward the car.

The journey to the city is fraught with tension and absolute silence.

I hold myself upright as I stare out the window, watching the city fly past in a blur.

Leo opens my door after we park in the underground parking lot at the building that houses The Commission. His mask lowers for a split second, highlighting concern and confusion. We are shielded by the car when he says, "Look, this isn't personal. I—"

"It's okay, Leo. I understand. You're just doing your job." Truth be told, him coming to fetch me was a courtesy bestowed by Ben. Usually, Commission soldiers are sent to retrieve people in these circumstances.

He nods, before taking my elbow and escorting me to the elevator. The ride is silent as we shoot to the top of the building. Leo guides me to the main conference room, and I focus on my breathing as I'm taken into the room where all members of The Commission are waiting for me.

Scrap that. Not all members. Massimo isn't here. I scowl at Gabe where he sits in between Luca Accardi and a smug Roberto Maltese. "Where is Massimo, and why are you in his place?" I ask, panic sluicing through my veins at the thought something has happened to my husband.

"Don Greco will be summoned in due course," Bennett says, nodding at Leo before he slips out of the room.

"I don't understand. Why is Gabe here? He's no longer a don."

Ben holds out a chair for me, but I stand, refusing to sit until I know what is happening. I have my suspicions, but until I'm accused, I'm saying nothing.

"There was a conflict of interest," Ben coolly replies, betraying no hint of emotion on his face. "In such situations, the predecessor steps in."

Thrusting my shoulders back and tipping my chin up, I level him with a sharp look. "What conflict of interest?"

"Intel has come to our attention that confirms you have been working with the Bratva for many years and that it was in fact you, not the Russians, who killed Don Salerno."

I don't blink or move a facial muscle as Ben drills a look into me. Tension bleeds into the air as I circle options in my head.

"Don't even think about denying it," Don DiPietro says, throwing a bunch of photos across the table and glowering at me. "You deceived me. You deceived all of us."

I glance down at the photos that seal my fate. They are shots of me meeting Anton that last time in the empty parking lot. Guess there was a camera after all. I pick up another photo, grateful my fingers are steady as I stare at the image of me exiting the warehouse after killing Salerno. I'm covered in blood. The next photo shows Renzo and one of my men carrying a body bag out the side of the warehouse. The photos are long lens, meaning someone was spying on us from a near distance.

Fucking Anton. He moved one final piece on the board before returning to Moscow to face his death. He must have had men following Renzo for some time. He never trusted him to betray me. He knew what he was up to all along.

Well played, asshole, I silently acknowledge.

I carefully set the photos down and turn to face Ben. There is no point attempting to refute this. There will be no talking my way out of it. I knew the risks when I came to New York with an agenda. I knew, no matter how much we covered our tracks, there was the potential it would come out.

I have never backed down before and I'm not going to start now.

I will own my actions and face the consequences.

It's time to reveal all.

Ben watches me closely, nodding as he sees the resignation and resolve on my face.

I sit down, keeping my spine straight and clasping my hands on my lap as I level a cool gaze at the four men sitting across my me. Out of respect, I wait for Don Mazzone to claim his seat at the top of the table before I begin. I clear my throat and let my eyes roam between all five Commission members. "I need to start at the beginning."

Massimo

"You should get that," Fiero says, cutting across our lawyer as my cell vibrates on top of the table for the fourth time in succession.

"I apologize for the interruption. Excuse me for a few minutes," I say, nodding at my friend. I hurry outside into the empty hallway, swiping my finger across the screen to accept his call. "This better be good, brother."

"We have a big problem," Gabe says, talking in hushed tones. "I can't talk for long. The session is about to start."

"What session? Where are you?"

"I'm at HQ. They have called an emergency sitting. Maltese

showed up at my place and told me Bennett was invoking the predecessor rule. All he said was it was a conflict of interest. I only found out what's going on when I got here."

"Shit." I rub the back of my neck as ominous dread washes over me. "Just tell me."

"They have taken Catarina in for questioning. It's bad, Massimo. Real bad."

I pace the carpeted floor, trying to remain calm. They have obviously discovered something. But what? "On what grounds?"

"Caleb Accardi passed intel to Don Mazzone. He said your wife has been in bed with the Bratva and she was responsible for the death of Don Salerno. From what I can gather, Bennett wasn't entirely convinced. Until photographic evidence was anonymously delivered to his office today."

"Fucking Cruz. I'm going to level that motherfucker."

I just know he's behind this. Catarina backed him into a corner, and he retaliated. I don't know how he found out about the Russians because I know Rina hadn't told him about that allegiance and we covered our tracks with Salerno, but somehow, he did. Perhaps Smirnov knew who he was to Rina, and he made one final power play before he was booted out of the US. I'm betting Cruz let the information slip to Anais knowing she would tell Caleb and he'd tell Ben. This way, Cruz gets what he wants without having to implicate himself.

"Did you know?" Gabe asks, whispering into the phone.

"It's probably best I don't answer that."

"Jesus fucking Christ, Massimo. What the hell were you thinking? She's a traitor, and she's going to pull you down with her if The Commission finds out you are involved. They are already suspicious you are."

"It's not cut and dry, Gabe. There is so much you don't know. When you do, you'll understand."

"I've got to go. She's just arrived. What are you going to do?"

"Save the woman I love." I end the call, pushing air from my mouth as I pace the hallway, churning options and looking for solutions.

I rush back into the meeting room, the door slapping against the wall as I charge inside. Fiero takes one look at my face and understands the urgency. He quickly gathers his things. "Gentlemen, we apologize, but we'll have to pick this up tomorrow."

We trade hurried goodbyes and stride from the room.

When we're safely in my car, Fiero turns to me as I climb behind the wheel. "What's going on?"

"Cruz made a move, and my wife is up to her neck in shit." I fill him in as I exit the parking lot out into traffic.

"Let's bury him. He's far from innocent. He was colluding with Rina behind their backs as well. Drag him into this, and it will help her cause."

"It won't be enough. I know my wife." I glance at him briefly, before I take a left down a side street and floor it. "She's telling them everything."

"They will kill her."

"They'll have to fucking kill me first." We're not going down without a fight, and we have leverage.

"What's the plan?" he asks as it formulates in my brain.

"Log into Rina's system, and pull up the dossier on Cruz," I instruct as I press call on my cell and put it on speaker.

"What are you doing?" he asks.

"Calling in reinforcements."

He quirks a brow as Natalia Messina answers my call. "It's Massimo. I need to speak with you urgently. It's a matter of life or death. How soon can you get to the city?"

Chapter Forty-Eight

Catarina

"Is that everything?" Ben asks after I have finished recanting my sordid tale. I gave them the CliffsNotes version, but I left little out. They know most everything, including my real identity.

My eyes lock on Gabriele's dazed gaze as he stares at me, utterly shell-shocked. "It is," I lie because I purposely kept mention of Cruz and Anais out of it.

I want to hang that cocksucker Cruz out to dry. Now I have the facts, I know he set this up. He must have been working with Anton. Anton knew Cruz was my brother-in-law, so I'm guessing he was the one to make contact. Cruz would have lapped it up. An opportunity to get ahead of the game. A chance to eliminate me and Massimo.

I could bury him. Tell them the part he played and that he's far from innocent, but then it'll all come out. Caleb has protected Anais, not revealing her as his source. If I involve Cruz, he will point the finger at my sister too. He will not go down alone.

I can't let anyone else I love die because of me.

Cruz gets a reprieve because it's the only way I can protect my sister—even if she is the one who betrayed me. She would know Caleb would go straight to his uncle and his stepfather. That hurts. A lot. But

I don't blame her. She's still grieving and the knowledge I killed her father would have sent her over the edge. I have always known where her loyalty lies.

"Did Massimo know?" Don DiPetro asks, looking slightly less hostile though only a bit.

"No." I shake my head and stare him straight in the eye, hoping he buys it. If he has photos of my husband at the warehouse, he will already know I'm lying, but I have to try. I will take the fall for this. Not Massimo. There's no point in both of us dying. I love him enough to protect him from that fate. Pain pierces me in the chest as all thoughts of my happy future evaporate in an instant.

"Of course, she'd say that," Maltese says, disgust lacing his tone.

"She came to New York to kill him," Accardi says. "Why would you think Don Greco knows anything about this?"

"Don't act the fool because you have sympathy for her," Maltese retorts. "Massimo is brainwashed and pussy-whipped. It's fucking obvious he helped to cover her tracks."

"Last I checked, Massimo doesn't do anything without Fiero," Don DiPietro says. "Implicate Massimo. You implicate Fiero."

"Don't you dare suggest my son had anything to do with this." Maltese slams his hand down on the desk.

"Enough." Ben's thunderous voice projects around the room, silencing everyone.

I have no problem holding on to my composure as I turn to look at the president. Revealing the truth has been incredibly freeing. There is nothing left but to pay the price for my actions. I always knew this day could come. I understood the risks. "I will accept responsibility for my actions and suffer the consequences," I tell Ben. "But this is on me and me alone. Massimo is not involved."

"We need to discuss this," Accardi says. "This isn't black-or-white."

"There is nothing to discuss," Maltese says. "She's a traitor. She planned to kill our president!"

"There were mitigating circumstances," Gabriele says, finally finding his voice. He has been enormously troubled since I dropped the bomb. "Donna Greco has apologized and explained how she changed her plans."

"If she's telling the truth," Maltese scoffs.

"She is," Gabe whispers. He stares at me with tears in his eyes. "It was you in the cage. I see it now in your face if I imagine you with blonde hair instead of brown."

"I dye it," I calmly explain.

"I'm so sorry," he whispers. "I'm so incredibly sorry." He turns his head to Ben. "She suffered unimaginable cruelty, and she was only thirteen years old. I am begging you for leniency, Don Mazzone."

"He's too biased," Maltese snaps. "And we only have his word for it that she is who he says she is. For all we know, she concocted this story to earn the sympathy vote."

"Gabriele is telling the truth. Ask Leonardo Messina."

Ben sits up straighter. "What has Leo got to do with this?"

I wet my dry lips. "It was Leo and Mateo who rescued me."

Shock splays across his face. "This is the first I'm hearing of it."

"I was the forgotten girl," I numbly reply. "It doesn't surprise me I wasn't mentioned."

Ben picks up his cell and taps out a message, drumming his fingers on the table while he stares at me with a puckered brow. He's troubled. Conflicted. A few months ago, I would have said that was unthinkable. If someone comes to New York to kill the president in revenge for something his father did, there is no gray area. It's simple. That person must die.

It should be uncomplicated for Don Mazzone.

But I know Bennett now.

He isn't prone to rash decisions, and he has empathy. It's written all over his face. He's torn. He believes me when I said I gave up that agenda once I got to know him. He understands I am no threat to him or anyone now I have had my revenge and made peace with my past.

"Let's park that for the moment," he says after a few silent beats. "I will need that evidence you have on Salerno."

"I can arrange to send it to you."

"If it proves what you say, that Salerno had been planning to kill me and he was going to make a play for Alessandro, it exonerates you for the unsanctioned murder."

"You are putting too much faith in a liar's words," Maltese says, and I would really love to gut that fucking spineless bastard. If I make it out of here alive, I'm taking that motherfucker down. "What is wrong with you?"

"Shut the fuck up, Roberto. I am sure I speak for everyone when I say we are sick of hearing your voice."

There is a knock on the door, and then Leo slips into the room, arching an inquisitive brow as he strides toward Ben.

"Leo. I need to ask you something," Ben says. "Do you remember rescuing Noemi Cabrini from the Grecoes' basement after Carlo Greco died?"

His brow pinches together as he bobs his head. "I do, yes." He glances around, looking thoroughly confused. "Angelo discovered her father had betrayed him because Carlo had kidnapped his young daughter and was using her to force his hand. His dying wish was that we rescue her and ensure she was looked after."

His words shake me to my core, and a sob rips from my lips before I can stop it. I clamp a hand over my mouth, trying to compose myself.

Leo looks at me and frowns before returning his gaze to Ben. "What is this about?"

"Do you remember the girl?" Ben asks.

Leo's face pales. "As long as I live, I will never forget the way we found her." He levels a glare in Gabriele's direction. "She was locked in a cage, naked and lying in a pool of her own vomit. The stench of urine was strong, and there were dried blood stains on the floor and fresh blood seeping from a festering wound on her back." His voice cracks. "I had already seen a lot of things at that point in my career, but that was the most shocking sight I have ever witnessed, and it remains so to this day."

His statement hangs heavy in the air. My heart pounds behind my chest, and I squeeze my eyes shut to ward off the images his words conjure.

"There wasn't an inch of her skin that wasn't bruised, scarred, or damaged in some way. Clumps of her hair had been pulled out. She was scrawny and malnourished. But it was the haunted, vacant look in her eyes that has remained with me." His eyes look suspiciously damp. "She was only a kid. Thirteen years old. If anyone treated my daughter like that, I would have burned the world down to save her and then burned it again to avenge her."

Tears leak down my face unbidden, and I'm powerless to stop them.

As if in slow motion, Leo turns to face me. I see the mounting horror cross his face as realization dawns. "My God, it was you? You're Noemi?" he whispers quickly figuring it out.

I nod through my tears.

"You were avenging yourself," he quickly surmises.

I nod as I mop my tears with the tissue Gabe hands to me across the table. "I was the only one who could do it. For years, I have been tormented by the things done to me in that dungeon. Those seven months altered me irreparably. I'd like to say things were better after I got out, but they weren't."

"Salerno and Conti," he says. I nod. "My God." He scrubs a hand over his jaw. "I am so fucking sorry, Rina. I failed you. I should have checked up on you, but Mateo died shortly after, and I lost Nat, and a part of myself died too. It's not an excuse. There is no acceptable excuse for not taking better care of you. I am incredibly sorry."

"I forgive you."

"I don't deserve your forgiveness."

"You weren't the monster who savaged me and broke my spirit. You weren't the one who shaped the vengeful creature I became. The people responsible are dead, and I was trying to put it behind me and move forward with my life. I always knew it had the potential to come back at me."

"She shouldn't be punished," Leo blurts, eyeballing Ben. "Fuck the rules. This isn't right, and you know it."

Eerie silence reverberates off the walls until the door slams open claiming everyone's attention. Massimo and Fiero race into the room, quickly followed by Natalia and Sierra.

Ben stands as Leo turns around.

Massimo rushes to my side.

"What are you doing here?" Ben asks his wife and his sister as Massimo crouches in front of me.

"What did you tell them?" he whispers in an urgent tone.

Although I'm shaking and upset, I know well enough not to say this out loud. I press my lips to his ear. "Everything except your involvement and Cruz and Anais's."

His eyes burn with anger. "Why the hell—"

"That's enough!" Don Maltese roars, jabbing his finger across the table. "They are getting their stories straight. This is a fucking outrage." He turns his venom on Bennett. "You are the president. Act like it!"

Very calmly, Ben rounds the table, coming to a standstill in front of Don Maltese. His arm whips out, and he wraps it around his colleague's neck, lifting him up in his chair. It's an incredible display of power and strength. A vein throbs in Ben's brow as he glares at Fiero's father, pressing his neck tight. Don Maltese grabs Ben's wrist as he gasps and struggles to breathe.

Everyone else has stopped talking, waiting with bated breath to see how this goes down.

"I am fed up with your lack of respect toward me. I am the president, and I'll handle this situation. Careful or my next action will be to raise a motion of no confidence in you." He shoves him back into his chair, and Roberto pants, sucking air into his lungs. "We are ascertaining the facts, and then we'll deliberate the best course of action. Unless you have anything valuable to contribute, keep your fucking mouth shut."

Fiero's lips twitch as he watches his father eat a large helping of humble pie.

"I mean no disrespect," Maltese says, rubbing his sore neck. "I just want to ensure we aren't letting emotions overrule us. What happened in the past should have no bearing on this, and all outsiders should be asked to leave. They can't get involved."

"I disagree," Gabriele says.

"As do I," Accardi adds.

"This isn't a typical situation," DiPietro agrees.

"It's true?" Natalia asks, walking toward me with tears in her eyes. "What Massimo told me on the way here is true? You were Rocco's daughter? The one Carlo kidnapped and tortured?"

Massimo stands behind me, placing his hand on my shoulder. I reach up and link my fingers through his, siphoning some of his warmth. "It is true. I am Noemi Cabrini. We met once as kids."

"I remember," she says, clamping a shaky hand over her mouth. "I see it now. I see the resemblance. I was very fond of your father. I used to sneak him cannoli."

"And apple cake. He loved it so much he asked you for the recipe. I used to bake it for him."

Sobs rip from her chest as she falls to her knees in front of me. "My God, Rina. I am so sorry. I feel partly responsible."

"Please don't." I let go of Massimo's hand and reach down to take hers. "It was in no way your fault."

"Carlo terrified me. He assaulted me several times, and I was sick at the thought of marrying him. He was a monster."

"He was the worst kind," I whisper.

She grabs me into a hug, and I cling to her. Behind her, I see Ben comforting his wife. Silent tears roll down Sierra's face.

Natalia breaks our embrace and climbs to her feet, pulling me with her. She holds my hand firmly as she addresses her brother. "I know Catarina has done things that are deemed unforgivable in our world, but I am begging you, Benny, please make allowances. The things she has endured are things no little girl should ever go through. You have to appreciate how that would transform a person. Can any of us here honestly say if we'd been in similar shoes that we wouldn't have been hellbent on vengeance? Because I know for damn sure I would have."

Sierra walks toward me, enveloping me in a hug. She stands on my other side as she turns to face her husband. "I support what Nat has said. Rina came here initially to kill you. I have a very good reason to want her to die for her crimes, but that is the last thing I want to see happen."

Letting go of me, she walks back to her husband. "This is the reason you are trying to change things, Ben. Women and children are still being hurt in this world, and it's got to stop." She glances over her shoulder at me before sweeping her gaze over all the men in the room. "If Catarina were a man, you would all understand. You would even applaud her for painstakingly exacting her revenge."

"But she isn't a man," Natalia adds, squeezing my hand as Massimo steps up behind me, placing his hand on my hip. "If she was, she would have done what she came to New York to do. But she's a woman. A brave, compassionate woman who had the balls to acknowledge she was on the wrong path, and she took steps to rectify it."

"There is merit in what you have said," Don DiPietro says, "but her crimes are too severe to go completely unpunished."

"Then punish me," Massimo says, eyeballing Ben. "I will accept the punishment on behalf of my wife. She has suffered enough."

"Are you insane?" I whirl around on him, anger rushing to the surface. I did not keep his involvement hidden so he could offer himself up on a platter even if it is quite noble and gallant how he's willing to suffer in my place.

"No, *mia amata.* I just love you enough to die for you."

Oh my God. He's a fucking moron, but I love the shit out of him. Before I can say anything, Fiero decides to get in on the action.

"You should know if Rina or Massimo die you will have chaos on the streets and lose half of your drug supply." Fiero shares a loaded look with his best friend. "There is more at stake than punishing someone for crimes against our organization."

Massimo jerks his head at his friend, giving silent permission for him to continue. Fiero tells them about Rinascita and everything the two men have been working toward since they were eighteen. Shocked faces fill the room when Fiero explains they have a shipping hub in the city and the ability to bring anything in and out of New York under the authorities' noses.

It's a game changer, and The Commission knows it.

"We need some time to discuss this," Ben says, staring at me and Massimo. He turns to Leo. "Please escort Don Greco and Donna Greco to the holding room." He eyeballs the rest of the uninvited. "The rest of you must leave. You can wait in the reception room downstairs, but under no circumstances is anyone to barge back in here. Do I make myself clear?"

The others nod and slowly filter out of the room. Fiero trades a silent communication with Massimo before he leaves. Then Leo takes us to a room, leaving us inside with an armed guard outside.

"Come here." Massimo props his back against the wall as he stares at me. "Now, *mia amata*. I need to hold you."

I run into his arms and cling to him. We don't speak for several minutes. I clutch his sides while he trails a hand up and down my back and presses kisses into my hair. "I almost died when Gabe called and explained what was happening."

"I almost died when you offered yourself up as a sacrificial lamb." I narrow my eyes as I look up at him. "Don't do that again. This is on me, and I'll pay the price."

"I'm not about to let them kill you, my love." He brushes hair back from my face.

"I think everyone's interventions will make a difference. They won't kill me. They'll find some other punishment." I can't be one hundred percent sure, but it's what my gut is telling me. "I can't believe Nat and Sierra came here to defend me and support me. Not after what I had planned."

"They were shocked when I told them, but they could understand it. The only thing that mattered to them is you changed your mind after you got to know Bennett. Just like you did with me and my family. They won't hold it against you."

"Maybe." I rest my head on his chest again. I wouldn't blame them if they never want to speak to me again. I will forever be in their gratitude for what they said in that room.

"You're very calm," he says, taking my hand and leading me over to the only couch in the room.

I shrug. "I have accepted my fate. Whatever it will be." We sit down, and he wraps his arm around my back as I lean into him. "In a way, this has given me closure. There are no more secrets now."

"That's not exactly true." He tips my chin up. "You didn't tell them about Cruz, and I know why."

"You do?"

He kisses my cheek. "I know you. You would do anything to protect your sister. If you accuse Cruz, he'll take her down with him."

"Yes. I can't do that to her."

"She doesn't deserve your love or your protection. If you confirm Cruz's involvement, they will have to show you more leniency or punish a don and a future New York heir. They are not going to do that. Don DiPietro would riot."

"You and Fiero have already achieved that. Did you see how their faces lit up when he explained? Rinascita and the port is too valuable to turn their back on it. If they want to open up the opportunities it offers, they need to keep me alive."

"I believe so, but I'm telling you now if they don't I'm hanging Cruz out to dry. There is nothing you can say or do to stop me. I will do whatever it takes to save you, like you tried to do with me."

"Fat lot of good it did me when you offer to take my place!" I link my fingers in his. "Is it weird I feel kind of peaceful right now?"

He chuckles. "Yeah, *mia regina*. It kinda is."

I grin. "I will accept whatever punishment they choose as long as I get to spend the rest of my life with you."

He looks at me with pure adoration in his gaze. "Ditto, sweetheart. No matter what happens from now, we are in this together."

"Always," I whisper before his lips descend.

Epilogue

Catarina – 4 years later

The baby monitor crackles a split second before an ear-piercing wail interrupts our sexy time.

"Goddamn it," Massimo groans, thrusting his hips forward with more urgency as he fucks me from behind. "Sometimes I think our son is the devil. He's got cockblocking down to a fine art form."

"Massimo! Don't say that!" I chastise as his fingers move to my clit and he rubs me hard. "Babies wake during the night when they're hungry."

"I'm only joking," he says in between pants as he ruts into me at full speed. "Kind of."

My arms strain from where they're cuffed to the bed, and I see stars behind my blindfold when he pinches my clit. I detonate the same time he roars and spills inside me.

Pulling out, he quickly cleans me up before climbing off the bed as our five-month-old son cries for attention. We only just moved him into his own room, and he has woken more regularly this past week in some form of baby protest.

"Massimo!" I hiss. "Untie me now!"

He swats my ass. "Patience, *mia regina*. I'll be back."

I'm cursing him under my breath as the door opens, and I hear the soft pad of his feet as he leaves to retrieve our little Rocco.

Massimo still calls me his queen even though I was stripped of my status and title by The Commission after they learned of my betrayal.

Dario is now don of what was once the Philly Contis' operation. He refused to do it at first out of loyalty to me. Until I explained I wanted it to happen. I was tired of all the shit, and my goals had changed. Eventually, I convinced him, and he has been the one in control ever since. He's doing an amazing job, and the men respect him. We are still close, and we regularly get together with our kids.

Nic had twins three years ago. A boy and a girl, and she's pregnant again now.

We adopted Renzo and Maria's two sons and daughter three months after The Commission's ruling. Their grandparents were too old to raise a then eleven-year-old, eight-year-old, and six-year-old. Especially when they were grieving their parents. Cassio, Armis, and Bella knew me, but Massimo was a stranger. It took them some time to settle, and we had plenty of small problems, but eventually they did.

My heart swells with pride and love when I think of them. They bring me so much joy, and Massimo is an amazing father. Cassio is fifteen now and already initiated. He looks up to Massimo, and I hope he will continue to do so as he grows into adulthood. Massimo bought him a motorcycle when he initiated, much to my consternation and concern. But I was overruled, and speed is their thing. The two of them regularly disappear for hours flying down back roads and giving me heart palpitations.

It will be Armis's turn to initiate next year, and he is champing at the bit for it. Armis has a close bond with Gabe. He relates to his sensitive nature best and is helping him to navigate the world he lives in. Interestingly, Armis recently died his hair platinum blond like Fiero's. No one knows what to think about it, but Fiero's and Massimo's first glimpse of it was priceless.

Cassio is the spitting image of Renzo while Bella is the one who most takes after him in personality. She is steadfast and full of inner strength with the biggest heart.

Bella loves to bake, and I'm teaching her all of Mom's recipes. She can already make Natalia's apple cake as good as I can. But she's also a natural at the hand-to-hand combat Massimo started teaching the kids the moment they moved in.

Watching him training with them brought back memories of Renzo training me, and it was incredibly nostalgic. It was the key to their bonding with him and instrumental in working out their grief. The day Bella flipped Armis, the pride on Massimo's face couldn't be rivaled.

Raising Renzo's kids and watching them blossom and grow went a long way toward helping me to reconcile what happened with him. In a lot of ways, it feels like I still have a part of him with me.

I don't know what my life would be like without them.

Life as I knew it tilted on its axis in the best way.

Family is my priority, and work takes a back seat. I could never have predicted how happy it would make me.

Although I was permitted to continue running the street trade within the Big Apple, it was increasingly difficult to do it without my donna title. Gossip and rumors were rife among made men, and I lost a lot of respect. Truth be told, my heart just wasn't in it any longer. I built my business to fuel my revenge. Once those dreams were exchanged for new ones, I didn't care about much of it.

Massimo took over initially until he formally succeeded Bennett Mazzone as president of The Commission.

Fiero forced his father to retire shortly after the showdown that day at Commission HQ, backed by Don Mazzone who was sick of Roberto Maltese's attitude and wanted him gone to pave the way for new blood. Fiero is a vast improvement on his father, and The Commission is more energized and dynamic these days. Massimo is currently working on plans to expand the board and add some other dons from different states.

Now, Fiero manages the street trade in conjunction with Diarmuid O'Hara, and I work part-time with Rinascita while the kids are at school. Fiero and Massimo are both still very hands on with their business, but they have a full management team in place made up of trusted advisers—a mix of skilled businesspeople and made men. I'm on maternity leave at the moment although I still do some work from home during the day when Rocco takes his nap.

Anais and Cruz are still in Vegas. My sister doesn't speak to me anymore, and I have given up trying. I did my best for her, and now she's on her own.

Cruz is at our mercy.

All our secrets are laid bare, but we have plenty of shit we are holding over him. He is over a barrel, and he knows it. I am sure, at some point, he will make a move, but for now, he's not someone we need to worry about. Massimo used our leverage to force him to concede on the DiPietro crown, leaving the path clear for Massimo to succeed Ben without contest. Now, Massimo is working closely with Cristian DiPietro and his father to map out a succession plan. The Accardi twins are due to take control of their family business shortly, and Cristian will step up then too.

It will be a younger and more vibrant Commission, and it's poised to effect real progressive change.

I talk regularly with Nat, Sierra, and Rena, and we regularly have all three couples over for dinner in our new, much bigger home and vice versa. I am grateful they could find it in their hearts to forgive me, and I value their friendship so much.

We moved shortly after we adopted our eldest kids. We needed to be nearer to the city for school, work, and The Commission, and we needed more space to accommodate our growing family. We still own the house on Long Island, and we spend a lot of our weekends there. I sold my sanctuary in Philly last year after holding on to it purely for sentimental reasons. I loved that house, and it was my safe haven for many years, but I don't need that anymore.

My husband and my kids are my safe place now. My family. My home.

"Look at Mommy," Massimo says, returning to our bedroom with a gurgling baby.

I whip my head in the direction of his voice, straining against my bound wrists in frustration. I will get him back for this.

"She loves it when I tie her up and whip her naughty ass. She loves letting me manage her pleasure and take control in the bedroom. She especially loves it when I drive my fingers in her ass and—"

"Oh my God, Massimo! Stop it. He's a baby. You can't say things like that to him!"

"Don't be ridiculous, *mia amata*." Rocco whimpers from close by, and my entire being strains toward my little son. "He doesn't know what I'm saying, and even if he did, he'll never remember it."

"You're an asshole," I say, as he uncuffs my wrists from the bed. I lean back on my heels and whip the blindfold off, instantly scooping our baby into my arms. I attempt to scowl at my husband as I lean back against the headboard, but it's virtually impossible to stay mad at him these days. I have mellowed a lot during our marriage even if we still butt heads on occasion. We will always be stubborn in that regard.

"But you love me," he croons, wrapping his arms around both of us as I cradle our precious, beautiful boy. Massimo hands me the bottle, and Rocco stops whimpering the second I place the nipple in his mouth. My husband strokes his cheek as Rocco suckles greedily, and we stare at him in amazement.

It took a couple of years and several failed IVF attempts before we finally had success. A lovely woman named Deanna was our surrogate, and everything went well with the pregnancy and delivery. We are so lucky. So blessed. We don't take him for granted.

"He is looking more and more like his mama every day," Massimo says, looking enthralled as he gazes adoringly at this perfect little human we made.

Speaking of mamas—Massimo's moved to Italy to live with her cousin almost four years ago. Once she knew who I was, she couldn't bear to be around me. I guess I reminded her too much of her failings. I'm not complaining, and we visit every summer. I won't ever be close to her, but I have learned to forgive her. She brought my husband into the world, so how could I not? Massimo and Gabe fly solo to visit her on other occasions during the year.

Gabriele and his partner Apollo live on the grounds of the Greco estate. Massimo ripped out the fountain like he promised, and they tore down the house and rebuilt a magnificent modern castle, which is jointly owned by the brothers.

Apollo was the architect they hired to design the new house, and it was pretty much love at first sight for those two. Although they officially have to keep their relationship under wraps, most made men in our circle are aware, and it hasn't caused too many issues within our world. It helps that Massimo is the president and he's laying down new laws. I'm happy for Gabe, and we're close now in a way I never imagined.

The house and estate will be divided equally between all Greco children in the future.

Cassio, Armis, and Bella are now officially Grecoes, but we only changed their names recently. We wanted to wait until they were all old enough to make the choice for themselves. The Greco name opens a lot of doors for them, but more importantly, it is who they are now. We are a united team, and it was important to Massimo and me that we all share the same name.

"Hey." Massimo tweaks my nose. "Where'd you go? You look like you are a million miles away."

"Just thinking about how far we've all come, and I think Rocco looks more like you." I stare up at my husband. He will be forty this year, but he's still hot as hell, and my lust for him hasn't dissipated in the slightest. In fact, I'd say I'm even more attracted and more addicted to him. He lights up my life in so many ways.

"He has your eyes and your lips," he says.

"He has your hair."

The day we took him home from the hospital, I swear we spent hours just staring at him in awe.

"I would've liked him to have yours," he says, fingering my dark-blonde locks. I stopped dying it a couple of years ago, having made peace with myself. I no longer want to pretend I wasn't the girl who worshipped her father, looked up to her big brother, and had ambitions to attend the Olympics.

I'm the sum of all the different experiences of my life, and they shaped me into the woman I am today.

I'm not sure I'd have survived the journey if it wasn't for the man who is by my side every step of the way.

Tears prick my eyes as I snuggle into my husband. Reaching up, I press a kiss to the underside of his stubbly jawline. "I love you, Massimo."

"Not as much as I love you." He leans in and kisses me softly.

Together, we watch our youngest child drink his bottle, his eyes turning heavy as sleep returns to claim him, and I contemplate how wonderfully strange life can be.

I thought I needed revenge and power to feel fulfilled, but I had it all wrong. All along, the only thing I needed to feel whole again was to become the queen of Massimo's heart.

Want to discover what Rina's erotic dream was all about? Read the bonus threesome dream scene, exclusively available to newsletter subscribers. Just type this link into your browser: https://bit.ly/3wrv3ew

The Accardi Twins Duet is slated for release in 2024.

Her teen crush is now a ruthless killer and powerful mafia heir. Will one life-altering night unite or destroy them?

Bennett Mazzone grew up ignorant of the truth: he is the illegitimate son of the most powerful mafia boss in New York. Until it suited his father to drag him into a world where power, wealth, violence, and cruelty are the only currency.

Celebrating her twenty-first birthday in Sin City should be fun for Sierra Lawson, but events take a deadly turn when she ends up in a private club, surrounded by dangerous men who always get what they want.

And they want *her*.

Ben can't believe his ex's little sister is all grown up, stunningly beautiful, and close to being devoured by some of the most ruthless men he has ever known. The Vegas trip is about strengthening ties, but he won't allow his associates to ruin her perfection. Although it comes at a high price, saving Sierra is his only choice.

The memory of Ben's hands on her body is seared into Sierra's flesh for eternity. She doesn't regret that night. Not even when she discovers the guy she was crushing on as a teenager is a cold, calculating killer with dark impulses and lethal enemies who want him dead.

Understanding the risks, she walks away from the only man she will ever love, stowing her secrets securely in her heart. Until the truth becomes leverage and Sierra is drawn into a bloody war—a pawn in a vicious game she doesn't want to play.

As the web of deceit is finally revealed, Ben will stop at nothing to protect Sierra. Even if loving her makes him weak. In a world where women serve a sole purpose, and alliances mean the difference between life and death, can he fight for love and win?

Reached #24 in the entire Amazon.com store upon release.

#1 Bestseller in multiple categories across the US, UK, Canada, and Australia.

Available now in ebook, paperback, and audiobook format.

Check your local Amazon/Audible store.

CLAIM YOUR FREE EBOOK – ONLY AVAILABLE TO NEWSLETTER SUBSCRIBERS!

The boy who broke my heart is now the man who wants to mend it.

Jared was my everything until an ocean separated us and he abandoned me when I needed him most.

He forgot the promises he made.

Forgot the love he swore was eternal.

It was over before it began.

Now, he's a hot commodity, universally adored, and I'm the woman no one wants.

Pining for a boy who no longer exists is pathetic. Years pass, men come and go, but I cannot move on.

I didn't believe my fractured heart and broken soul could endure any more pain. Until Jared rocks up to the art gallery where I work, with his fiancée in tow, and I'm drowning again.

Seeing him brings everything to the surface, so I flee. Placing distance between us again, I'm determined to put him behind me once and for all.

Then he reappears at my door, begging me for another chance.

I know I should turn him away.

Try telling that to my heart.

This angsty, new adult romance is a FREE full-length ebook, exclusively available to newsletter subscribers.

Type this link into your browser to claim your free copy:

https://bit.ly/TITMHFBB

OR

Scan this code to claim your free copy:

About the Author

Siobhan Davis is a *USA Today, Wall Street Journal*, and Amazon Top 5 bestselling romance author. **Siobhan** writes emotionally intense stories with swoon-worthy romance, complex characters, and tons of unexpected plot twists and turns that will have you flipping the pages beyond bedtime! She has sold over 2 million books, and her titles are translated into several languages.

Prior to becoming a full-time writer, Siobhan forged a successful corporate career in human resource management.

She lives in the Garden County of Ireland with her husband and two sons.

You can connect with Siobhan in the following ways:

Website: www.siobhandavis.com
Facebook: AuthorSiobhanDavis
Instagram: @siobhandavisauthor
Tiktok: @siobhandavisauthor
Email: siobhan@siobhandavis.com

Books By Siobhan Davis

NEW ADULT ROMANCE

Kennedy Boys Series

Rydeville Elite Series

All of Me Series

Forever Love Duet

NEW ADULT ROMANCE STAND-ALONES

Inseparable

Incognito

Still Falling for You

Holding on to Forever

Always Meant to Be

Tell It to My Heart

The One I Want

REVERSE HAREM

Sainthood Series

Dirty Crazy Bad Duet

Surviving Amber Springs (stand-alone)

DARK MAFIA ROMANCE

Mazzone Mafia Series

Vengeance of a Mafia Queen (*stand-alone*)

*The Accardi Twins**

SCI-FI & PARANORMAL ROMANCE

Saven Series

Alinthia Series ^

True Calling Series ^

---

*Coming 2024

^Currently unpublished but will be republished in due course.

www.siobhandavis.com

www.ingramcontent.com/pod-product-compliance
Lightning Source LLC
Chambersburg PA
CBHW030350310726
48979CB00001B/243

* 9 7 8 1 9 5 9 2 8 5 2 2 9 *